The Realms Series

Book Five

Realm of the Snow Queen

Emory R. Frie

Realm of the Snow Queen by Emory R. Frie

© 2020 Emory R. Frie

ISBN: 978-0-9974354-6-7 (Paperback)

Cover Design: Emory R. Frie
Cover Images © Shutterstock

www.emoryrfrie.weebly.com

For Madison, who takes this world by storm.
Keep moving forward; you'll become Legendary.

At the end of all things, there was no song;
So the legends lived on, until all that remained
were the stories she must tell...

Chapter One
The Girl Who Kissed Roses

Light streamed through jagged cracks in the frozen walls, harsh and blinding across her eyes. Some of the openings were so large they could have been windows. But they were never so large as to allow escape – she'd unsuccessfully tried to crawl through before. Even if she could've squeezed out, she wouldn't get far before being discovered. There was nothing but sheer open ice outside her prison.

Nothing to stop her.

Nowhere to hide.

The ice that encased her chamber was dark as iron with crystalline patterns crawling up the surface in sharp angles. There was no need for chains or shackles. All the same, she swore she could feel the imprisonment binding her in a suffocating straitjacket. Most days she felt like a mind apart from her body, an observer of her own life. This was one of the few moments she felt grounded in her own skin. She tried to never waste them.

Buried in the ice across from her hung a mirror as large as she was tall, a fellow prisoner. She hated it. Still, she always forced herself to look at it even as she tried to ignore its reflection. The mirror was composed of cold, reflective fragments pieced together in a jagged, incomplete puzzle. Over the time in her captivity, she'd watched it progressively become whole again. Little change had occurred in months. The mirror was practically completed.

The only real change was in its reflection; this being what she loathed most about the mirror. Tentatively, she stood to approach it. Long ago, years it felt like, when she woke one day to find the mirror in her cell, she wondered why it was so important to the Snow Queen. Perhaps if she could figure out its mysteries then she would be able to use that information to somehow escape or defeat the Snow Queen.

But these were fantasies, she realized. Remembering these old dreams was like remembering a child she'd long left behind. This bitter isolation had changed and enlightened her. The mirror's purpose would never bring her freedom. It would only ever destroy her. Every reflective fragment fitted back in place only strengthened the prison she was trapped in. The mirror grew whole, the ice grew thick, and she herself grew in ways that made her increasingly wary of who she was becoming.

Gerda looked in the mirror and saw someone she hated, someone she feared. She was afraid it was herself.

Chapter Two
The Unreliable Escort

The wind whistled in the stretch of silence that followed as Kai Ødegård took in his surroundings without moving a muscle, every nerve on edge. Brittle shrubs grew from the apparently desolate terrain. Short hills seemed to slope into each other around them with a blanket of snow that crunched underfoot like dry grass. He supposed they were on some lip of a valley in the southern mountains that would rise and plummet at a moment's notice should they walk far enough. More immediately surrounding them were stacked rocks and unmarked headstones. He wondered who died here and how long ago.

But Kai knew better than to stand still for too long. The cold was so harsh in some places that it could settle forever into the bones of any sorry wayfarer who stood idle. There was nothing natural about this kind of chill.

Still, there was the smiling devil to deal with.

Lowering his voice to an even rumble, Kai questioned, "Whose side do you claim now?"

The intruder made a face at his tone. "Side? What side? Everyone's so obsessed with sides these days."

"Frost," Kai interrupted tersely. "Whose side—"

"I'm on my own side!" Frost thundered as snowflakes stormed around his neck and ears.

Kai didn't flinch. "Friend or foe?"

The flurry settled as his expression calmed to apathy. Frost cocked his head. "Friend. For now."

Flexing his stiffened fingers, Kai addressed the matter no further. Frost was flighty and intolerable. Kai couldn't even begin to fathom the implications of why he was there, no matter what he might've tried to imply with his greeting. Instead, he turned to his friends who watched them cautiously from a safe distance.

"Don't stand still too long," he advised. "Keep the blood pumping. You can't let the cold settle."

"Frost bites," Frost chipped in, baring his teeth in a sinister grin. "Not that I have anything to do with it anymore."

Wendy Darling inched closer to Red Daim, both shivering under their fur coats. Beside them, Alice Liddell studied Frost in curiosity as the lean fellow took two long steps toward the person standing closest to him, Jack Caldwell, in order to examine him. There was a tense moment of narrow-eyed scrutiny that caused Jack to straighten his shoulders.

Frost quickly returned to his hospitable façade, crystal eyes sweeping over the group. "So, who's who? Legacy and prophesy proceed you, but names fail to be interpreted on the winds."

Kai felt the urge to protest, clenching his fists. His disdain must've proved obvious as those crystal eyes flicked to him.

"Do you really think she doesn't already know who you are?" Frost chided. "Ha! Even you cannot be so blind."

Agitation flared up his neck, but he refused to respond.

Frost turned back to Jack and his expression instantly changed even as there was still a dangerous gleam in his hard eyes. "Who are you, then?"

Jack hesitated, glancing at Kai for confirmation. He gritted his teeth before dipping his chin. If Frost was right, then it didn't matter if they revealed their identity. The Snow Queen probably already knew they'd arrived.

Kai frowned as in the next moment Jack himself underwent a change of expression, pulling a bright grin, hiding the pain still fresh from what was left behind in Giant Country.

He hides it too well, Kai thought in remorse.

Jack stuck out his hand. "I'm Jack."

Frost raised an eyebrow at the outstretched hand, not inclined to take it even if he knew what it meant. "Jack, eh? Nice name... Mind if I take it?" Without allowing for a response, he raised his arm as if he could see the words in the air. "*Jack Frost.* It has a nice ring to it."

"Are you human?" Alice questioned, something strange in her voice.

"No. Yes. Or, used to be, I think. Word of advice: Don't ever kiss the Ice Maiden."

"Ice Maiden?"

"I suppose she goes by the Snow Queen now." Frost shrugged it off. "Now, who are you?"

"Alice."

Frost made a slight grimace and sucked air through his teeth at the thought. "Eh, not a terribly bad name, but not quite as audibly appealing."

Kai shook his head and turned away while Frost continued requesting introductions. He looked around at the white layers folding over the expanse, dustings of snow sifting through the wind. He couldn't entirely place where they were relative to where they needed to be. The longer he looked, the less certain he became.

"Are you done now, Frost?" he questioned, ready to move on from their idle conversation.

"Perhaps," was Frost's indifferent response.

Kai turned on him, eyes darkened. "What's the real reason you're here?"

"I'm the welcome party!" Frost exclaimed grandly as if he hadn't already said so. He shrugged at the insufficient appreciation. "I'm also the escort, but that's not nearly as exciting."

"Escort?"

"There was no telling how much you'd remember your bearings when you got back. Besides, there's a whole slew of spies and hunters about. Can't be too careful."

"Where do you mean to take us?"

Frost made a face. "You're too suspicious for your own good."

Before Kai could retort, Frost twisted his head around like an indecisive snake then turned away and started walking off, his feet barely leaving any footprints in the snow. Kai huffed, hesitant to follow. Frost was as trustworthy as ice – he might hold your weight, but he could also break and trap you under. But one look at his friends and he knew they had to get going if there was any chance of finding shelter and warmth. Already Red was stained rosy about her nose, cheeks, and chin.

"Who sent you?" Kai called after him.

Frost never broke stride, pivoting once to face him with arms widespread. "Everyone!"

Kai frowned in suspicion but begrudgingly trudged after Frost, his friends falling into step behind him.

*****

Hiking up the mountainside with a gnarled hand clasped around her walking stick, the Finnish Witch raised her nose in the frigid air and frowned deeply. Something dangerous and bitter reeked in the wind. Something like petrification. Something like death.

"Noaidi," she beckoned sharply, "come."

Behind her hobbled the Lappish Witch whose cloaks layered were as colorful as a field of wildflowers, her features soft and round. The Finnish Witch herself only wore one thin brown cloak and a scarf wrapped around the back of her balding head, cheeks hollow and nose sharp, aged skin hanging loose over her bones.

"What is it, Taika?" the Lappish Witch asked, her voice just breaking a whisper.

They'd been wandering through the southern mountains for weeks without a word passed between them. After a brief reprieve, the Snow Queen's powers had grown stronger, her reach stretching farther and becoming more toxic, forcing the two witches to flee their respective homes into the mountains. They informed anyone who asked that they were trying to prevent the Snow Queen's treacherous influences from advancing further south. Despite this, they hoped to appear suspicious, as if they were looking for someone.

"I've a feeling our troubles have come to fruition," the Finnish Witch informed gravely, her fishlike eyes staring hard into the swirling snow before them.

The Lappish Witch gave a small sigh and grasped her shoulder. "Do you believe they'll resolve this without us? Are we abandoning them in their greatest time of need?"

The Finnish Witch wisely patted the Lappish Witch's hand. "No power we can give them is greater than that which they already have. If they cannot discover this themselves, then there is no help we can provide."

Despite the softness in her eyes, the Lappish Witch nodded knowingly. They both harbored a fondness for the boy Kai and the Finnish Witch knew that her friend secretly hoped to see him one last time. But as the foul scent agitated her nostrils once again, she knew this was not to be.

She sensed rather than saw the figure standing in the snowy wasteland before them. A sour knot formed in her stomach.

"Come, my friend," she said, taking the Lappish Witch's hand and leaning against her walking stick. "Our time has come."

Together they approached the ferocious woman who stood tall amidst a plane of bowed trees laden heavy with snow. The witch, Häxan, peeled back her lips in a wide smile.

"A little far from home, aren't we?" she leered, electric blue eyes as startling as the aurora borealis. She had an unnatural rise and fall to her voice like she was tempting children into her rose garden or a bear trap.

"Are we? Please, I could have sworn we've only been walking for an hour," the Finnish Witch insisted in grave sarcasm.

Häxan narrowed her eyes. "What are you doing out here, Taika?"

"It seems we might be lost if we're a little far from home. That tends to happen in our old age, so I hear."

"You're lying."

"No, it's true," the Lappish Witch spoke up indignantly, her soft voice barely audible over the wind lapping against their weathered bodies. "I've heard plenty of people go wandering about when their old. You ought to know; you're here lost with us."

"Where is the boy?" Häxan snapped. The Finnish Witch could sense her temper rising, saw the way her long fingers curled into claws.

She shrugged, deciding the best lie was the truth. "We do not know."

Häxan sneered like a fox. "You are a deceitful old crone."

"And you are a treacherous old viper," the Finnish Witch retorted through her teeth.

"May your teeth rot out and your eyes sink into the back of your head," the Lappish Witch added with as much venom as she could muster.

The Finnish Witch squeezed her hand. "Now, now, Noaidi, we don't want to wish longevity on the old woman. Better she keels over tomorrow than live to see a ripe old toothless age."

Despite the insult, Häxan cocked her head thoughtfully – a bad sign. The Finnish Witch could often outwit the heinous fiend, but Häxan was clever. She'd figure out their ploy in the end.

"So, you do not know," Häxan determined. "And you think to distract *Snödrottningen* with your vagabond wanderings."

Pressing her lips firmly together, the Finnish Witch said nothing. But Häxan did not need her affirmation. Death was in the air and she knew it was theirs.

9

Without any hesitancy, Häxan flicked her wrist as if signaling an execution. The snowflakes around them swirled to life, gathering together into the humanoid figures of the Snow Queen's guard. They surrounded the two women and came upon them in a vicious blizzard, swallowing them whole, tearing them apart.

The Finnish Witch raised her head to the sky and whispered, *"Täällä tulee aurinko."*

Here comes the sun.

*****

The winds picked up soon, bringing with it the biting chill of snowflakes tossed into the air. Kai readjusted his furs to better trap his body heat. He wished he'd thought to transfigure hats out of the giants' old cloaks when he had the chance. Heat had a tendency to escape through the uncovered head, and with the wind building he knew they'd need all the heat they could salvage.

Hopefully this wouldn't rage into a storm. They couldn't afford to be blinded without shelter. Of course, Kai thought darkly, it could be Frost's fault. It wouldn't be the first time a blizzard was brought upon him due to the lithe devil's powers. But if Frost was meddling with the weather, he didn't show it.

Wendy hiked beside Kai, nearly as light on her feet as Frost was. She'd managed to wrestle a hood out of her fur wrappings to protect her face from the abrasive wind. Upon his recommendation, she kept an eye on the ground in search of a long stick to use to test the snowy floor as they walked – an issue that would inevitably arise once they cleared this plateau and traipsed through varying levels of accumulated

10

snow. She never complained, though, not about the harsh cold or their uncertain path. None of them did.

Alice stumbled on loose rock and would've fallen to her knees if Kai hadn't caught her. She nodded thanks when he helped her up, but her distracted look wasn't lost on him. Frowning in concern, he watched as she retrieved the escaped pocket watch from its landing place, brushing its damaged face with her thumb. The broken glass scratched her skin, smearing blood. She didn't seem to notice.

When Alice looked up at him, he saw such worry staining her cornflower blue eyes that he understood immediately what was wrong. Their only ticket home was gone. For good this time.

Kai placed a hand on her elbow to lead her on, but she shook him off, preferring to walk on her own.

As the neared the slow decline marking the edge of the plateau, Kai readied himself to recognize some mark in the terrain that would determine where in the mountains they were exactly. If he could somehow get an idea of where they were heading, then perhaps they could somehow shake off Frost. He wasn't completely willing to follow him blindly to an unknown location.

Cresting the mountainside, a blast of icy wind bashed into them and threatened to shove the small group onto their sides. Kai barely had time to brace himself before the storm followed right on the wind's heels, throwing them in a blinding haze of snow. With a frustrated shout, Kai hastened to gather his friends together so they wouldn't lose each other in the confusion, struggling with their coats to fashion hoods to protect their exposed heads. He could just barely see Frost silhouetted before him ambling onwards into the blizzard.

11

There was no choice now. Whether they trusted him or not, they had to follow Frost wherever he was leading.

Chapter Three
The Waiting Crows

Time obliterated in the swirling white mess of the storm. Kai led his friends in a line linked by their clasped hands, eyes squinted to the wind yet still able to discern their impervious guide ahead of them. After an endless trek, Frost seemed to head straight for an indistinguishable dark mass in the distance. Kai began to strongly suspect a trap when Frost suddenly thrust open a short door and held it ajar for the group to stumble inside.

The difference without the wind pummeling against them was instantaneous. He could breathe easier, feel the ache in his muscles. Outside the storm still raged, but its screams were muffled now to mere whistles against the sloped roof.

From what he could tell, the small lodge they'd entered was humble at best with short wooden walls and a creaky floor, beams supporting a steep triangular roof like a ribcage. Snow piled up over the windows on either side of the house. One window remained uncovered above the door, the glass so frosted that everything beyond appeared crystalline. A large stone fireplace graced the back wall like an open mouth, empty but promising.

Kai looked around with a frown as the others fumbled together shivering. A threadbare quilt hung from a shelf on the wall, yarn unraveled like a kaleidoscope of spiderwebs.

"I know this place," he murmured.

"At least your memory's intact," Frost said, wrinkling his nose at the few wooden furnishings that weren't broken or shredded. "Used to belong to one of the witches; the Lappish one, I think. She's not here anymore."

Kai ran his hand down the wall, tracing scars from icy winds sharp enough to shave wood. The Lappish Witch must have been run out of her own home. She'd helped him once on the final leg of his journey to find the Snow Queen and rescue Gerda. He recalled how bright the cabin had been, so full of light. Looking at the shambles it was in now, he realized this was probably his fault.

"You look a little blue," Frost observed, stooping over Red who sat with her knees tucked to her chest. She glared at him. With a quick jerk of the head, he indicated the fireplace. "You'll find everything you need right over there. Pull out the fifth stone from the right at the bottom."

Jack hastened to do so, finding flint and steel. Wendy found the firewood stacked beside the mantle. While they worked to get a fire going, Frost casually made his way to the farthest corner of the room where he ended up standing near the short doorframe. Jack struggled against his shaky hands to get the flintstone to spark, so Wendy had to take over. Sparks quickly showered over tinder and caught flame. Quickly, the five friends swarmed around the welcomed heat.

Behind them, Frost grimly stared out the icy window into the storm. His silence and watchful look made Kai anxious. Reluctant to leave the fireside, he stood and approached Frost.

"Watching for friends of yours?" he questioned, allowing a dark edge to sharpen his tone.

"Friends of yours, actually," Frost answered cryptically.

Working his jaw, Kai growled, "Are you going to tell me what the devil is going on here?"

"As I told you, I'm the escort."

"Where are you taking us?"

"Once the storm clears, I'm taking you to your army."

Kai furrowed his brow at that. Nothing was making sense. Any army he had was standing in this room, or else shivering by the fireplace.

Frost rolled his eyes as if he read his mind. "Surely you didn't think you were the only ones fighting against the Ice Maiden."

"Are you included in that statement?"

"Yes."

"Why do I find it so hard to believe you?"

"Because last time you were here, I led you into a trap after saving you from another one."

"Some would call that betrayal."

"I think most anyone would call it that."

"How do I know you're not doing it again?"

"You don't." Frost looked sidelong at him out of the corner of his eye. "I could be helping you in your rally against the Ice Maiden for any number of reasons. Revenge, rebellion, justice, the sheer fun of it, because it's the right or wrong thing to do; or maybe because I just woke up this morning and decided to shake things up a bit. It doesn't matter which; take your pick. This time you don't get the luxury of knowing *why*."

Kai narrowed his eyes but didn't press the subject any further. Frost casually reverted to searching the swirling blizzard outside the window. Even now, Kai didn't know what to make of him. Any minute the prickly devil could stab him in the back, and he wouldn't be the least bit shocked. He wished he could be certain of Frost's allegiances. But he should've known better than to pray for things to be so black and white.

Leaving Frost to his silent staring, Kai returned to his friends by the heat of the crackling fire. He encouraged them to try and rest while they could. As soon as Wendy tucked herself in a ball, she was pleasantly asleep. Alice was staring at Frost with a frown, the firelight blazing amber against the side of her face.

"I've seen him before," she muttered.

Kai raised an eyebrow, but Alice didn't venture to explain any further before she settled down with an arm under her head and drifted off as well. He couldn't come up with any reason why Alice would find Frost's face familiar. Frost was practically a slave to the Snow Queen – or at least he was until recently, if Kai could take him at his word. Besides, Frost might very well melt if he ever ventured too far from the Snow Queen's chill. But Kai knew better than to write off one of Alice's wonderings. She hardly drew up on a dead end.

Leaning against the wall close to the fireplace, Red had to warm up a little longer before she eventually nodded off.

Jack didn't fall asleep. He sat silently staring into the fire, the light dancing against his dulled eyes. Kai felt a pang in his gut. Just last night, Jack had lost one of his childhood friends for the second time. They'd sent her body away on a funeral raft that morning. Grief was bound to come in some form or another. Kai wished he could help ease the pain for his friend, but knew it was fruitless.

We all must come to terms with our pain, he thought forlornly. *And we must each learn how to carry it.*

Knowing he needed to keep his strength up, Kai leaned up against the wall and folded his hands over his chest. "Keep an eye on him," he warned Jack, flicking his eyes to Frost. Jack momentarily blinked out of his stupor to nod in comprehension.

Closing his eyes, Kai willed himself into a dreamless sleep.

A latch flicked in place, and Kai woke sharply at the sound to find Frost wrenching open the window above the door. Snow blew inside with a gust of wind. The sudden chill was enough to wake the others and cause the fire to shrink back.

"What are you doing?" Kai demanded, shuffling to his feet.

Frost didn't bother to answer before something black and hectic swooped inside. The window slammed shut, the latch firmly locked. Kai touched the hilt of his sword before he realized what the intruder was.

A large, disheveled crow flipped onto its feet after the ungraceful crash landing, a loaf of bread on the wood paneled floor nearby where the bird had dropped it. Cocking its head at Frost, it hopped around until it had Kai in its sights. It flapped its wings and cawed excitedly.

Frost frowned, peering suspiciously out the window. "Where's the other one?"

The crow squawked one last time before it bowed its head, stretched out its wings, and began to grow. In only a few seconds, a man stood in place of the bird. Short and stocky, he was as dark as the crow's feathers with beady eyes, no hair, and strange clothes that reflected deep blues and purples in the flickering light.

"She's on her way," the man responded, his voice scratchy. He stooped over to pick up the bread loaf and dusted it off. "She insisted on carrying jam along with her load. I tried to tell her it wouldn't do any good if the bread ended up hard as a rock, but she wouldn't listen to me." With a sheepish grin, he offered Kai the loaf. "Welcome back, *dumskalle*."

Kai couldn't help but smile. Ever since he'd met the crow and confessed his determination to save Gerda from the Snow Queen, the crow had called him *dumskalle* – a fool. The name stuck.

"*Tusen tack*," Kai said, gratefully accepting the bread.

He pressed the loaf to Wendy so she could split it between the five of them with her knife. When she offered a sixth piece to Frost, he shook his head with a scowl.

"Who are you?" Jack asked the crow-man, who stood at least two heads shorter and three times wider than him.

The crow-man waved his hand absently. "Agh, you can't pronounce my name in this ugly language."

"Alright then, Mr. Crow," Jack held out his hand, "I'm Jack."

Beady eyes brightened instantly, and he wagged his finger in interest. "Oh, I like that. Jack. Call me Jack."

"I already claimed it," Frost spoke up from his corner of the room.

Mr. Crow gave a deep frown in disappointment. "But it's such a refined sound, it is. Almost pleasant to the ear. And you already have a decent enough title. Everyone goes around calling me *Mr. Crow* like I'm some common animal – and I'm no common animal."

Agitated tapping shook the glass window above the door. When Frost forced it open again, a second crow hopped in with another bread loaf and a small jam jar tied to its ankles. Slipping out of the bundle with a few firm kicks, the crow grew similarly the way Mr. Crow had, except this time a woman stood in the center of the room. Of equal height and width to her predecessor, she had feathery black hair framing her round face.

"Sorry about that, Mrs. Crow," Frost said as he latched the window shut again.

She ignored him, turning on her husband in a fervor as she retrieved her bread and jam. "And what did you hope to achieve by leaving me behind?"

"Getting out of the cold faster," Mr. Crow muttered.

She shot a cool scowl at him and pinched behind the ear, earning a deserved flinch. After a last huff of annoyance, she kindly smiled at Kai and pressed her goods into his hands with a tender pat. "There you are, *kära*. Don't mind Mr. Crow; he's just grumpy about having to take off at a moment's notice these days. Comes with the job."

"It's Jack now!" Mr. Crow proclaimed resolutely, pointing to Jack like he'd given him a prized possession. "He's letting me take it."

"Would everyone please stop taking my name?" Jack muttered to himself. Kai struggled to keep back a laugh.

As Kai reached to borrow Wendy's satchel in order to store the extra loaf for later, Mrs. Crow insisted with a squawk, "Eat it! There's more where that came from. After scrounging around all day with empty bellies, best sleep now with filled ones."

Kai nodded and again divided the bread between the five of them. The jam was unfortunately frozen solid, so they placed it near the fire to defrost. At least they'd have something for breakfast.

While the others ate, Kai drew Mrs. Crow closer to the fire and kept his voice low, "What's going on?"

Affectionately, she patted his arm. "We've been waiting for you, *kära*."

"Who has?"

"Just about anyone you can think of. The nomads, the forest people, the princess, the witches, some animals, Frost." She made a sour face. "I'm sure even *Snödrottningen* has been waiting for your return."

"Then who sent him?" he questioned, jerking his chin toward Frost whose crystal gaze lay forebodingly on the fire from his dark corner.

"Everyone." Her casual answer mirrored Frost's which shocked him. His confusion must have shown because she went on to explain, "Frost was the only one who could determine where you'd show up. He could've chosen to take you either to us or to Snödrottningen. He betrayed her and has paid the price for it. For reasons I cannot say, he's chosen us. It was a risk we had to take."

Kai narrowed his eyes. "What price did he pay?"

"My immortality," Frost spoke so suddenly, Kai almost didn't catch it. Steel flashed in his eyes. Without another word, Frost walked outside into the blizzard and slammed the door shut behind him.

Mrs. Crow sighed, pity creasing her brow. "He's cut ties with Snödrottningen forever. I think he loved her once."

"Hogwash!" Mr. Crow spat with venom. "Nothing can fall in love with that devil; not even a treacherous trickster like Frost."

20

A chill ran down his spine. Kai recalled flashes of his conflict with the Snow Queen before he'd been wrenched from this place. Ice encasing, glass shattering, and the devil herself in all her monstrous fury. All he'd ever wanted was to save Gerda. And she was still there, trapped in the Snow Queen's clutches.

But so much had changed, and he along with it. This was bigger than Gerda, it always had been. Even back when he'd first ventured through the Snow Queen's realm, when he became sympathetic to the plights of people he'd never expected to care about – he should've known this didn't stop with Gerda's kidnapping. He had his friends, these people who had become like family to him. He had so many promises to keep. And now, apparently, he had an army.

Where did that leave Gerda?

Perched on the hearth's edge, Alice stared into the pocket watch's broken face like it might begin to speak its secrets to her if she looked hard enough. Wendy sat cross-legged beside her, taking the melted jam and scraping some over her bread piece. Red huddled next to the fire with her eyes suspiciously on Mr. and Mrs. Crow. The color on her cheeks had finally normalized. As for Jack, still baffled about the confusion regarding his name, he settled back down to maybe get some sleep at last.

Kai looked over them all with a tinge of concern.

What would become of them after all this was over?

The storm cleared with the grey of dawn, and at such opportune time, Mr. and Mrs. Crow bade leave with assurance of their prompt return with more food. The remaining jam served as a small breakfast along with whatever canteens of water they'd taken from Giant Country. Kai encouraged everyone to stay hydrated. After drinking his fill, he drained the rest of his own canteen into the others until his was sufficiently emptied, then he stepped outside to fill his container with fresh snow. No sooner had he ducked back inside than the door was flown open again. Frost stood there with a devilish grin and a jerk of his head, as if he hadn't disappeared all night.

"Come on," he announced, "we've got ground to cover."

Kai didn't bother to be hasty. Once he tucked the snow-filled canteen into his coat so that it pressed against his ribcage – a tactic his father taught him, using body heat to melt the snow into suitable drinking water – Kai made sure his friends were sufficiently covered before they doused the fire and braved the cold.

Fresh snow blanketed the landscape. The sparse trees weighed heavy with it, many leaning to the side as if conformed by the wind, others completely enveloped by rime ice.

Though now Kai knew roughly where they were, he wondered at their direction. Frost was eastward bound not northward, which was unexpected, but he supposed it was also a good sign. It meant Frost wasn't taking them to the Snow Queen.

The morning sun seemed to arouse spirits all around. Frost walked with a bounce to his step like a child, and Alice seemed to have put the incident with the broken pocket watch to rest. She was transfixed with their escort – Kai could practically see the gears spinning in her head. But he'd already determined that either Frost had some likeness to someone else whom Alice knew, or else she had another wild explanation for the familiarity. He decided not to trouble himself about it until Alice herself came upon a conclusion.

They skirted the edge of a few sturdy spruces that stood under a lipped snow cornice, afraid the overhanging would collapse at any moment. The trees themselves braved the danger, standing tall and dusted in powdery frosting. Kai stopped at the trees despite the threatening cornice overhead. Frost tried to walk onward, but Kai investigated one of the closest spruces, bowing under the needled branches to run a hand down its bark.

"What are you doing?" Jack asked behind him.

By way of answer, Kai dug his fingers into the trunk's ridges and pried away the bark until a teardrop-shaped plaque fell away. Ropes were attached on the inside. The tree remained unharmed behind the object, as if he'd removed a second skin. Resolutely, Kai found the other hidden contraption easier, completing the pair of roughly constructed snowshoes.

Jack had this awed look on his face like Kai had just pulled a rabbit out of a hat.

Alice peaked around at them. "How'd you know those were there?"

"The nomads used to have these made and hidden in case later travelers needed them," Kai explained, wrenching out another pair of snowshoes. "The Lappish Witch showed me how to find them."

After he'd collected just enough in fair condition – that is, those he managed not to break or weren't missing ropes – Kai helped the others strap on the snowshoes. Frost tapped his bare foot impatiently. For good measure, Kai also collected a thin branch for each to use in testing the snow's depth. In this part of the mountains where the terrain appeared as series of gentle slopes, it was easy to miss the sudden ravines and concealed sinkholes they might come across.

He hoped the snowshoes would make travel easier. Of course, it took two steps before Jack fell flat on his face and Wendy tripped into a brittle shrub. Red looked like she was on the verge of shifting form to experiment walking over the snow on the Wolf's four paws.

Kai discouraged the idea instantly. "Do you have a winter coat?"

Red frowned in answer. She'd probably never considered the notion before.

"Then don't risk it," he advised, helping Jack to his feet. "This is how you walk... Step wide so you don't trip over the other shoe."

"Point taken," Jack grumbled, dusting the snow off his arms and knees.

"Use your staff for balance if you need to," Kai continued. "Use your toe to kick into the snow when going uphill, and use your heels going downhill. Going along the sides of these slopes, put your weight on the higher foot so you don't slip."

He tried to demonstrate with his feet the different positions. As he instructed, Frost leaned against a spruce with his arms crossed, watching and laughing whenever anyone tripped or fumbled. Without warning, Alice grabbed a hunk of packed snow and launched it right into the branches above Frost's head, knocking heaps of snow right on top of him and wiping the smug grin off his face.

"Not so funny now, is it?" she shot spitefully as a laugh bubbled up. But she slapped her hands over her mouth suddenly in shock, as if she couldn't believe what she'd just done.

Frost shook off his hair. "Hilarious."

Alice dropped both her hands and her gaze. Her facial muscles seemed to twitch, contorting into confusion, like she couldn't decide which expression to wear. With a smirk, Frost spun on his heel to lead them onward once again.

Kai frowned in concern. He'd seen this happen before with Alice, at least recently, where she burst into unexpected fits of impulsivity, or where her mood seemed to swing from one face to another. She once said that she found herself acting increasingly spontaneous. This time, however, she seemed to be keenly aware of some confusing inner battle that was becoming harder to contain.

"Are you alright?" Wendy asked her softly, stepping close enough to touch her elbow.

Alice nodded, but didn't seem too convinced.

They trudged on, often waddling side to side like penguins. Better that they walked on top of the snow than knee deep in it.

As the morning brightened, sunlight glared down in a yellowed haze and made everything around them glow. Kai could see the mountain peaks now rising from the snow-covered hills, rock bared only on cliff faces; their crests seemed so close despite their great distance. To the left, when a tall slope did not block the view, he could sometimes see the treetops of what he knew to be a dense forest, and inside this forest he knew there was a river that led to the Snow Queen's castle – this being the path he'd taken the last time he'd left the Lappish Witch's house.

He'd never traversed over the slopes like this. They'd been the strip to cross from the mountains to the forest, from the forest to the Lappish Witch's house, and from there down the river to the Finnish Witch and then the Snow Queen. Perhaps it was smart, then, to have been given a guide. Kai might not have been as adept to the terrain as he'd care to admit. This wasn't like Alice's Wonderland and Wendy's Neverland where the place was home to them, nor was this like Red's Enchanted Forest and Jack's Giant Country where they'd been forced to know the territory due to years of survival. Kai's visit to the Realm of the Snow Queen had always been a means to an end. He knew only what would take him to that end, and now that knowledge wasn't enough.

Frost came to a halt at the top of a hill where there was nothing but air surrounding him, and the sun hit him like a spotlight. Even when the rest of them caught up, he remained still, staring north. Kai sucked in a breath.

Sugar coated pines inked down the slopes and collected into a crowded forest in the valley. A strong river churned from the mountains and twisted through the trees, its power raging from the snowmelt. The river fed into a blinding white lake, frozen solid, like a great crystal mirror. Beyond the lake in the distance was a barren wasteland of ice and the snowy skeletons of trees bowed into frozen arches. Protruding from the center of this iced lake rose a monstrous castle like a thousand stalagmite icicles.

Kai sighed in dismay, breath clouding. Gerda was still in there. She was there and he was going the wrong way.

Stay strong, min älskling, he wished and hoped that God would pass on the message.

When at last he turned from the view, the intruder crested the hill, coming toward them.

Chapter Four
The Runaway Captives

Greetings, hjältar.

The voice echoed pure and warm inside Kai's head. He couldn't help but smile as the white-haired reindeer approached, stepping forward to greet him.

"Bae," Kai said softly as the reindeer pressed his muzzle against his palm.

A pleasant hum filled his mind, radiating from Bae like a private melody. One look at his friends, though, and Kai knew that they too could hear Bae's voice. Jack seemed particularly shocked, and Alice blinked as if she just realized that the voice in her head was not a figment of her own imagination.

Bae was twice as large as a normal reindeer with massive antlers that pinked in comparison to his albino pelt. Kai closed his eyes and let Bae's hum warm him. They'd been through much together when they journeyed across the Snow Queen's realm. He didn't realize how much he'd missed his old friend.

"As I said," Frost spoke up, pulling Kai out from the waves of nostalgia. He looked back at Frost who extended his arms and gave an exaggerated bow. "I'm on your side."

Bae regarded their lanky guide with warm brown eyes. There was something deep and perplexing about his silence that made Kai wonder if the reindeer knew more about Frost's intentions than he'd confess. Or perhaps Bae was sending a private message to Frost through his telepathy.

"Does he transform like the crows?" Red asked cautiously.

In response, Bae laughed gently like a warm glow. *No, hjältinna, I am as you see me.*

Kai vaguely wondered why he continued to call them as such. But he knew Bae's eloquence often broached a wisdom he could not understand, and he wasn't sure he wanted to know why Bae dubbed them as heroes.

"What are you doing here?" Kai whispered, breathing in Bae's earthy scent that somehow reminded him of home.

I am to lead you forward, Bae responded.

"Where?"

That is for you to decide.

Somehow, he knew those last words were for him alone. "I will go where I am needed."

You are needed in more places than you can ever fathom. This is your choice to make.

Stomach clenched, Kai realized the crossroads where they stood. Beyond was an uncertain future, behind was home, and now he faced an end that he could choose. There was Gerda, there was the Snow Queen, and there was Anders. Whatever came next had to be of his own volition. Nothing could force him onward but himself.

"Why now?" he asked.

Because it is about to begin.

Kai looked back at his friends, all of whom had already stood where he was and made their choice to be here, to keep on this path. Now it was his turn.

"Take me to the army," Kai said, glancing at Frost who remained unfazed.

Bae blinked his large brown eyes in understanding. *We shall go as you eat.*

"Eat?" Jack perked up.

The reindeer hummed in amusement, turning so they would descend into a shallow flatland.

Overhead, two crows appeared carrying netted bags of bread and carrots. Both cawed in greeting, circling briefly. Mr. Crow accidentally dropped the carrots in the snow and earned a sharp jab on the head from his wife. Kai and Red retrieved the food to distribute it while Mr. and Mrs. Crow contented themselves in perching on Bae's antlers as he led them on.

Frost again refused any food, taking instead a handful of snow and crunching it between his teeth. Mrs. Crow clicked her beak at him.

Bae translated, *You will not be able to eat like that for much longer, Frost.*

He gnashed his teeth. "You don't seem to realize that just because I'm mortal now doesn't mean I'm human."

Mr. Crow says to take caution when talking to his wife like that or he shall show you how mortal you are.

Frost extended his arms daringly. "My apologies. I meant every disrespect."

With a wild shriek, Mr. Crow took wing and catapulted straight for him. Frost raised his hand just before the crow could reach his hair, and Mr. Crow plummeted head first to the ground, a block of ice sealed around his beak. He flapped around angrily but couldn't so much as hold his head straight with such a heavy muzzle.

Kai shot a disapproving look at Frost before he scooped up the fallen Mr. Crow and set him on Bae's broad back. The bird slumped in frustration while Mrs. Crow fussed about his feathers.

Frost said nothing, stomping ahead, his breathing heavier than before. Kai huffed. Gently, someone slipped a hand in his and gave it a squeeze. He turned a small smile to Wendy before moving forward through the light.

The ravine came suddenly, invisible up until the moment before they found themselves inside its gaping trench. Spruce trees and shrubs lined the steep sides so Kai did not fear so much an avalanche as he did the exposure. Anyone could be watching them, concealed by the snow and evergreens, waiting to ambush.

Bae seemed unconcerned. He led them through the ravine on limber legs without hesitancy, humming all the way. Despite this, Kai kept a hand on his sword.

Red, too, was clearly unnerved by the situation. She regularly looked over her shoulder, eyes darting to the trees, as if she heard something following them. Even without considering those from other realms, the Snow Queen had many spies. Kai was glad for Red's heightened senses, as she was most likely to discover any intruders they happened upon.

The wind whistled down the ravine, kicking up snow in its icy chill. Kai shivered, hoping not to get caught in another snow storm. He hoped that wherever Bae was taking them, it included shelter and hot drinks.

Alice attempted to drink from her canteen but came up dry. The water had frozen around the nozzle, blocking its contents. Kai offered her his canteen, the snow having melted from earlier that morning, and took hers in exchange to try to thaw the frozen spout.

"How are you?" Kai asked, noticing the purple hue to her lips.

She shrugged. "A little chilly. You?"

"I've been worse."

"How do you know him?"

He blew warm air into his hands and rubbed them together. "We were both held captive by a band of nomadic robbers, I believe I've told you about them. Bae and I were kept like pets for this girl's menagerie; Mr. Crow, too. We traveled together after she set us free."

Alice accepted this information, but she corrected easily, "I meant Frost."

Kai felt a knot form in his stomach, bitter and harsh. "He helped me escape the witch Häxan's trickery, gave me some directions."

"Then why don't you trust him?"

"Because he lied," he said in a low growl. "The last time I saw him, he led me into a trap; right into the Snow Queen's arms. He'd do anything for her."

"Even play both sides?"

Kai cast a glance behind where Frost tailed the group with shifting eyes. "I don't know."

When Alice drank her fill, Kai suggested she hold the canteen upside down. That way, if the water decided to freeze again, the ice would congeal on the bottom of the container and leave the spout untouched.

Deeper in the ravine where the spruce trees formed a fine patchwork along the sides, Bae came to an abrupt halt. His round ears flicked back and forth. On his antler, Mrs. Crow squawked worriedly.

Kai broached them. "What is it?"

She has been following us.

Fuming, Kai whirled on Frost with knuckles clenched, ready to pummel the traitor for deceiving them once again. Frost scowled at the sudden aggressiveness, like he was on the verge of denial.

Snow exploded from the left, and both men flinched away as a massive lynx pounced, claws extended. Kai's anger vanished as he realized the situation. In an instant, he shot forward and shoved Jack out of the lynx's trajectory just as an arrow slammed into the lynx's shoulder, bashing her to the ground. Kai landed hard on Jack as they hit the floor. He looked up in time to see another shaft bury itself in the ground beside the spotted predator, prompting the lynx to wheel around and bound off into the snow.

Panting, Kai lifted himself onto an elbow. Ambushers surrounded them, each wearing hardened leather clothes and fur-lined hoods, each holding drawn bows aimed straight at them.

Frost raised his hands up and behind his head in annoyance. The girls hesitantly followed suit, except for Red who seemed to be evaluating how many of the intruders she could take down before someone got shot. Beside him, trapped face down under his arm, Jack lifted his hands so they hovered on either side of his head. Kai groaned, rolling his eyes back to Bae.

"Were any of them aware of this plan of yours?" he questioned. "Or did you decide to improvise and hope for the best?"

"Sounds like something I would do," Jack muttered into the snow.

Bae merely hummed in response, the coy beast.

"*Det är på tiden att du kom tillbaka till mig,*" a sharp voice said easily from the surrounding ambushers.

Kai craned his neck as he looked around from his awkward position, finally spotting the girl standing over him. Grey fur encircled her round face, black wisps of hair escaping her hood to blow over her cheeks. Narrowed onyx eyes scrutinized him. Her thin lips rested into more of a pout than a frown. She pressed her gloved hands into her padded hips. Even with her looking down on him, she looked significantly short.

"*Du är sen,*" the girl jabbed.

Jack squirmed and asked under his breath, "Did she just threaten us? Please tell me she's not going to kill us."

Kai shifted up to both elbows, regarding the girl. She couldn't be more than twelve now. "You've grown up."

"You got old."

The comment made him grin. He was glad that at least some things never really changed. "How are you, Inga?" he asked.

"*Präktig,*" she said sarcastically.

For a moment they remained as they were, staring, waiting to see who would make the first move. Kai's arm slipped out on the snow from under him, breaking eye contact. Inga smirked. She cast her steely gaze over the others who remained with arms raised in submission.

"They're all with you?" Inga questioned, eyebrow raised.

Kai nodded. "*Ja.*"

"Even Frost?"

He hesitated but resigned. "Even Frost."

Inga gave a grunt as if she couldn't quite believe it but would accept it all the same. With a broad wave to her companions, the other nomads lowered their bows and relaxed their shoulders. Kai rolled onto his feet, pulling Jack up after him.

Promptly ignoring him now, Inga made a beeline for Bae and her face brightened in a way she didn't with anyone else. Like she was still a little girl who only wanted to be loved. The reindeer pressed his forehead against hers affectionately. She grinned and scratched his ears.

Behind him, Jack hissed, "Kai."

The robbers closed in around them and steered them ahead in a way that felt both like protection and captivity. Bae crouched down onto one knee for a moment, allowing Inga to hop onto his back before he walked on again. Inga held Mr. Crow securely in her lap.

"Kai," Jack whispered again as they started forward. "Kai. You never answered my question. Are they threatening us?"

Kai shrugged. *"Det är svårt att säga."*

"You know I don't speak Swedish!"

Chapter Five

The Little Robber Girl

The nomads took them along the ravine until the ground began a steady incline, bidding them to jam their toes into the snow for traction as they ascended. Kai's thighs took the excursion in toll. Covering distances like this through snow doubled the accrued fatigue. But he was used to the wear on his legs, the strain of his Achilles tendons as his feet were forced to extended angles, the burn up his hamstrings with every step. His friends, on the other hand, were beginning to lag – except for Wendy, who hardly made a dent in the snow as she climbed.

Thick fog rested over the valley below the slopes, blocking the forest and castle from view. It resembled the cloud sea wherein they'd pushed Jill's funeral barge. Jack refused to tear his eyes from the hill before them, his feet shoved into the snow with a rhythmic trudge. Kai looked away. Sometimes he forgot how his friend was still mourning.

"Are you exhausted already, *gubben*?" Inga asked, mocking in her tone.

Kai was not, but he humored her. "You might be as well if you walked down here with the rest of us."

Inga shrugged impassively as she stroked Mr. Crow's feathers. With a jolt, Bae dropped to his knees, causing her to squeal and nearly be thrown off his back. Bae chuckled at the jest even as Inga puffed out her flushed cheeks and smacked him on the shoulder blades. Mr. Crow flapped his wings in annoyance, beak still frozen shut. Kai laughed when Inga shot him a nasty glare.

It was strange, the déjà vu of it all, the unraveling of things. Kai could still remember a time when Inga held them all captive, Bae chained to a post, Mr. Crow held in a cage. He remembered how she would take a birdcage holding a yellow dusted siskin, a scarlet crowned redpoll, and a bullfinch with a broken wing, and she would demand them to sing for her. She'd shout so hard she'd start to cry. She used to tickle Bae's neck with her knife to discourage any escape. She'd poke a stick at Mr. Crow through the cage bars until he was in a frenzy. She treated Kai like a slave, forced him to sleep on the ground just under her bed where she kept a blade pressed to his back. It was hard to tell that was all nearly two years ago.

Now here they were, returned, reunited. Bae explained to Kai once why he would return to Inga after everything, why he never tried to escape until she'd let him go. She was only a girl who didn't know how to love. She was still learning.

As they crested the hill, they entered a hollow glen where fabric-covered lavvus and goahtis crowded into each other, thin curls of smoke twisting invitingly from the tents' peaks. Reindeer wove in among them, all brown, mute, and normally sized. More nomads were scattered throughout the camp, bundled in heavy padding, going about their daily business until they noticed the oncoming travelers.

Kai felt his stomach tighten with each step. Excited shouts rose from the camp, a chant repeated over and over until it became a collection unit: "*Här kommer solen! Här kommer solen!*"

He'd heard the phrase before like a victory cry, a hope for a distant future. For the robbers, it was *här kommer solen*; for the witches, it was *täällä tulee aurinko*. It meant the same. This time, though, he knew it was for him.

"What are they saying?" Alice asked, nearly losing her footing.

Before Kai could answer, Frost spoke up dryly, "They're welcoming their long-awaited heroes."

Ignoring him, Kai translated for Alice's benefit, "*Här kommer solen* – Here comes the sun."

"It's old fashioned, if you ask me," Inga added from Bae's back, wrinkling her nose. "But no one liked my idea."

"What was your idea?" Wendy questioned.

"*Välkommen tillbaka, ditt ägghuvud*," Inga answered, cutting her eyes to Kai. "Welcome back, you egghead."

He huffed amusedly. "Hard to believe it didn't catch on."

"They're so hard to please. I even tried to welcome you as my runaway pet. They didn't like that either."

"Your pet?" Jack frowned, out of breath. "Am I missing something?"

"Yes, probably."

Red couldn't contain the bark of laughter she tried to cover with her hand. Jack didn't know whether to be impressed or take offence.

Leaning forward, Inga scratched behind Bae's ears and up his fuzzy antlers. "Tjuv gave Kai to me as a present."

"So he was your slave?" Jack clarified.

"Pet," Inga insisted.

Jack looked at Kai inquisitively. Kai shrugged and said, "They are almost the same thing."

"*Pet*," she pressed. "But then I let you go out of the sheer goodness of my heart. And because I am so good, I released all of my other pets so they could be free and live happy."

Bae hummed pleasantly.

"I had to convince you to let me go, and then promise to return once I completed my journey," Kai added.

Inga rolled her eyes. "It is called a compromise. Besides, the others come back to visit me. You have dragged your feet."

"I've been busy."

"Ungrateful," she muttered with a pout. "*Otrolig!*"

"*Lilla Rånareflickan.*"

"*Gubben.*"

"Alright, children, calm down," Jack cut in. He probably enjoyed watching them banter so long as he could understand what they were saying.

Coming upon even ground in the glen's bowl, Inga led Bae and the rest of them through the crowd that awaited, parting the waters. All around them hands reached out to touch Kai and his friends as if in their very nature they held some warmth or promise of deliverance. Kai frowned, his skin crawling with discomfort. He'd seen these people before, even lived with them for a time, and they had not treated him like this.

Inga brought them to a stop where the nomads formed a ring around them. A hardened elderly woman stood before them, jowls sagging, hair shot through with veins of silver, grey, and black, all braided into a tight knot at the back of her head. Walrus tusks hooked through her earlobes. She had the same thin lips and narrow black eyes as Inga.

"So," the woman spoke, her accent heavy, "my granddaughter's pet returns."

Kai swallowed a lump in his throat then approached her carefully. "I have come to finish a long journey."

"That is why we have all come," she responded, arms spread to those around her. Her inky black eyes regarded each of them in turn, from Kai to Jack, Red, Wendy and Alice. "I am called Tjuv. I speak for us all. Welcome, *hjältar*."

"*Tusen tack*," Kai thanked, bowing his head slightly. His jaw remained tight at the excessive attention.

Tjuv noticed his discomfort. "You did not expect our greeting?"

He shrugged. "Last time you were not so civil."

"Last time you were a wanderer with no purpose," Tjuv answered, as if that justified them capturing him before. "Now, you are a warrior who will save us. A warrior who is almost ready to go home."

Kai didn't know how to respond.

Beside them, Mrs. Crow gave an enthusiastic squawk as if to second Tjuv's statement, Mr. Crow attempting to join in with strange guttural sounds as his beak remained clamped shut in ice. Bae filled his mind with melodic humming. The nomadic robbers surrounding them began to chant again in low, growing hope. Kai's friends shifted uncomfortably. Only Tjuv and Frost remained silent, staring.

Kai looked up at Inga, seeking some sense of familiarity. This praise seemed strange and awful all at once. There was no part in him that felt deserving; if anything he felt repulsed, as if this warmth were a betrayal of who they were and who he was.

Inga merely shrugged. "*Välkommen tillbaka, gubben*."

The vague insult eased his spirits somewhat. But this other cry echoed in his ears, rattling him with expectations he couldn't fulfill and promises he wasn't sure he could keep.

Here comes the sun...

Here comes the sun…
Here comes the sun…

*****

Gerda shrieked when she awoke, cold sweat pricking her skin.

The mirror was no longer in jagged pieces. It was solid, a perfect glass without scratch or blemish. The Snow Queen had finished it at last.

Cautiously, she approached the mirror, running her fingertips over its surface and hoping the wholeness was a trick of the light. But there was no crack she could find. The mirror was seamless. She jerked her hand back as something sharp nicked her finger, drawing blood. Wherever the imperfection was, it was too small to see. In the end, it didn't matter. It was complete.

Terror filled her like a rod behind her ribcage. Had the Snow Queen finally won, then? But if she had, then would Gerda even be here? She supposed she'd be dead if the Snow Queen won; unless this imprisonment was to be her damnation, a lifetime of half-consciousness, only just awake enough to witness the Snow Queen's destruction.

Nej! she scolded herself sharply.

Despite the Snow Queen's efforts to keep her from eavesdropping, Gerda could often overhear her from this prison. She grabbed on to the last thing she'd learned like it was her lifeline.

Kai had returned to the realm, and the rest along with him.

Stay strong, min älskling.

41

His voice came to her like a spring breeze, the closest thing to warmth she now knew. She choked on a sob. Longing clutched in her stomach, aching. Squeezing her eyes shut at the homesickness, she had to lean against the mirror with her hand so she wouldn't fall over. She couldn't even remember home. There was only Kai, and even his face began to blur at the edges.

With a sigh, Gerda opened her eyes and saw the woman staring back at her in the mirror. She gasped and shrank back as far away as she could. Gerda hated when that woman appeared in the mirror, the jade eyes, the straight ginger hair. She didn't know the woman's real name.

She'd always called her Anne Christiansen.

*****

"We shall move on once the storm clears," Tjuv informed as she gave silent commands to those they passed, encouraging the reindeer to be moved into shelters, prompting everyone to get inside soon.

Inga scowled at a blank sky. "I do not see a storm coming."

"It is coming," Tjuv said simply, harsh. "Ask Frost."

When Inga cast a frown at him, Frost spared only a curt nod in his indignant silence. He'd been more irate and steely ever since they joined the robbers, acting even more uncomfortable than Kai had been. Kai didn't know of anything specific Frost might've held against the nomads. As far as he could tell, Frost had a simple dislike for people in general. Not that the nomadic robbers had any warmth for Frost, either. Former as it may be, Frost's reputation as the

Snow Queen's devout servant preceded him. They had good reason to distrust him.

"Where are we moving to?" Kai asked. He was ready to get some straight answers after being unsuccessful with his inhuman companions' responses.

Tjuv checked that the fabrics covering the goahtis and lavvus were securely fastened. "They have told you of your army?"

"*Ja.* But not what this army consists of or where it is."

With a grunt, Tjuv hefted a basket of roots that had been abandoned in the hubbub. She shoved it into Inga's arms. "The princess has taken charge of the preparations. She gathers her forest people who have not yet been tainted," she spoke with a bluntness that ground against stone. "We will join the princess's forces once the storm clears."

"If there is a storm," Inga muttered.

"Inga, go chip the ice off *Herr Kråkan*," Tjuv ordered coolly.

Sticking out her lip in a pout, Inga stuck the basket on her hip, cradled Mr. Crow in her arm, and scampered off. Mrs. Crow flew after her to land on the girl's shoulder.

Heart pounding in his ears, Kai stepped closer to Tjuv and lowered his voice, "Have you heard anything of Gerda?"

"The girl you sought after before?"

He nodded.

Tjuv frowned, looking at the others standing behind him. "She is not with you?"

Furrowing his brow, Kai shook his head.

She narrowed her eyes. "We have heard nothing."

Kai sighed but expected as much. The engagement ring weighed heavy around his neck. He was so close to getting her back, safe and home, that his insides hurt. He could bear it so long as Gerda was there at the end of all this.

His scar burned ice cold.

The storm was rolling in now, clouds rolling in over the sky like a sheet, the wind sharp against her skin. Few remained outside to get the last of the preparations done before the blizzard hit. Alice wondered if it would sleet. She wondered what it would feel like to be pummeled by tiny flecks of sky-ice.

At the edge of the glen, she found Frost sitting in the snow and watching the pale grey sky, the swirling snowflakes flitting down on his face. He looked like what she imagined a body would appear when it froze to death.

"Shouldn't you be inside?" Frost asked blandly as she approached. He didn't drop his skyward gaze.

"Shouldn't you?"

"As I said before: I'm not human."

"But you used to be."

"Supposedly."

Alice stopped just beside him, standing so her boot was parallel to his bare foot. "No, not supposedly."

Frost didn't react. Snowflakes caught on his bleached eyelashes but didn't melt.

With a huff, she watched her breath cloud. A dragon on her lips. "I know how I recognized you. I saw you in a vision, this blind girl accidentally showed it to me, one of two faces. You looked different."

"Not so frightfully handsome?"

"Not so bitter and pale."

Frost frowned, cutting his eyes to her for a moment, but he said nothing. Alice took that as a sign to continue.

"You had ginger hair, freckles," she explained as best she could, trying to remember the vision. "You were laughing with someone; I couldn't see her face. But you were making a toy house, I think. And the girl said your name, but I can't—"

"Please stop." He said it so softly she almost didn't catch it in the growing wind.

"I thought that maybe you could explain—"

"The last thing I want right now is to be reminded of a life I can't remember and asked questions that I can't answer."

"I just wanted to know who the girl was."

"You should go."

"I think it's important."

"Please go."

"Rudy, if you could just—"

"*THAT'S ENOUGH!*" Frost burst to his feet, snowflakes swirling around him, eyes hard as ice.

They stood a hand's breadth apart, tension so tight she could hardly breathe. They remained frozen like that for the split moment it took for her to realize she'd used Frost's real name. Without another word, Alice turned away steadily and walked toward one of the tents where she would wait out the storm.

Frost was still standing outside alone when the blizzard hit.

Chapter Six
The Tainted Water

The wind beat against the side of the goahti, causing the fabric to ripple between the wooden poles. Inside, the ground had been dug out into a shallow circle, furs and blankets strewn over the floor to keep the bare dirt from sapping their body heat. A small fire snapped in the middle, keeping them warm.

Kai watched as Inga threw a scarlet and blue patterned blanket over Bae's back. She was so tender now with the animals, so different than before. She even held Mr. Crow's icy beak until it melted from her warm hands. A soft glow filled his chest. He always knew she had goodness in her. She just had to grow a bit, learn to love and show kindness. Maybe they both did.

Much has changed, hjälte, Bae's voice swept through his mind, his soft eyes observing him. *As have you.*

Kai didn't respond; he knew it was true. He was almost afraid that at the end of this journey he would find he'd become someone unrecognizable. Would his mother and grandmother know him when he returned to Anders? Would Gerda?

He shivered until he shook himself out of the sullen hole of doubt. Whatever happened to him, it did not change what mattered in the end. He would defeat the Snow Queen and keep his promises, he would save Gerda, and he would return home. Of course he would be different; everything changed with time. Gerda would be different, just as his mother and grandmother would be, and Anders itself. He just hoped he remembered the way home, and that there was still a home to go back to.

Jack sat close beside him with a newly acquired woolen blanket, coughing a little from the smoke. "So, do you think this bloody ice queen is trying to hold us up?"

"What do you mean?" Kai asked in concern.

"You know, with all the blizzards. Or are we just unlucky?"

He huffed a laugh. "Not unlucky, just a subject to the weather."

"So Old Frosty can't just, *poof,*" Jack made a kind of explosion with his hands, "magic snow storm?"

"She can," Kai admitted. "But this is more likely a natural occurrence, if not a side effect of her power, than the Snow Queen's influence alone. If she wanted us, she would probably do something more direct, like send her guards or Häxan. As is, I'm not sure she even knows where we are."

"Let's hope," Jack muttered, crossing his arms over his chest and tucking the blanket under his chin.

Kai looked him over warily. "You don't look well."

He didn't really smile, though he tried. Smiling didn't seem to come as easily to him anymore. "I'm not well," Jack confessed as easily as he could've said that he was cold. He didn't bother to blame the smoky room or the chill; he didn't even shrug it off like he might've a few days ago. He just let the fact sit there between them, bare and true. He was not well.

"I'm sorry about Jill," Kai said softly. "I never told you before."

"Thank you." Jack sighed deeply, looking at the smoke twisting out through a hole in the roof. "It's strange mourning her again. It's worse this time around."

Kai said nothing. He knew loss, but this he could only imagine.

"But I can live with missing her this time," Jack continued, surprising him. "I don't want to waste away lingering on things I no longer have control of. Maybe her death was my fault, but she had choices too. We all do."

Setting his jaw, Kai watched him cautiously, recognizing a tipping point where Jack unknowingly stood. Grief had ways to break or remake its casualties. But sometimes what it remade wasn't the strength one might hope for.

"Be careful not to let the grief turn to vengeance," Kai warned, voice low. "You can't control that either."

Jack let the words sink, nodded. "I want to live. I don't want to be scared anymore. That's all."

Kai followed where Jack's gaze drifted, where Red lay shrouded in blankets. He gave a grunt, but didn't say anything, trying to suppress the smile tugging the corner of his mouth. It was about time.

Wendy and Inga were talking in hushed tones, exchanging stories, leaning against Bae's soft body. He tried not to think of the possibly embarrassing tales they shared about him. By the way Inga's black eyes shone with mischievous laughter, he figured it was best not to know.

Bae gave a gentle hum just before he drifted off to sleep. Mr. and Mrs. Crow perched on either antler, beaks tucked into their wings.

On the far side of the goahti, Alice sat in stoic contemplation. Long lemon blonde hair swept over to one side of her head, leaving one ear exposed, her head tilted slightly. She stared at the firelight with eyes half closed as if she saw answers there to the questions flicking through her mind. Kai wondered if she would get any rest tonight.

A gnarled hand rested on his shoulder. Tjuv looked down on him, flicking heavy lidded eyes to Jack also. "You must sleep. The night is cold, and tomorrow will be long."

Kai didn't argue, and Jack was smart enough to follow his lead. Without a word, Kai lay down on the covered floor with arms crossed, quickly falling asleep the way he usually did, dreamless, always on the brink of waking.

Except this time was different.

This time the biting chill down his scar never ceased.

By morning the storm had cleared to wisps of snowflakes, and Kai woke to the taste of blood in his mouth. He ran his tongue precariously over his teeth. But the sensation was gone in an instant, so he thought nothing of it.

Within the hour, the nomads had dismantled their lavvu and goahti structures, secured them and their belongings to the domesticated reindeer, and began the trek out of the glen and down the slopes. To give him a break, Inga didn't ride Bae as she did yesterday. Her curl-toed boots helped her walk through the snow with ease.

Kai tugged on his new leather gloves, catching up with Jack to walk beside him. He seemed distracted, hands shoved in his pockets, stealing glances at Red who walked ahead of them.

Nudging him, Kai pestered, "I thought you didn't want to be scared anymore."

Jack wrinkled his flushed nose. "I'm waiting for the right time."

"Ah, the right time."

"Maybe when I'm not freezing my bloody toes off. Or when we stay in one place for longer than a pleasantly stormy evening. Or when I'm not wearing a ridiculously furry hat," he said, indicating the fur-lined beaded hat he now donned that sat on his head like a badger.

Kai huffed humorously, "Good luck with that, *bror*."

Jack pressed his lips firmly together, looking again in Red's direction. Kai felt a pang in his chest, all humor lost. He sighed, pushing back memories of stealing glances at Gerda down the streets of Anders, her sleeves rolled up to her elbows after helping her father with a patient, the sun in her hair. Or holding her hands as she pulled him into their *smultronställe*, the flowers she put in her pockets, behind her ear. Or when she'd smile at him from her bedroom window where their houses nearly touched, roses grown between them, letting the curtains fall.

Swallowing through a tight throat, Kai told his friend, "Take it from me. You never know when anything can be stolen away, and you never know when you are given the opportunity to put yourself together again."

Jack raised an eyebrow. "That was good. Where'd you hear that one from?"

"My grandmother," Kai admitted, remembering her papery hands over his, how she looked at him through watery eyes, how she sometimes mistook him for the son she lost. The father he missed.

Jack managed a smile.

With the southern mountains at their backs, they neared the edge of the slopes where the trees awaited them. The forest seemed to hold its breath at their approach, foreboding, cold. The terrain began to level out at last a good distance before the inevitable plunge into the forest.

Frost appeared behind Alice, shadowing her for a span of three heartbeats before he said in an even rush of words, "Her name was Babette."

Alice caught him a sideways glance. "So you do remember."

He scowled and marched off, but he didn't disappear. Alice couldn't help the slow victorious smile that stretched across her face.

Inga sauntered ahead of the pack, Mr. Crow on one shoulder and Mrs. Crow on the other. Kai watched her warily. Something squirmed in his stomach, suspicious. The distance grew. He picked up his pace.

A sharp crack split the air, shooting out in jagged bolts around her feet as Inga froze stalk still. The Crows cawed wildly, taking flight to hover above her. The nomads gave panicked cries behind.

Kai pitched forward to get her, but a deep groan beneath his feet caused him to halt. He looked down, realizing they were at the edge of a frozen pond, the ice so white and cracked that they mistook it for snow. Behind him, Tjuv gave a shout that made the robbers retreat to solid ground.

Inga's wide eyes met his as she grasped the horror of her situation. Kai took another cautious step forward, then stopped cold when he recognized the muted thumping under his feet. His heart sank. Dropping to his knee, he brushed aside the snow to expose the naked ice. A fist met the opposite side, knocking against the frozen surface repeatedly from under the water. He finally made out a face there, white eyes inside an inky face, blue ice bleeding from the corners of his eyes. When the girl showed herself, with pale moon skin and thin white eyes, Kai looked away, back to Inga and the webbed ice around her.

Before he could risk crossing the expanse to get her, Wendy rushed past him, footsteps hitting the ice light and quick. A hand burst from the ice behind Inga. She screamed. The Crows dove towards the protruding arm to keep it away. Wendy jumped, slid, and grabbed Inga, the two girls rolling out of the way.

When Kai glanced back at the ice below him, the shadows beneath were drifting away, joining others in congregation towards Wendy and Inga who tried retreating to him. Realizing their plan, he lunged forward. Someone shouted a firm, "Stay back!" behind him, but he didn't bother to check if it was directed at him or not.

Craggy, frost-bitten hands shot out of the ice and locked onto Inga's leg. She screamed as she tripped. Wendy slid to her knees to turn back for her. The Crows were in a frenzy, flying closer to help. More hands shot up, damaging the ice, water leaking from the cracks. Kai aimed at full speed, grabbed both girls, and used his momentum to propel them across the pond.

The attackers under the lake's surface were silent as they drifted after them, a horde of reflections. With no time to reevaluate, Kai launched the lot of them into a snowbank, earning a squeal from Inga.

The snow threatened to bury them upon collision, but Kai didn't allow much time to rest. Shaking off the snow, he crawled up the bank and pulled the girls after him. The Crows landed nearby. Thumping drew his attention and he noticed the congregation at the edge of the lake, pounding against the ice. Kai hardly spared them a second glance. Now that they were off the pond, they were safe.

Catching his breath, Kai grimly helped a pale-faced Inga to her feet while Wendy sprang up with little difficulty before he could offer a hand. He raised his head and locked eyes with Tjuv who stood on the opposite side of the pond. Solemn, she bowed her head in gratitude. She then led the nomads in circling the pond at a safe distance. The trio gathered themselves before meeting them.

Mrs. Crow flew up to land on Inga's shoulder and fuss at her hair. Shaking off the shock, Inga finally muttered, "*Tack.*"

Wendy took Kai's hand and gave it a squeeze. He tasted blood again.

Rejoining the others, Inga trotted up to Bae, kissed him on the nose, then pulled herself onto his back. Jack, Alice, and Red hastened forward.

"What are those things?" Jack asked Kai, scowling at the crystalized hands slipping back into the pond.

Tjuv's rough voice answered, "Water people; the tainted ones who are poisoned by Snödrottningen."

"Those are people?"

"People of earth?" Alice piped up, having heard about them from Kai before.

Kai nodded, explaining, "They are people bound to nature, usually water or tree. Sometimes they live as such for centuries. Not many forest people are tainted, though."

53

"Why are these tainted?" Alice asked.

Kai shrugged, but Tjuv answered for him, "Water is easier to freeze."

The nomads ahead of them stirred with nervous hubbub as they broached the forest. Narrowing her eyes, Tjuv shoved her way through the crowd.

When he noticed her shivering, Kai wrapped one of his scarves around Wendy's neck, helping arrange it to get the most warmth. Beside him, Red frowned with her eyes to the floor, listening. Kai turned to her expectantly and folded his arms.

At last, she met his eyes. "They're calling for you."

When the whispers reached his own ears, Kai understood what she discerned despite the language barrier. But he shook his head and corrected, "They're calling for us."

By the time they made their way through the crowd, Tjuv was glaring at the forest with Frost standing cross-armed beside her.

"You're a quick lot," Frost commented, turning to face them.

Kai ignored him. "What's this about?"

"The *hjältar* must enter first," Tjuv answered with an aggravated huff. "We are still forbidden otherwise."

"Why?" Alice asked; her favorite word.

"Because despite our alliance," she said it as a sneer, "they think that we will abuse our right of entry by hunting in their trees."

"The trust here is overwhelming," Frost leered sarcastically.

Tjuv jabbed a thumb at him. "And then there's Frost."

He laughed. "Being forbidden never stopped me from intruding."

"It comes with consequences."

"When you're mortal."

"Which, as I recall, you are."

Jack nudged him with his elbow. "Welcome to the club."

Frost gnashed his teeth with a scowl but didn't pursue the discussion.

Scanning the woods before them, Kai felt a chill ink down his spine. He wondered if the forest people were watching, waiting to see what would happen. He wondered if Lovisa was standing in a tree's shadow. A memory pressed behind his eyes.

Deep brown eyes looking up at him, silently searching, wordlessly asking.

"Lovisa... I can't."

His scar stung, throbbing.

Someone slipped a hand in his. Kai didn't need to look to see Wendy beside him as his friends linked hands, Alice to Jack to Red. Whatever happened, they were going in together.

Setting his jaw, Kai stepped forward into the woods with his friends beside him.

*****

The mirror was bleeding.

Bleeding.

It had never done that before.

At first, for the briefest of moments, Gerda thought that it was melting, and that perhaps this meant the Snow Queen's plans were foiled. She hated how quickly she jumped at hope, desperate. Then she realized.

Dark, sticky crimson leaked from the missing sliver in its surface. Then it poured from the mirror's sides, from the ice encasing it, until blood flowed freely down the wall, pooling, expanding. Gerda's heart sped in her throat. She scrambled back, pressed herself against the opposite wall. The ice hissed and steamed upon contact with the amassing blood.

Still, the mirror bled, drenched and shining. Blood covered the floor, steam filling the room. Gerda couldn't escape it.

When the flood reached her at last, she couldn't hold back the cry as the substance burned her toes. A crack split the air, followed by another crash. Her head jerked up. The ice split, webbing away from the mirror, like it was breaking free. But the heat had split the wall leading outside, fragments falling from the opening and splashing onto the bloody floor with a hiss.

Her eyes widened in realization. The ice was opening. A way out.

Without waiting a second longer, Gerda bolted for the gaping hole, slick blood burning her soles. She broke into a run as soon as she passed through the severed wall. Crimson feet flapped on ice. She never stopped, never looked back as she made her escape. Her heart pulsed in her ears.

She was free.

She was free.

Chapter Seven
The Princess

The child glared at them as they passed through the forest, crystal white eyes peaking over the edge of her creek. Kai placed a hand on Wendy's back to guide her away. She'd been lingering too long, staring back at the young girl in the water, concerned. Kai didn't blame her for her sympathy. The girl was just a child, skin so pale the veins shone translucent violets underneath, hair colorless against her head like snow. So young, and still incredibly dangerous.

Icicles like daggers hung from the snowy tree branches. Frozen leaves crunched underfoot, frosted pine needles, patches of snow. Sunlight raked the air, breaking parallel through shadows.

Inga wrinkled her nose. "It's not really exciting."

You're not looking hard enough, Bae hummed patiently.

"I mean, it's pretty. But for a forbidden forest, it's a little boring."

You're not looking hard enough, Bae repeated as Mr. and Mrs. Crow settled on his antlers. *Listen. Everything is in tension, holding its breath, unknowing what may fall from the sky or barge through the trees or break from the earth. They wait, anxious to what the day brings, what the ice will claim next. Some dare not sleep for fear never to wake. Others have no choice. It is fear, Lilla Rånareflickan, which plagues these woods. Fear is a reaction to anticipated pain, whatever form the pain may take. You can feel this vibrating in the air.*

Inga frowned, eyes now roaming. "It's still quiet."

Quiet is not the same as boring, young one.

Bae and Inga walked beside Kai, leading the group through the woods, hoping not to lead them astray.

The first time he'd plunged through these trees, he was with the reindeer. Mr. Crow had led them onward so that he would be reunited with his wife, who lived with the forest people and worked for the Princess Lovisa. Kai had come because Mr. Crow had told him of the rebellion against the Snow Queen, and he hoped the princess would help him. Bae had promised to aid him on his journey after they fled the robbers, and indeed he upheld that promise up until they reached the Finnish Witch's house where they parted ways so Kai would save Gerda from the Snow Queen.

Now here they were, retracing their journey to the forest people. Except now they brought the robbers with them.

Alice trotted up beside him, launching instantly into her questions, "How do you know this princess who's gathering your army?"

"Our army," Kai corrected.

"That's not how Tjuv keeps putting it."

"Mistranslation."

"You're avoiding the question."

"Not avoiding," Kai countered, lowering his voice. He cleared his throat. Alice raised an eyebrow at him, but he shook his head. "It's not a secret. I met Lovisa after I left the nomads. I hoped she would help me save Gerda, and she wanted my help reclaiming this land for her people. We were using each other to further our own goals against the Snow Queen. But…"

"You spent too long together, and things changed?" Alice guessed.

"Not in the way you're thinking," he admonished. "We parted as friends."

She stared sidelong at him for a moment. "I believe you. Let's just hope this princess feels the same." Then Alice leaned towards him, raising an eyebrow, lowering her voice, "And do you really want to assume that you know what I'm thinking?"

Kai merely grunted in response. With a smile, Alice fell back, leaving him alone again.

Noon found them deep in the woods, still walking, hoping to find something. Diamond dust glinted in the air, tiny ice crystals all around in an invisible fog, pinpoints of reflected light. Kai found his gaze drawn to them, a moment of beauty.

He stopped dead in his tracks.

Standing in front of him was a man, still as a tree, erect and grim. Branches crawled over his bare chest, looped around his biceps. Dark green inked up his black arms and stained around his eyes – not the icy white of the tainted. But he remained planted directly before them, menacing.

Kai met the man's gaze, his jaw set. Behind him, he heard the nomads shuffle to a halt upon noticing the sudden obstacle, nervous whispers, hands held tight. Most had never seen the forest people, besides the tainted, and the legends were enough to make them wary even of one lone man. But Kai knew better. He spotted the hidden folk in the surrounding trees, peeling from the bark to observe them, camouflaged perfectly against the rough surface. A passing glance would miss them entirely. Looking intently enough and he could make out the faces, cheek to tree, hands splayed up and around the trunks. The man who stood before them was striking enough to draw any attention away from his disguised comrades.

Bae stepped up beside Kai, silent. Not even a hum resonated.

When the man spoke it was in a low and indistinct language like rushing leaves or the sound of tree bark stretching up and outward. The robbers muttered nervously, afraid of witchcraft or deceit. Kai narrowed his eyes.

"Frost," he spoke, waiting for the lanky imp to appear. As soon as Kai felt the cool gust beside him, he asked, "Would you interpret?"

Frost grumbled, "Just because I forfeit my loyalty to the Ice Maiden does not mean I am now in your servitude."

"Did I summon you with a bell?" Kai snapped under his breath. "I ask a favor."

"I don't do favors."

"You do now."

Frost shrugged with a smug frown. "Not likely."

"You are Kai Ødegård?" the man spoke up, unfazed as he shifted language to interrupt their argument.

Kai ignored Frost's self-satisfied look. "I am."

"And the rest of *hjältar*?"

Recognizing the term, Wendy stepped up with Alice, Jack, and Red, answering for them, "We are here."

"Are you here to take us to the princess?" Alice spoke up. Kai could tell she'd found the hidden forest people surrounding them, her eyes flicking to each trunk, finding even those he'd missed himself.

"There is no need," responded another voice entirely.

Kai stood straighter as the speaker stepped out from the trees behind the man. Willow vines and fireweed blossoms circled her head, twisting through the gathering of black curls pinned up at the base of her long neck. A fern green dress hung loose over her shoulders and flowed over bare feet. Twigs wove up her ankles like they grew from her footsteps. An elegant black tree inked into her brown skin stretched up her spine, the branches wrapping down her bare arms. She regarded Kai with warm brown eyes.

"I am glad you have come," the princess, Lovisa, said at last. The small smile at the edge of her mouth soon disappeared. "We have much to do."

Before he could step forward, one of his ears popped as the air pressurized just beside him. Frost had tensed, fists clenched, the snowflakes frozen midair around his head. The diamond dust was sparking everywhere now.

In a voice so thin it was nearly inaudible, Frost hissed, "She knows."

Wind whistling, the icy mist harshened the light in a glaze. Kai's stomach tightened. The nomads were warning cries of "*Häxan!*" But this wasn't Häxan. The diamond dust was blinding white, now. This was the Snow Queen's guard.

Kai shouted as such, but it was too late. The swirling white snowflakes swelled up around them, toiling through the trees with a sharp buzzing. He could just make out the humanoid forms in the ice cloud ready for the attack. The snap and groan of lumber entered the chaos, shooting through the buzz, and all went dark.

She held a snowy grey fox in her lap, rocked it back and forth as she sang softly in its ear. One hand, laced with the black branches that inked up her fingers, pressed against the somber creature's broken ribs. Nothing spectacularly magical seemed to happen. No glowing palms or ozone changes. Yet as her song ended, the fox slipped from her arms and scampered off, completely healed.

Looking up, she met his eyes – and that's when the air seemed to tighten. She was standing, a breath away, so close he caught the spruce scent of her skin. Heat itched up his neck and down his palms as her fingers intertwined with his and her breath warmed his jaw.

They had one moment. One moment of her mouth against his, his fingers through her hair, her hands cupping his neck. Then he broke away, steadied his breathing, still close.

Deep brown eyes looked up at him, silently searching, wordlessly asking.

"Lovisa…" he whispered, gently pulling her hands from his neck. He held them like a barrier forever between them. "I can't."

Her gaze dropped to what had slipped out from under his shirt collar. A ring like crushed moonrock. A promise. She looked up at him one last time. "I know."

She released his hands, walked away, and left their moment in the woods behind them.

Kai woke with a jolt, scattering the pinecone shavings and spruce needles which had blanketed him. He was in a shallow dip in the ground like a crib, a thick layer of moss lining the floor, thick between his fingers. Snow patched the ground, though the chill didn't bite so much here. With a scowl, he ran his tongue over his teeth. It was the first time in a while where his mouth didn't taste like blood.

"You've changed."

He whipped around. Lovisa sat beside his mossy bed, perched on an arched tree root. She no longer wore the gauze dress from before, donning now a beige blouse plated with leathered bark and leggings. Her feet were still bared, ankles encircled with twigs. Her black curls were hidden under a colorful headscarf shot through with threads of violet, eucalyptus, and burgundy, revealing the ebony tree tattoo stretched up her neck.

Kai blinked, regaining his composure and bearings. "What happened?"

"We were ambushed by the snow bees," Lovisa explained, using the nickname for the Snow Queen's guard. "Frost's warning came just in time for us to get you out."

"And the others?" Kai asked anxiously, not fond of how singular this sounded.

She didn't seem fazed. "We brought everyone here."

Despite himself, he looked around though he could not see anything beyond the small alcove where they sat. He pushed down the unease of not knowing where Wendy, Jack, Red, or Alice were. In this part of the woods, the circular dips in the forest floor were arranged in such a way that one could feel enclosed and isolated, even if someone were resting just a few meters away. For Kai, he always felt as if he were being watched, on the brink of ambush. He never liked being caught unawares.

But he knew this was for the forest people's protection. They could hide easily and keep enemies from finding the groves where their bonded trees grew. This part of the forest was on their side. It kept them safe.

Even so, he didn't like being separated from his friends. Not here. Not after everything they'd gone through and everything they knew.

Lovisa tilted her head, examining him as if he were a new creature who'd wandered into her path. "So, you have become one of the awaited *hjältar*."

Kai passed a hand over his face and leaned forward over his knees. "Please don't say that."

"Why not? It is what you have become. The heroes destined to bring freedom, to save this country and its people."

He cut her a sidelong glance. "You know it's more than that."

She said nothing, but her unchanged expression confirmed his suspicions. This wasn't just about saving one country; much more was at stake. And now it was all coming to rest on his shoulders, on his friends' shoulders, all five of them.

He remembered when the White Rabbit had called them children. That this journey they were going towards was too dangerous. Did the rabbit know? Did he know what that rescue mission would lead towards? Did he know there was more waiting ahead of them than what they left behind? Kai had argued with him, insisted that they had gone through more hardships than most. Who was he to argue? Look where that got them. It was never supposed to come to this. Five people shouldn't be responsible for saving worlds.

He huffed, shook his head. "You know I'm not destined for anything."

"Maybe not," Lovisa admitted with a shrug. "But the hope your name brings has gathered the peoples of this country together for the first time in history to reclaim our homeland

64

from a common enemy. That's power enough to the name *hjältar*, no matter how at fault destiny may be."

Something pulled the corner of his mouth. There was fire in her eyes. Blazing. "You've changed, too," he said.

Her gaze fell briefly to his resting hand as if she might hold it. She didn't. "We changed each other."

The words hung in the air, heavy and true. She'd taught him to look beyond himself and his situation. Kai didn't know how he changed her, but there was that fire, and though he couldn't take credit for that, he had not seen it before now.

Lovisa straightened her shoulders. "But I believe you've changed within the past year or so even more than I."

"It's the scar, isn't it?"

She broke into a smile. "It does stand out."

Kai rubbed his jaw self-consciously, wondering about the numb sensation down the scar.

She didn't look away. "But it's more than that."

Heat crawled up his neck under her gaze. Dropping his eyes, he cleared his throat. "Where are they?"

"Waiting. I will take you to them."

"Am I the last to wake?"

She shook her head. "Many of the robbers still rest, exhausted from the journey. And one of your friends is talking in his sleep."

Kai huffed a laugh, knowing perfectly well who that was. "Jack."

"He should wake soon. Only three were unaffected by the spell," Lovisa explained. "Bae, Frost…"

"Not surprising."

"…and Alice."

He frowned. He didn't know much about the magic the forest people used to get them away from the Snow Queen's guard, but if it was powerful enough to make everyone slip out of consciousness, then he didn't know what to make of this. Bae was at least twice as large as any of his human companions, and Frost was still teetering on the edge between immortality and humanity. But Alice was neither of those things.

Lovisa noticed his confusion. "She told me her name."

"I guessed as much. But how did she…?" His voice trailed off, unable to form a coherent thought.

Lovisa merely shrugged. "She has a restless mind."

Kai wasn't sure how that explained it, but he decided not to question any further. She certainly wasn't wrong.

Snow started falling lightly down from the sky, slipping past the canopy of branches, landing in his lap. Lovisa was looking intently at him again, as if filled with words she couldn't say. Snowflakes caught her ebony eyelashes. She didn't blink them away.

Gently, she asked, "Who did you come back for? For us? For them? Or is this still for her?"

Kai sat in silence for a long time, watching the snow collect on her headscarf, melt in his hands. There was a hollow pit behind his breastbone. Strange and uneasy.

"I don't know," he said in a low breath. "For all of it, I think. You, your people, the nomads. For Alice, Jack, Red, and Wendy. For Gerda. Everyone."

Her dark russet eyes softened knowingly. "That's it. That's how you've changed."

He wasn't sure he understood, but he let the words settle over him all the same.

With a sigh, Lovisa rose to her feet, revealing a thin skirt she'd been sitting on which she promptly wrapped around her waist and tied off at the hip, the long beige fabric flowing over her leggings. "Come," she beckoned. "We've left them waiting long enough."

As Kai stood, he reached out and touched her arm. "Wait."

She turned back expectantly.

"Tell me the truth," he said, lowering his voice. "Do we stand a chance at winning this?"

"Do you still love her?"

The ring swung lightly against his chest. "I do."

She dipped her chin. "Then yes, I believe we do."

Chapter Eight
Advices and Arguments

Kai followed Lovisa into an enclosed clearing where the bordering trees stood so close together that their branches intertwined. Roots ruptured the ground in peculiar arches, sea serpents in a snowy lake, dipping and rising. He immediately tasted tension like a bitter rag on his tongue.

Tjuv sat silently on one of the protruding roots, lips pursed into a multitude of wrinkles which ringed her mouth. Beside her, Inga held a meatless plate in her lap which she picked at with a sour expression on her face mirroring her grandmother's. The nomads were hunters, reindeer herders, robbers. Anything they didn't kill to cook was stolen, or else scavenged. Kai had only known one recipe they used consistently that did not involve meat, that being the spruce bark they ate to prevent starvation when winter was especially harsh. Their pine needle tea was hardly delectable either, to say the least.

But the forest people were vegetarians. They prevented any hunting from transpiring in their woods. The meatless plates they provided were admittedly far better than the nomads' – which might attest to Inga's cooking more than anything, as hers was the only food Kai was allowed when he was captured by her – but that did little to convince Inga that anything presently on her plate was actually edible.

On the edge of the clearing, Frost stood leaning against a tree, arms crossed in his typical brooding fashion. Red appeared uncomfortable with the whole situation, while beside her Alice seemed especially thoughtful, like she was too busy seeing nothing in particular to focus on what was or was not happening right in front of her. Deciding not to disturb them, Kai joined Wendy on a mossy root, earning a smile.

Lovisa had no sooner sat at the head of this ring of knotted roots than Bae arrived, the Crows on his antlers and Jack at his side. The green-armed man who'd met them in the woods was also with them, unchanged except now the branches seemed to comb over his head from his neck like spindly fingers, conforming easily to his movements.

Jack pulled something of a smile. "Did I miss something?"

When he received no answer, he settled himself awkwardly on the closest available spot, that being beside a grumpy looking Inga. Jack's smile waned, looking with some desperation at Kai. He could only shrug.

Lovisa did not allow the tension to dissuade her. She turned to look expectantly at Tjuv, waiting.

The elder woman's lips hardly moved. "We had an agreement."

Folding her hands neatly in her lap, Lovisa nodded. "I am aware."

"We were to bring the *hjältar* to your little haven in the woods," Tjuv went on bitterly. "We would join in this rebellion as allies to defeat Snödrottningen once and for all. We have been honorable in that bargain."

The way she jabbed her gnarled thumb at Inga, Kai knew that *we* did not include the forest people. He shifted in his seat, suddenly understanding why Red looked so uncomfortable. He felt like this was an argument he shouldn't be privy to.

Tjuv continued, pointing accusingly at Lovisa, "Yet we found ourselves again barred from your forest. We traveled long and unprotected before finding your body guard."

"I am Latham," said the green-armed man solemnly, as if that changed the title bestowed upon him.

Tjuv ignored him. "And you failed to hide our whereabouts from Snödrottningen, Häxan, or whoever else sent the snow bees to ambush us."

"We saved your lives," Latham said with the same steady tone as before.

"A treacherous devil who belonged to the enemy saved our lives," snapped Tjuv.

Behind her, Frost scoffed and feigned offence. "You're welcome – despite that backhanded thanks. I've never been so flattered."

Inga muttered something under her breath, still stabbing at her plate with a pout.

Gaze steadily on Tjuv, Lovisa leaned slightly forward. "I know our agreement. I have no misgivings toward our alliance."

"I've got a few," Inga grumbled.

"Our woods are not closed to you."

"I know how your woods work," Tjuv interjected tersely. "No walls bar the border, but we sense the spell. The moment my people enter, we are targeted like mice to a hawk, noticed and hunted by your people and that of Snödrottningen."

"But we would know you and find you," Lovisa implored.

"As would everyone else."

"And it was she who stipulated the conditions of the spell's eradication."

"*Vad?*" Inga asked, face scrunched up in confusion as if the princess was spewing nonsense.

Lovisa took a deep breath, refocusing herself. "This was the Snow Queen's doing. The moment the *hjältar* entered the forest, the spell which you speak of was broken. My people sensed its absence, as I'm certain our enemies did, which is how we knew you arrived. I assume the Snow Queen and the witch sent the snow bees out as soon as they discovered this themselves." Her hand curled into a fist, the only sign of frustration beyond her calm façade. "While the spell was intact, no friend or foe could enter without our knowledge. Now we are blind."

Kai felt his own fist dig into his thigh. They could be ambushed again without warning. They couldn't afford to be caught off guard again. He felt the weight of what dangers lay before them settle over his shoulders.

Red leaned forward so her elbows rested on her knees, looking between Kai and Lovisa. "I thought the witches were on our side," she said hesitantly.

Inga frowned at her. "How did you know that?"

With a shrug, Red responded, "Overheard Mrs. Crow talking with Kai."

"Snoop," Inga mumbled.

Red tapped her ears. "Good hearing."

The Lappish Witch and Finnish Witch are, as you say, on our side, Bae hummed to answer her inquiry. *They have gone to the mountains in order to keep the influences of Snödrottningen from advancing further south. The witch whom the princess speaks of is Häxan, and her powers are much different. She aligns herself with Snödrottningen.*

"Frost saved my life from her once," Kai added, looking up at him coolly. He didn't mention the betrayal afterwards, the trap Frost led him into by tempting him with the mirror and a way to break it, by using Gerda as bait, by lying.

Frost said nothing.

Tjuv cut through the offhand topic with another curt finger at Lovisa. "If we are to proceed in this alliance, from now on you will trust us with the whole truth."

"I never lied," Lovisa insisted.

"That is not what I requested. You will trust us with the whole truth. All further discussions regarding this revolt, I or my granddaughter will be present for. Our voice will be heard. I expect to know as much about the war to come as you do."

"There is no war to come. It is the same war my people have fought since the Snow Queen first abused her power." Lovisa paused, gathered her composure, tasting her words. "But to the best of my capabilities, I will grant your request."

Tjuv lowered her accusing finger and set both hands in her lap, apparently accepting this without further discussion. The only sign of gratitude was in her silence.

With a short flutter, the Crows hopped over to Inga and began picking at her neglected plate.

Then Alice looked up from her stupor as if oblivious to the previous conversation. "What does it mean: *hjältar*?"

Bae again answered in serenity, *Literally, it means heroes. You are long awaited, destined to save us from Snödrottningen.*

Alice seemed to take this as mere definition. The weight of it, perhaps, wasn't as important or daunting as it was to Kai. "Why are we the *hjältar*?" she continued, ticking off boxes in her head. "Why does the Snow Queen want us?"

72

Lovisa opened her hands helplessly, an expression of pity. "I wish I knew. You were chosen."

"I don't think it matters anymore," Red muttered. "We're here now."

Alice took this with a frown, retreating to her silence. Maybe Red was right in that it didn't matter why they were here so much as what they would do now moving forward. Maybe there were more pressing questions. Still, Kai remembered back in Giant Country sitting in Liesel's attic trying to hash out the answers to Alice's questions. She was determined to figure out the *why* behind it all. For her sake, he hoped she did uncover the mystery. Before it drove her mad.

"Who are we up against?" Tjuv questioned, her gruff voice demanding attention once more.

Leaning back, Lovisa's dark eyes flicked to Frost as if offering him the question.

"I suppose this is when I really earn my keep, eh?" Frost said. With a groan, he peeled himself from the tree he'd stood against, taking two lanky steps into the circle. "You know the Ice Maiden, Snödrottningen, Snow Queen, whatever she wants to be called these days. She's got the mirror, the witch, the snow bees, the spies, and now she's tainted all of your water folk, even some of the tree ones."

"And you?" Inga asked, nose scrunched up. "Are there any more like you?"

He flashed his teeth. "There's no one else like me."

"She means wind people," Lovisa clarified. "Are there any others?"

"There's no one else like me," Frost repeated, voice lower, reverberating from the back of his throat. "You say *wind people* as if such a thing exists. You think what I am is so simple as being bound to the wind? The wind is wild, unpredictable, untamable. It's not like attaching yourself to a tree or a puddle. Don't try to make me out to be the same as you. I'm not."

Lovisa said nothing more on the subject.

Twisting his head, Frost continued with his report, "Then there are her gathered forces: the mad witch, the seafarers, the wolves – there was talk of giants, but I'm not sure if they've yet arrived."

"They're here," Jack spoke up, voice strained. He cleared his throat. "We saw them leave."

Kai heard Wendy make a kind of sigh as if she wanted to reach out and hold Jack's hand, squeeze it in hers, let him know she was there for him. Jack must have sensed it. He offered her a small smile as if to say he knew.

Inga shrugged nonchalantly at the news. "Doesn't seem so bad."

"Not so bad?" Frost burst in agitated exclamation. "Have you not compared the numbers? All that power raging against us, and then there's us. We have yet-to-be tainted forest people, a band of wandering robbers, two witches who aren't here at the moment, two crows and a reindeer. But oh yes! I forgot, we have our destined heroes! Maybe they can explain the intricacies of their respective enemies?"

"Well, when you put it like that," Inga grumbled into her fur-lined collar.

"If you're so faithless in this fight," Kai said with a hard glare, "then why leave? Why choose to help us?"

Frost scowled. "I told you before. You don't get the luxury of knowing the answer to that question."

74

Anger flushed hot up his face. He balled both fists now, struggling to contain his frustration.

Inga huffed deeply. "So what now?"

Then Alice made a noise, almost like a bark of laughter, so short and sudden that all heads turned sharply to her. She was stoic, eyes wild, staring at nothing. Silence followed as if they held their breath collectively, wondering if she really made such a noise.

Without warning, Alice shot up to her feet and slammed the frozen pocket watch on the arching root before her.

"Make it work," she said, eyes locked on Lovisa who sat rigid under her stare. "They need a signal."

"Who—oh." Jack groaned, rolling his eyes back. "You mean Long Ears."

Alice didn't take the opportunity to banter, which was how Kai knew something was changing in her, something that confirmed her restless mind.

"You don't care why we're here? Fine." She pressed her finger firmly against the watch's pearly face. "But we need them. We need all of them."

Then she turned on her heel and walked away.

*****

The shifting black mass shrunk away at the torchlight hovering above the open lantern, ensuring its captivity. Gold eyes glittered. Lupa imagined the Shadow's silent scream in pain, voiceless and agonizing. She'd never seen such an entity before. The pirate said that it was some link between a boy and his island, a bridge, an anchor. She didn't much care for what it was so much as what it could do.

Gently, she reached into the lantern, careful not to let the writhing Shadow escape. Pointed nails scraped against glass with a sharp screech, like a scream the Shadow couldn't cry. Her fingers came away laced in a soot-like substance. Before the Shadow could recover enough to launch out of the lantern, Lupa slapped the lid down and sealed it shut. The torch dropped to the ice in a shower of sparks, but she ignored it as it sputtered out.

Her gaze remained transfixed in fascination by the stuff on her hand as she brought forward a bone bowl from the scattered mess of her table. Steadily, she dusted the soot into the bowl and let it settle there.

Behind her, a dreadfully annoyed voice prodded, "Could you be more insufferably slow?"

"Patience, Queen," Lupa cooed without looking back. She reached for the knife and dish of sticky golden liquid. A pleasant reek hit her nostrils, metallic and warm, making her mouth water. "Nothing was ever really accomplished out of haste and impulse."

"I prefer calculated unpredictability."

"And look where you are now."

Lupa could hear the tight huff behind her as the Queen of Hearts shifted her weight from foot to foot in frustration. A smirk pulled at her mouth.

Her boney fingers wrapped around the knife, its blade soaked in giant's blood. Luckily, the giants brought prisoners with them. Nozrok's people seemed intent on keeping their blood inside their humungous body-sacks of flesh; and though the idea of taking one of them down pleased her, Lupa knew that the full moon was soon to rise. She thought it best not to mingle the poison of her bite with the potency of giant's blood. It could ruin her concoction.

She tapped a few drops of the golden liquid into the bowl, running her tongue over her pointed teeth. With the knife, she stirred them together, shadow and blood.

Satisfied, she took a cup filled with sleet she gathered from the storm, pouring the tiny frozen water droplets into the bowl. They did not melt immediately. The sleet swirled into intricate patterns, like a dance of chasing rabbits.

"And what has brought you this far other than calculated unpredictability?" the Queen shot. As if such things mattered to her. As if questions for were made to satisfy one's pleasure, not knowledge in its own right.

Remaining calm in the face of the Queen's bubbling rage, Lupa said simply, "Instinct."

"Another word for impulse," the Queen leered. "We are not so different as you claim."

Lupa scraped the flat of her blade along the bowl's rim, setting the knife aside. She licked her fingers as she turned to her companion at last.

"Ah, how wrong you are," she crooned. "I am free, here by choice. I have always been here by choice. But you, on the other hand, you are here by necessity. You are shackled to your desire for power and revenge – neither of which I've found tasteful, other than their use as tools to achieve greater things."

"You do not also seek power and revenge?" the Queen of Hearts growled. "You who overpowers those weaker than you, who hunts after a girl who's thwarted you since she was a child?"

"I seek pain and enlightenment!" Lupa flashed her filed teeth. "There is nothing purer than pain. There is nothing more inevitable. I was created an instrument of transformation, the peak of evolution from which the weak will not survive. You falsely call it power, but it is knowledge in its truest form. Humanity is destined to fall. I serve greater things."

The Queen scowled, her pretty face turning scarlet, her fists curled into her sides.

Lupa tilted her head. "You will have to seek out your feminine companionship elsewhere, little queen. You waste your breath trying to relate to me. Perhaps the Captain would provide better assistance in that department."

Lips pursed in agitation, the Queen glared daggers at her. But Lupa merely extended the bone bowl out, waiting expectantly. One more ingredient was all she needed. That's what the Raven Sorceress, Carabosse, had told her: a shadow's remnants, gold blood, crystalized water, and now a lightning strike.

The Queen of Hearts swept her onyx and ruby cloak over one shoulder, revealing the creature curled around her legs.

"So dramatic," Lupa murmured, but her arm remained extended.

The creature opened one fiery reptilian eye, lifting a scaly head. Lupa lowered to her knees. The creature was only a cub, but already as large as a wolf and twice as long. It huffed, both eyes wide now. Curious, it crawled forward to sniff the bowl Lupa offered.

"There. It is time for the young jabberwocky to play his part."

"Jabberwock," the Queen corrected.

Lupa raised an eyebrow but ignored the statement. "Shall you make him sing, or shall I?"

Her lips tightened again. For a moment, Lupa thought she would have to do it herself. Maybe thrust her sharp nails into the meat of its shoulder. Or yank out a claw from its foot.

But the Queen raised her hand, fingers extended in tense display of power. The young jabberwock shrieked, writhed, then spat a burst of braided lightning that electrified the concoction in the bowl. The Queen released the jabberwock from her magic, and the creature instantly retreated into the folds of her cloak behind her legs. Lupa stood with the sparking mixture, shaking off her shocked arm, not allowing any discomfort to line her brow.

"A word of advice," Lupa voiced as she turned away, "do not attach yourself to that cub. There are no pets here, only weapons."

"Do not underestimate me, dog," the Queen spat. "I don't rely on the information and talents of others to survive. I hold my own."

Lupa didn't look back as the Queen of Hearts stormed off with the jabberwock. She shook her head. That cub would not survive this war. She doubted the Queen would either.

Now she had to wait for the Snow Queen's word.

She paid no mind to the missing lantern.

*****

"You left quickly."

Alice whipped around with a jump. Something in her wanted to do it again: jump. She restrained herself.

Frost had just stepped onto the mound between the bowl-like clearings where she stood hidden by bordering trees. She'd been staring at the little pale blue berries in the branches which grew despite the snow. Her fingers were twitching.

With a smirk, Frost shrugged. "Not that I blame you. I'm sick of the lot, too."

"No, I…" Her voice rushed up and came like a train wreck in her throat. Too many words. Too many thoughts. "I can hear them. *There she goes again barking up a tree that doesn't matter anymore.* They don't care about *why*! They only care about how to keep going forward and what to do next. As if it's not connected."

She noticed her twitching hands, tried to cover one with the other. It was like she had too much energy trying to break out of her skin.

"But we can't go on until we know where we've been… It's important." She jabbed a finger at Frost. "You're important."

He gave a sharp laugh. "*I'm* important?"

"Did I stutter?"

"You're out of your mind."

"I'm deep into my mind – I'm lost in my mind!" Alice rubbed her head, ruffled her hair. She didn't usually do that. "I've seen you before. *Before* before. When you were still a freckled ginger Rudy making toy houses with Babette."

At the mention of both names, Frost growled in frustration or pain, slapping a palm to his forehead and wincing back.

"You're important," Alice repeated, certain. "I saw you. You hold the key, I can feel it. It'll unlock this puzzle, and everything will make sense."

"I'm not who you think I am."

"Then *who are you*?"

"I am Frost!"

"Then where is Rudy? I'd like to speak with him."

"Rudy is gone!" Frost exclaimed, stomping his foot. "He died ages ago at the bottom of a frozen lake and left something bitter and cruel in his place. I don't remember him anymore."

"And what about Babette?"

"*I destroyed her!*"

Every snowflake in the air snapped into crystal, dropping like pebbles. Alice didn't flinch when they bounced off her skin. Head bowed in frustration, Frost kept his fists clenched at his sides. She wanted him to tell her everything. She was sure he had the answers, somehow, hidden in his past where he didn't want to return.

Throat tight, Alice lowered her voice, "Why are we here?"

Frost looked up, eyes glazed over like the frozen lake he'd drowned in.

She repeated it, desperate, "Why are we here?!"

Easily, he cocked his head. "Are you sure you're asking the right questions?"

He left her alone while her mind filled with shadows.

Chapter Nine
The Body in the Snow

Footsteps slapped against ice, then snow, hoping not to leave footprints but too scared to look back to check. She couldn't afford to let anyone see her run. She couldn't let anyone see her at all.

*****

Red found the forest princess in a grove filled with light. The trees here stretched high overhead, branches weaving together in a grand canopy, sunbeams leaking through the multicolored leaves. Hardly any of these trees should've been alive in this cold, that much Red could tell. Still, winter was only clear in the dustings of snow on the floor and the sharpness in the air. A paradise in this world of white.

Lovisa moved from tree to tree, taking a small twig or leaf from each as if they were offered to her. The collection was stowed in a colorful scarf which had formerly wrapped around her head, leaving her hair loose, cascading down her back. The frozen pocket watch swung from her wrist.

"It will take all of our voices to wake this timepiece," Lovisa spoke without turning to face her.

Red frowned, pressing her palm against the closest tree. The trunk pulsed under her skin in a familiar rhythm. "It's a heartbeat," she breathed in astonishment.

Focusing, she could hear it, the steady thrum of a thousand drums beneath the bark of a thousand trees in the grove. The sound vibrated through the tree sap, humming in the ground from their roots, making the leaves dance. Life was in chorus, beating not in sync but in harmony.

"Why were you looking for me?" Lovisa asked, pulling her from the hypnotizing sound.

Taking her hand from the tree, Red realized that tears had escaped her eyes. She blinked them away. She hadn't cried since the Enchanted Forest when the wolves had escaped and Quasimodo was dead along with Carabosse, when she'd fought a phantom and carved into her friend's face. Jack didn't know all that at the time, but he held her then like it didn't matter why she was crying, only that she was there hurting, falling apart in his arms.

She steadied her breathing, followed after Lovisa. "How do you know we can survive this?"

That was the question, shed from her lungs at last like it'd kept her from breathing properly. Not if they would win this war. Not if the Snow Queen could be defeated. But if they could survive, and somehow live beyond this.

Lovisa's answer was anything but satisfying. "I don't."

Red frowned. "Then why?"

Lovisa looked at her for the first time, evaluating. She didn't ask for elaboration, which made Red want to trust her for some reason, like she saw something familiar in the way Lovisa held herself and accepted Red's ambiguous questions, the stoic grace. It hit her that, in a way, this princess reminded her of Kai. Like someone she could trust.

Averting her path, Lovisa moved through the grove, expecting Red to follow. "Do you know how my people are bound to nature? Should either human or tree perish, or water dry up, then the other will die as well. With near immortality there is extreme vulnerability."

Red felt the heartbeats under her feet, singing in the back of her mind. How many souls were bound to this place?

"Can you imagine if this grove were discovered? Light a match, rip up the earth, split ice up through the core. Genocide." Lovisa sighed, "We cannot delay the inevitable. It's not enough to hide anymore, and we cannot run."

She emerged from the grove, stepping over a snowbank and moving into the grey and white surrounding wood. The heartbeat was here, too, but faint and far between. Lovisa easily approached the trees hidden amongst the others, accepting offered branches and pinecones. Red wondered why these were separated from the grove.

Lastly, they came to a single tree which stood farthest from the grove. Rime ice clung to its black bark and lined each green needle. Red heard the pulse in this, too, despite its distance from the others.

Lovisa circled this tree slowly. "Now we must save ourselves from the very force who should've protected us in the first place."

Red noticed the way the tree seemed to lean towards Lovisa as she walked. Needles wrapped around her fingers when she reached to touch them. Grass grew from her footprints, bursting through the snow.

"Why does your tree stand hidden at a distance from the others?" Red asked.

When Lovisa looked at her, Red knew she'd caught the real question. Was the separation to save herself should her people burn or to save her people should she burn? Red didn't let her expression slack.

"There are those of us who have volunteered to stand apart," Lovisa explained calmly. "Leaders are called to do so. My mother did before me, and my cousin Latham will after me. His stands just beyond here, where we have come from. We do not hide. We are stationed."

Red dropped her gaze, ashamed for assuming the worst.

Brown eyes looked at her in their permanent state of evaluation. "Why do you hide?"

Red felt suddenly like she was exposed, her insides turned out until the darkness spilled. The Wolf was on the brink. She could no longer tell which part of her held the reins.

Shifting on her feet, Red said, "It's easier to hide when you're losing control."

Lovisa continued her level stare. "There is a part of you that is wolf, just as there is a part of me that is this tree. We are tied to something other than ourselves. Call it strength, call it weakness; it's an inevitability that is better accepted than fought."

Stomach tightened, Red narrowed her eyes. "What are you getting at?"

"I think you know."

"He's just lost someone."

"We're all about to lose someone," Lovisa said with impossible serenity. "That's what keeps us living."

Red clenched her jaw, not sure why her eyes began to blur and sting, or why her throat seemed to swell into a knot. She hated feeling this vulnerable. And of all the people to expose her vulnerability, this stranger had done it without so much as lifting a finger.

"How did you know?" Red managed shortly.

Lovisa remained calm, holding no delicacy but no condemnation either. "I didn't. You just told me."

"*Why?*"

"I needed to know if you have one person to fight for." She stroked the tree with the back of her hand. "That's how we're going to win."

Red scowled. "Fighting for one?"

"Fighting for one."

She looked down at her fisted hands. She couldn't understand what philosophy the princess was following. She'd always fought for all; she would've died fighting for all. She'd fought the world before, and she'd fought for the world, or at least pieces of it. But it wasn't enough. Her parents had died by a mistake she'd made; her efforts to save captured girls from Bluebeard and disfigured people from Lupa always came up short; sacrificing herself to defeat Carabosse backfired with Quasimodo's demise; and Jill died because she couldn't reach Jack in time to help him. Time and time again, Red was reminded that she wasn't enough to save her world.

Her voice felt small. "And if it takes one sacrifice to save the whole?"

Lovisa was steady. "Then it will be me."

Red saw it, then, the burning in Lovisa's eyes. A fire she didn't have to understand to trust.

"If everyone fights for one person, each of us has a tangible goal," Lovisa continued. "If enough of us fight for one person other than ourselves, then we cover the whole." She held out her arms. "I fight for my people. I fight for my country. But that means nothing if I can't fight for one. And through that, with everyone fighting for one, our roots entangle and we are all connected stronger than ever."

Red looked up at the icy tree which stood alone and separate. "Who do you fight for?"

She didn't bat an eye before responding, "Kai."

"But he doesn't fight for you."

"He fights for a girl who cannot fight for anyone. He is the last branch, connecting us with the end goal. Because of that, we have a chance at surviving."

Red looked at this woman, a stranger one moment who quickly became someone she would willingly follow into battle. Her strength didn't come from hiding. Her strength came in being open, not gentle. There was ferocity in her grace. Red could read her like a book only because she didn't conceal it.

"You love him," she observed.

There was no denial, no shame. Lovisa merely raised her head slightly as if she were talking to the tree. "Enough to know he'll never fight for me. Enough to help him save the one he loves."

"Enough to hurt."

"Everyday." She paused, fingers brushing the pine needles. "Love isn't possession. I don't need to have him to love him."

Though Red admired that strength, she wasn't sure she could bear that kind of pain. It would eat her alive.

*****

She slinked through the underbrush even at the brittle branches smacked her face, scratched her hips. Out here, all was shadows and snow. She reminded herself to keep breathing.

Keep breathing.
Don't get caught.

*****

The Crows came in a flurry without explanation, just noise like a battering cage against his skull. Kai only had a moment to process their presence before they were off again, expecting him to keep up. Panic seized his chest.

Without hesitation, he followed after them through branches and snow, further away from the alcoves and the forest people. He could sense the distance as the cold sharpened around him, enticing him to draw up his hood. Every breath clouded before him. The snow deepened in some places which made him regret leaving behind his snowshoes. Still, he labored on as quickly as he could.

The Crows rounded back every so often to make sure he was on their trail.

Red smelled her first.

She'd left Lovisa to find Jack when the hair on the back of her neck pricked and the scent hit her nostrils. Something in the back of her mind suggested she should go back and get Lovisa to come investigate with her. But instinct crept in. This was something she had to seek out alone.

Slinking deeper into the woods where the underbrush thickened and air chilled in such a way that goosebumps spread up her arms, Red took the risk of letting the Wolf take over. Instantly, her senses expanded. She was thankful to discover that she had a winter coat. Silent, she hid herself in the snowy shrubs and waited.

Footsteps padded over snow and spruce needles. Breaths struggled to stay muffled, exhaustion in every huff. Red wondered if this was what fear smelled like: musty sweat and dirt under fingernails.

The wolf stepped into Red's sight, her rusty brown fur powdered with snow and snagged with twigs. Red narrowed her eyes. She knew this was one of Fang's pack, could smell it despite the matted fur and mangled appearance. Steeling herself, Red emerged from the underbrush bristling and snarling. The smaller wolf faltered, ears lowered.

Red circled her, testing to see if she'd attack or run. But the wolf remained stalk still, and when Red faced her once again, she changed. Brown skin, messy hair, amber-shot eyes. Her stance was submissive, nervous.

"Red?"

Waiting half a moment, Red shifted form, still ready for a trap.

"Fang sent me."

She didn't allow her expression to betray any confusion. Her chest pressurized and her stomach tightened. She remained silent.

The girl went on, desperation edging her tone, "Something's happening. I managed to get away, but I can't stay."

"Why would he send you?"

"He wants to warn you. She's preparing something."

"The Snow Queen?"

"And Lupa."

Her breath caught short.

The girl chewed her lips as if to stop them from trembling. Her cheeks were hollow, and shadows circled her eyes. Ruddy patches hit each cheekbone and the bridge of her nose where the cold bit her skin.

"We're being forced to fight," she pleaded, voice scarred with fear. "We have no choice."

"*Why did he send you?*"

"He wants you to kill her."

Red huffed. "Not hard to persuade—"

"You don't understand..." The girl sighed, shivered, hesitated. "You have to kill a wolf twice."

She scowled, throwing all pretense to the wind. "What?"

"I won't say it again." Amber-shot eyes shifted around nervously, as if someone were listening for the secret to hunting down wolves.

"But I don't understand."

"Just trust me! Make sure you kill her twice."

"Why should I believe you?"

The girl pulled up her sleeve, revealing violent white scars on her forearm. A wolf bite. "I want her dead just as much as you do."

Red sifted the new information around in her mind, comparing it to what she already knew. She wanted to believe her, but she didn't want to be tricked. As the girl covered her arm again, she said, "I thought the Pack never turned on its own kind."

"When it's a matter of life and death, we make exceptions," the girl admitted. "Fenrir, Lupa..."

"Me."

She nodded sheepishly.

With a sigh, Red conceded, "I will think about it. I'll do my best."

The girl relaxed slightly in relief, then tensed as if she heard something, anxiety down every muscle. "She can't know I'm here. She can't know..." Before she turned away and ran off, the girl said, "Fang also wants to say that he's sorry it's come to this."

As the rusty wolf disappeared, Red whispered, "So am I."

Kai didn't realize how far he'd run, but every step became more anxious as the air chilled around him. He didn't ask the Crows where they were taking him. Then again, they never lingered long enough for him to get a word in.

When he burst through the next thicket with a shower of fallen snow and leaves, he stumbled to a halt. Bae lay on the ground just below the slope, snow surrounding him, dusting him. In a flurry, the Crows made a racket overhead. Bae raised his head. Kai's heart pounded in his throat. The reindeer stood, revealing a figure he'd wrapped himself around.

I tried to keep her warm, Bae explained. *She is as cold as ice, and her feet...*

The world fell away.

Kai rushed forward, collapsing to his knees beside her body. He brushed the snow off her face. Every tendon in his hands shook.

"Gerda."

Quickly, he swept off the rest of the snow covering her, scooped her in his arms, held her close.

"We have to take her back to camp," Kai said anxiously, unable to tear his gaze from her. "How long has she been like this?"

We found her this way, Bae informed.

Her lips were blue, her skin marred with ruddy frostnip. She was barefoot, gloveless, coatless. Black stained her toes, blisters formed on the tops of her feet while the bottoms were skinned, raw, bloody.

Kai's throat tightened. He gritted his teeth. "We have to get back."

Without question, Bae knelt so Kai could climb on, balancing Gerda in his arms. He wrapped her feet in his scarf, slipped his gloves onto her hands, and took his hat off for good measure, pulling it over her ears. At his prompting, Bae was off. The Crows circled overhead as lookout.

Legs pressed tightly against the reindeer's sides, Kai tried his best to keep Gerda as close as possible, cradling her head in the nook of his neck, keeping her tight against his chest. Cold air filtered in and out of his lungs.

"Just hold on, *min älskling*," he whispered under his breath. "You can make it. Just hold on."

Chapter Ten
The Changing

Jack blinked in bewilderment. "Is that—?"

"How can I help?" Wendy pitched in.

Kai hardly registered the words coming out of his mouth even as he said them, "I need blankets and warm water, now."

"*Blasted bloody* – What's wrong with her feet?"

"Frostbite. We need to wrap them."

"I'll get the blankets and water, rags, too," Wendy stated, calm and commanding. "Kai, keep her close. She needs body heat."

"Jack, find Tjuv or Lovisa," Kai said. "She could lose her feet if we don't reverse the effects of frostbite."

Jack nearly rolled his eyes. "Sure, leave it to me to find the headstrong, powerhouse women who look like they want to strangle me every time I open my mouth."

"Isn't that your specialty?"

"Shut up, Wendy."

"*Sticka!* Go!" Kai urged.

Jack shook himself off. "Right; be back as soon as I can."

Mr. Crow followed Jack as he scampered off while Mrs. Crow led Wendy to get the supplies. In the mossy dip of the alcove, Kai held Gerda close between him and Bae who lay with his head rested on Gerda's bare feet, trying to instill warmth in her again. Her skin was frozen to the touch, the shallow breath on his neck holding an unnatural chill.

As the silence dwindled to only inhabit their breaths – Gerda's terrible shivering, Kai's desperate anxiety, Bae's calm huff – Kai felt the shock that wrapped his mind and prompted him to action melt away. His heart pounded in his head.

Gerda was here, in his arms, barefoot and frostbitten. But she was alive. She was here.

But how did she escape? Did the Snow Queen know of this? Did she try to stop her? How long had she been like this?

The questions came and went, disappearing as he focused on the pulse under Gerda's skin and the small twitch near her eye. She was alive and she was here. That's all that mattered.

*****

Diablo came flying into the cavernous room they'd been cooped up in for ages, crying a hoarse warning just in time. Quickly, Quinn was hastened into the thick crowd of wolves, her shivering form hidden from sight. She'd only recently returned from meeting Red, only enough time to have a cloak thrown over her shoulders and nod confirmation that the message was delivered before she was rushed into hiding.

Fang steeled himself. The raven perched on Fang's shoulder, whispering in his ear with tongue against beak.

She knows.

Fang shot a look at Lycaon, a threat to remain silent. Lycaon shrunk back but remained near. Despite his influence, Fang didn't trust him enough to let the wolf too far out of his sight. Thaddeus and Lev flanked Fang on either side.

The plan was clear. Everyone was to remain in human form until all suspicion had blown over. Since Quinn had snuck out as a wolf, she wouldn't be recognized or singled out based on her silhouette. Fang wasn't taking any chances.

An iron rod seemed to slide down his chest as a lone figure appeared in the open entryway, her electric blue eyes framed in a stain like black ice that bled over her jutting cheekbones. Knotted fingers and birdlike hands were inked dark as frostbite. Her lips peeled into a smile.

"Are all the dogs in the doghouse tonight?" the witch, Häxan, asked with that strange lilt to her voice.

Despite himself, Fang clenched his fists. "All save one, as always."

"No, no, no, no, no, I don't mean your *big bad wolf.*" Häxan slid forward through the entrance, shaking ink-dipped hands like a conductor. "I mean your dogs."

He tried to remain rigid, calm and in control. "What do you want, witch?"

She clicked her tongue. "So demeaning. For a traitor."

The word shot against him like a mallet. He didn't move, narrowed his eyes. "What are you implying?"

"You really think no one would notice one of your little dogs cross the lake and slip into my woods without permission? Hm?" she hissed, so close he could smell her rosewater breath.

"Whatever it is you're accusing me of, my Pack had nothing to do with it."

"Did you forget your little agreement with Snödrottningen?"

A chill ran down his spine. "No."

Häxan cocked her head like a hawk eying its prey. "Well, since I've been feeling so generous after killing the oldest friends I know, I'll make this easy for you." She backed away, arm sweeping over the expanse of the Pack. "Pick one. Guilty, innocent, I don't care. Surrender one over to me as atonement for your poor judgement."

A deep scowl curled his lip up in furry. "I'll do no such thing."

"Then I will choose."

"Take me."

She laughed sharply. "Sorry, not how this works. Either you choose or I will, and you'll have no control over the outcome." Häxan spread her arms wide. "What'll it be? Choose."

"No."

"Choose!"

"I won't."

"Last chance, dog." Electric blue eyes reflected the light as she inspected the Pack for her victim. "Choose!"

Just before Fang could round on Lycaon, Thaddeus stepped forward and proclaimed, "It was me. Take me."

Panic sent a jab to Fang's abdomen, ice water down his scalp. "Thaddeus, what are you doing?"

The elder man ignored him. "I crossed the lake. I thought that if I could find a way out, then I could convince Fang to lead the rest of the Pack in escape." He sighed deeply through the nose to hide the tremble in his voice. "But there's no refuge for us out there in that cold."

Häxan looked intently at him, eyes narrowed, her lips peeled into a leering grin. "You're a foolish old hound. Dig deep enough, you'll always find refuge."

"In your own grave, maybe," Lycaon grumbled behind.

Thaddeus worked his jaw and lowered his head, the knot of grey hair resting against the nape of his neck. He met

Fang's gaze. "There's no other way. Sometimes you need to seek refuge with an enemy in order to escape the devil."

Fang's throat tightened. "Thaddeus…"

His small eyes widened, every wrinkle a deep crack in his face, the light reflecting silver off the scar slashing the olive skin around his right eye. Thaddeus's hands flew to his throat as his face grew beat-red. Gagging, he collapsed to his knees.

Someone unleashed a scream from the Pack behind them. Snapping out of his stupor, Lev had to rush to stop Quinn as she bolted from the crowd in hysteria.

The shock faded to raging fire. But before Fang could grab hold of the situation, a thorny stem burst from Thaddeus's throat, blood spraying. Dried yellow roses and thorns emerged from his open mouth. He froze, a corpse suspended, then fell onto his side, blood dripping from his eyes and drooling down his chin.

Quinn screamed, tears bright down her face, wrestling against Lev's hold. Lycaon stood aside with his mouth hung open. Breathless, Fang fell to his knees beside his friend, pain shot through his kneecaps. He couldn't believe his eyes.

"Lesson's over," Häxan crowed, her voice battering against his eardrums. "You're being moved to first defenses. We'll see how you behave as guard dogs."

Then she left, but her presence still hung heavy over the room.

A numb chill leaked into Fang's veins, spreading through his weak muscles, leaking from his burning silver eyes. This wasn't over. Even so, he knew his friend had gone beyond his reach.

Clearing his throat, Fang tried to steady his voice, "Get him outside quickly."

"But what if—?" Lev began, hoping.

"No." Fang shook his head. "Thaddeus is gone."

*****

Gerda arrived two days ago, and since then tension strung tight as a high wire over the alcoves. No one seemed to know what this meant for the future of the rebellion. The very thing that tied Kai's motives to their struggle against the Snow Queen hinged on Gerda's rescue. Now she was here.

The forest people were afraid to lose the nomads' loyalty, the nomads were afraid to lose their *hjältar*, and the *hjältar* were afraid to lose their friend. What's worse was that Kai did nothing to confirm or deny their worries. So there the tension hung, high and vulnerable.

Having finished redressing Gerda's wounds, Wendy washed her hands in a basin of melted snow and thanked God that Lovisa was able to reverse the effects of frostbite so Gerda wouldn't lose her feet and fingers. She caught either side of the basin and released a long breath.

The silence was suffocating, like walking on eggshells hoping not to draw blood in the process. Wendy wanted nothing more than to dash it all aside. The nomadic robbers had pitched their tent-like structures in the largest clearing in the alcoves, hardly sparing a word to the forest people. They kept close watch on their tamed reindeer, afraid the forest people would try to set the herd free when their backs were turned.

As for the forest people, they slipped in and out. Wendy didn't know where they slept, though once she saw one peel away from a nearby tree trunk, skin the exact texture of bark.

None were much for conversation. Latham was kind and provided her with any herbs she required, and she often saw Lovisa. They paid more mind to their guests than most.

Red was often out on her own, probably acquainting herself with the terrain, and Alice was in her own little world. Wendy would've tried to reach out to them if she wasn't so busy helping Kai with Gerda. As it was, her only breaks were spent with Jack and Inga. The surrounding tension seemed to lighten with those two, managing to lift her spirits.

Earlier that morning, Jack's usual joking smile waned to the mask Wendy learned to recognize.

"Can I ask for some advice?" he asked her. "You know, from my elder."

Inga stuck out her lip. "Is that supposed to be funny?"

But Wendy felt a smile tug her mouth in amusement. "What kind of advice?"

"Just, uh." He raked his fingers through his hair. "I've been meaning to talk to someone about something…"

"That's cryptic," Wendy teased.

"…but I think she might be avoiding me."

With her cheek swollen with salted fish, Inga stated, "If you think she's avoiding you, then she is."

Wendy raised an eyebrow at her. But Inga merely shrugged. "That's my advice."

"Thank you," Jack said, hands clasped. "Your wisdom is astounding."

"*Gubben.*"

"Gesundheit."

Inga leaned forward, her mouth still full of fish, and annunciated, "*Gubben.*"

Jack made a face. "What does that even mean?"

99

"Jack," Wendy interjected, trying not to laugh, "you're avoiding your own question."

"*Old man*," Inga translated.

Before Jack could retort, Wendy gave him a look of warning. He lowered his head to evade Inga's smug expression.

"How do you know she's avoiding you?" Wendy asked.

"I already told her," he admitted.

"She might need some space."

Jack's jaw tightened. It had only been a few days since Jill died. The wound was still raw, reopened after years of thinking she was already gone. Wendy wanted to hug him and promise things would work out, but she knew that would hurt worse than anything.

"Or maybe," Inga cut in, using her fork as a perceptive baton, "she has better things to occupy her mind and time with other than romance – this war, for example – like a rational person."

Jack raised his eyebrows. "You hear this girl? Expecting us to be rational. I think she needs to spend some more time with Alice."

"She spends enough time with you; I think she gets the idea," Wendy countered with a smile.

Now she stood staring at her face in the water's reflection. A pang wound itself into her chest like a fist pulling her throat inwards. She longed for bare feet and freedom, for laughter and light-hearted adventures, for unfiltered words and unlimited love. She longed for her family, the Lost Boys, Tink, Peter. She longed for home.

Her face frowned back at her with those strange eyes, eyes older than the years she held, years that her face would never show. And suddenly it was like she couldn't breathe. Like the unspoken words held in tension around them became a weight in her lungs.

Impulse driven by an overpowering need to breathe took her to the closest tree. Gloveless hands found knobs and edges to bring her higher until she reached branches to grab. On she climbed, pulling herself up, bringing the sky closer. She needed that sky. She needed to breathe.

What she wouldn't give to release the bark under her fingers, to feel weightless as gravity yanked her down, to catch her breath and defy all constructions, to spread invisible wings and fly above the treetops. For now, she settled for the wind in her face and the distance she put between herself and the earth.

Breaking through the canopy, Wendy breathed in the frigid air. Sunlight settled on her skin. Moisture frosted her eyelashes. The sky stretched on forever, and she felt free.

Yesterday, Lovisa and Tjuv had stopped her to ask about the allies they would be calling in once the pocket watch was aroused. Wendy figured they'd come to her since they didn't take Jack seriously and the others were too preoccupied. So she told them about everything: The Wonderland army, the gypsies and knights of Grimrose, the belowlanders and giants, the Lost Boys and Panther Tribe, even the ghosts who Kai had promised to save if they could be summoned.

She wasn't sure which part sounded most unusual to the two women. Tjuv frowned deeply at the mention of giants, while Lovisa seemed particularly unsettled by the ghosts. If all went as planned, this was going to be the most peculiar of armies.

Scatterings of snow drifted past her, brushing her ears. Wendy sighed. Though her homesickness grew nearly unbearable these days, she prayed that the Lost Boys wouldn't come when the pocket watch called. For every ally they had, there was an equal enemy. She was scared how this would all turn out in the end.

Breath clouding in the wind, she caught sight of the distant castle like a beacon in the sun, and noticed the dark swarm crossing the frozen lake the castle sat upon, moving for the woods.

Chapter Eleven
The Remembered Home

Kai left her side for the first time in days after Tjuv practically shoved him away saying he smelled like reindeer and sweat. She did promise to get him if Gerda woke again, though. So after he left, he found a wash basin waiting for him in the robbers' camp and let the water wash off the grime of the past few days. The haze clouding his mind melted away in the steam. His scar throbbed bitterly, a sharp pulse with every heartbeat, getting worse by the day. But at least now he felt like he could breathe.

When finished, he dressed in the fresh clothes laid out for him, slipping on the chain around his neck he'd worn since this whole journey began. He'd never had the chance to give it to Gerda – not that now was the time for such things. But he'd always worn it as if the ring were already hers. He wanted her to have it. The question still lay unspoken.

For the first time, he wondered if he was still ready to ask. He dashed the doubt out of his mind before he could mull over it too long and finished getting dressed.

Lovisa waited for him outside the tent.

"How is she?" Lovisa asked. He hadn't seen her since she helped reverse the effects of frostbite in Gerda's body, though even then he hardly processed what was happening.

"She's getting better," Kai said, breathing in deeply. "*Tusen tack.*"

"Don't thank me."

But the gratefulness was there all the same, clogging his throat. If it wasn't for Lovisa, Bae, the Crows, and even Tjuv, Jack, and Wendy, Gerda might not have made it this far. He couldn't bear to think about what could've happened otherwise.

Lovisa looked at him for a long time, respectfully letting the moment pass. "Has she spoken yet?"

"Not yet. She's still recovering."

Kai thought back to when Gerda first woke, how her eyes settled on him and she choked on a sob. He hadn't been able to hold the tears back. He held her close and rocked her gently as she clung to him, as if she was afraid he'd melt under her fingers. They stayed like that until she fell asleep in his arms. Since then, she'd only been awake for fleeting moments. Not a word had yet passed between them.

Lovisa turned away, facing the lake and castle that lay beyond the woods out of sight, but which held an unmistakable presence. "This changes things," she breathed.

"I know," Kai admitted.

She paused again, evaluating. "I'm going to meet with her."

"Gerda?"

"The Snow Queen."

Ice settled in his stomach. "What?"

"I will send an emissary to settle a meeting with the Snow Queen," Lovisa continued, looking at him now, as if that made the news any easier to swallow. "We no longer face a rescue mission. A battle is approaching, and I will exhaust every opportunity to avoid bloodshed no matter how slight."

Though he didn't care for the idea of meeting the Snow Queen peacefully, he didn't argue with Lovisa's resolve. "Will she meet with you?"

"I don't know."

"You could be walking into a trap of your own making."

"And she could be walking into hers," Lovisa said. "The moment we face each other, she will try to probe me for any hint of our plans just as I will for hers. But I will not ask strangers to fight by my side until I've attempted diplomacy."

"Diplomacy," Kai echoed dubiously.

"She wasn't some power unleashed from the depths of hell," she pressed. "The Snow Queen used to protect us under her rule. But then she found a way to extend her life and power; now she's abused every duty she'd been given. We are both leaders. Perhaps she has some remaining desire to have subjects of flesh and bone by the end of this."

Grimly, Kai nodded. He realized attempting peace was the best choice if it came down to it. But he couldn't believe for a moment that the Snow Queen would ever agree to terms – at least they would try.

"I'll let you return to her," Lovisa said then, turning to walk away, gossamer flowing around her ankles. "Let me know as her condition improves, or if signs of frostbite return. We won't lose her."

She shouldn't have been up. She needed rest and time to fully recover. But when Gerda woke and began to get up, Kai didn't stop her.

He followed her, hand in hand, as she distanced herself from the cramped quarters of the trees and trekked up the mountainside where this part of the forest washed up onto, where snow and air surrounded them. But at least she could breathe. When she could no longer walk, she sat on the edge of a rock that jutted out over the wooded ravine. Kai joined her.

The view stretched out before them like a glittering white canvas. She'd never seen the castle from a distance. It looked like sugar and glass from here. A shining gemstone on a mirror. She'd always hated mirrors.

The sky erupted in brilliant gold and rose. She leaned against Kai as if to convince herself he was still there. That she wasn't alone.

"I'm afraid to close my eyes," Gerda whispered.

He didn't say anything, waiting patiently for her to continue.

"I'm afraid I'll wake up and I'll be trapped again."

"I won't let that happen," he said – she had desperately missed his voice. "I promise."

She used to tease him about his impulse to promise. She used to say that one day he would end up making a promise he couldn't keep. She felt the urge to say it now, but she didn't. Too much had happened. She couldn't remind him of something so painfully true.

"How long has it been?" she asked.

"Two years."

"My parents must be worried sick."

Kai was silent for a while. "I haven't been home either."

Gerda looked up at him, trying to count the ways he'd changed since last she'd seen him. His eyes were lighter, his hair unkempt – though thankfully still not long enough to cover his ears. The vaguest memory of a much younger Kai flicked through her mind, of a time when he hadn't received a haircut for nearly a year. She couldn't help but smile. She'd teased him about his ridiculous ponytail until at last his mother chopped it off herself when his back was turned.

The scar was new. It ran along his jaw, stark white. She wanted to touch it but refrained. Though the scar was the largest change to his face, there was something else, too, hidden beneath the surface. She couldn't put her finger on it.

"Your mother and grandmother…?"

Kai shook his head. "I don't know."

He's been searching for me.

For two years she'd been imprisoned, and in all that time he was out here trying to get her back. Gerda supposed they had both been through countless things in such time, unforgettable things, unforgivable things. But right now, sitting with him, it was as if nothing and everything lay between them. And it didn't matter. She just wanted to be with him, hear his voice, remind herself that she wasn't dreaming.

"Do you remember it, Kai?" Gerda asked softly, nuzzled under his arm. "Home?"

Kai nodded slowly.

She sighed, blinking back the blur over her eyes as she disclosed, "I can only remember glimpses, moments, faces. But it melts in my hands like snow. I can't hold it. I can't make it real."

She choked and couldn't continue. She wanted to ask him. She wanted him to remind her of things she could only imagine.

So Kai told her.

He spoke of Anders, the colors that glowed down the village, how their houses nearly kissed at their windows. He said she used to kiss the roses to help them grow. In the winter it got so cold they had to keep a fire going for weeks on end. Ice clung to the windows and formed circles on the glass. He talked about their *smultronställe* in the summer, their hidden paradise in the mountains, her bare feet, the flowers she braided in her hair and stuffed in her pockets.

Sometimes they would both join her father on his physician calls – once her father had to pull a rotten tooth and Gerda held the patient's mouth open only to get a nasty bite as result. Kai rubbed the scars on her fingers. She got her unusual eyes from her grandfather. Brown on the left. Blue on the right.

He explained the callouses on his hands, his training as a blacksmith, how he was sore for months before his arms and shoulders got used to the swing of a hammer. She used to poke him in his sore spots and refused to rub out the ache until he'd promised a sufficient foot rub in return.

Kai was still talking when the sky grew dark and Gerda fell asleep on his shoulder.

Chapter Twelve
The Confessed Heart

Alice plopped down in the snow and started making little snowmen.

"I'm ready to talk to Frost now," she said loudly, rolling a head in her hands.

It wasn't long before she got a response. "Do you ever give up?"

Alice shrugged, not bothering to raise her head as the white-haired boy stepped into the clearing. She put the snowball on top of her second snowman. There was nothing for eyes or mouth, so she left it faceless.

His voice came with an edge of forced agitation. "What do you want now?"

Calmly, she looked at him. "What's your story, Frost?"

His face contorted into a scowl. Before he could say anything disquieting, however, Alice interjected, "If you're so intent on avoiding my questions, why bother coming?"

"Stupidity," he grumbled.

"No, I'm familiar with stupidity. That's not why." Alice cocked her head but kept building her snowmen. "I'll just keep asking you questions until you answer them. I'm annoying that way."

"As if that's not abundantly clear."

"Again, you're the one who keeps showing up."

One of the snowmen's heads fell off, smushing on the ground like a soft tomato. Alice couldn't help but think of the Queen of Hearts. Weren't heads supposed to roll, not splat?

Frost sat down cross-legged before her, clusters of snowmen between them. He placed a hand on each knee. Snowflakes danced around his ears. "What do you want to know?"

Alice sighed and rolled her eyes, finding it exhausting how often she had to repeat herself. "What's your story?"

"My story?"

"Honestly, I feel like either everyone's going deaf or I'm developing a slur. Yes, *your* story. Frost, Rudy, whoever you want to indulge – I'm getting a headache trying to keep everything in line. How did you become you? How'd you destroy Babette? How'd you get wrapped up with the Snow Queen? Why did you leave her?"

"You're walking on thin ice there."

"I'm tired of walking on eggshells, so thin ice is a step up for me."

Frost narrowed his eyes, but she didn't relent. She was determined to find out why he had shown up in the vision she'd seen from Kezia. The blind gypsy girl saw Lupa and Frost when witnessing the end of this brewing war. Alice already spoke with the Big Bad Wolf. Now she needed Frost's piece of this puzzle. She was certain of it.

"You can start at the beginning," Alice prompted. "How did you become you?"

"I kissed the Ice Maiden. She put ice in my chest and eye."

"See? That was easy."

Frost looked away, gnashed his teeth. "I used to be human. I built toy houses, I loved a girl named Babette, and I was called Rudy. The Ice Maiden killed my mother and claimed me as her own."

Alice frowned, but refrained from interrupting. The way he spoke was like reciting a list of facts and memories he could no longer remember naturally.

"Growing up, I saw her everywhere, beckoning me to follow her. I finally set out when I was eighteen. I wanted revenge for what the Ice Maiden did to my mother. I'd discovered a way to destroy her. But Babette followed me. She said I was doing exactly what the Ice Maiden wanted, but I didn't listen, so she tried to stop me.

"When Babette finally caught up to me, I was crossing the lake to exact my revenge – it wasn't completely frozen back then. I'd reached the icy center, got out of my boat, but Babette called out from behind me and I fell into the water under the ice." Frost scowled, his eyes glassy, swimming like churning ice. "Babette made a deal with the Ice Maiden: her life for mine. So when I woke again, I was in the ice castle with the means to forever end the Ice Maiden in my hands. But I couldn't do it."

He paused, debating, as if about to relay a secret he'd never spoken aloud before. "The Ice Maiden hasn't lived for so long by merely binding herself to some tree stump or scummy pond. She takes on a vessel, inhabiting it like a parasite, completely taking over. So when I faced the Ice Maiden with the means to destroy her, I didn't face a demon or my mother, but my own Babette."

Rubbing his hands together, he took a deep breath. "I kissed the Ice Maiden. She put her devil's ice in my heart and eye. She claimed me as her own."

Alice frowned. She wondered if the ice was melting inside him, if that's what happened when he chose to help them, the reality behind his loss of immortality. "So if Babette is the Ice Maiden, why did you leave?"

"I've been used by her until I lost myself," he muttered, no longer looking at her but at his hands open now in his lap. "Why did I leave? She's not my Babette anymore."

Since recounting fond memories of growing up during the sunset last night, Kai seriously debated bringing Gerda home to Anders. Her feet were healing, and she was eating well enough, but her skin was so pale and cool to the touch. He feared what the years in the Snow Queen's captivity may have done to her.

He knew about the worries shrouding the robbers' camp and the alcoves. They were afraid he'd return to Anders now since Gerda was with them. Only a few days ago, Kai was ready to take down the Snow Queen and all her followers. He would've led the army.

But now, he wasn't sure.

He wanted to keep Gerda safe. Hadn't that always been his goal? Save Gerda. Bring her home. He never expected to get tied up in a war, to get attached to people along the way, to make so many promises. Why did everything have to get so complicated?

Turning to Gerda while she was eating her vegetable stew, Kai proposed, "What if I sent you to Anders with Bae, and then joined you after this war is over?"

She stared at him uncertainly with her brown and blue eyes. "What do you mean? Wouldn't you come with me? Aren't you ready to go home?"

Kai sighed, a knot forming in his chest. "I have to see this through."

"Surely no one expects you to stay."

"I've made promises."

"Then break them."

He frowned. "Break them?"

Gerda dropped her gaze to the bowl in her hand, but she didn't eat. "No cause is worth sacrificing your life for."

Gently, he shook his head. "I'm not—"

"You don't know her like I do," she interjected. "You don't know what she's capable of."

Pain shot down his scar, a bite so sharp he winced. "What did she do to you?"

Her hands gripped the bowl so hard her fingers were white. She set it in her lap. "It doesn't matter."

"It matters to me." Kai took her trembling hands in his, gave her an imploring look. She hardly met his eyes. She seemed petrified.

"She showed me things," Gerda confessed quietly. "Frozen deserts, tainted soldiers, bodies so cold they shattered like porcelain at the touch. She wants to live forever. Which is why we must leave, go home, forget this place so she'll never find us."

"That's why I must stay," Kai urged. "We must stop her before she gets too powerful. I was close before; I can do it again."

"If she wants you, then you should be running as far away as possible instead of right into her arms."

"If she wants us, then there's nowhere far enough to run. We must stop this."

Pressing her lips, she looked away. "I wish we'd never been tied up in all this."

Before Kai could respond, she turned back to him and kissed him. He hardly caught his breath. Then she pulled away again, so close, closer than they'd been for two years. He longed to kiss her again but didn't want to push her. Instead he remained, searching between her brown and blue eyes, wondering where this urgency to run away came from.

Closing her eyes, she whispered like a fist in his chest, "You never should have tried to save me. At least then you would've been safe."

Jack had grown tired of waiting around for the right moment, so in a sudden burst of stubborn decision, he took off. Maybe the cold was making him impatient. Maybe that little robber girl was getting on his nerves. Either way, once he got to his feet there was no stopping him – no matter how many times he told himself he was being wildly ridiculous. There was no way this would end well.

He ran into Wendy.

"Where have you been?" Jack asked in mock agitation. "I haven't seen you all morning. You've completely missed the opportunity to prevent me from doing something stupid."

Wendy didn't smile, which made his wane. It was never a good sign when she didn't brighten up at his teasing.

"I was talking with Tjuv and Lovisa about something I saw yesterday," she confessed.

Jack huffed. "How is it that I'm never invited to these meetings?"

"I was going to tell you," Wendy said, still serious. "The Pack was moving from the castle, crossing the lake into the surrounding forest. I don't know what it means. But Lovisa is still going through with sending an emissary to the Snow Queen for a diplomatic meeting."

"Because when I think of an ice monster, I think of diplomacy."

"Maybe not. But maybe we can get some of her followers on our side if we're seeking peace. Apparently, a wolf reached out to Red the other day cautioning her about how the Pack is forced to fight for the Snow Queen because of Lupa. Fang sent a message asking Red to kill her."

Jack's stomach tightened so hard he barely processed what Wendy said. "Wait, Red was there?"

She nodded.

His heart pounded in his ears. "Where? I need to talk to her."

Her smile appeared then, sly and knowing, as Wendy jabbed a thumb over her shoulder. Without explanation, Jack kissed her on the head, thanked her, and started down the way she'd indicated. He faintly heard her wishing him luck.

Stepping over the lumps and dips of the alcoves, Jack ran through what he wanted to say to Red once he found her. Dread filled his lungs

What in the blazing world was he going to say to her? Did he confront her head on or ease into it?

Hey Rubes, how've you been? Haven't seen you in a while. By the way, I've been in love with you for so long I can't remember what it felt like to not be in love with you. I figured I'd let you know in case you didn't catch it the first time.

115

He grimaced. It seemed so blunt. Would she ever talk to him again? What if she was avoiding him to pretend that he hadn't already confessed how he'd been pining for her? What if this was her way of letting him off easy?

Hey Rubes, remember back in Giant Country when I basically told you I'm crazy about you? Yeah, I was wondering how you felt about all that, because if that freaked you out a little too much, we can just forget that ever happened and go back to being friends.

Nothing sounded right. It was all a mess in his mind. He raked a hand through his hair, took a breath.

All around, everything seemed to come down to this:

Rubes, I love you. Please talk to me. I care about you too much to let my feelings come between our friendship.

Then he was suddenly facing her, and every preconceived conversation vanished from his mind. Their eyes locked. The air charged. Something seemed to boil in the base of his throat.

When Red dropped her gaze, it was like a jab in the gut as he realized she was going to walk away again. He couldn't take it.

"Why are you avoiding me, Rubes?" Jack blurted, hating the break in his voice that revealed the swelling hurt inside.

Red grimaced at the accusation. "I'm not avoiding you."

"Please don't," he said, hating when she lied – but at least he knew when she was lying. "You haven't talked to me since we came here."

"That's not true."

"Yes, it is! You look away every time I'm around. I've barely seen you at all. You never even told me about this wolf that apparently found you a few days ago. You've been

116

avoiding me since we've come here, and I can't stand it." Heated, he raked his hands through his hair. "Was it me? Did I do something?"

"No, Jack, it's not—"

"You know how I feel about you." He choked, and the buzzing silence that followed swelled up around them. It was all out there again, his truth bare before her, waiting to see if she'd leave his words in the cold or take them close where they belonged.

He stared at the ground between them, trying in vain to swallow the lump in his throat.

"But when I needed someone..." Jack forced himself to look at her again. He refused to look away. "When I needed you the most, you fell away. If it wasn't me, then why?"

She bowed her head, wringing her hands.

He stepped closer. "Why, Rubes?"

"Because I'm scared," she whispered.

"Because you're scared?"

"My parents died because of me. The last man I cared about betrayed me. It's the pattern: I let people get too close, they get hurt, and I get hurt – and there are people out there who will use that against us."

Jack felt a knot of agitation in his abdomen. "First of all, don't go using this people-close-to-me-get-hurt card. Because gushy couples use that excuse all the time to not be together, and we are not about to be that gushy couple."

"Jack—"

"Bad things happen. Terrible, horrible, awful stuff happens regardless of whether you let people close to you. And you're not the only one who suffers."

They were so close he could touch her wringing hands if he tried. She still wouldn't look at him, but she didn't move away either.

Lowering his voice, he added, "Secondly, I would never betray you."

"I know."

"And I'm not planning on dying anytime soon."

Instead of pointing out the obvious impending war, Red stated, "Lupa is going to come for me, and once she figures out that I love you, she's going to hurt you to get to me. I can't let that happen."

Jack's heart leapt to his throat. "You love me?"

Scarlet flushed up her face, but he was grinning like a fool. Now she was really avoiding his eyes.

"You just said you love me."

"Jack, I'm serious," she said with an edge to her tone. Her bottle green eyes shone bright and desperate. "I can't lose you."

Cautiously, he reached up and cupped her cheek, thumb brushing her cheekbone. "Trust me, Rubes, the feeling is mutual."

Before he could kiss her, she pressed her mouth against his. He suddenly didn't care if they were the gushiest of couples, because the world had now fallen away, and it was just her.

It was always her.

Chapter Thirteen
The Lost Mind

After her talk with Frost, an itch whittled its way into the back of her head. Thoughts like rocking-horse flies were buzzing madly around, and Alice wished they would just stand still so she could discern what they all led to.

She tried to tell someone about it. Maybe with some help, they could piece this all together. But she couldn't find Red, Jack, or Wendy. So when she ran into Kai, she tried to get him to follow her. She wanted to tell him everything, wanted him to be there when the big discovery came – for she was certain that's what it was tickling her brain. A big discovery. Kai, however, was busy.

"Later, Alice," he'd said, not unkind but distracted.

She hated that word: *Later*. It was a word with bars. Like *Never* or *Impossible*, *Later* was just as imprisoning and intangible. But unlike *Never* or *Impossible*, she had yet to find a way to break it.

So again, she found herself alone with Frost; two outcasts trying to unravel a mystery.

"What other visions did this blind girl show you?" Frost asked absently, picking at his nails with an icicle.

"She showed me an abandoned Facility where people like me were sent. The place looked as if it never existed," Alice huffed. "But it did; we were there."

"Why'd she show you that?"

She scrunched up her face in thought. "To prove something. To prove that the five of us were brought together for a reason. Like pigs for the slaughter… But what about the other pigs? The other pigs who didn't get tunnels? Where did they go?"

"You're losing me."

"Why us? Everywhere I turn, it all points to the same bloody question. Why us?!"

Frost's eyebrows shot up defensively. "Don't look at me! I may have worked for the icy devil forever, but that doesn't mean I know everything."

"She showed me visions."

"The Ice Maiden?"

"No, Kezia. The blind gypsy girl. She showed me visions of each of us. But I can't find the common thread between them, except that we all came from the same world and found ourselves in a different one. But others have done the same! The Facility was filled with other people like that. So what's special about us?"

"Beats me."

"And why these moments? I saw Wendy flying, I think, for the first time. Then Red caught by Fang the night she became the Wolf, and Jack being tortured by giants – that was when he got gold in his blood. There was Kai when he faced the Snow Queen and shattered a mirror. And me putting Remus's heart back—"

"Kai shattered the mirror?" Frost interrupted, crystal eyes suddenly attentive.

"Yes," she nodded, pulling her legs under her, "that's how he got the scar."

Frost fell silent, eyes narrowed, working his jaw.

With a firm poke to his kneecap, Alice prompted, "What?"

"Nothing."

She glared at him until he caved.

"The mirror is a source of the Ice Maiden's power," he explained. "Way back when we were still mildly getting along, I told Kai he had to break the mirror. But I didn't tell him how to destroy it."

"Which is why you're not buddies anymore," Alice guessed, rolling her eyes. Trust was such a rare thing these days that to squander it on the finer points of smashing mirrors didn't make sense to her. "You may need to tell him how to destroy it, then, at some point."

Frost shrugged. "I just thought that it may not be such a good thing if Kai got a piece under his skin. The mirror can influence you. It's how the Ice Maiden claimed me, by putting a piece in my eye and heart until I found her. Once she had me, she replaced the mirror shards with her own devil's ice."

Alice's mind surged into a whirlwind of images. Wendy flying. Red turned Wolf. Jack with gold pumping in his blood. Kai getting a piece of the mirror under his skin. Alice binding her heart to Remus's. It ran through her head like a song. Or a recipe.

"What did Babette look like?" Alice asked before she could fully process her thoughts.

Licking his lips, Frost took a handful of snow and cupped it in both hands. He furrowed his brow until the snow began to change form, a bust in his hands, faint with color that clung like a memory. Alice's jaw dropped open. Staring back at her, formed by snow, was Anne Christiansen.

Everything fell into place.

She had to warn the others.

They were on their way to find Bae to see what his thoughts were on bringing Gerda back to Anders, when Gerda suddenly froze stalk still, forcing Kai to backtrack.

"It's too late," she whispered.

"What's wrong?" he asked when he reached her.

Her face had paled to a near blue color and her wide eyes stared at nothing. Kai wondered if something had triggered a kind of traumatic reaction. He remembered a night when his father returned home from the military, never quite the same, forever dreading vast open spaces that left him exposed on all sides. His mother was always gentle with his father when he lapsed into states of terror. So now, Kai tried to do the same.

He touched Gerda's arm lightly. "You're safe, *min älskling*. I am here."

"Will you promise me something?" she asked in a breath, still in her strange daze. When Kai agreed, she continued, "Promise me that you'll do whatever it takes to defeat the Snow Queen."

Just this morning she was ready to run away together, to leave everything behind. He frowned in concern but nodded. "Of course; I promise."

Closing her eyes, she breathed a sigh of relief. He didn't know what changed her mind, but he would do everything in his power to keep the shadows from forever chasing her. Gently, he slipped his hand down her arm to take her hand, assure her that everything would be alright. But she flinched away.

"Don't!" she screamed.

Kai stumbled back. "Gerda, what's wrong? Talk to me."

She backed away, her face contorted with fear and pain like he'd never seen before. She pressed her hands to her head. "Stay away from me!"

"*Lugna ner dig*," he soothed. "It's only me."

"She's coming back."

"She can't get you from here, *min älskling*."

"I can't fight her—"

Icy scales flicked over her fingertips and began spreading up her hands. Gerda screamed in terror, tried in vain to rub them off. Kai's stomach tightened. She turned and took off.

Snapping out of his stupor, Kai ran after her. "Gerda!"

Somehow, she was faster than him, despite her still tender feet. By the time he reached her, she had paused with her back toward him. The strange ice was creeping up her shoulders now. He faltered, heart pounding in his throat.

"Gerda?"

At first, she didn't move. He almost reached for her, almost took her in his arms, pulled her close to his chest. But then she turned to face him, and he stepped back. Her eyes shone brighter, like colored glass, reflective and fantastic. The crystalized second skin was blooming over her cheekbones now. He desperately tried to ignore the impending recognition rising up in his chest.

She smiled in a way that Gerda never would've. "Did you really think that she was merely the bait?"

His stomach lurched.

The Snow Queen.

Gerda grimaced. The ice retreated from her eyes. He wanted to run to her, but his feet felt frozen to the ground.

"It's not me," she whispered.

And then she was gone.

Numbness spread like water over his body. By the time he realized he was flanked by forest people in a semicircle around him, Kai had collapsed to his knees while Lovisa stood still as a stone beside him.

Alice didn't know how far she'd run before she realized that the trees were repeating themselves. She stumbled to a stop, noticed the footprints. Over and over again, a loop before her and behind her, all her size. Somehow she'd left the alcoves instead of going further in. It was colder here. Her head began to spin.

"Wendy!" she shouted. She tried to run again, but the trees were taunting her now, a perpetual coil. "Kai!"

She tried not to lose it, the great discovery. Every heartbeat brought another revelation. The plan, the recipe, she felt it growing inside her. But with every puzzle piece that fell into place, something else seemed to slip away.

"Jack! Red!"

Borogove! The footprints were laughing again. All hers. She was circling. She couldn't control it. A never-ending spiral, and she couldn't break free.

There was a pattern; she could see it now. Every moment they changed, a special chemistry, special spices to the soul. They were oysters prepared for harvest, and it set them apart.

They were never in control.

"Kai!"

"You're losing your mind, Alice."

Alice whirled around at the voice. The tick tock in her head slowed.

"It's you," she breathed, not surprised, but still disappointed. She didn't tell them in time.

The Queen of Hearts smiled from her fur-lined cloak, dark eyes shining. "You've figured it all out, haven't you?"

Heart pounding like a hammer, Alice released the revelations pressed to her throat, "It's a recipe. We're the ingredients for her rise, not her destruction."

She didn't bother to clarify. By the look of the Queen of Hearts' face, Alice had discovered the truth to it all. They weren't the heroes. They were the means to an end.

"Clever girl," the Queen of Hearts said, her voice smooth and confident. "I warned them about you. You'd be the one to unravel everything. Shame."

Snow swirled around them, turning pink. The trees stripped away like tissue paper.

Alice narrowed her eyes in scrutiny. "Are you real?"

"I may be the only thing that is real."

A baby jabberwock slithered around the Queen of Heart's legs. There was something like a scalpel scraping in Alice's skull, present but not painful. Now the sky was falling, flipping, swimming.

Alice pressed her fingers to her temples. "I'm losing my mind…"

The Queen of Hearts grinned knowingly.

Lowering her hands, dread filled Alice's stomach. "You're stealing my mind."

She shrugged. "You'll give it to me willingly."

"Like the rest of us."

"Mostly."

Pink snowflakes stuck to Alice's skin like scales. She squeezed her eyes shut, forcing concentration. "This is all in *my* mind," she demanded.

The scales expanded and floated away as bubbles.

The Queen, however, didn't flinch. "But I'm in control now."

The bubbles hardened and dropped like lead, falling on the ground, and Alice suddenly found herself in a field of decapitated heads. Unsure where to go but away, she picked her way around the heads. Her heart pounded in recognition. There was the White Rabbit and the Brothers Tweedle, the Dormouse, Dinah, the March Hare, Boojum the snark, flowers with faces, animals with human eyes, so many people.

Scream, Alice.

She ignored the voice inside. She didn't trust it. She didn't trust this.

In the field of heads, a lone figure stood erect. She approached it, realizing this was Celeste, the White Queen, staring at her with bulbous ghostly eyes. Blood fingered down her throat from a wound ringed around her neck. Afraid she was going to faint, Alice grabbed Celeste's arms. The White Queen's head fell backwards, clean off her shoulders, rolled across the ground. Alice's lungs thickened. The body didn't drop under her hold.

Scream, Alice.

Shaking her head, she tried to regain some control over herself. She released Celeste's headless corpse.

"I don't believe this," Alice choked. "I don't believe any of this."

"How can you believe anything if you can't believe what's inside your own head?"

At the sound of this new voice, the decapitated heads and corpse melted into an expansive pool of blood that foamed at her ankles. Playing cards floated on the surface, the faced ones crying crimson streams, wails so quiet they were mere ripples.

Alice spun around to find the source of the voice. Atop a gargantuan mushroom of bleeding cards sat the Blue Caterpillar, massive and looming. He smoked his hookah pipe, but the smoke he blew was black and hung low over his head like storm clouds ready to unleash. Sulfur dioxide stung her nostrils.

"I've lost my mind," Alice whispered.

"No," the Blue Caterpillar drawled. "You're lost *in* your mind."

"I need to get out."

"You know better than anyone there's no getting out of your head once you've already wandered off the path. You've fallen down the rabbit hole. You're in your own Wonderland now."

Panic began to creep into her bones. She imagined the blood tears sliding down her own cheeks.

"I want to go home," she whimpered.

The Blue Caterpillar leaned forward until his face was a hand's breadth away from her own, his breath hot. "Then *scream!*"

Smoke billowed around her, filling her lungs, clouding her eyes. Alice coughed, gagged. She couldn't catch her breath as it burned her chest and choked grey tendrils around her esophagus. Tears blinded her. Then she hacked up something which dislodged from her throat, landing heavy in her open hands, and she could breathe again.

Gasping, she recovered herself and wiped her eyes. The thing in her hand was a watch like a penny in her palm. She frowned at it just before it floated away, up in the air, and disappeared in the fading smoke.

Familiar singing echoed once her ears stopped ringing. The smoke cleared. Alice found herself standing in blackness, white clock faces ticking in the distance like stars. The singing grew louder.

"*Scream, scream, scream,*" the song went on until a smiling cat swirled into existence, floating around her in pulsing color.

"Why would the Queen want me to scream?" Alice asked.

"When you scream, you lose control," the Cheshire Cat hummed. "You let it go."

"Let what go?"

"Oh, nothing important. Just your sanity."

"So, if I scream…?"

"You lose your mind!" The Cheshire Cat cackled, rolling through the air, a firework of brilliance. "You'll be just like the rest of us, really. Except worse."

"Worse?"

"You'll have lost your sanity. We never had it to begin with. True, we may grow to become more than the madness we were born into. But you who adopted it, who embraced it so fondly," the Cheshire Cat's smile stretched, "you'll be left with nothing but the madness."

He vanished in a vacuum, and there was nothing. No color, no sound, no light, no darkness, no time. There was only Alice.

It took everything in her not to scream.

"Alice!"

Her eyes flashed open. She was in the snow again, right where she'd fallen asleep. Sitting up, she rubbed her eyes and shook away the haze of dreams that fell from her memory like sand in an hourglass.

"Alice!"

She turned towards the voice curiously. Her heart stopped. Running from the pinstriped trees came the Mad Hatter, wild and panicked and calling her name. Alice felt something glow inside her with excitement. With a smile, she stood to meet him.

He paused, twisting her way, and his sky-blue eyes passed over her. Her breath caught short, a marble in her chest. But he kept running and calling her name.

With a start, Alice ran after him.

"Remus," she called.

He didn't turn back. She was so close to him.

"Remus," she shouted, louder.

He tripped but kept going, desperate and oblivious. They broke into a clearing like a plateau in the mountains.

"Remus!"

He turned, saw her, and didn't see the lip.

"*REMUS!*" she screamed, lurching after him as he toppled like a pinwheel over the cliff's edge and into oblivion.

The Queen of Hearts snatched the air victoriously.

In horror, Alice clamped her hands over her mouth. She fell to her knees. She lost.

"Thank you," the Queen said, fist clenched, "for your cooperation."

Everything melted away.

Alice lay in the snow alone, staring at nothing, her mind like a tooth scraped of enamel.

She laughed at the sky for crying.

Chapter Fourteen
The Undoing

Kai was vaguely aware of Wendy beside him as she wrapped a blanket around his shoulders and kept Inga from pestering him with questions he had no intention of answering. A cloud had fallen over his vision, making his ears ring. His scar throbbed. Gerda's words ran through his head like a cyclone.

"Promise me that you'll do whatever it takes to defeat the Snow Queen."

"Of course; I promise."

I promise…

He shuddered, shoved the heels of his hands into his eyes. He should've taken her away as soon as she told him to this morning. He should've listened. Would that have made a difference?

Whatever it takes, is what she said. Because she knew. She knew what this could come to.

Kai may have just promised to kill the woman he loved.

Rage blistered inside, a toiling geyser, straining to be unleashed.

From the surrounding woods emerged Jack and Red, pink faced and hands locked, both utterly confused at the chaos going on around them. The nomads were panicking at the news, gossip like a wildfire. Tjuv tried to calm the masses. The forest people ringed the clearing in stoic formation, as if expecting an attack.

Kai didn't know how many times Jack said his name before he finally flicked his eyes up in acknowledgement. The ringing in his ears sucked away to harsh reality.

"Kai," Jack repeated, his brow knit. "What happened?"

What a question. *What happened?* That's what he wanted to know. Kai looked between Jack and Red, the two of them, together. Their swollen lips, their messy hair, their linked hands just before they hurriedly broke apart under his gaze. What happened. Rage festered into a deep aggravation.

"The Snow Queen," Kai growled as he slowly rose from his seat, "has somehow possessed the woman I love, the very woman who just ran away to protect the rest of us from herself and whatever that devil might force her to do."

"Kai…" Wendy spoke cautiously, reaching out to pull him back.

He ignored her, stalking forward so close to Jack that he had to take a hasty step back. A crimson tint edged Kai's vision. "All while you were off snogging in the woods."

"That's not fair," Jack countered, flustered.

"Gerda is gone *again*! Captured *again*. Only this time it's worse than before, because now she's got the bloody Snow Queen infecting her insides like a bleeding parasite."

"You know we couldn't have done anything about that," Red spoke up.

Kai turned on her, a cool burning in his tone, "I suppose we'll never know. You weren't *here*."

Red shrank back.

"Hey," Jack cut in, "it's not her fault."

"*Ja*, you're right, it's not her fault." Kai's hands were fists now, clenching and unclenching. "After all, it wasn't her fault

132

that we wasted time in a useless realm even after we knew it was the Snow Queen who was behind all this."

Jack's eyebrows shot up. "You can't seriously be blaming me for this."

Boiling, Kai accused, "If we came here earlier, I could've gotten Gerda out in time. We should've left that country as soon as we arrived."

"You chose to stay," Jack pressed, standing his ground as Kai moved dangerously close. "*Of course I'm bloody staying* – remember? Those were your exact words."

"I could've saved her!"

"But you didn't!"

Kai bashed him full in the face, throwing him backwards nearly off his feet. Jack hardly recovered before he shot forward and barreled into Kai's stomach, sending them both rolling on the floor in crimson-tinted chaos.

Snow clumps sprayed into his eyes and mouth. Kai jabbed Jack in the ribs before an explosion of stars burst into his right eye. Blinded, he wrestled to get on top and land a blow to Jack's jaw, a rush of released rage. Kai felt something give in his chest, and he could breathe. His fist ached.

Then Jack's knee shot up and knocked him in the spine. Kai recoiled enough for Jack to scramble away and get to his feet. Heart pounding against the walls of his tight chest, Kai jolted up in time to be rammed again. Arms locked in a violent wrestle to get the other to collapse. Kai shoved Jack away, balled his fist, sent a blow again for Jack's head – and landed a punch right across Wendy's face as she shot between them.

Heat flushed up to his ears when Kai realized what he'd done. A tense, horrible silence strung tight around them as they stood in frozen suspension.

Wendy righted herself with baffling sharpness, a glare boring straight through him. Already a welt was forming below her left eye. "I said *enough*."

Kai fumbled, "Wendy, I—"

"I don't want to hear it," she shot.

He wondered if she even felt the blow, or if maybe his fist rebounded off of her like steel. But there was the welt, and there were her fists against her sides like her body was telling her to be in pain, yet she wasn't having any of it. Like she was too angry to be in pain.

"I am extremely disappointed in you," Wendy said coolly. "I understand you're hurting, but that gives you no right to blame people for things they had no control over."

Ashamed, Kai hung his head. Every breath helped dissipate his anger.

Wendy turned to Jack, just as stern. "And you, fighting your best friend like an animal."

"He punched first!" Jack said defensively.

"So? Don't punch back."

"But—"

"No."

"Yes ma'am."

Wendy huffed, looking between them. "Now, though I should just let your egos fester, I'm going to get something for your bruises. I'll be right back. And has anyone seen Alice?"

"I saw her this morning," Kai admitted. "Haven't seen her since."

She took this with a nod, then marched off to get whatever supplies she needed to patch them up. She still seemed oblivious to the welt by her eye. Casting a sidelong glance at Jack, Red followed after Wendy.

With a groan, Jack plopped down on the ground with his legs stretched into lanky arches before him. Kai remained standing, flexing his bruised knuckles. Jack flicked his bleeding nose with the back of his wrist. His upper lip was swelling.

Guilt wound through Kai's stomach. "I'm sorry, *bror*."

Rubbing his hands together, Jack shrugged it off. "Me too. And I'm sorry about Gerda. I didn't know."

Kai dropped his gaze to his flexing hands. "No one did."

He could barely wrap his head around the situation himself. Could the Snow Queen have really possessed Gerda? Or maybe she used her as some sort of messenger, a megaphone – but that didn't account for the icy scales that flicked up Gerda's arms. He'd only ever seen such an exoskeleton when he fought the Snow Queen, and admittedly the crystalized skin distorted any features beneath the surface. He couldn't have known what the Snow Queen really looked like.

A gnarled knot formed in his chest. Last year in the moment before he plunged from this realm, he'd seen Gerda's eyes, brown and blue, like a vision before him. He always assumed he'd imagined it, like what people said about seeing one's life flash preceding deathly experiences. What if Kai had been fending off Gerda the whole time while the Snow Queen inhabited her body? What if it wasn't chance that sent him from this realm, but Gerda in an effort to save him? What if he was so desperate to rescue her from the Snow Queen that he couldn't bring himself to believe where she'd been this whole time?

Gritting his teeth, Kai shook his head violently. He was driving himself mad. Jack looked up at him from where he sat, brow knit in concern, watching helplessly as Kai wrestled with all the doubts and confusions that came with this confuddled revelation.

Kai forced himself to focus on the regularity of his breathing, staring intently at a spot on the ground between Jack's foot and his own. Silence stretched between them. The wind soon cooled his skin and filtered through his lungs. Salt stung his eyes, but the rage was still there. A cold and despairing rage.

"So," Jack spoke, the gold in his eyes reflecting like fractured light, "what happens now?"

Kai took a breath, but someone else answered.

"Now," Lovisa stepped up beside him, her neck in a strong arc from collarbone to chin, "I go meet with the Snow Queen."

The chill that passed through him was like ice water fueling his rage. "What?"

She regarded him for a split moment. Her eyes seemed darker, resembling obsidian. She responded in a kind of calm finality, "The emissary returned. We are to meet at the Finnish Woman's house by dawn."

Jack scoffed. "You can't seriously be considering peace with the bloody witch now."

"We are accounting for recent events," Lovisa said evenly. "The terms we present will include Gerda's permanent freedom from whatever possession the Snow Queen has over her."

Kai stepped closer. "I'm coming with you."

Without hesitation, Lovisa shook her head. "That wouldn't be wise."

"Why not?"

"Yeah, why not?" Jack echoed, rubbing the bridge of his bleeding nose. "The man can be pretty convincing."

Lovisa cast one sweeping glance over Jack's beaten form before cutting her gaze at Kai once again. "You are unstable."

"I'm stable enough," Kai growled.

"And if the Snow Queen wants the five of you, as you have proposed, then it is in our best interests that you stay far away from her grasp."

"But she was here," he snapped. "She was here among us this whole time."

"A mistake I won't readily make again," Lovisa said, a sharp edge to her steady tone. "Taking you to a meeting to negotiate a peace treaty puts too much at risk."

Fists to his sides, Kai knew all arguments were in vain. "You're seeking a deal with the devil."

"And she'll accept my terms if she still wants a kingdom by the end of all this." There it was, the blazing wildfire behind her eyes. Lovisa sighed, shoulders dropped, then squeezed his arm gently. "I'll be careful."

Her touch lingered like an apology before she turned and walked away. Kai watched the grass gradually return to a stand from her footprints.

Wiping the blood from his nose, Jack rose to his feet with a groan. "So what do we do? Just wait?"

"*Nej*," Kai muttered, mind turning. "I think it's time we found out why the Snow Queen wants us."

"Ah," Jack dusted off his hands, "so we find Alice."

Kai nodded. Whenever she decided to show up again, he'd have to find out what she made of this chaos.

A bushy grey Himalayan wolf sniffed her face to see if she still lived despite the icicles in her tasseled hair and the minute rise of her chest. A snowball hit him square on the nose. With a growl, the wolf scrambled away into deeper woods.

Frost approached her in grim caution, the crystal flecks of his eyes dull, afraid of the discoveries she made and what they meant. But her body in the snow proved his darkest dread, that history was repeating itself. This was his fault. This right here, this innocent girl on the ground whose only mistake was in asking too many questions, in seeking a home, in following a pink-eyed rabbit down a hole... He gnashed his teeth. Everything that's happened, everything that would happen – all because of him. One decision. He still witnessed the consequences.

What brought him to follow after her? He couldn't discern if it was guilt or shame, or even some amusement from her constant badgering and inquiries. Maybe it was something else, a desire of sorts to be seen and heard, to be wanted for something more than the monster he'd become. Maybe that newfound need had turned to fondness.

He should've known not to get attached.

Gingerly, he thumbed the snow off her face and scooped her up in his arms. She was blue. The icicles in her hair broke and clattered like windchimes. Frost wished he could give her warmth, but all he could do was take the freeze threatening to eat her nose and appendages upon himself. The cold had never disturbed him before, so he took it all at once, not expecting the faint wedge of pain that twisted up his stomach. He grunted, shook his head, then walked on. He parted the snow like a curtain around them even when his breath grew short with the effort, carrying Alice limp in his arms, praying he wasn't too late and knowing that he was.

Chapter Fifteen
The Girl Who Spoke Riddles

Lovisa was gone. So when Frost entered the alcoves with Alice unconscious in his arms, it was Tjuv who stepped in. She had a lavvu cleared out, sent Inga to get food and warm water, and with the look of a beady-eyed bear she left Frost alone to watch Alice as she left to personally inform Kai and the rest of the *hjältar* what little she knew about the situation.

It seemed to Tjuv that something rotten had infested this day and leached into the night, first with the girl Gerda and now this. Still, she remained sturdy in the knowledge that this wouldn't be the end of such tragedies stacked up against each other like rolling stones. But for the boy's sake, and for the sake of his friends, she lowered her voice respectfully around their fire, pressed her gnarled fingers around Kai's tense shoulder, and nodded toward the designated lavvu. She left them to their own devices.

By the time the four of them arrived, Alice was awake.

She stood with her back toward them, her long hair loose and wet, wearing only one shoe. With her bare foot she drew shallow troughs in the ground where she'd kicked aside the mats and furs, her big toe caked in dirt. In a cheery yet forceful tune, she sang, "Mind, heart, breath, bone, blood. Mind, heart, breath—"

Wendy stepped toward her friend. "Alice?"

Her singing ceased abruptly. Casting a look over her shoulder, Alice cautioned, "Don't fall in."

"What?"

Cornflower blue eyes swept from the markings on the ground to Wendy's concerned face. "Your feet aren't as sticky as you think."

Wendy blinked, but Jack huffed a halfhearted laugh. "Whoa. We leave you alone for a few days and you've already boarded the crazy train again?"

There was something feline about the way she twisted to face them, the way she crouched down and stared unflinchingly at Jack. Kai's shoulders tightened, his hands at his sides, unsure what to prepare for.

"We're all mad," Alice pressed her fingers into her temples so hard that it left halfmoon imprints from her nails, "here."

Jack clamped his mouth shut and gulped.

Wendy tried again, "What happened?"

"Typical. Heart goes in, mind goes out. Scream! *Scream!*"

Her fingers turned white from the pressure she put against her temples at her final screech. Wendy rushed up to pry Alice's hands away from her head, afraid she may hurt herself. But before she could reach her, Alice plopped down on the ground, cross-legged and stoic, oblivious to Wendy hovering directly in front of her. She hummed to herself and rocked from side to side. Wendy looked back at the others, worry written across her brow.

Red stood in dead silence, her fists clenched against the back of the tent. Jack frowned in disbelief.

Jaw tight, Kai turned to Frost who had placed himself with arms crossed near the entrance. "What happened?" he asked in a low growl.

Frost didn't look at him, only the girl swaying on the ground. "She got to her."

"Was this your doing?"

He huffed, working his jaw out to the side in a space between aggravation and annoyance. Crystal eyes cut back to Kai. "As much as you don't trust me, believe that I would never do anything to hurt Alice."

"Why?"

"Because, sadly, she's the closest thing to a friend I have."

Kai narrowed his eyes in suspicion.

Frost sighed, righted himself, and clapped Kai on the shoulder. "Try not to get too jealous."

Then he left. Kai stood dazed for a moment wondering what could have happened to make that tricky devil care about anyone, let alone Alice.

When Inga came in with stew and pine needle tea, she eyed Alice in a guarded silence, clearly not wanting to come any closer. She had the same expression when Bae came back to her for the first time after he was freed, like he was a wild animal, a creature who would hate and harm her. Red must have recognized the look for she took the stew and tea from the girl, volunteering to present them to Alice herself. With a nod of thanks, Inga gratefully made her leave of the lavvu.

Red squared her shoulders and held the teacup out upon approach. "Here Alice, this may help you feel better."

Alice raised her chin from where she sat, sniffed. Pupils dilated.

"Don't drink!" she screamed, leaping up and slamming the teacup away. Tea sprayed like a firecracker, and most of the soup spilled over. Red flinched back.

"Poison. *Poison*," Alice ranted, spinning wildly around. "It's going to tear out your throat."

She wrapped her hands around her own throat and squeezed. She choked, tongue over teeth, but didn't let go. Kai shot forward to stop her, but Red and Jack were already there, prying her stiff fingers away until she released herself. Somehow Wendy ended up with the soup bowl cupped in her hands, face pale.

As soon as Red and Jack got Alice's hands away from her throat, each with one arm, she ceased struggling and skipped over to the pile of furs that made for a bed, singing the same song as before. "Mind, heart, breath, bone, blood…"

Jack took in gasping breaths, shaking his head in bewilderment. "Blasted bloody—" He raked his hand through his hair. "What happened to her?"

Kai pressed his lips firmly together, dropping his gaze to the maze of markings Alice had traced in the dirt ground. There was nothing discernable. A patch of loops and dashes.

"The Snow Queen got to her," he said in response.

"And now, what, she's officially got straw on her head?"

"I don't know."

Again, Wendy approached Alice slowly, the soup bowl in hand, its lip stained brown from the spill. Still humming, Alice remained still while Wendy came to sit beside her. Crisp blue eyes watched her curiously. With a sigh, Wendy took a spoonful of stew and held it up to Alice's lips, repeating the gesture after every accepted bite. It went on like this in mesmerizing display, Wendy's diligent and gentle spoon feeding, Alice's strange unblinking stare. When the bowl was scraped clean, Alice reached up to wipe the stray tears off Wendy's cheeks and whispered something Kai couldn't make out.

Dazed, Wendy stood and returned to the others who'd watched the whole scene in resigned silence.

Jack shrugged. "Well, maybe Rubes was just never meant to be a nursemaid."

Red hit his arm.

"What did she say?" Kai asked Wendy softly.

She blinked as if it was difficult to focus. "She said that I'm the heart."

"But what does that mean?" Jack asked in a harsh whisper. "What does any of this mean?"

Unable to answer, Kai looked back at Alice. She chewed her fingers and stared at nothing. His stomach felt hollow. He wanted to hope that this was temporary, that Alice would wake up when the sun rose again and she'd be back to normal. But this felt irreversibly wrong. Something happened to her, something that went deep and left permanent damage in its wake. Kai didn't know how to fix this.

"We shouldn't leave her alone," he said grimly, looking at each of his friends. "We'll take it in turns."

Wendy nodded. "I'll go first, see if I can get her to eat some more."

Though the rest agreed, they were hesitant to leave. Red's jaw was so tight the tendons stuck out down her throat like wire. She looked at Alice for a long time before leaving quickly, the fabric flap beating back and forth upon her exit.

Jack's face twisted with the effort of trying to make sense of an unacceptable situation. Kai couldn't blame him. Nothing about this felt justified. Alice was really the youngest of them. Now, she was the most damaged. How was that right?

Before he left, Wendy caught his arm. "When Lovisa gets back," she said, "we need to make sure that pocket watch gets working. I have a feeling we're going to need some help from Alice's Wonderland friends."

Kai put his hand over hers in agreement. "Maybe that Mad Hatter can reach her better than we can."

She managed a tight hopeful smile, but Kai recognized the hurt. This was out of their control. They were helpless – they could do nothing for her now.

*****

Gerda felt the change like sandpaper against her palms. Things were different now, because this time, Gerda was more than just an eavesdropper put to sleep for the Snow Queen to play with, only catching glimpses of the horrors and snagging stray thoughts and plans which flitted through the thin border between their consciousnesses. She didn't wake up in her ice prison with the bleeding mirror and Anne Christiansen's reflection staring back at her.

This time, she was awake. Fully conscious. Completely without control.

A voice wrapped around her soul like a winter wind, *I want you to see the greatness we will become.*

Gerda recoiled, repulsion like a rose vine in her core – but she couldn't recoil. The nerves died before they could flinch down her muscles into action. She wasn't in control of her own body. But she was aware of the cool lick of ice scales over her skin, the air like barbed spearmint in her lungs, the failed signals when she tried to run. Her heart sped in panic yet remained steady in her chest. Her whole body wrestled under countered instructions, and Gerda was losing the battle.

She processed her palms pressed over the mirror's surface. There was a scream under her fingertips, a vapor washing over the reflective ice before sinking into it like a sponge. She inhaled the raw power this new tie brought, this new cage which both inhibited and strengthened her. It was like she was wound wrist to wrist, knee to knee with the Snow Queen. A puppet tangled with the puppeteer. They would no longer take turns pulling the strings.

With everything she could muster, Gerda cried out to the frigid mass in her head, *Why are you showing me this?*

The cool voice clouded over her senses again, chilling her soul. *This will all go easier if we work together, don't you think?*

Work together? I don't want this. You're controlling me.

Bitter laughter swirled around in her head. *The more willing you are, child, the smoother this will be – and the less people get hurt.*

She stewed in this as she watched herself step away from the mirror, wrap a polar bear pelt around her shoulders, and pass the wiry witch who lurked in the corner of the throne room with glittering eyes and wringing hands. Häxan remained behind as the Snow Queen left the castle into the grey morning.

A low mist hung over the frozen lake, curling from her feet. Swirls of snow bees formed humanoid figures standing guard on either end of the castle door, shifting and churning into each other like self-contained blizzards. The Snow Queen walked past them all, across the bare expanse of blue-grey dawn, through the parted line of wolves at the lake's edge. She traveled along the river even upon reaching where the ice dwindled to rushing waters, her crystalized foot meeting newly formed ice with every step, the river groaning into solidity at her touch. Shadows stretched in black lines, prison bars on the ground.

The Finnish Witch's house was completely iced over, glass shattered in the windows, the door sealed shut. Icicles clung along the edge of the lipped roof and reached nearly to the ground like white yarn hung to dry. *Taika* – Gerda sensed the Finnish Witch's name more than she knew it, the information leaking into her awareness without drawing much attention to itself. There was a tone to the Snow Queen's thought at the name, sharp and dry and satisfied. Taika was dead. Whoever she was.

The door broke loose with a strong push of her arm. Wind whistled through the cavernous skeleton of the house. Furniture that had not fallen to rot was frozen over in hoar frost, delicate patterns branching up the walls and across the floor. Pale sunbeams slanted inside to provide dim light to the grim interior. The Snow Queen stood by an open window, facing the door, so the light hit the right side of her face. Blue eye shone like ice in a crystalized face. Brown lost in dark shadow.

Gerda stirred when the door creaked open again, though the Snow Queen stood in stone composure. The Princess Lovisa calmly stepped inside, head high, elegant and rigid. Immediately Lovisa's gaze found and fixated on the Snow Queen while her coupled entourage were late in realizing her presence and flinched back in shock. Amusement pricked Gerda's consciousness. At least she could still distinguish between which thoughts came from the Snow Queen and which came from herself.

Lovisa donned an evergreen cape over a loose jade dress which fell to her branch-wound ankles, gold armbands glinting in the dull light. She regarded the Snow Queen without revealing any discomfort upon seeing Gerda blanketed in ice shards and polar bear skin. A lump formed in her throat. This was the woman who saved her from frostbite not a week ago. Now, look where they stood. Lovisa should've let her die.

Gerda wished she could tell her to take Kai and run far away from here. A rumbling snicker smothered her consciousness.

"You are alone," Lovisa finally voiced, not a waver to her tone.

The Snow Queen's voice edged from her throat as if her vocal chords were edged in rime frost, "I do not need anyone else."

Lies, Gerda thought bitterly. She was living proof of the Snow Queen's dependency. But the Snow Queen brushed away the accusation with ease.

"You have summoned me," the Snow Queen spoke, "to discuss terms of your surrender?"

"I wish to discuss terms of peace," Lovisa corrected, head high, regal like a general.

A cool flush hit Gerda from the Snow Queen, recoiled agitation, a cobra. *Are you intimidated, Snödrottningen?* Gerda asked slyly. She nearly shrieked as a sudden steel wall shot up between them, blocking all emotion from leaking into her awareness. Settling back into submission, Gerda watched the rest of the negotiation.

"My people have suffered centuries under this violent tension between us," Lovisa continued. "Enough lives have been taken. Let us settle this dispute without further bloodshed."

The Snow Queen let a silence stretch, stepping away from the window and angling herself so the light fell full on her reflective face, both eyes mismatched in the pale sun. Diamond dust flitted through the sunbeams like pinpricks of starlight.

"I agree," the Snow Queen said at last.

Gerda's attention pricked in suspicion. Lovisa didn't let any surprise show, but surely she couldn't have expected compliance. The harsh wall between their consciousnesses thinned down to cheesecloth, filtering unnamed emotions that heightened Gerda's misgivings.

The Snow Queen continued evenly, "Bloodshed should be the last resort. What good comes from killing each other but to prove who is stronger in the end?"

You're playing her, Gerda struggled to understand. *You have to be. Is this a game to you?*

She didn't respond, but let the thought linger like an echo in the cavern of her mind.

Dipping her chin, Lovisa shifted to stand flanked between her two companions. "I am pleased to hear you also see reason, which leads me to proceed with my prepared terms for negotiation."

The Snow Queen raised a hand, allowing the Princess to continue.

Squaring her shoulders, Lovisa recited, "We require that every one of our peoples tainted by your ice will be released from your power, and that no individuals may be controlled in such a way from now to forever."

The Snow Queen had expected this, Gerda knew. But instead of finding loopholes to the terms, she actually seemed to be listening to them. There was no toying with the ideas, no mulling. They passed in and out of her thoughts with mere acknowledgment.

"We require that an elected individual from the nomadic clan, the forest people, and the witches – each elected by their respective population – be involved in the ruling council of this land and kingdom."

Gerda hardly felt a snicker at the assumption that the witches were still alive. Häxan was the last of them. Even so, surely the Snow Queen wasn't compliant enough to consider these terms.

"We require that you pull back from your pursuit to spread your power past the mountains to the realms beyond."

What are you planning? Gerda asked, afraid what the answer may be. But the Snow Queen remained at ease and silent.

"Finally, we require that you release Gerda Vår from your parasitic control," Lovisa concluded, "never to inhabit an unwilling host again."

Gerda felt her chest swell to bursting. To be free after two years of fighting for control of her own body seemed too unbelievable to consider. That last term had to have been for Kai – it wouldn't make sense otherwise. The Snow Queen could never make herself so vulnerable as to surrender Gerda, and Lovisa was too smart to believe such a thing was considerable. But Kai would. Gerda knew then that this woman, this powerful general, she would do anything to protect him. Just as she would.

Oh child, the Snow Queen said at last with a breath that encased her with frosty chill. *It matters not who protects him. This all ends the same.*

"In exchange," Lovisa stated, "we will allow you to rule, as permitted under our terms, without further rebellion or bloodshed. You may then continue to govern this kingdom under ice and snow as you wish."

The Snow Queen nodded, twisted, let the shadow fall over half of her face again. "I will consider your conditions," she said slowly, ever calculating. Gerda knew the act was eroding away. "Shall I now propose my own?"

Lovisa's eyes narrowed ever so slightly, the first outward sign of her suspicion. But she inclined, "Of course. This is a negotiation."

"Yes," the Snow Queen hummed, tilted her head. "As to your first term regarding the *tainted*, as you call them, they may be released so long as a draft be permitted should the need for an army arise."

Lovisa dipped her head. "Understandable."

"Your elected council may be allowed so long as I may elect my own additional representative to even the numbers – but a more specified account of this council may be drawn up at a later time." The Snow Queen waved it off absently. "As for the expansion of my power, well, this is not so simple to compensate. I have other agreements to consider."

"Surely there is a way to satisfy your allies in order to regain the loyalty of your people?"

"Perhaps. I shall think on it."

You give her a false sense of control, Gerda observed. *Why?*

Don't spoil things, child.

151

"As to your final request," the Snow Queen continued, "I cannot promise that she isn't willing to host me. After all, what little girl doesn't want to be a queen?"

I don't.

Do not lie. I know you better than you may know yourself.

Stern, Lovisa said nothing. Her tight lips and rigid neck expressed how unrelenting she was on the subject.

"As for my own conditions for this proposed peace, I only have two. Firstly, I would require that the pocket watch be eradicated."

Gerda felt something cinch in her stomach. She couldn't remember anything about a pocket watch, but the vague breath of knowledge came from the Snow Queen's consciousness, a beacon, a key and door in one.

Lovisa's eyebrows twitched. "If the pocket watch were eradicated, how do you expect them to leave?"

She didn't have to explain who they were. Gerda wanted nothing more than to be free to go, leave this place far behind her, to return home to Anders with Kai and his friends.

The Snow Queen smiled as if revealing a secret. "They can walk."

She narrowed her eyes. "Walk?"

"Where did you expect your *hjältar* came from? Their homes lie beyond the southern mountains. They are of the very people I have always protected you from. They are the reason you hide in this land."

The forest people behind Lovisa shifted were they stood, tension coiling at their feet, pulling back their shoulders. Lovisa stiffened as if she could brace through a hurricane.

A cold film of ice whitened the Snow Queen's hands. "I would like to spend some time alone with your *hjältar*."

Dark russet eyes hardened. "No."

"Think this through," the Snow Queen cautioned, thin veils of fog emitting from her icy fingertips. "I am not going to kill them. That has never been my intention. I merely wish to retrieve something as a return on investments I made a number of years ago."

"No, this is out of the question."

"You understand that I cannot accept your terms if you do not accept mine."

"I refuse."

Something brittle seemed to snap around Gerda's consciousness, needled icicles breaking in her eardrums. The pretense was up.

The Snow Queen's hands clinked now with ice, cracking and forming with every muscle's movement. "Then you will watch your world shatter when I come to full power."

"So, you would sacrifice peace for your own power?" Lovisa asked sharply.

"No, it is you who sacrifices peace for what you claim as heroism. You sacrifice the whole for the sake of mere individuals who are not even your own people. I ask for a simple trade. What are six children in exchange for peace?"

"If it is a sacrifice you want, then take me."

The Snow Queen laughed, not bothering to grace the offer with a response. She tilted her head so the light shone on her teeth. "I do not even wish to kill them, so *sacrifice* is not so much the expense as a sacrifice of their time."

"What of Frost?" Lovisa asked.

A strange stir brushed against Gerda's awareness – a memory, so subtle she barely noticed. But then it was gone, destroyed, as if all traces of a previous host were eradicated once and for all. Gerda recognized it. Anne Christiansen.

As if she too could sense the stirred memory, Lovisa pressed, "What of your loyal servant, traitor, betrayer? You make no demands for him?"

"He will find his mortality to be punishment enough," the Snow Queen said without any trace of nostalgia. "I made him. He can be replaced."

In the tense silence that strung between them, Gerda wanted to scream at Lovisa, wanted her to betray this peaceful meeting.

Kill her!

She fought with every ounce of strength she could muster to push the thought forward, to move her tongue, to wince, to whine, to do anything that would regain some sort of control over her own body again.

Kill her!

In her struggle, sweeping cold laughter surrounded her. *Child, you do not see? They can never kill me – all they see is you.*

Gerda froze.

"Surrender," the Snow Queen spoke slickly. "You cannot win this battle."

Though the words were spoken to Lovisa, Gerda knew they were meant for her as well. Any attempt to fight was hopeless. The truth of it hammered into her chest with every heartbeat.

Lovisa raised her chin. "We shall see."

No, Gerda thought as the waves of the Snow Queen's consciousness lapped over her, revealing plans already in motion. The Snow Queen was ahead of them all, unfazed. She could see the next move like pawns on a chessboard: the preparation, the sacrifices, the means to an end. Every loss on her end only meant a deadly strike on theirs. And the Snow Queen would win it all in the end because Gerda was the final piece.

As Lovisa turned to leave, flanked by her escorts, Gerda sent a final pleading thought before she sank into the abyss of the Snow Queen's mind:

Kill me.

*****

Kai took the last shift, stepping into the lavvu to find Red kneeling with her knuckles pressed against her mouth, her gaze constant and shadowed towards Alice who lay sprawled on her back with eyes wide to the small opening above where the tent-stakes crossed. Starlight flicked in her eyes. When Kai broached Red and placed a gentle hand on her shoulder, she flinched, startled.

"*Jag är ledsen*," Kai apologized.

Red waved it off, rubbed her face, made as if to stand but didn't. Kai knelt beside her on the array of mats and furs covering the floor, waited.

"I just…" she started but cut herself off. Her thumb tapped anxiously against her knee. She wouldn't tear her eyes away from Alice. "Wendy tried talking to her. But she couldn't get it, what Alice says, whatever version of reality that's wrapped up in her head. And you know Wendy, she never gives up, but this," Red held her knuckles briefly against her lips like she could keep back the cracks in her voice, "this is beyond any of us. Then Jack tried the usual antics, the joking, the pestering,

155

whatever it takes for him to see light or, or what's funny. This isn't funny. Even he couldn't laugh about this."

Her eyes shone black in the lamplight like ink blooms. Jaw set to grinding. Kai couldn't tell if she was ready to shatter or tear the world apart.

"And you?" Kai asked, voice low.

She huffed, dropped her hands. "I'm angry. I'm angry that this happened to her. I'm angry that I can't understand her. I'm angry that I can't fix it, I can't help her, I'm just sitting here helpless staring at her while she's losing her mind."

Her words rang in the air, electric and fuming. After sitting rigid in the bitterness of them, Red stood suddenly and left the lavvu as if she had held on as long as she could. Kai watched her go, then turned back to Alice as she rolled over, legs over head, until she sat poised on hands and knees with her eyes fixed on him.

He thought about what Red said, about how hard it was to understand Alice's version of reality through the madness. But she couldn't be lost. She was still there behind this insanity. Or maybe she was inside the insanity, but it was like a language barrier lay between them too high to climb and too thick to breach. Kai folded his hands over his knees. If this was a matter of misunderstanding, like a foreign dialect, then maybe he should believe it all, every word she said no matter how insane, to crack the code. Afterall, the madness was all true to her now. He had to try something to figure out what happened to her and why.

When he finally rose, Alice leaped up to him so they stood face to face. "*Blood mirror*," she sang in place of greeting.

Kai opened his hands calmly. "Alice, please."

"Alice please," she echoed.

He frowned. "What?"

"What?"

"What are you—"

"What are you doing?"

At this, he clamped his mouth shut, lips in a firm line.

Eyes glittering, Alice leaned uncomfortably close and whispered, "*Blood mirror.*"

Kai flinched at her hot breath on his cheek. She laughed hard enough for her nose to crinkle, then she hopped back and began skipping in a loop. All the while, she lifted her voice up and down, "What *are* you doing? *What* are you *doing*? What are *you* doing?"

Passing a hand over his face, Kai huffed out a sigh. This was going to be difficult.

"*Whoooo arrrre yooooou?*"

He shook his head at the irony. "You're always asking questions."

"I have no more questions!" Alice cried, arms stretched wide like a freed bird about to take wing. "Just all the answers floating around in my head."

"Is that what got you here?" he asked.

Alice pulled a scarf from her neck, let it trail on the ground, and wrapped it around and around her head like a turban. "I'm wearing all the hats," she said with a grin.

"What did you find out?" Kai pressed.

"In! In!" Alice threw the tails of her scarf over her shoulder. "What did you find in?"

"I don't understand. Is that a clue? What answer did you discover?"

"Magic splinter."

"What is that?"

Her scarf slipped over her face and onto the floor. She crouched down, looking at him through her eyelashes. "*Blood mirror.*"

Kai scratched his throbbing scar. He wished he could understand, but this was a mess of hats and mirrors and riddles.

"Look who's asking the questions now," Alice spoke.

He looked up to find her in front of him again, reaching gently up to his face, caressing his chin. Her touch lingered. Kai searched her eyes for any sign of the Alice he knew. Her pupils seemed to pulse in the dim light.

"Alice," he whispered. "Please try."

"*Try,*" she echoed softly. She pulled away, shook her head from side to side like the word had twisted into sour coils around her tongue. "*Try try try try try.*" She froze. "Try." Blue eyes turned to him, pleading, vulnerable. "Try."

He swallowed the raw lump in his throat. "I will."

Satisfied, she nodded and began to hum. "*Mind, heart, breath, bone, blood.*"

Kai watched silently, gathering his thoughts, as Alice plopped down and started plucking individual hairs from the furs on the ground. She gathered them in her palm, a delicate cloud. Kai took a seat on Alice's makeshift bed.

Clearing his throat, he said, "You know something. You solved the mystery or discovered something worse. Did you know about Gerda? Were you trying to warn us?"

She tossed her palmful of hairs into the air so they showered over her head. Closing her eyes, she blew at the floating strands. "Anne Christiansen," she said lightly.

A jolt shot down his spine. He hadn't thought much about that name since Wonderland. Leaning forward on his elbows, he asked, "What did you find out about Anne Christiansen?"

"Blood mirror," she whispered to herself. She was chewing on her fingers again. "Blood mirror."

"She helped us escape."

A sharp laugh shot from her gut.

Kai frowned. "Didn't she?"

"Little oysters skip into a walrus's mouth if they think they're being saved." Alice rolled her head around. "Little fishies, Mister Crocodile, into your jaws we go!"

His heart pounded in his temples. So they'd been tricked, or that's at least what Alice was suggesting. Anne Christiansen wasn't the friend they thought she was. But why? What did this have to do with the Snow Queen, with Gerda, with what happened to Alice? She was speaking in riddles – the answers were in there somewhere, he just had to listen for them.

Alice stopped humming, stock still, her hands tense against her kneecaps. She turned to look at him, pain pulling at her face.

"I'm trying," she whimpered, strained. "I'm trying. Sparks fly all in my head, and I try to catch the right one, but touch the wrong spark and it explodes. They all explode. BOOM!" She trembled like the sound of her own voice shocked her. "I'm trying."

Anxious to take advantage of whatever window of control this was, Kai asked, "What is the Snow Queen planning?"

"She's cooking, crawling in the oven."

"How?"

"Wrong question. *Wrong question!*" Alice exclaimed. Everything was shaking now with the effort of holding against this mental battle. "You didn't listen. You didn't care."

"I care now."

"Bread and glitter. Bones don't break."

"Alice, what did she do to you?"

"Raised an anchor. Lost control. Scream!"

"What did you find out?"

"The last you give, the first you take…" She shook her head. "You weren't listening."

Kai raked his fingers through his hair. "I'm listening now."

Alice clicked her tongue. "Tick tock, tick tock, tick tock…"

He hated this, this helplessness. It felt like he was too late. He was too late to save Gerda, too late to save Alice, too late to pay attention. Guilt tightened his chest and throat like a beast pressing its paw down on him to break his breastbone, squeeze his lungs.

"Blood mirror," Alice repeated. "*Mind, heart, breath, bone, blood.*"

"I'm sorry," he whispered.

But the words fell off her without notice.

160

Chapter Sixteen

The Right Question

Frost had disappeared after bringing Alice back to the alcoves last night. Once he decided to show himself again, Kai determined to talk with him about what Alice talked to Frost about before she lost her mind. Maybe she had told him something that would make these riddles clearer.

Mind, heart, breath, bone, blood. Alice's words played in his head like a melody, haunting and constant. Kai relayed as much as he could to the others what all she had told him last night, just in case they could see something he couldn't. But his friends were just as confused as he was. Alice hadn't spoken with them about Anne Christiansen or oysters or mirrors. There were other phrases and riddles which were just as confusing: *death lies, tear reaper, bread bone.*

As for the warning which Alice had repeated relentlessly, *blood mirror*, she had not told anyone else this. Just Kai. He had an itching suspicion that he knew why.

"*Gubben*," Inga called, tottering up to where he sat trying to down some lunch. Wendy had just left to take her shift watching Alice. Neither Jack or Red looked to have gotten any sleep last night, shadows hanging under their eyes. They hardly touched their bread and eggs.

Kai looked over his shoulder at Inga, strained to pull a smile and tousled her black hair. "*Goddag, Lilla Rånareflickan.*"

"What was that?" Jack asked, jerking his head up as if he'd drifted into a trance state between sleep and awake.

161

"Good day, Little Robber Girl," Kai translated patiently.

"Ah," he mumbled, eyes droopy. "Good day."

Inga rolled her eyes and thumped Kai on the shoulder. "The Princess is back."

Suddenly wide awake and anxious, he back snapped straight. "When?"

"When do you think? She arrived, I saw, and I came here. Did you think I'd let you mull about unawares before I told you?"

"Where is she?" Kai asked, standing now.

Pointing with one gloved hand behind her, Inga said, "Two or three alcoves down. She didn't look happy."

Kai nodded in thanks, gave her the last of his lunch, and started off.

"We're right behind you, old man," Jack called out weakly.

"I will come back for you later," Kai countered, not breaking stride.

"You do that."

Kai marched out of the robbers' camp, past the silently watching forest people in the trees, until he found Latham guarding one of the smaller alcoves where Inga had indicated Lovisa to be. The thought of peace with the Snow Queen made Kai's blood boil.

First Gerda.

Now Alice.

The Snow Queen was going to pay for what she did.

Latham looked at him silently, hands wrapped around a gnarled spear of braided wood, but he did not stop Kai from passing and entering the alcove. The space was blanketed in fir needles, empty of anything besides Lovisa. Her mess of

162

obsidian curls was pulled up in a bun on her head. An evergreen cloak lay piled on the floor while her jade dress swished around her ankles as she paced. Hands folded at her mouth, she didn't bother lifting her gaze at his approach. She wasn't surprised he had come.

"What did the bloody witch say?" Kai growled, stomping into the alcove.

"Let me think," she responded distractedly with a wave of her hand.

"Think?" He clenched his fists, rage churning. "While you were out proposing peace with that devil, she went behind our backs and did something to Alice."

"Yes, I know."

"You know? You know that one of my closest friends is talking complete nonsense, is seeing things that aren't there, is unable to remain alone or else she may hurt herself? You know about that?"

"I know."

"And you have to *think* about what she said?"

"Be silent!" she snapped.

He ground his teeth, shaking with anger. Alice had gone mad, and it was the Snow Queen's fault. Jack used to joke about how Alice was going crazy. But Kai had never questioned her sanity, not even when she herself was questioning it. There was no denying it now – Alice lost her mind.

Though Frost had been the one who found her, who brought her back, Kai couldn't help but think that it should've been him. He'd been so preoccupied with how Gerda was hosting the Snow Queen that he wasn't there to protect Alice when she needed it. He'd even seen her that morning. She wanted him to join her, to help her answer whatever mystery she'd been unraveling. But he ignored her. If he had gone with her, would things have turned out differently?

"Tjuv told me about Alice," Lovisa spoke up at last. "So I went to see her. She wanted to tell me something."

Kai's heart jumped. "What did she say?"

"Mind. Heart. Breath. Bone. Blood."

He sighed, having hoped for something different, something that would actually solve that particular riddle. Or any riddle. "She's been saying that ever since Frost brought her back."

"I can't get it out of my head. It's like what the Snow Queen had said, or at least just as curious." She twisted her hands as she spoke like she was trying to unravel the tangle of her thoughts with her fingers. "One of her demands was to spend time with the five of you as a return of investment—"

"Return of investment?" Kai repeated with a bitter scowl.

"She also said that I will watch my world shatter when she comes to full power."

"So there is no peace treaty?"

"No, of course not. Focus. She admitted that she is not at full power, and there's something she needs from the five of you, something she invested in."

"Gerda mentioned that the Snow Queen wants to live forever," he admitted, though his gut twisted knowing how she knew that.

"That is not surprising, as she has been trying to extend her life and reign for centuries. But it has come at a cost. She cannot be at her full power and live forever as she has. She wastes her energy clinging to her host. Her magic was tied to her mirror – the mirror you destroyed. Unless…"

"Unless she found a way to have both," Kai finished, his scar burning. "Unless she put the mirror back together."

It hit him like a tidal wave.

Blood mirror.

"The kind of power it would take for her to regain the magic from her mirror, permanently tethering herself to this world, and still manage to live forever," Lovisa breathed, narrowing her eyes trying to fathom it. "This would take years of precise preparation. It would be the kind of spell that would be unstoppable for a thousand lifetimes."

The question snuck into his mind, slipped from his lips in a whisper, "Why us?"

It was the inevitable question, the one all paths seemed to lead to, the mystery Alice had always been trying to answer. Now, he realized it was the one question that led her to lose her mind.

"Get Tjuv, Inga, Bae, and Frost if we can find him. We need to talk to Alice," Kai said in a low rumble. "And we need to get that pocket watch working."

They soon stood in a halfmoon around Alice who sat cross-legged and swaying in the center of the lavvu, humming to herself about drowning time and rolling heads. Bae lay to one side with his head erect, Inga beside him with her pudgy hand looped through an embroidered leather harness around his neck. Tjuv stood near her granddaughter with gnarled hands folded before her. Wendy, Red, and Jack waited on the opposite side close enough for their shoulders to brush.

Linking between the two groups stood Kai and Lovisa. Frost had yet to show himself.

Kai waited patiently while Lovisa explained the details of her meeting with the Snow Queen, relaying her suspicions about the Snow Queen's plan to use the five of them to regain her full power.

"We believe that somehow Alice discovered this plan, maybe even how the Snow Queen would accomplish it," Lovisa speculated, "and this is what prompted the Snow Queen to get to her."

"She found the answer by asking the question," Kai spoke up, looking at each of his friends in turn. "But we never noticed how important it was."

Red's head was lowered, nails in her palms. Jack swallowed uncertainly and Wendy turning watery eyes to their friend sitting unawares before them. Kai looked at Alice, her relaxed face for once peaceful.

He took a deep breath. "Why us?"

Cornflower blue eyes snapped open, dilated. "Checkmate."

Jack started back, and Inga clutched Bae's shaggy scruff in her fist.

Alice swept her gaze over them, the air charged. She sniffed. "Something's cooking. Smells like pork, cabbages and kings."

Aware that all eyes were on him, Kai stepped forward and lowered himself to a crouch in order to meet her at eyelevel. Like an incantation, he recited slowly, "Mind. Heart. Breath. Bone. Blood."

Alice leaned forward in interest.

He started again, more intentional. "Mind."

In response, Alice gave a long trailing whistle, ending with a sharp clap of her fist to her palm.

"Heart."

"Bird tarts. Fly away!" She wrestled with her tongue like it was going to fall from her mouth.

Afraid he was about to lose her attention, Kai reached out and grabbed her hand. "Blood mirror," he whispered.

She stopped, her eyes shining. "When little girls cry, we all die."

Tjuv muttered something under her breath like a curse or a prayer.

Kai sighed, licked his lips. "Breath."

"The last you give, the first you take." She leaned forward and whispered loudly, "Boom."

"Bone."

"Bread and glitter," she sang.

"Bones don't break," Jack finished in awe. Kai glanced back at him to find his face had paled. This wasn't the first time Jack had heard the riddle.

Kai turned back to Alice. "Blood."

"*Sh!*" She pressed a finger to her lips. "Secret ingredient."

"Blood mirror," growled a voice behind him. All heads whipped around to the figure standing in the lavvu entry way. Sunlight hit him like a halo, but his face was washed in shadow.

"He's the key," Alice whispered before she started ticking.

Rising slowly to his feet, Kai said, "What do you know, Frost? Did you know about this spell your beloved Ice Maiden is after? Did you know why she wanted us?"

Frost stepped forward until the tent flap fell shut behind him, crystalline eyes trained on Alice. She ticked

167

continuously, oblivious to his stare. He didn't bother answering Kai's question.

"I could've stopped her long ago. But I didn't. Now it's happening again, but worse. This is all my fault." His cheeks seemed to have hollowed since yesterday, his eyes deep in his skull. He lifted his gaze to Kai. "You need to do what I told you before."

Stomach cinched, Kai ground his teeth. "You mean when you lied?"

"I never lied. I just didn't tell you the truth."

"That'd be a lie," Jack muttered.

"The *whole* truth," Frost corrected. "In order to destroy the Snow Queen, you need to destroy the mirror – properly this time."

"So," Tjuv observed in a forlorn grumble, "she has put it back together."

"Blood mirror," Frost echoed, ice in his voice. "You know I'm right."

"Then tell us what your plan is, Jack," Jack spoke up impatiently.

Pulling his lips back in a grin at the name, Frost thumped him on the arm. "See? Catchy, isn't it?"

"Well, it's my bloody name," Jack mumbled.

"Frost," Kai snapped.

Alice's ticking grew louder, a time bomb.

Gnashing his teeth, Frost explained, "I won't bore you with details – Alice already wrestled my sob story out of me. But before I was *this*, I found a way to destroy the mirror not just break it. There's a pickaxe, the very one the devil himself used to chop the ice that made the mirror. It wasn't so hard to find the first time. Before me, the Ice Maiden never had cause to hide it. When I joined her and she made me what I am, my first task was to secure the pickaxe inevitably so no one else could use it against her. Häxan helped with the finishing details."

"Where is it?" Wendy asked warily.

"Closer than you'd think."

"And?" Lovisa urged, waiting for the catch.

"And," Frost shrugged, "anyone who goes to access it will burn alive. Humans, animals, even witches would die before they could even touch it."

"Ha!" Alice shouted, pointing straight ahead. "The key!"

But Kai narrowed his eyes at Frost. "So, you give us an impossible mission?"

"Difficult, not impossible. Or have you not learned anything from your friend here?" He nodded to Alice who sat with a disappointed scowl. Kai felt a tinge of guilt in his gut.

Frost tilted his head. "Some things burn slower than others."

Aggravated, Kai barked, "Enough riddles, Frost!"

"Sacrifices must be made if you want to win this."

"I will not lose anything or anyone else to that bloody devil."

Frost shook his head. "Then you've already lost."

Calmly, Lovisa spoke, "I will go."

Kai's head snapped around to her. Anxiety built up in his abdomen, speeding his heartbeat, heating his neck. "No, this is not happening. Frost put away the bloody thing. He'll get it back."

Frost's eyebrows shot up. "You think I would reach it?"

"Short of the Snow Queen herself, you're the coldest person I know. You'd reach it."

"As flattering as you are, that is where you're wrong. Or did you forget about the price I paid to defy the Snow Queen? I am *mortal*. And I'm thawing. The phoenix could not lick me up fast enough."

"Phoenix?" Inga squeaked.

"Then it's decided," Lovisa said, a shadow over her eyes.

Kai's heart sped in his throat. This was not happening. He was not about to let someone else he cared about be sacrificed for the sake of the Snow Queen. He couldn't lose her. Not after Gerda. Not after Alice.

"*Nej*," he argued, throat tight.

"I will burn longer, brighter," Lovisa assured, stoic, head high. "I will make it."

"I won't allow it."

"It's not your decision to make." Her eyes were ablaze already. "I'll burn, and she'll melt. It will be her world that will shatter."

Before Kai could step toward her, beg her to change her mind, argue that they would find another way, Alice gave a shrill scream. His ears rang even when he quickly covered them. She'd never made a noise like this before. Finished, she coughed twice, then began ticking as she had been. Kai pressed the topic no further, but he was still seething.

"She's been one step ahead of us this whole time," Red said solemnly. "If we're going to get this weapon before the Snow Queen finds out, we need to move fast."

She is right, Bae hummed, his voice like a soothing melody. *We must be swift, and we must be united. We are facing violent days ahead. We must do all within our power to minimize the suffering.*

Sullen, Wendy added, "We need to call the others."

Lovisa nodded. Without looking at Kai, she produced the pocket watch from the folds of her cloak. It rested cocooned in a nest of twigs and leaves which twisted around the silver surface like a stroking touch.

"I do not know how to activate it," Lovisa admitted. "But it is ready. Our magic will be powerful enough to call through the fabrics of realms."

"Beware," Alice said eerily, rocking back and forth. "Ghosts and giants, breath and bone. One handed mirror breaker. Roaring fire. Blood spills like tea on powdered sugar. Don't cry, my friends. Don't cry."

Silent, Lovisa approached Alice and offered the frozen pocket watch shrouded in its living nest. Alice's pupils contracted. Gingerly, she took the watch and cradled it in her hands like a babe. She began to hum the same tune she had been since losing her mind.

"Mind, heart, breath, bone, blood," she sang softly, brushing her fingers over the silver.

She popped open the pocket watch. The branches moved to wrap around the lid and porcelain. Holding her fingertips around its edges, she twisted the starry face around to the right and left, producing strange clicks and winding gears, like a codebreaker and a lockbox.

"Earth, stars, song, shadows," Alice added in the same tune as before, "time."

Once the last word lay spoken, she pressed the diamond button. The clock's hands spun wildly. Ice melted, dripping from her hands. Branches turned to dust. A sudden wind swirled around them, filling the lavvu, picking up speed as the spinning hands did. Alice burst out in gleeful laughter. Kai felt the urge to take the watch from her, afraid it would take her to another land, one where they could not follow.

Before he could rush forward, screams erupted outside in rising symphony. The wind had only barely died down. Alice was still sitting before them.

The tent flap flew open.

"Would someone please take care of the situation out here before some terrified buffoon gets trampled?" the rabbit in a waistcoat exclaimed, forelegs folded tight over his chest. "Great Uncle Jackrabbit! You'd think they've never seen a giant before."

"Good to see you, too, Long Ears," Jack said, breaking out of line to face him.

The White Rabbit shivered. "You couldn't have given us warning about the cold? Some of us haven't grown our winter coats in."

"Well, we would've written a letter, but we've been a bit preoccupied lately."

White opened his mouth to retort, but his black eyes caught sight of Alice who still sat laughing with the pocket watch cupped in her hands. He twitched his whiskers.

"Miss Alice?" he said cautiously.

But she didn't respond. Didn't see him. Didn't hear him. The White Rabbit frowned though he did not make to approach her. It was as if he knew, somehow, that something was different.

Snapping out of his stupor when another scream split outside, White hastened, "Someone needs to get out here and tell these giants where to settle. It's about to get quite crowded once the others catch the signal."

172

Chapter Seventeen
Friends and Strangers

As far as the White Rabbit explained, once the five of them had left Wonderland, he had set to work on acquiring the necessary number of portals for each potential realm that the Master might have been found in. Once completed, they divided into groups in order to travel to individual realms to either collect allies or else find the five friends and the Master. Boojum the snark took the Dormouse and Dinah to Neverland – an easy trip for a flying beast. The Brothers Tweedle went on to the Enchanted Forest through a looking glass, and the White Rabbit ventured to Giant Country with his cousin the March Hare. Each of them was supplied with a magic bean, an enchanted mirror, and an ice crystal just in case they were summoned to a specific place.

As for the Realm of the Snow Queen, most access points had been cut off like a locked door. All they needed was a signal and the right push. The pocket watch provided just that.

Naturally there would be a delay on the others' arrival, so the White Rabbit said. For though many of his company were larger in size, they were unexpectedly few in number.

"It seems that many of the giants were taken captive before I arrived, or at least the ones who would stand with us," White stated as he led Kai and his friends to the newly arrived crowd. "They've also suffered a great tragedy in their mountains which also contributed to their loss in numbers. As for the human inhabitants, I will say many were not nearly as enthusiastic to join us. But I'll let their leader speak for himself."

The giants formed a ring around the huddle of belowlanders, curious nomadic robbers milling around them while the forest people warily kept their distance. Kai half expected to see the Fiddler standing rigid among them, terse and glaring. He counted nearly twenty giants and no more than thirty belowlanders.

Standing out from the others and taking in his bearings like he was on another fascinating adventure, Harry Silver came rushing toward them with a laugh. The Fiddler was nowhere in sight.

"It's bloody good to see you, friends!" Harry proclaimed with a broad grin, clapping Jack into a tight hug. "I half expected you were kidding about the talking bunny when you left. But lo and behold, not even a week after you left, Toothy here shows up speaking just like you and me. Who would've thought it?"

"I figured this one was a friend of yours," the White Rabbit grumbled with a twitch of his whiskers.

Clasping Kai's forearm in greeting, Harry nodded between White and the belowlanders. "He's the only reason half of these blokes showed up. I thought for sure the Fiddler was going to see me swing from a rope before I could take more than two warriors from him. Still, we managed to scrounge up a few more than that."

Jack's gaze passed over the small crowd. "They didn't believe you, did they?"

Harry shrugged. "Didn't matter whether they believed me or not. The Fiddler was furious, turned most of the belowlanders against me. Liesel had to sneak Tom and Blue out of town, afraid of what could happen while we're gone. The boys are staying with ole Marie and the few giants who stayed behind. But once Toothy arrived with his scruffy pal, you wouldn't believe who ended up coming."

Kai frowned at the woman who stepped up behind Harry, recognizable by the thick scar spitting her right eye and the hard set of her jaw. She was flanked by none other than Brann and Spider.

"No way," Jack gawked, open mouthed.

"Giant Slayer," the woman grunted in acknowledgement.

"Cat," he greeted in turn. "Never in a million years would I have expected to see you here."

"Some things are more important," she said simply.

Liesel appeared beside them, a fist on her wide hip, raising an amused eyebrow at the general. "It's unreal how people see reason after a pair of talking rabbits show up."

"Actually, just the one rabbit," White spoke up. "March is a hare. But I can see the confusion."

Cat ignored the interjections, continuing grimly, "I'm not about to see the Fiddler take us down the same gutless path as the late King Cole before him. Cowards do not survive long. Those who willingly follow them are even more fruitless."

"So, you've come to your senses," Jack quipped with a slight smile.

Before the general Cat could retaliate, someone else emerged from the crowd. Scroungy, brown, and missing a toe, Kai could only assume this was the March Hare. Beady eyes darted around, long ears twitching. "Where is Alice?" March asked in a jittery kind of way.

Wringing his paws, the White Rabbit bowed his head. "March, something's gone terribly wrong with Miss Alice."

"Don't tell me she's been finding her marbles again."

"Quite the opposite, I'm afraid."

Furrowing his brow, the March Hare's fidgety grin faded. "You don't mean it. Not our Alice."

Wordless, the White Rabbit looked up at Kai imploringly. His throat tightened. Together, he led the leporid cousins back to the lavvu where Alice was actively rolling across the furs and mats on the floor, back and forth, over and over again. They stood at a distance, watching.

The March Hare's ears drooped down his back. "Not our Alice," he lowed, head shaking. "She was our bridge, our ambassador to reality. She kept the humanity in our madness."

"You can see it, can't you?" the White Rabbit asked, pointing at something Kai could not see. "Her sanity's been ripped from her, shredding her mind."

March agreed forlornly, "Never seen anything like it before. A bloody mess that is."

"Will she heal?" Kai asked, hopeful.

"Heal?" The March Hare shrugged and held out his paws with a grimace. "Returned to normal…"

Alice lay flat on her back covered in dust, staring at the ceiling, whistling through her teeth.

The White Rabbit sighed. "Best wait for the Hatter. Don't let any of the others see her until then – especially the twins. I won't have them whiffling after the Red Queen and getting themselves killed in the process."

"You think the frumious bighead is behind this?" the March Hare questioned with a frown.

"I've only ever seen the likes of this during the Underland Wars," White relayed grimly. "I haven't a doubt in my mind whether she did this."

"It's only the beginning," a voice said lowly, grabbing the attention of the cousins instantly. Frost was the only one who'd stayed behind with Alice.

"And who might you be?" the White Rabbit questioned, his nose twitching.

"A friend," Frost responded. The word ran coarse out of his mouth, like he was still getting used to the phrase. A shiver ran visibly down his spine. "Someone else is coming."

Heeding the warning, Kai tore open the tent flap and looked around expectantly. The forest people were working tirelessly to grow a shelter between the trees and the mountainside large enough to house the giants comfortably. Trees groaned and bark cracked as the woods moved to provide space for its new large guests. The nomadic robbers eyed the belowlanders in distrust as if they emitted a repelling odor. In turn, the belowlanders stared at the forest people with wide eyes and grit teeth, unsure how to process a people covered in various growths of foliage, who could blend in with the trees as easily as an owl. Kai wondered how everyone was going to work together with any sort of harmony.

Before he could dwell long on the thought, a flash of light blinded the crowded space.

"Cabbages and kings!" someone exclaimed as the light receded. "It's bloody freezing."

"Did you expect the place to be all sunshine and palm trees?" exclaimed an agitated Frenchman in a flurry.

"Borogove, I hate it when things make sense."

Even in the vast new crowd, it didn't take long to find the Brothers Tweedle badgering the wiry Clopin Trouillefou until he was scarlet from his neck to his eyebrows. Just behind him stood his sister, Esmeralda, her face marred in thin silver scars, her brilliant smoky eyes now dull and vacant though sharp. The Woodsman, Jim waited nearby with both legs still attached – a miracle considering they'd left him in the Enchanted Forest with one leg stuck deep in the earth.

All around swelled the mass of gypsies and knights. Grimrose's entire military seemed readied with allies from Chliobain to Lille-Havfrue, even a band of soldiers from the port kingdom Belle who remained loyal to the Prince Ingénu. King Thrushbeard led the armor-clad men alongside his Queen Euna whose hand rested lightly on her husband's arm. Amid the chaos, the massive Bear Wizard, Isbjørn stood at least a head taller than those around him, his black eyes taking in his new surroundings.

Red made a beeline for the Princess Aurore and her husband Ingénu, colliding into the both of them in a tight embrace.

Kai ran his fingers through his hair, found Lovisa across the glen, met her eyes. Even she seemed shocked at the numbers spilling through the alcoves. A blast of light signaled another arrival. He shielded his eyes in vain.

Instantly, a voice crowed, "Wendy?!"

Bells chimed up in the cry along with a chorus of other boys echoing like sealions, "Wendy? Wendy?"

She burst forth from the masses and slammed into Pan with a tight grasp around his middle, her face pressed into his chest, eyes squeezed shut. He seemed shocked at the greeting but held her anyway. Oblivious to Wendy's distress, the six Lost Boys who'd arrived surged in around them in a collective group hug. Tinker Bell sat perched on Pan's hat with her delicate wings wrapped into her warm clothes to prevent them from freezing.

Of the Neverland party, Tiger Lily was the one who brought the numbers, her warriors from the Panther Tribe flanking her on each side as if ready for an immediate battle. Their Wonderland escorts stood close, the Dormouse and Alice's old cat Dinah astride the gigantic snark Boojum who shook out his feathers and wagged his spiked tail pleasantly.

"Cheese and whiskers!" the Dormouse squeaked, running her paws up and down her forelegs. "I'm freezing my tail off here."

"That's what I said!" Tweedle-Dum spoke up from across the alcove.

"More or less," agreed Tweedle-Dee. The brothers would've been indistinguishable if it weren't for the clawed scars across Dee's face from his time spent under the Queen of Hearts' torturous outbursts.

Dum looked around, moving through the crowd. "Where's Alice?"

"I think she's in there," Dee pointed to the lavvu where the White Rabbit and March Hare had just emerged from.

White stepped protectively in front of the tent's entrance. "No, wait! You can't go in there."

"Why not?" both brothers asked at once.

"Because..."

"Because Alice is sick," the March Hare spoke up fervently, twitching his ears. "Very sick. Don't want to go in there, nope, nope, nope."

Boojum approached and settled beside the Wonderland group. The Dormouse slipped off of his back, bounced off his knee, and landed before the rabbits with a concerned tilt of her head. "Sick?"

"I don't care if she's having tea with the old Mock Turtle," Dum proclaimed as he and his brother stepped easily past White and March into the lavvu, Dinah and the Dormouse at their heels.

Waiting outside, Boojum stared at the giants, wagging his tail and panting. He was just the right size to be a giant's pet dog.

It wasn't long before the twins stormed from the lavvu, viridescent eyes alight with fury and ears nearly as red as their hair.

"I'm going to kill her," Dee growled, fists clenched and ready for a fight.

For a moment, regicide seemed exactly what they were going to do. The Dormouse and Dinah remained in the lavvu while the White Rabbit followed after the brothers in desperate argument that they should wait before getting themselves killed.

Kai felt frozen in the overbearing crowd, unable to stand farther than an arm's length from anyone, a mere observer. He hardly noticed when Frost appeared by his side until the brittle voice hit his ear, "Are you expecting more?"

He looked from the forest people to the slow growing trees moving through the earth in their alcove's expansion. In response, he nodded. "We'll have to ride each other's shoulders in order to fit."

Frost wrinkled his nose. "Stifling."

"They're trying their best."

"It's not enough. They're fighting winter. The way they're going about it, we'll be exposed if we expand much more."

"Then what do you propose?"

Frost didn't answer, but he suddenly began to pale until his skin was nearly blue and steam rose from the coldness of him. Light flashed once again in blinding array, this time accompanied by a gust of frozen wind as if the snow bees had found their haven.

The light dissipated to reveal the mountainside shaved of trees and rock layers, a cavernous space deep enough to shelter the giants, glazed in permafrost. The forest lay bared in wide open space ringed with sloping ice barriers and hidden stalagmite icicles ready to impale any enemy invaders. Trees still spotted the terrain, but the ground was leveled off. The lavvus and goahtis stood glittering in a coating of rime ice.

Knees buckling, Frost leaned on Kai with a hand on his shoulder. His touch was cold in the way ice thawed in a bare palm. Sweat shone on his brow, face greyed.

"Are you alright, lad?" Isbjørn asked, coming up behind them to help hold Frost up with one massive hand.

Frost shivered from his spine to his knuckles. Kai frowned. Was he cold? When Frost couldn't even bring himself to speak, Isbjørn glanced at Kai in concern and led him away.

Blinking in his new surroundings, Kai noticed the last group had arrived. A regiment of black armored cards headed by the White Queen in gleaming chainmail and the vorpal sword at her hip. Animals were well suited and armed, standing at attention. The Mad Hatter was the only one without armor, his hat cocked low over one eye, his long tail coat tailored to his figure. If he hadn't been standing by his imposing sister, he would've looked far more intimidating than the entire Wonderland army behind him.

Arms spread wide, the Hatter flashed a smile. "We have arrived, and we brought tea, so I hope everyone's thirsty because we're not taking *no* for an answer."

"I don't know who you are," Aurore spoke up from across the clearing, her ginger hair glowing in the afternoon sun. "But I like how you think."

"Hatter," Kai said urgently, broaching the man. "I need you to come with me."

"It's Kai, right?" the Hatter greeted. "Glad to see that leg healed up nicely."

"You need to come now."

"You'd best come, too, highness," the White Rabbit spoke up to the White Queen, appearing beside Kai. "I'm afraid the twins will do something regrettable."

Before they could ask, Kai added, "It's about Alice."

The Hatter's smile dropped. "What's happened?"

"You go," the White Queen said, patting his arm. "I'll take care of the Tweedles."

Quickly, Kai led the Hatter to the lavvu where Alice was kept. Inside, she was lying on the ground, her body curled around Dinah as she stroked the cat's orange fur. The Dormouse sat at her head with a paw on Alice's hair, ears drooped. Watery brown eyes raised to meet the two men upon entry.

"Oh, Hatter," the Dormouse sniffed, wiping her pink nose with the back of her wrist.

Dinah nudged Alice with her head and meowed. Alice was humming to herself, pleasant.

The Hatter didn't ask questions about what happened or how. He stepped forward as if this was normal for him, as if he'd suspected this all along. Maybe he had. Maybe the link between their hearts had informed him ahead of time what to expect. But there wasn't a lick of concern in his voice when he asked, "Alice?"

She stopped humming, stopped stroking Dinah's soft fur. Cornflower blue eyes pinned on Remus. Without looking away, she raised herself up to her palms, her knees, her feet. When she stood before him, her hand crept over her heart to feel its beat. Remus approached, closer. Alice reached out and placed her free hand on his chest, let it rest there, watched. His hand covered hers until she could feel the joint heartbeats under both palms. With his other hand, Remus held her face, encouraging her to meet his eyes again.

"What do you feel?" he asked, soft and gentle.

Her face twitched from frown to smile to grimace, eyes squinting and growing wide, as if she couldn't decide which expression would take over.

"Anything," she said at last. "Everything. All at once."

He tilted his head, brushed her hair back. With both hands, he placed his hat on her head and planted a kiss on her brow. When he pulled away, his eyes matched hers. The steadiness, the shifting, the indecision, the madness.

With a small smile, he assured, "You learn to get used to it."

Chapter Eighteen
The Converged Plans

"This doesn't feel right," Wendy said softly, her shoulder against Kai's arm as she cupped her tea in her lap, "without Alice."

Kai nodded grimly. Lovisa had bade a meeting with the leaders of her new allies, all while the Dormouse and the March Hare dutifully passed out tea to all on the premises. Everyone held a teacup in hand before entering the alcove where a newly constructed table formed from interwoven bush branches awaited them. Deciding to stick together, Kai sat with Wendy on one end, Jack and Red on the other. They'd deemed it best to leave Alice in her lavvu with the Hatter.

"She always helped us make the plans," Wendy continued. Her cup was lavender in her lap, empty. Kai traded hers for his untouched one, having found no appetite for the complimentary hot drink. Sipping gratefully, Wendy pressed, "And she clearly still knows things. How else could she have called everyone here? I didn't even know the watch could twist like that. Her mind can't be as far gone as we thought."

Beside Wendy sat Pan with Tinker Bell perched lightly on his shoulder, the two Lost Boys called Slightly and Nibs standing behind with arms crossed and faces frowned in mock imitation of Tiger Lily's dueled entourage who stood tall next to them. The White Queen, Celeste, sat winged by the Brothers Tweedle with the White Rabbit to accompany her.

Two giants, Ajaal and Trell, were seated at the edge of the alcove where only their knees touched the center table.

184

Because their leader, Balthaz, had been captured by the Giant King, these two acted in his stead as representatives of the giant allies. On the opposite side of the giants' knees sat Harry sandwiched between Liesel and the general Cat. Of those from the Enchanted Forest, they'd settled on sending King Thrushbeard with Aurore and Ingénu along with Esmeralda and Clopin. Isbjørn soon joined them, bringing Frost who appeared less grey though still shadowed under his crystalline eyes.

Lovisa headed the table, her cousin Latham standing at attention behind her while Mr. and Mrs. Crow perched on either side of her chair. Tjuv and Inga sat to her right next to Red, Bae standing with head high behind them, while Frost remained on his feet at Lovisa's left. He placed one hand on the table as if to balance himself or else seem formidable. Perhaps both.

"What if she knows something that can help us?" Wendy asked worriedly.

Kai thought on all the things Alice had said in her madness, the riddles and hidden meanings. There was a key to unlocking her messages. He just had to pay attention.

"She's already told us what to do," he voiced, and he knew it was true. Alice had given him the pieces, tried to relay the answers that buzzed in her head. Kai just hoped he understood.

"Greetings," Lovisa spoke, rising to address the whole. "I am Lovisa, princess of the forest people. As you are all here, I assume it is because you are aware of the present danger that threatens each of our worlds. Thank you for joining us, for joining our cause and our fight. The Snow Queen has been gathering forces in order to expand her rule and power. What we now know is that she has taken over the body of Gerda Vår and seeks our friends here –Wendy, Kai, Jack, Red, and Alice – in order to accomplish her desires to rise to full power without the need of a host."

"She is a parasite?" Tiger Lily clarified.

"A demon," Clopin growled, a fist on the table.

"In a sense, yes," Lovisa confirmed on both accounts. "The Snow Queen cannot live long without a host. But her magic is tied to a devil's mirror. It's been broken before, but we have strong reason to believe she has pieced the mirror together again and is now trying to regain power from the mirror without being bound to it."

"So, we destroy this mirror before she rises," Ingénu concluded, earning a nod from Lovisa.

"A certain pickaxe was used to create the mirror, so it is the only thing that can destroy it. Frost knows how to reach where the weapon is hidden, and due to the severity of the situation, it's been determined that I should be the one to retrieve it."

King Thrushbeard shifted so his elbow rested on the table. "How do we know the Snow Queen has not already obtained this power from the mirror?"

Lovisa answered, "Because, in order to accomplish this kind of spell, she needs specific ingredients."

"Us," Kai raised his voice, speaking for his friends. His scar throbbed with every heartbeat. "She needs us. Or something from us. Alice knew, which is why they got to her first."

The Brothers Tweedle balled their hands into fists at their sides. Celeste leaned forward in order to meet Kai's eye and asked, "What does the Snow Queen want from you?"

"I have only riddles," he admitted. "*Mind, heart, breath, bone, blood.* It's what Alice has been chanting since we found her. Five ingredients, five of us. I can only assume Alice was the *mind*, and by the look of things—"

"But that's ridiculous," Cat interjected with a scowl. "They couldn't take her mind, else she would be dead. Her brain has to still be in her head."

Tweedle-Dee raised a scarred eyebrow. "You think you have to lose your brain to lose your head?"

"It is possible that the Red Queen stripped Miss Alice of her sanity," the White Rabbit explained carefully, thoughtful despite the disturbed wringing of his paws. "Her magic is a deadly blend of Wonderland and Underland training, in addition to whatever this Snow Queen may have taught her. Perhaps in the darkest of her studies, she found a way to make sanity tangible, if of course it's freely given. There is always a free will element to delicate things such as minds and hearts."

"We need more troops," Red spoke up urgently. "Better yet, we need to take some from the enemy. Which is where the wolves come in."

"*What?*" Clopin burst.

Ignoring him, Red continued to press her case, "The Pack is under the Snow Queen's control against their will. Lupa is the enemy, not the others. If we save them, they will fight for us."

"What of my people?" Ajaal asked, his voice cascading down on them. "Our leader was captured with many of our warriors when we helped you save the Giant Slayer. We must rescue them. Their added numbers will do us well, if it is a battle you seek. You cannot fight giants without giants."

"Well, that's not really true," Jack muttered to himself.

187

Dum smirked and elbowed his brother. "I'd bet one good sized shrinking pastry should do the trick. Level the playing field."

"What makes you believe the wolves will fight for us?" Clopin asked, still not finished with Red's earlier proposal.

Straightening her shoulders, Red stated, "Because I'm going to kill Lupa."

Clopin threw his hands up. "Ah. Brilliant."

"Or at least distract her," she added, "so we can rescue the Pack."

"Except the wolves have been moved to the front lines," Frost said lowly, leaning into the table. "They're guard dogs. And the giants will be imprisoned at the castle. You don't just have this Big Bad Wolf to look out for, but you've got Häxan."

"Add it to the agenda," Jack said with a huff.

"So, let me get this all straight," Aurore spoke, poised on her fingertips. "In order to defeat the Snow Queen, we need to break her magic mirror before she gets hands on any more of these five, so that she doesn't rise to full power and take over the realms. But the only thing that can break the mirror is a magic pickaxe that only Frosty knows how to get to and only this warrior tree princess can actually get. But even if we do manage to break this mirror, we've still got a whole slew of villains out there ready for war. And in the midst of all that, we need to rescue the wolves and the giants."

"Yes, that sounds about right," Lovisa agreed.

"That's a quest, stealth mission, rescue attempt, and battle," Cat summed up bluntly. "That could take weeks to pull off, assuming nothing else occurs in the meantime."

Pan shrugged as if he didn't see what the problem was. "Why not just do it all at once?"

Celeste nodded. "He's right. There are enough of us to successfully divide and conquer. It would certainly make tracking us down a chore."

A lopsided grin spread across Harry's face. "Alright, friends. Who's up for a relay race?"

While Celeste updated the Hatter on the outcome of the gathering, Kai and Jack returned to Alice's lavvu where they watched their friend follow Dinah from the pile of furs to the matted floor in a loop on her hands and knees. Jack broached Alice with the cup of tea they'd brought her, held it out to her until she noticed. With surprising gentleness, she took the teacup from him, sat cross-legged, and sipped the beverage delicately.

"It's kind of funny," Jack started, still watching his calmed friend, "how our plans match up with what Alice was saying earlier."

Kai frowned. "What do you mean?"

"Before she started messing with the watch. You know: beware ghosts and giants, breath and bone. Something about breaking mirrors and fire and blood, tea, sugar. Anyways, it's like she knew."

"But we didn't talk about ghosts."

Jack shrugged. "Maybe we should have."

Curious, Kai stepped closer to Alice. She'd finished her tea and was trying to balance the cup on her nose.

"Alice, what did you mean by *ghosts*?" he asked.

"Use your skull," she said without lowering her gaze to him. "It's hard as a rock."

Jack laughed, "That's nothing new."

"You mean Neverland," Kai guessed, cutting eyes at Jack. "How do we summon them?"

"Sleepy stars. The rumors are true."

"What rumors?"

"Giant ones!"

"What do you think the difference is between her riddles and her puns?" Jack asked.

"Giants, giants, ghosts and pirates," Alice chimed. "Fee-fi-fo-fum, and a bottle of rum."

Jack cringed. "I don't like that."

"But how do I get the ghosts here?" Kai pressed. "Can Lovisa do it?"

"Wrong princess," Alice hummed as she turned up the floormats to expose the bare earth. She began to bury her teacup.

Furrowing his brow, Kai looked at Jack. "You think Celeste?"

Jack made a face. "Eh, she's a queen. I've been told it's not the same thing."

"Then who?"

"Isn't Aurore a princess?"

"Can you... can you... can you...?" Alice's voice trembled.

When Kai turned, he found her with her hands held before her, palms bloodied. He came forward and pressed his scarf into her wounds. "What did you do, Alice?"

He noticed the flipped rocks in the dirt like small arrowheads. The teacup had broken into shards. Alice was shaking.

"I don't feel it," she stammered, a tear dropping from her eye like lead. "Can you feel it?"

Kai shook his head. She dropped her eyes in disappointment.

Chapter Nineteen
What the Night Brings

That night, Lovisa joined the four of them around their small campfire where they were finally able to speak in private. Amber firelight brushed across her cheekbone, her bare arms. Kai couldn't help but think of this phoenix that would inevitably consume her. Jaw tight, he tried to swallow the thought.

Lovisa's darkened eyes raised to each of them, her tattoos invisible in the dim light. "You will need to split up."

"What?" Jack frowned, his hold on Red's hand tightening at the suggestion. "After everything that's happened, I thought we were supposed to stick together. That was the plan."

"Nothing good ever happens when we're separated," Wendy agreed, legs crossed under her. She looked like she wanted to list every example she could think of since their adventures in Wonderland.

Lovisa remained silent. She knew she couldn't force them to do anything they did not want to. But her gaze flicked to Kai. He wondered what she would do if he refused to agree with her.

"She's right," Red said softly. When Jack looked at her with raised eyebrows, she shrugged. "It makes sense."

"Why?"

Lovisa turned to him. "Because in the end, all that matters is that we keep the Snow Queen from getting to you."

"And we've been so successful at achieving that goal, have we?" Jack snapped. "If you recall, splitting up is exactly how she got Alice in the first place."

"We cannot risk her finding all of you at once."

Jack huffed a sigh, turning to Kai like maybe he would speak some reason. "What do you think about all this?"

Hands folded, elbows rested on his knees, Kai thought a moment before responding, "We already have different missions. If we separate, we lower the chances of the Snow Queen finding us."

Jack groaned and practically rolled his eyes.

Before he could protest, Kai added firmly, "Like it or not, she needs something from each of us, and if she succeeds, then everything we've been through and everyone we've lost will have been for nothing."

A grim silence settled over them, and Kai didn't have to say their names to remind them.

Quasimodo.

Jill.

Gerda.

Alice.

If they didn't act soon, the list would add up.

"Alright," Jack clasped his hands together, "what do you propose?"

Kai squared his shoulders, glanced at Lovisa who gave him an encouraging nod. "Red handles Lupa. Wendy goes with Lovisa and Frost. You and me, Jack, we've got the stealth mission."

"And Alice?" Wendy asked.

"She'll remain here," Lovisa spoke up. "We'll keep her with the infirmary."

At this, Jack laughed and shaking his head.

Lovisa frowned slightly. "What is so humorous?"

"If there's any Alice left in her mad head," Jack answered, "then that's not going to fly well. She belongs on a battlefield, and once she decides that's where she needs to be, then good luck keeping her here. She's as uncontrollable as a squirrel."

Something like a smile tugged at her mouth as she shrugged. "Then we'll keep her armed."

Red ran a hand over Jack's shoulder until his eyes lazily swung open from the nightmare she knew he was having. She said nothing, just let her touch linger until he fully woke. He squinted his eyes, trying to focus on her, how she kneeled over him in the dark of the goahti, her long black hair swept over one shoulder.

Gently, she slipped her hand in his. The warmth of his palm was welcome in her cold one. She pulled lightly until he stood, silent but unsure, and she led him from the tent. She noticed the flash of icy blue eyes as Kai noticed them leave, but he did not stop them. It was as if he too knew, as Red did, that this calm would not last the dawn. She was becoming increasingly aware that life was much too short to remain stagnant.

There was a spot beyond the camp where the trees caved in on a small covered clearing where no snow had settled, and the trunks bowed into comfortable slopes and pine needle dustings. Red took Jack to one of these trees and pulled him down close beside her. He looked at her, still unsure what her intentions were. But she took the time to memorize his face, brush a brown lock from his brow with her fingertips, trace the arc of his cheekbone. He smelled faintly of timber and honeysuckle. His eyes held a thousand golden rivers, each one a scar she could recognize in her own past. She tried to find constellations in his freckles, thinking maybe she found Orion across his cheek if she tilted her head to the left, and the head of Canis Major craned over his lips.

She kissed him there softly, then under his eye, the curve of his nose. His breath hit her throat and her nerves electrified. Holding his face, she brought her mouth to his. His arms wrapped around her, held her waist, her ribs. There was nothing in this moment but him.

A cackle rippled through the sky, causing Red to jerk back and twist to find the source. Rolling through the air floated the Cheshire Cat grinning from ear to ear, laughing at his interruption.

"Quack and Scarlet, what a scandal," sang the lilting voice of the Cheshire Cat.

Jack's ears pinked as he hissed a curse. Red bit her lip, trying not to laugh.

"Oh, have I come at a bad time?"

In response, Jack threw a rock at him. It passed straight through like he was nothing but mist, earning a final giggle and grin before the Cheshire Cat disappeared. This time, Red did laugh, which made Jack's frustration melt away.

She kissed him again, then settled in next to him until her head found the soft spot on his shoulder. Jack held her hand over his chest, his thumb running over her knuckles. They watched the northern lights through the gaps in the tree branches until they drifted off to sleep.

195

When it was time for the quest to set off, the sky was dusted in coal and ash. There was not a sound in the alcoves nor an official sendoff. Any attempt at discretion could lessen the likelihood of the Snow Queen discovering their plans.

But Kai did meet them. He clasped Frost's hand grimly as if handing him his trust. Frost betrayed nothing in his expression, but he nodded, and Kai knew that whatever his intentions were, Frost would do his part in this.

Wendy threw her arms around Kai's neck and he held her as tight as he could. Dropping her back to the floor, he pressed a kiss to her brow. Her eyes watered. They knew. He prayed he'd see her again at the end of all this. With a sigh, Wendy returned to the others, Peter Pan and the Lost Boys, the Crows and Frost.

When Lovisa came to him, there was such fire in her eyes as if she was already burning. He swallowed his swollen throat. He almost spoke then to tell her not to go, to prevent her from sacrificing herself. But she held his gaze, and he knew this was it. He would not hold her back. And she would not ask for it.

Gingerly, she touched the side of his face, thumb along his jaw, fingers round his neck. A warmth spread there, sliding over his skin and congregating until a small black leaf marked the nape of his neck. Breathless, she pulled away. He blinked but didn't look away from those burning eyes until she left him.

Shadows filled the glen, the silent forms of the forest people gathered in solemn farewell. The traveling party disappeared into the woods. Kai could still feel Lovisa's touch. A heartbeat on his neck. A gift.

Chapter Twenty
The Dog Star

Red woke when a shock split down her spine, a bristle. The Wolf sensed something even if she wasn't sure what. She waited, cheek against Jack's chest, for the noise again. Like a footstep or a breath.

Cautious, she sat up so as not to disturb Jack who lay against the tree trunk with his scarf tucked under his head like a pillow. No nightmares this time. She brushed a snowflake off his cheek, then slowly she kissed the spot, light against his skin. She was still figuring this out, how to love him. It was one thing to let herself feel the love and another to learn how to show it. This was new, and despite the pressing danger, she wanted to take it slow.

For a moment, the wind shifted as if flicking a tail her way, and there was a whiff of something familiar in the air that was gone before she could place it. Stealthy, she grabbed her bow and quiver from where she'd left them nearby and rose to her feet. She hesitated, looked back at Jack who still lay sound asleep. She'd only be gone for a moment, Red reasoned. She didn't want to disrupt his much needed rest. Light on her feet, she left.

The sun was pale and dripping. It was colder the farther she went, snow spotting the forest floor like birchwood. There weren't many icicles here but there were enough to catch the morning light. If it got too cold, she would turn back.

Something brushed over pine needles. Red's eyes snapped, an arrow nocked in her bowstring. Shadows stretched long before her, footsteps moving among them, steady and sure.

"Why don't you put that bow down," a croon slid through the space between them as Lupa emerged from the woods. "We wouldn't want anyone getting hurt."

Instead, Red drew her bow taunt, her heart pounding in her ears, her jaw clenched without a word.

Lupa exposed her empty hands with a raised eyebrow. "I am unarmed. I don't wish to fight you – not now."

Red refused to move.

"I just want to talk."

Again, silence. Her muscles tightened in their held stance, but she kept herself at ease, breathing steadily.

Lupa sighed, dropping her hands at her sides. "This isn't exactly going to be the most productive conversation if I'm the only one making an effort."

"You want to talk," Red growled. "I want to kill you. Seems we're both in a position to get what we want."

Lupa chuckled. "You are still so young, Little Red. Pity."

"What do you want?"

"I have a gift," she said, "and a proposition."

Red scowled. "What kind of gift?"

"I deal in information, Little Red, and I have some to ease your mind so you may find peace before the end in knowing that you were never in control of your circumstances."

"How comforting," Red huffed. "And the proposition?"

From the folds of her skirt, Lupa produced a vial pinched between her thumb and forefinger. "Drink this."

"Poison?"

"In a sense."

Red laughed humorlessly. "Why the devil would you expect me to take that willingly?"

"Because you wouldn't let anyone else take it, either." Lupa ran a pointed nail down the glass. "I know you're aware of our master's little ingredients. I'm here to fetch one, and frankly, I don't care who I have to get it from. But wouldn't it seem so deliciously poetic if it was you?"

"What does it do, the poison?"

"I think you know what this does. I'm after a *last breath*, Little Red. In many respects of the word, you will die." She leaned closer, whispered, "But it's you or it's someone else. The Wendy Bird, perhaps? Or that charming young man you left sleeping back there?"

Red felt gooseflesh go down her arms.

"It wouldn't take much to convince them to take the vial in your stead or else pin them down," Lupa continued easily. "But they would die, Little Red. Either of them. You at least have a chance. Only part of you will die."

"What do you mean?"

"I mean the Wolf, my cub."

Something twisted in Red's gut, nearly causing her to lose her stance. Lupa noticed. Her gold eyes glittered with the knowledge that she'd hit her mark.

"Did you really think she wouldn't fight back?" Lupa leered, exposing her filed teeth. "You think you work in such harmony, that you are one. But when you die, Little Red, only one of you can die at a time. She'll turn on you. Only one of you will come back."

Red remembered what the wolf had told her in the woods, words that rose in her chest like a ghost. "You have to kill a wolf twice."

Lupa smiled, calm.

Aiming the arrow once again, Red asked, "And what if I just kill you now?"

"I will not be the only one with a poisonous vial and a mission," Lupa answered. "And many others are not nearly so merciful as I am."

Red wanted to retort that she was wrong, that they would never hurt her friends. But even the hope of such a thing felt like a lie. The Snow Queen had already gotten Alice, now Lupa had found her and knew where Jack was. If it was a breath they were after, a final breath, then Red knew she couldn't let them reach the others. But she didn't know what to think about fighting the Wolf for her life.

Clenching her teeth, Red imagined the feel of losing her arrow once, twice. But she found herself lowering the weapon. Taking the vial. She fingered the stopper, raised her head. "And what is this information?"

Lupa tapped a nail against her teeth. "Ah, Little Red. The only time you ever told a good story was about those sad little stars. Did you ever think about who gave you that bomb to send your parents into the sky?"

Her breath hitched. Something like pitch fell over her eyes, like maybe she'd plunge into the darkness of time and space to find that very moment when she'd orphaned herself. When a bomb was placed in her hands and called a magic box. A rescue. A way for her parents to never have to live in the shadows again.

Red forced herself to breathe again. "It was you?"

"Everything you've been through has led you to this, Little Red. It's all led you back to me, to fulfill your purpose."

Golden eyes glittered in the dripping sunlight. "Carabosse got it wrong. Go now and face your worst enemy."

Fingers around glass, Red looked down to find the vial uncapped and burning in her palm.

I'm sorry – she sent the thought to Jack, hoping he knew.

She downed the vial, every drop of it. Lightning and frost ran down her throat, squeezing, choking. She couldn't breathe. Darkness swam before her eyes. She gasped, collapsed hard on her knees, face swelling. The vial landed in the snow as her hands flew to her throat. Something formed there, she felt it, a glass marble collecting her breath that wouldn't reach her lunges, and there was the sun dripping on her face. So much light and burning.

"*Gubben*," Inga called her usual greeting, her voice flat.

She found Kai after he'd just finished speaking with Aurore about the ghosts, conferring what both Alice and Lovisa had suggested in order to adjust their plan accordingly. Strangely, Aurore didn't seem fazed by the proposal, though she was anxious to talk it over with Isbjørn to get his advice on the matter.

When Kai turned to face Inga, he found her winged by the familiar blonde haired, brown eyed siblings, Hansel and Gretel.

"*Lilla Rånareflickan?*" Kai said suspiciously. He felt like she was ready to gang up on him, like she'd recruited the gypsy kids as her bodyguards. Of course, Hansel's hedgehog-like fairy pet was curled up on his shoulder and Gretel gave him a shy smile in greeting, so Inga was rapidly losing her intimidation.

She folded her arms across her chest. "It's about this plan of yours."

Kai tried to keep a straight face. "*Ja?*"

"We feel that you are not utilizing your resources well."

"Is that how you feel?"

"*Ja,*" Inga said curtly. "I said so."

"We can help," Gretel offered, her tone softer.

"We can fight!" Hansel added. He bounced on the balls of his feet in anticipation.

"They say they killed trolls," Inga relayed, "and a flesh-eating witch. I didn't believe them until they said the house was made of sweets, which reminds me of how Häxan tricked you with her flower garden—"

"It was a little more than flowers, *Lilla Rånareflickan,*" Kai said defensively.

"It doesn't matter. They can fight a witch, they can fight Häxan."

Raising an eyebrow, Kai mimicked her stance of folding his arms across his chest, playing along. "And you?"

Inga puffed her cheeks out at if appalled that he had not thought of her usefulness yet. "You are going on a stealth mission, I am a robber, and yet I am not going with you."

"This may be just beyond your talents."

"Why? I stole you. That was not so hard. Breaking a mirror won't be difficult."

"Tjuv gave me to you after she kidnapped me," Kai corrected. "And you should know breaking this mirror will be harder than you say."

"But you are going. It can't be that bad."

Kai sighed, looked between the three of them: Hansel ready for action, Gretel anxious to help, and Inga determined to show her worth. If it were up to him, he'd send them all far away from the mess that was to come. But he couldn't shelter even them. He knelt down on one knee so he could meet them at eyelevel. Inga pouted her lip.

"I know you think I underestimate you," Kai said. "As much as I want to protect you, I cannot. Which is why you must remain here with the infirmary."

Inga wrinkled her nose at the suggestion.

But Kai continued, "When the battles come, the Snow Queen will find a way to attack our weak spots. She will come for the helpless, the wounded, the healers. You can help protect them."

"But what if she doesn't attack here?" Hansel implored.

"Then all the better for it," Kai admitted, casting a sidelong glance at Gretel. "But should the need arise, you'll be ready."

Gretel nodded grimly, taking hold of her brother's hand, ready to carry out their task. Kai raised an eyebrow at Inga. Rolling her eyes, she sighed deeply though her slack shoulders betrayed her surrender.

"Fine," Inga huffed. "We will stay. And when you are injured, you will thank me for saving your life."

Kai smiled, ruffled her feathery black hair. She grimaced but didn't pull away.

Hjälte, Bae's smooth hum filled Kai's mind. He turned to find the white reindeer approaching at a near trot, shaking his antlers back and forth anxiously.

Kai stood to meet him. "What is it?"

Your friend, he is looking for you, Bae informed, brown eyes deep in concern. *He fears the other has gone missing.*

A pit formed in his stomach, a heartbeat in his jaw. "Take me to him," Kai said, but his voice felt distant, like he already knew they were too late.

Jack's throat was raw, every vocal cord strained, from calling her name all morning. His trousers were damp around the ankles where he'd stumbled into snow banks and slushed puddles, never having tucked them into his boots. A pale ring formed around his mouth.

In the end, it was Jim who found her, a body sprawled out on the snow staring at the sky. He carried her, limping, until he ran into Jack just outside the alcoves. A grim exchange passed between the two men. Jack stumbled, landed wet on his knees, every muscle trembling and brittle. Tears blurred his vision. Jim met him on the ground so Jack could take her, hold her, but he could not carry her. Jack sobbed over her, a trembling blue hand on her brow, in her hair – and nothing hurt as bad as this, like his lungs were shriveling in his capsizing chest, and his face burned into a blazing hellfire, because those brilliant green eyes would not see him anymore.

Somehow they were no longer alone, and Esmeralda stooped gently to close those sightless eyes into eternal sleep. As neither Jack nor Jim could bear to stand, Ingénu pulled away from his weeping wife to lift the limp body of his old friend into his arms and carry her to camp. Kai helped Jack to his feet, steadied him.

On the verge of falling apart, they followed.

Chapter Twenty-One
The Stages of Grief

In the goahti, Kai tried his best to focus in on the embittered and anxious words around him. Tjuv stood silently by his side, shadows deepening the wrinkles down her sour face. She was the only one who didn't badger him with questions.

"What the devil are we supposed to do now?" Clopin exclaimed, throwing his hands up in a frenzy.

Stoic, Esmeralda tried to intervene, "Clopin."

"It's too late to call off anything, what with half the plan already underway across this blustering snowscape. Right?" He whirled on Kai. "Right?"

Kai looked up from his crossed arms for a moment, nodded, but couldn't yet bring himself to speak.

"Right. Just what I thought."

"Clopin."

"And who's going to distract the Big Bad Wolf tonight now? On a *full moon*. What luck!"

"Clopin."

"Not to mention this bloody queenie is one step closer to getting whatever it is she wants. Who's to say she hasn't already snagged the little one, too?"

"Will you shut up," Jim snapped.

Clopin pursed his mouth shut, glanced broodingly at the ground as if reminded why they were even gathered here. The air stilled around them like the moment before a thundercrack. Kai swallowed the pit in his throat.

In a separate lavvu, Aurore, Celeste, and Liesel were preparing the body. Jack waited outside where they worked, unable to speak since they'd found her. Harry was with him. Despite wanting to be with his friend, Kai couldn't stay – they should have already been prepared to leave by now. With Lovisa gone, the others looked to him to figure out what to do next, what plans needed to change. But he felt numb, like after Gerda left him covered in the Snow Queen's icy second skin and when Alice came back insane. Only this was worse.

He forced himself not to think of Red's limp body in Ingénu's arms, her eyes closed by Esmeralda, how Jack begged and pleaded over her to somehow not be dead. Why did she go off on her own? What could have prompted her to venture so far away from the camp? There were no signs of a fight, no wounds, no missing arrows. If he didn't know any better, it looked as if Red had walked into the woods and died on her feet. Except there was fur in her mouth and scratches in her throat as if something had tried to pull out her tonsils, and her eyes were blotched with crimson hemorrhages. Like she suffocated.

"Everything will go on as planned," Esmeralda spoke easily, smoky eyes focused on nothing. "I will deal with Lupa."

"No, I'll do it," Jim interjected.

"Why?" Ingénu asked, frowning. "Because you think you can repay your debt to her by avenging her?"

Jim squared his shoulders. "Because I have nothing to lose."

"Ha!" Clopin barked, alight with a manic scowl. "Nice try, Jimmy. Everyone has something to lose. Even you."

"I will go," Ingénu spoke up.

Jim growled, "So pretty boy can play hero?"

"Neither of you fools are going after Lupa because neither of you are suited for it," Clopin stated sharply. "You'll be dead or wolfed before you could get a shot. You have to be valuable to get her attention and keep it long enough for the rest of the plan to work. And I'm sorry to burst your heroic egos, but you don't hit the mark."

"And you do hit this mark?" Ingénu questioned, eyebrow raised.

"*Oui*, but I'm not going out there. I'm too hot-headed; I'd rush things, try to kill her too soon. No, no, Lupa needs someone with valuable information and the cool patience to not lose her head." Waving a hand at his sister, Clopin said in finality, "Which is why she's going to do the job."

Esmeralda said nothing, though she looked to Kai as if waiting for his permission. Tjuv, too, raised her beady black eyes to him in silence. She did not offer her support beyond this small compliance, this respectful turning even in the midst of his observational haze. Grimly, Kai nodded to the gypsy woman.

"Then it is settled," Esmeralda said steadily. "I will leave—"

Light flooded the goahti as the entrance flap was drawn back in haste. Aurore stood there, her face stained pink, pale blue eyes bloodshot. Stillness washed over them. It was time for the burial.

But instead, Aurore said gravely, "We have a problem."

Dropping his arms, Kai instantly followed her outside where the yellow sun assaulted his eyes. He froze when he saw her, ice down his veins. On the ground in the center of camp rested Red in a nest of intertwined branches and flowers,

208

her face washed clean and hair brushed to silk. She was dressed in a crimson gossamer gown and her scarlet riding cloak. A bow and arrow were held over her breast. And perched over her body stood Alice baring both the vorpal sword and the Sword Kladenets, a fire in her eyes.

"We thought she just wanted to say goodbye," Aurore explained beside him. She pressed the heal of her hand against her forehead, took a breath, brushed the ginger wisps away from her face. "But now she won't let anyone near the body."

Kai watched Celeste try to broach their friend, her hands up in caution. But Alice scowled and bared her teeth.

"Alice, please," Celeste tried to reason.

"*Back!*" Alice barked, poised. "*Back! Back!*"

Frowning at the sight, Kai asked, "Where did she get the weapons?"

Aurore shrugged. "I don't think anyone thought to keep them hidden."

Kai huffed. He wished he could assume that Alice wouldn't harm anyone, but the way she wielded those swords showed tense readiness for violence. Whatever had overtaken her maddened mind had the fearsomeness of a mother bear.

Jack stood by silently, staring. Kai approached him and asked, "Have you tried to talk to her?"

Expressionless, Jack said, "I don't want to bury her any more than Alice does."

"What about the Hatter?"

Jack nodded to where Remus sat watching, arms propped on his knees, grounded from when Alice had pushed him away from her. He looked almost as confused as the rest of them.

"She could hurt someone," Kai muttered.

"Then we'll wait; bury Rubes with the others. This bloody war can't be finished with us yet," Jack grumbled. "Alice can't guard everybody."

Chapter Twenty-Two
The Phoenix Bird

The traveling party had to make fast shelter when a snow squall rushed over them, harsh wind gusts beating against their bodies, fresh snow soon covering everything in sight. Frost had sensed it coming and Lovisa bade two pine trees to bend over in a tight arch for protective shelter. The squall lasted maybe ten minutes. Once Lovisa had coaxed the trees back to their standing height, they were on their way once again.

Ice crunched under Wendy's feet, her ankles sore and stiff from the long walk over uneven terrain. Peter and the rest of the Lost Boys followed close behind her while Frost restlessly led far ahead through the woods and Lovisa bridged the gap between. Most of the Lost Boys had stayed behind in Neverland, but the oldest of the lot had come along for the adventure: Slightly, Nibs, the Twins, Curly, and Tootles. Tink sat snuggled in next to Peter's neck under his newly acquired scarf. Wendy had already assured that each of the Lost Boys wore hats that covered their ears, mittens tucked into their coat sleeves, and extra socks supplied by the nomadic robbers. She was not about to have a case of frostbite on her hands again.

It'd been strangely quiet since leaving the alcoves and the snow squall. The temperature dropped the farther they traveled, wind whistling through sparse trees. But there seemed to be no spies or snow bees or any other creatures about. Wendy hoped the reason for such silence was that Frost was leading them down a safe path and not that the Snow Queen's patrols had better things to do, or they were better at hiding than anticipated. She couldn't decide which alternative was worse.

The Lost Boys made a game out of who could leave the least amount of footprints, hovering a bare inch above the ground, trying to subtly shove each other into the snow. Slightly kept pushing Nibs a little too hard, often causing him to fall to his knees rather than touch to floor. The Twins kept score. Tootles was winning.

When Curly tried to thump Slightly into the snow, Slightly leaped away to fly out of reach. Curly huffed in frustration.

"Hey, that's cheating!" Nibs accused.

Slightly swept down and shouldered him in retaliation. Nibs landed on his knees in a snowbank by Wendy's feet.

"*Oof,*" Nibs groaned, righting himself quickly before joining the game again. "Sorry Wendy."

The Twins tallied the score against Nibs.

Wendy laughed in amusement, wishing she could join the fun. But she didn't have her happy thoughts back, the trinkets that allowed her to fly, so she had to reside herself to ground travel and sore ankles.

As much as she hated the situation and circumstances, Wendy was relieved to have Peter and the Lost Boys with her. Breathing came easier when they were around. Her feet felt lighter. She knew there was so much to tell them, so much unknown between them because she had moved through time while they had only moved in perpetual suspension. There were months of adventures, memories, and stories she had now that they didn't. Once this war was over, she would tell them about it all.

The thought settled strangely in her mind: Life after this. Wendy and her friends had spent so long searching for the

Snow Queen, preparing to defend the realms from her cruelty – what would it be like to finally stop? Would everything go back to the way they used to be, before the hunt for the mysterious Master, before the Facility, before the world got so complicated? Wendy didn't think it was so easy. Besides, too much could happen between now and life after that could further change how the future looked. She had spent so long outside of Neverland, trekking through time. Was she ready to return to timelessness?

Wendy rubbed her reddened nose, breathed into her cupped gloved hands, trying to restore warmth. Once the war was over, she had to make a trip to London first. She owed it to her parents, her brothers and sisters-in-law, her nieces and nephews. But she realized that much more had changed now than she'd ever anticipated. She had changed. Though Wendy knew she needed to see her family, it couldn't be the same as before.

And the boys at Hangman's Tree, Neverland's timelessness, the ceaseless adventures – she wasn't sure that she wanted those in the same way. There had to be change, now, *after*. Maybe something like the peace before the feud when Hook was just James and pirates were just Lost Boys grown up and the Panther Tribe could be allies and tradesmen. Wendy saw a world of opportunity *after*. A better world.

Wendy paused briefly so Peter would step up beside her and slipped her hand in his. "When all this is over," she said softly, swinging their arms, "I want to visit the Mainland, see my family."

With a nod, he pulled one of his dimpled smiles. "Okay."

"I want you to come with me."

He didn't speak for a long moment, clearly surprised by the request. But after furrowing his brow in careful consideration, he nodded again. "Okay."

Her heart leaped. "Really?"

"Yeah." Peter squeezed her hand. "Besides, your mom loves me."

Wendy grinned, not bothering to remind him that her mother always thought Peter Pan was a figment of her own dreams and bedtime stories, a kind of angel boy. She wondered how her father would react. Would her brothers remember Peter from their forgotten childhood? She couldn't be sure, but she was excited to find out.

"Can I come?" Slightly whispered behind them as if he hadn't just eavesdropped on the whole conversation. "Parents love me."

Nibs made a face. "You've never met a parent."

Slightly pushed him into the snow.

One of the Twins started, "We haven't seen Michael—"

"—Or John since they left the Island," finished the other.

"Do you still have the dog?" Curly asked, wringing his hands wryly.

Even Tootles appeared beside her and lifted his eyes up in question.

Wendy laughed. "Of course, you're all welcome."

"I'll pass on that," Tinker Bell jingled from her cozy perch. "Or at lease keep a safe distance. Last time I saw Mister Darling, he swatted at me like a fly."

"Yes, yes," Frost spoke loudly ahead of them, bitterness edging his tone, not even bothering to hush his voice. "Everyone's invited to the Darling house for tea, given that you don't die beforehand. Everyone satisfied? Good, because we're here."

They walked into open wasteland.

Kai waited alone at the edge of the frozen lake, his gaze rested on the icy spires reaching for the evening sky, the violet grey hues. All seemed calm on the ice, breathless. He knew it could all snap awake at any moment.

This close to the Snow Queen's castle, the risk heightened in potentially running into the Pack on a full moon; but from this vantage point, Kai would be able to see nearly any hostile coming in on where his troops were stationed. Should anything go wrong before they were ready, he could easily provide direction.

Footsteps approached from behind. Kai refused to move else draw attention to himself until a gentle hum filled his mind, easing his stature. He turned to meet Bae, Aurore astride his broad back.

"I don't know if this is going to work," she admitted as she slid off Bae onto the snow. She placed her hands behind her hips and stretched out her lower back, the sunlight arching over her rounded abdomen. Kai hadn't realized that Aurore was with child, though maybe Wendy had mentioned it once.

"We have a backup plan," Kai assured her. "But I'd rather not resort to the backup plan."

A small army stood readied below to serve as either distraction or rescue. Preferably, they would only need the distraction.

He tried to remember all he knew about the ghosts at Skull Rock. Their curse forced them to reside in such a place because the pain was too much to bear anywhere else, and night brought the worst hurt. Kai wasn't sure how much the distance and dusk would affect them, but he steeled himself as best he could.

Drawing his sword should any danger approach, he asked, "Are you ready?"

Aurore nodded. With a deep breath, she opened her hands, and as her palms began to glow with silver light, her summer sky eyes darkened into the swirling depths of the Milky Way. The world flickered. Reality seemed to haze. An eerie blue silhouette formed, then vanished just as quickly.

"Come on," Kai pressed, urgent.

In an instant, she appeared standing before him in full form as if she still lived. Sylvia Hook. She flicked off like a candle.

The sensation hit like frigid seawater ripping through him and stealing his breath away. Suddenly Kai was in limbo surrounded by the living corpses of pirates and children, and before Sylvia could kill him, he was thrust back to the ice with Aurore and Bae. Only Sylvia remained, a lone ghost scowling in furious agony.

"What are you doing?" Sylvia cried, a ghoulish screech in her voice. "You're supposed to free us."

"Control yourself," Kai demanded sharply. He feared that the ghosts would try to lash out again, this time with Aurore, and he didn't want to risk what that kind of impact could have on her or her unborn child.

"You lied!" Sylvia shrieked again. "You promised an end for us."

"I never meant to hurt you. I know the distance is straining your curse, but you must fight past it."

"I want to be free!"

"You will be free. All of you will be free." Kai's gaze flicked from Sylvia to the other figures slowly becoming clear in the evening. He recognized Long John Silver propped up with his crutch, a hat pulled low over his gruff face. Even the dog ghost was taking form in the clearing.

Working his jaw, Kai added, "But you're going to do something for me first."

Sylvia's eyes churned like dark pools, but she waited for him to continue. As Kai explained to the ghosts what he required of them, Aurore at last dropped her arms and her eyes returned to their normal shade of blue. She leaned against Bae who stooped to his knees so she could climb his back again.

I will return for you, hjälte, Bae hummed to Kai as he trotted off to take Aurore back to camp.

Soon, the leaf marking on the back of his neck began to burn.

Frost came to a halt at the edge of a rocky wasteland, his bare feet on the tiny obsidian pebbles that covered the terrain. Lovisa stood gravely just behind while Wendy and the Lost Boys flanked them. The air was stifling, windless. Though still considerably cold, this seemed to be the warmest place in the whole country. The sky stretched grey above them like a hanging smokescreen.

"There it is," Frost announced, swinging out his arms in presentation. "There's a large ring-like stone in the center with

217

a pool of these." He kicked up the black pebbles. "The pickaxe will be at the bottom."

He didn't mention the phoenix. No one wanted to bring up the ritualistic sacrifice they were about to witness.

Slowly, Lovisa removed her cloak and leathery armor, baring her back to expose the tree inked up her spine and over her arms. She now only wore a juniper gossamer shift, her feet bared on the pebbled ground. Every inch of her gave the impression of a goddess, yet there was nothing more human than the look in her eyes as she turned back to her companions.

Wendy didn't know what to say. The chance that Lovisa wouldn't come back from this was more than she could comprehend. Wendy hardly knew her, but she recognized that Lovisa had no real friend with her when she most needed one. This fact made Wendy so terribly lonely for her, this woman who was willing to walk into fire to save them all. Before she could overthink it, she stepped forward and pulled Lovisa into a hug, holding her tight so she would know that she wasn't alone.

"God be with you," Wendy whispered before she pulled away.

Lovisa smiled gently in thanks. With a final look at each of them, she turned and walked out into the obsidian wasteland.

Nothing happened at first. Lovisa simply walked, one foot after the other, getting further away from the forest. Wendy heard anxious heartbeats in her ears. Holding her breath, she squeezed Peter's hand tight. Frost stood motionless.

Time stretched on, and soon Lovisa was half way to the center. Still, there was only breathless silence. Wendy swallowed the lump in her throat.

A shrill shriek ripped through the air. Panicked, the Lost Boys ducked for cover. Even Peter's knees buckled, jerking Wendy down to a crouch. In the distance, a fiery explosion slammed into Lovisa, erupting in a pillar of flame where she stood. Wendy screamed and lurched forward, but Peter held her back. With a sigh, Frost shook his head as the fire battered the sky. They couldn't see anything from this far away.

The flames shrank, smoke rising to the grey sky, and there – *there!* – was Lovisa, a flicker just beyond the fire's haze, her dress smoldering tatters. The smoke was rising from her body. Flames flicked up between her toes. But she walked on, a steady beacon.

Again, the shriek came with the speed of a firecracker, and this time when the fire hit, Lovisa's bitter cries pierced the air. She was burning now, the flames licking up her skin, singeing her hair until her curls charred at the tips. She glanced back at where they stood on the forest line and Wendy could see how it glowed in her mouth, how her eyes turned amber and black, as if the phoenix was consuming her from the inside. Rising to her feet, she walked on. A burning ember in a field of smoke.

Wendy wanted to call her back, but she held her tongue. She didn't think Lovisa could take another hit. Frost was biting his fingernails now. Was he more afraid that Lovisa would fail or succeed?

Limping now, Lovisa was so close to the center when for a third time the phoenix's shriek tore through the atmosphere, and instead of bracing herself, Lovisa turned to meet it head on. Branches burst from the volcanic ground, encasing her extended arm as she grasped the firebird by the throat. Wendy could see it now, the bird, its wings aflame – and Lovisa stood burning as she choked this pulsing fire. The wood cracked, blackened, sparked around her arm. There was a scream like wind through a wildfire before the fire snuffed out and Lovisa dropped onto a pile of ash, smoke twisting above.

Frost dropped his arm. "She's done it."

Wendy gasped in relief, feeling as if she hadn't breathed in hours. "She's alive!"

But Frost didn't hear her. His face slacked in astonishment, his voice barely a whisper, "She's burned away her immortality."

Upon arriving at last to the ringed stone, Lovisa reached into the pocket of obsidian pebbles up to her elbow and produced the pickaxe they'd come all the way for. The weapon was large and heavy, its head and handle lined in violet ice. Lovisa returned to them as quickly as she could despite her many injuries. Wendy threw her cloak around her shoulders as Lovisa pressed the pickaxe into her hands.

"We haven't much time," Lovisa urged. "Go!"

Chapter Twenty-Three
The Big Bad Wolf

"Have you come to kill me?"

Esmeralda turned at the sound of Lupa's voice, her long raven hair pulled back from her face with two twined braids. Despite the risk of frostbite, she'd come dressed in as little extra layers as she could bear; if there was a duel to come, she wouldn't have her speed and agility impeded by restricting attire. Lupa's pointed teeth gleamed against the darkening shadows.

"*Oui*," Esmeralda confirmed grimly. Both hands remained empty at her sides, both scimitars sheathed.

Lupa tapped her sharpened nails against the tree truck she stood beside. "That is a dangerous proposition, seeking revenge on a full moon. Nights such as this bond wolf and woman as one."

"But I am a gypsy, *louve*," Esmeralda spoke smoothly. "I have come to see your soul."

"And what would you tell me? My future? My past? I care not for such things."

"Your fears."

"My fears?" Lupa raised an eyebrow, amusement staining the back of her voice. "And what would that bring you? The last time you read someone's fears, you misinterpreted. Or why else would you have carved your own face but to imitate the monster that Carabosse dreaded?"

Esmeralda kept her feet firmly planted as Lupa stepped closer into the clearing. Gold eyes glittering, Lupa cocked her head like she knew she'd hit a nerve.

"You sacrifice yourself again and again, yet it is your loved ones who pay the price," Lupa said darkly. "Throw yourself to hellfire, and your husband wanders alone for the rest of his days. Mar your face to permanent disfigurement, and your best friend dies protecting you. Kill a wolf on a full moon, but Little Red has already died. This is why you've come, is it not? To continue the cycle. But she's already gone."

Esmeralda's mouth remained a firm line. The depth of Lupa's knowledge caused her gut to clench, but she refused to let it intimidate her.

Feigning a bow, Lupa removed one of the many charms around her waist, dropped it to the ground. "If it is fear you wish to see, then by all means look. I do not intend to let you escape with the wolf this night. This is my mercy to you."

With a shallow breath, Esmeralda narrowed her smoky eyes and looked right into Lupa's soul. Most have different depths to their fear, mild phobias on the surface, deep traumas at the core. Lupa only had one image to represent her fear.

Calmly, Esmeralda spoke, "A wolf fears the lamb? I have never seen such irony."

Lupa shook her head in pity. "Ah, and here is your weakness, gypsy. You see but you do not understand. This is how I have bested you all of these years in the Forest, and how I will best you again."

"My people have hidden from you for years," Esmeralda disputed defensively.

"Did you ever suppose I never found you because I was not looking?"

"You worked for Carabosse. You killed the deformed."

"I did. And I killed many. But I need insurance. Carabosse could have betrayed me any time she wished. I needed leverage that she could not find, and your people always housed so much leverage."

Esmeralda glared, jaw tight. "I do not believe you."

With a shrug, Lupa admitted, "I do not care if you believe me. I have provided you information. I am known not to lie, but who is to say the truth of that claim except for me? Truth is only what you make of the information presented to you."

"You are giving me much information tonight."

"I do not expect you will live long."

Lupa began circling her as if unable to remain still for any longer. She looked Esmeralda up and down, nostrils flared, stalking her prey. Esmeralda refused to move.

"I do not fear the lamb, gypsy. I fear the shepherd who guards it and what she represents. It is the shepherd who protects the lamb, hence it is she who is most dangerous for she will do anything to defend her flock. The same is said for the parent and the child, the lover and the loved, the true and the friend – the one who has something for which she would do anything for. The shepherd is the most fearsome creature of all."

"But you do not fear the shepherd," Esmeralda countered easily. "You fear of becoming it."

The statement brought Lupa to a standstill, head cocked in mild interest. "So, you do understand."

At first, Esmeralda said nothing, letting the revelation linger before she began to circle Lupa in turn. "Shepherds are dangerous creatures, not only to everyone else, but to themselves. They have something to love and protect, but that means they have something to lose."

Arching an eyebrow, Lupa admitted, "You impress me – to a degree. Tell me, is your sight limited to only the person standing before you? Or could you see anyone's fears you wish?"

"Is there someone you wish to frighten, *louve*?"

"Information is insurance. It also prolongs your life."

"Whose fears do you wish to see? Mine? Your nephew's? The Snow Queen's?"

Lupa chuckled, stroking one of the charms at her waist. "You refuse to answer my question by asking your own. Clever tactic. But I have my own tricks, gypsy, and when I say that I know your true intentions without your having spoken a word – no, you won't believe me until I say it." She leered in the twilight, gold eyes shadowed. "You may indeed intend to kill me, but you're stalling me on a full moon because your little friends are starting a war tonight and you're here to distract me."

Esmeralda betrayed nothing in her expression or unchanged stance, yet Lupa smiled in confirmation, turned on her heel, and ran into the forest. Drawing her scimitars, Esmeralda followed in swift pursuit as Lupa shifted into a Mongolian wolf ahead of her and sent a droning signal skyward.

The two merged armies had just reached the edge of the frozen lake when the howl echoed through the air from the west. A sharp chill ran down Jim's spine. Clopin cursed in French under his breath at the sound.

"If she's dead," he growled next to Jim, his black eyes drowned in shadow, "I'm going to kill every last one of those howling scoundrels."

"You have a lot of anger, friend," Harry spoke with an amused lilt to his voice. "You should see someone about that."

Jim laughed at the prospect of Clopin treating his anger management issues, but Clopin scowled in response.

"I don't need to see anyone," he snapped. "And we are not friends. What would you do if your sister was murdered by a pack of bloodthirsty monsters?"

At that, Harry's smile waned, and the air seemed to tighten. But he merely shrugged. "I don't know, friend. Let's hope it doesn't come to that."

Twilight stained the sky in indigo and tiger's eye, sending black shadows to spill across the ice and darken the trees. Silhouettes moved over the frozen lake like arrows. The Pack was responding to the call.

"Weapons!" Clopin barked, drawing his rapier.

"Remember your orders," Ingénu shouted.

Jim touched the pistol at his waist but drew his club. For Red's sake, he wouldn't kill a wolf tonight. After everything he'd done to her, she'd given him a second chance to redeem himself, so if it was within his power he would give the Pack that same chance.

"You heard 'em, friends," Harry spoke up to the crowd of eager belowlanders behind him, earning an agitated sneer from his righthand general Cat. "This is one bloody negotiation."

As a horde of wolves rushed in upon them, a metallic *whoosh* set off from behind as an enormous net was cast into the air and landed on the fastest wolves, trapping them under the weighted ropes. The beasts growled viciously, snarling. A roar battered Jim's ears as Isbjørn broke out onto the ice in full polar bear form, circling the net to swat a massive paw at any who tried to escape by chewing the ropes and to guard against any wolves attempting to rescue their fellows.

"Don't get bit," Jim warned the men standing beside him, bracing himself for their plunge into battle. Clopin hardly acknowledged the statement as he barreled forward at the second wave of wolves.

Harry, however, saluted him with a lopsided grin. "Right back at you, friend."

Brandishing his club in one hand and shield in the other, Jim charged into battle. A wolf ran headlong into him, standing on its hindlegs to press against his shield and drive him down. Jim shoved the shield into the wolf's chest to keep its snapping teeth above his head.

"We're here for Red," Jim shouted above the wolf's brutal snarl. "We don't want to hurt you."

The wolf didn't relinquish, putting its full weight against Jim's shield. When he tried to throw the beast aside, he felt his footing give way and he slipped backwards on the ice, shoving himself away from the wolf as its claws raked over his shield. Quickly, Jim regained his footing and bashed his club over the wolf's shoulders.

A snap and shout from behind caused Jim to bolt out of the way as another net was thrown by the giants in the forest, pinning more wolves to the ice. Urgently, Jim managed to pull someone out who'd been caught with a weight on her back.

"Are you good?" Jim asked, though he did not recognize her. She had onyx downturned eyes and pitch black hair, a brace on her wrist. He assumed she belonged to the belowlanders.

"I'm fine," she snapped, pulling her arm away from his grip. She didn't seem particularly thankful that he'd just helped her.

"Spider," someone called in the distance, "come help with this!"

Then she was gone.

With a huff, Jim looked around at the battle they'd started. No one was getting anywhere as far as negotiations went. Isbjørn paced the nets, but others had to join him in trying to keep the wolves from escaping. The Pack still pressed on in the attack, emerging from the woodworks, some thankfully avoiding the use of their teeth in light of the full moon. The giants would soon run short on nets.

Subtly, the ice beneath his feet began to tremble. Twilight was darkening to grey dusk, forcing him to squint and blink to notice the gigantic silhouettes in the distance. He hoped these were the reinforcements, the giants they'd come to rescue, but these figures moved steadily without haste – and Jim knew better than anyone what an escaped prisoner should look like.

Licking his lips, Jim drew his pistol. He'd never fought a giant before, but he hoped a bullet would still do the trick.

Chapter Twenty-Four
The Convicted and Redeemed

Wendy ran, the pickaxe strapped to her back wrapped in vines and cloth, still far behind Nibs who sprinted ahead of her. Having met them after Lovisa's battle with the phoenix, Mr. and Mrs. Crow flew overhead to keep watch over the lot of them after the group had scattered from the obsidian wasteland. They figured it'd be harder for the Snow Queen to discover who held the real pickaxe in their possession. Tink had stayed behind with Lovisa to see her safely back to the alcoves, readily able to provide pixie dust for an emergency escape.

Feet pounding against the shallow snow, Wendy heard the buzzing in the distance. Her breath hitched in recognition. She ran faster.

"Nibs!" she shouted, heart pounding. "Fly! Quick!"

Though she couldn't see him, she knew he would've done it. He would've leaped and soared full speed ahead as soon as she demanded it. Nibs didn't need to hear the buzzing behind or know the snow bees were after them. Just her voice.

Pushing forward, Wendy realized the elation pulsing through her veins, the thrill that came in place of the fear that should've been bursting inside. It was like she'd returned to Neverland, fleeing from the dragon on Neverpeak, running for a waterfall, taking on the world. The thought made her run faster, lighter. And Peter was there – she couldn't see him, but she knew they shared these woods, and her Lost Boys too, and Tinker Bell. The pewter grey sky seemed so big and welcoming and familiar, stretching on to hover over her homes, her family, her friends who'd become her family. And suddenly she realized it, how her legs cycled and her feet never touched the ground. She was flying, really flying, and it hit her that Alice was right this whole time. Wendy laughed in delight.

A blast crashed behind her, white ice colliding through the trees, launching Wendy forward. She hit the ground, rolled, remained flat on her back. The snow bees missed and passed. Elated, Wendy gave a crow to the sky. She'd flown! Alice was right: her feet weren't as sticky as she'd thought.

Breathing heavy and unable to stop smiling, Wendy rolled to her feet. The pickaxe had snapped off her back in the fall. She picked it up by the handle. Maybe she could fly again, even without the talisman to represent her happy thoughts, just like Peter. She sniffed, trying to catch her breath. All this time, the trick was all in her head – or her heart.

"Nibs," Wendy shouted as she continued forward, hovering longer with each stride. "Look at this!"

She tripped, stumbled, caught herself in time, then looked up to find that someone had appeared before her. Her smile faded. Her feet felt the weight of gravity again.

Breathless, Wendy asked, "Why are you here?"

Jane stood stiffly in the dusk, chin out but frozen. Her hair had grown since leaving Neverland, her bangs long enough to tuck behind her ears. A damaged wooden pendant hung over her chest and a spotted leopard mask swung from her belt. A Lost Boy mask.

"Why are you here?!" Wendy exclaimed, suddenly so angry she could hardly contain it.

"I..." Jane couldn't get her words out. Her stature wouldn't budge, but her eyes lowered, fumbling for a response.

Wendy felt her blood boil. This girl had lived decades longer than she, trained on the edge of Neverland's borders, raised by pirates to destroy the Pan, and still Jane was nothing more than a child. Wendy hated finding that similarity, hated that she felt an empathy for this girl who betrayed everyone she cared about. That mask signifying her place in Hangman's Tree was evidence enough of Jane's betrayal.

Clenching her fists, Wendy went to slip by her. "Just go away."

"Wait."

Wendy paused, looked from Jane to the bundle she produced swinging from her hand. Anxious, Jane set the bundle on the snowy ground between them. Wendy didn't recognize the shape as it was covered in a velvet drape. But something tugged in her chest. Jane stepped back, still staring at her offered burden.

"I never asked for this," Jane said at last. "I never expected..."

When her voice droned off, Wendy pressed, "Never expected what? That you were wrong? That the Lost Boys would feel like family? That you would fall in love with Peter? That you would forget and remember and regret it forever?"

"I never meant for a lot of things. I can't do anything without betraying someone now. But there you go."

Wendy waited, watching Jane's face for any sign of a trap. Cautiously, Wendy knelt before the item, lifted the drape to expose a lantern with glass stained in soot. The blackness inside shifted like smoke. A sigh escaped her chest.

Jane looked down at her, eyes shining. "I can't bear to see him hurting."

Wendy didn't respond, but the words hung in the air regardless. This small gesture was only that. Nothing could fix the rift Jane laid the moment she walked away from them in the dark of the brig. Jane would only ever see Peter Pan in pain from now on. Nothing would change that.

As she turned to leave, Wendy called, "Jane."

Bidden to stop, Jane met her eyes for the first time.

Wendy swallowed past her tight throat. "Walk away. It only gets harder from here."

She looked so helpless, on the verge of tears. "It's too late."

"You always have a choice," Wendy said, imitating Peter's warning back in Neverland.

Jane recognized it, squared her shoulders, and said in a raw apology, "I've already made my choice. I'm continuously making my choice. Now, I have to bear the consequences."

Jane turned to go, then paused to reach under her collar and pull something over her head. She stared at the trinket in hand, then held out a fist to Wendy, dropped it in her open palm. Though she didn't say it, Wendy knew. The apology lay in her hand. Then Jane was gone. Wendy dropped her eyes to the silver thimble and bronze acorn in her palm. She didn't feel any different.

After slipping on her happy thoughts around her neck, she took the lantern in one hand and the pickaxe in the other and started forward to continue her journey once again, hovering just above the ground until something latched into her foot and yanked her down.

"Brann," Harry shouted, sprinting across the ice. "Give me a boost!"

Brann pulled instantly away from the wolf-man – leaving Spider to deal with him alone – and crouched on one knee with fingers interlaced. Harry leapt forward, used a rock and Brann's hands as a launching pad, before he was airborne, limbs wheeling, flying straight for an enemy giant. He caught a beltloop, swung briefly, then scrambled up the giant's back like a squirrel. With a yell, the giant reeled back as he tried to reach for his attacker. Harry dodged the groping hand and managed to crawl over stooping shoulder blades.

An earring made from human femurs dangled from the giant's lobe, which was unfortunate for him because Harry grabbed hold of it and used the ornament as a swing to get to the giant's ugly face. The stench of his breath made Harry want to gag. Snatching the curved fishhook of a sword from his side, Harry hooked the giant's nose and drove his momentum into the ground. The giant plunged down head first, somersaulted on the ice, landed flat on his back. Harry yanked his hook free while Brann finished the giant off.

Harry whistled as Liesel ran past him into the oncoming flood of giants. She took a mechanical orb from her belt, twisted it until an artificial light halved it, then launched the device at a giant barreling her way. The orb exploded on impact, erupting the giant in flame. Liesel threw two more, each meeting their mark and bringing down the colossal assailants with roaring screams.

Harry grinned like a fool. "That's my wife!"

"You're not married yet," Brann retaliated.

"Small details."

Brann blinked in awe at the sight, rubbing the black flames tattooed up his wrists. "Can you imagine if the Fiddler knew about this?"

"Knew about what, friend?" Harry asked.

Brann waved a hand at the sight of fiery giants. "That Liesel can make explosives."

Wiping off his fishhook sword on the dead giant's sleeve, Harry asked cryptically, "You think he didn't already suspect it? He came to the house every now and again to ask about her late husband's work."

Spider approached having wrenched her sword free from a giant's gullet. "She could've saved a lot of lives if she shared that weapon."

"She already saved a lot of lives because she didn't," Harry corrected, a sharpness in his tone that he rarely used.

Brann frowned, confused about the predicament, while Spider gave a huff just short of rolling her eyes. They didn't pursue the subject.

"I suppose she'll have to be renamed," Spider said, her black eyes reflecting sparks and embers.

"Mouse." The answer came from beside Harry where he hadn't realized General Cat had been standing. Her grave face splattered in blood, nothing in her expression revealed how long she'd been listening to their conversation. Spider grunted in agreement.

But Harry knew she would always be Liesel.

Leaving the belowlanders to resume the battle, he jogged forward until he reached his fiancé where he found her standing in the middle of her burning giants and at her feet knelt a man with a hand to the ground. Harry slowed his pace, looking around to assure no one was trying to sneak up on them. Somehow, he knew this was a wolf-man. He steeled himself to leap into action.

Liesel and the strange man held each other's gaze for a stretch of time. She had this ability – Harry didn't understand it – to level someone with this look like she could read their mind. Often, he witnessed this with the boys, Tom and Blue, or else with Harry himself. He suspected this was some kind of supermom power.

"You don't have to stay," Liesel said at last, steady and knowing.

The man waited long enough for Harry to realize that this must be the wolf-man leader they were looking for. "Is she dead?" he asked in a low rasp.

Harry couldn't tell if he was talking about Red or the other big bad wolf, but Liesel seemed to know. As she does.

"I don't know," Liesel admitted.

"Red is, though," Harry spoke up, still looking out for intruders. "Thanks to your wolf pal."

The man frowned, his silver eyes black and amber in the blazing dusk. He glanced again at Liesel whose face remained unchanged. Then he turned, shifted into a lone grey wolf when he was only a shadow, and disappeared. Liesel looked back at Harry just as a howl droned through the sky.

"I hope that's a call for surrender," Harry said.

She pulled a strained smile. He wrapped an arm around her, rubbing her shoulder, kissed the top of her head. Warmth nestled in his abdomen. Then he saw it, a haze on the horizon.

Frowning, Harry asked, "Do you see that, too?"

Liesel narrowed her eyes, nodded. The haze grew brighter, eerier, illuminating the growing silhouettes barreling their way. The strange light overtook one of these figures, crawling up to encompass the giant, glowing blue in his eyes, his nostrils, his mouth. No scream. And the giant collapsed.

"If that's not a horde of ghosts," Harry said, unsure whether to be excited or scared out of his mind, "then I don't know what is."

Indeed, the ghosts became more distinct the closer they came, and behind them rumbled the giants they'd rescued. From the forest came a victorious roar from Ajaal and Trell's giants, welcoming their escaped kin. Harry pumped his fist in the air.

"We did it!" he whooped.

"Harry," Liesel cautioned, looking behind them. "Those aren't just cheers."

That's when the frozen zombies started to stumble out of the forest.

When Bae returned, he allowed Kai to ride on his back. On the battlefield, the ghosts succeeded in freeing the imprisoned giants and now drove the enemy into fierce retreat. Kai watched as the ghosts swarmed into a giantess to bring her down. If their victims weren't dead, their bodies remained trembling on the ice. Before pulling back, some of the enemy giants managed to dislodge the nets holding down the Pack, and the escaped wolves quickly disappeared into the surrounding forest.

Bae moved carefully, skirting the forest's edge. The tainted forest and water people had begun to emerge, and he couldn't afford being discovered. Kai leaned his head back to stretch out his neck.

Aurore's spell would soon wear off and the ghosts would disappear before long. Their duty to him was complete, their curse of suffering fulfilled, and Aurore's magic freed them. Kai tried not to think about how Sylvia tried to kill him, how she screamed at him and would have split his soul to pieces if she wanted to. He knew her reaction was out of pain that the night and distance from Skull Rock caused. He just wished they could have ended on better terms before she at last moved on from this half-life she existed in.

A doleful howl rose in the distance. Kai perked at the sound as if he expected to see a black wolf run into battle. But he remembered suddenly, and the unshakable heaviness returned inside.

Bae began to hum, filling his mind with a melancholy song, and Kai felt his throat tighten.

You are thinking of your friend.

The howl still lingering in his ears, Kai pressed his thumb and forefinger against the bridge of his nose. "It could've been anything," he admitted, voice gravelly. "Lupa could've escaped or killed Esmeralda. Fang could be calling retreat or attack. Any number of those blasted wolves could've howled – maybe even a new one. *Jag vet inte.*"

I see, Bae hummed, weaving around the icy trees.

Icicles gleamed in the faint light as dusk waned to night. The sky had cleared, exposing the first smears of starlight, the marble disked moon. Bae waited in comforting silence before he spoke again.

There is a reason why morning follows night, hjälte. *After times of great darkness, we must take time to mourn all we have lost and all who were lost, even as hope rises with the sun.* Twitching his round ears, Bae twisted his head around to see Kai through one bright eye. *All this time, you haven't had time to mourn. But such a time is coming. Then, you must let the darkness wash over you so you can stand in the light again.*

Kai pressed his lips together, but he nodded. He knew there was truth in Bae's words even if he couldn't see how. Tangling his fingers in the shaggy pale scruff of Bae's neck, he allowed Bae to press forward into the night.

Jim tore the pistol from his belt and shot the frozen man barreling towards Clopin. Though not enough to kill the humanoid creature, it gave Clopin an opening to finish him off with a few quick slashes of his rapier. No one had warned them about the frozen people. They slipped from the forest, one or two at a time. Jim was afraid to even touch the things – their frostbite looked infectious.

"Help!" someone cried desperately near his feet. "Help me, please!"

Jim whipped around to find a man pinned halfway under a weighted net filled with wolves. The man squirmed haplessly, palms slapping ice.

"They're going to eat me!" he screamed.

Rushing over, Jim dropped his shield, locked hold of the man's arms, and managed to pull him free before the wolves started snapping at his ankles. Jim helped him to his feet. The man was out of breath, a hand on his shoulder to keep from falling.

"You alright?" Jim asked above the noise of snarling wolves.

The man made an exhausted head motion, a shake to a nod. "Thank you. Thank you." Stringy bold hair hung over his fair face and amber eyes. Something smelled like cinnamon.

"Hey," Jim tried to get a better look at the man's face. "Do I know you?"

The man smiled at the ground, still breathing heavy. "Should've just played along, kid."

Jim tried to shove him away, but the man's nails dug into his shoulder in a death grip. In one move, the man whipped Jim backwards onto the ice, jerking his shoulder out of socket with a painful crack and launching his pistol across the ice. Jim cried out, the breath knocked out of him. The man, the very same who had blocked their passage to Chliobain and exposed Red as a wolf, sneered down at him as his teeth elongated. Jim tried to twist out of the way, but his arm erupted at the movement.

Suddenly, a shining mass like fog came barreling towards them, yelling out a rising baritone before slamming into the man and throwing him back away from Jim. The man's expression turned to panic, eyes and nostrils and mouth glowing from the light that swarmed him from the inside. Heart pounding, Jim's stomach twisted in fear. The man's muscles seized, veins bulging, then collapsed dead to the floor.

The strange light lingered, a ghost, looking back at Jim. He looked like a pirate, large and gruff with his left leg gone at the hip, and he leaned into a crutch under his arm. Jim blinked. It was like the pirate had stepped out from one of his grandfather's stories about an island filled with treasure and his adventures at sea.

Face softened, the ghost turned to face him, and with a hopeful tang he choked, "Jim?"

Then he faded, a smudge in the air, and was gone.

Jim's throat tightened. Lights all around him began to fade into oblivion. Ghostly faces turned heavenward, peaceful at last.

Jim wondered about the ghost who saved him, how he knew his name, before he realized that the ghost had seen someone else in his place. His grandfather. Jim should've told him the truth, that he wasn't the heroic cabin boy but the lost woodsman. In the end, it didn't matter. Long John Silver saved the life of Jim Hawkins and could rest knowing he finally did something right.

Chapter Twenty-Five
The Witching Hour

Jack waited alone hidden in a thicket of brittle bare bushes, itching to race into battle. He wanted to hit something until his knuckles bruised and arms grew sore, or else let something hit him. Anything to distract him from the twisting black knot in his chest.

But he knew the plan. He had to wait here on the lake's northeastern front for Kai or the pickaxe to arrive; whichever came first. The castle looked closer from here, and when the sun was still up, he could see the details etched in the spires and turrets, the arches curving along the walls like a cathedral. In the dark, the ice emitted a faint glow.

Jack's guard was down, but he didn't care. He wasn't being as careful as he should. If anyone came at him, whether tainted or wolf or giant, it would be the best thing to happen to him all day. Everything in him wanted to run until his feet bled because he couldn't feel anything but this empty, suffocating, hollow ache.

A twig snapped and he leapt to his feet, sword drawn. Nothing came. He remained exposed anyway, practically begging for something to show up.

"Come on," he growled, shaking his sword anxiously. His throat tightened and eyes welled. *"Come on!"*

Nothing answered. He swiped the air with both hands wrapped around the hilt. His knees buckled and he fell to the ground, shoulders shaking, arms limp. Tears rolled down his face, unable to stop himself from sobbing. Silence pulsated on every side. His mind clouded in a deep and drowning haze, and he couldn't find the strength to break himself out.

Memories like fragments rose to the surface: the amber flecks in her eyes he could only see up close, the way her face felt in his hands like a heartbeat, her palm on his chest as the northern lights cast emerald reflections across her fingernails – and she was staring at the sky when they found her, and he couldn't save her, couldn't even carry her body in his arms, and she wasn't the first. Green eyes, gold eyes, blue eyes. He couldn't save them, not Red, not Jill, not his parents. They were gone, slipped from his fingers just after he got them.

Jack screamed at the moon until his voice broke and he could only breathe the frigid air. That's when he noticed it was snowing. Flakes on his eyelashes. His breath in clouds overhead.

Someone answered with a laugh all around him.

Jack shot to his feet, sword raised again. Tear lines down his cheeks crusted on his skin. He spun in a tight circle but only saw trees and snow.

"Show yourself," Jack barked, his voice weak at the edges.

The laugh continued in a woman's singsong voice, "Oh Jackie, Jackie, Jackie, my little broken boy. You laugh, you cry, your friends all die, and now you're my new toy."

Jack scowled. "Who are you?"

"I'm the voice in your head, the monster under the bed—"

"Stop it!"

"*Jack and Jill go up a hill to fetch a pail of water.*"

There were flashes in his head now, Jill stumbling out of the mist, dragging a bucket to meet him.

"*Jack fell down...*"

Jill swung the bucket at him.

"*... and broke his crown...*"

A burst of light, the fall down the hill, giants all around.

"*... and Jill came tumbling after!*"

"Shut up!" Jack cried, for he was suddenly holding her again, then his sword stretched before him, and her head was on his shoulder, but both hands grasped his hilt. "What are you doing to me?"

The woman chuckled again, homing in at last on a single focal point. "I'm only speaking, Jackie. Anything else is of your own doing."

He was shaking, but he fought against it. A panic loomed on the edge of his mind he didn't recognize, but the more he focused on the rising anxiety, the worse it became. And that scared him.

He could see the woman now in the early night, her electric blue eyes, the blackness inking up her pale birdlike arms. She lingered like a wraith in the darkness. "Do you miss them, Jackie? Your parents, your sister, your lover? They died for you, you know. Trampled, poisoned, suffocated. How can you live with so much blood on your conscience?"

"*Shut up!*"

"If it wasn't for you, they'd still be alive."

"Stop."

"It's your fault. Yours! You may as well have sent the blows with your own two hands."

"Please..."

"Are you going to let someone else die for you? Can you live with yourself?"

Jack closed his eyes, his heart throbbing in his ears. A pressure built behind his forehead and threatened to burst. Weakly, he asked, "What do you want?"

"Fee fi fo fum, Jackie," the woman said, teeth flashing. "I've come to bake my bread."

Jack swallowed the knot in his throat. "You're sick."

"Maybe. But you're going to give me what I want."

"Why?"

"Weren't you listening? I'm sparing you guilt. I could've gone to anyone."

"That's not true."

"No one else knows that."

Jack's heart sped. He knew Alice's words were for him, about the bone, just as Red probably knew the breath was about her. But if this woman got to one of the others and convinced them otherwise, none of it mattered. Wendy would do anything to protect her friends – gosh, she didn't even know about Red. Alice would lop off a bone herself in the state she was in. And Kai, after everything he'd already cost his friend in delaying their arrival and ruining the chance to save Gerda, Jack would never be able to look him in the eye again.

"I'll get what I need all the same," the woman said in casual confidence, extending her hand as if to make a deal. "This is less messy. But I can promise you this: anyone else, I'll make it gruesome. Yours I'll make quick. I won't touch any of the others."

The overbearing panic threatened to pull him over the edge again. Jack stared at the offered hand. He was beginning to hyperventilate.

"You won't hurt the others?" he asked, tears welling again.

"I won't hurt them," she affirmed. "Do we have a deal?"

Jack swallowed, a metallic taste in his mouth. "Deal."

He shook her hand, and in one swift movement she produced a blade from her side and lopped off his right arm at the elbow.

Kai arrived just as Jack fell to his knees screaming, trying to stop the bleeding with one hand. Häxan stood over him like a vulture, locked eyes with Kai, and smiled with the severed arm firmly in hand.

Before Kai could react, her eyes iced over, and her voice became familiar but not her own, "You still don't get it, do you? You were never in control."

Häxan shuffled away with a sneer, raising her free hand until it deepened to purple. Bae reared to throw off her aim as a blast split the air between them. Thrown, Kai fell backwards to the ground before Bae lost his footing and collapsed sideways on the snow. Wrestling to get back on his feet, Kai caught sight of Häxan as she waved the severed arm and slipped out of sight.

Heart pounding in his throat, Kai jolted for Jack who lay writhing on the floor.

"I'm sorry! I'm sorry!" Jack sputtered, a squeal tugging the back of his voice. "I didn't – *blasted bloody* – Kai, Kai…!"

He hushed him sharply, tearing off his belt to tourniquet Jack's bicep. Blood wetted his hands, stained Jack's side, pooled in the snow. Kai ripped off the first of his layered shirts to stop up the exposed wound.

Someone stepped into the clearing and Kai nearly jumped up to attack until he realized it was Frost.

"What happened?" Frost questioned, the real pickaxe ready in his hand.

"Häxan cut off his arm," Kai said gruffly, pulling the belt even tighter.

Jack spurt out another stream of indistinguishable panic, tears streaming down his face.

Without asking, Frost kneeled beside him while Kai tightened the tourniquet. He held his palms up for a moment, skin turning blue and steaming with cold, before Frost clasped both hands around Jack's open wound. Jack gave a guttural wail. The effect was searing, vapor rising from his grasp. When Frost pulled away, the wound was sealed from severe ice burn, marks like fingers scarring Jack's bicep.

Breathing deeper, Kai pressed his forehead to Jack's brow and tried to steady the anxiety pulsing through him. He grabbed Jack's remaining hand, the left one.

"I'm here, *bror*," he assured gently. "It will be alright."

Jack cried softer now, eyes squeezed shut.

As a tender hum filled his mind, Kai looked back to find Bae still lying on his side, an icicle spire dripping from his abdomen. The reindeer's eyes were glossy, and steam puffed heavily from his nostrils. Kai raised his head but already he knew it was too late to do anything. Bae's melodic hum continued. He saved Kai's life.

You do not see it, Bae said, brown eyes watching him warmly, *but the sun is coming.*

His humming faded, eyes drooping to a close. Kai's jaw tightened as his face grew hot, stifling a sob, tears leaking off his chin and dropping to his lap. He looked up at the sky but only saw the stars.

Chapter Twenty-Six
The Sacrifice

Red woke up nose to nose with the Wolf, her riding hood draped over them like a blanket. She felt the Wolf breathe against her arms and stir as she too began to groggily wake. Stomach tight, Red tried to take in her surroundings without alarming the Wolf, but all she saw was a forest around them, pine in her nostrils, and slowly the cloak began to itch. Almost immediately Red realized her limitations: her heightened senses, her super human strength, it was all gone. The Wolf lay beside her. They were no longer one.

Slowly, Red pulled away, keeping the cloak around her shoulders. There was a bow and a single arrow in her hand. She tried to steady her breathing. Nothing about this place seemed familiar, and the trees hazed if she tried to focus on them.

Gradually, her cloak began to burn, prodding her to turn back. The Wolf was awake. Rising to her paws, the Wolf yawned deeply to expose her long canines. She shook her black fur thickened in a winter coat, sniffed around her immediate environment, then caught sight of Red. Their eyes locked. The space buzzed between them. Red recalled Lupa's warning, that the Wolf would turn on her, that only one of them would come back from this.

The Wolf smelled the air, bobbed her head. As if she too remembered Lupa's words, her ears flattened to her head, and slowly her lips curled back into a low snarl. Red gripped her only available weapons and ran.

Immediately, she felt awkward in her own body. She felt the difference in her muscles like the strength had been sapped from her limbs. The faster she sped, the shorter her breath came. Judging by the distance between them, the Wolf was experiencing the same adjustments. Together they'd shared combined strength, but apart they were restricted to normalcy. But Red knew that before long the Wolf would overtake her. She only had one arrow. She had to make it count.

When her cloak burned to overbearing intensity, she whirled around just as the Wolf pounced. Red used her arrowhead like a dagger, slicing an ear, cutting a leg. In the scramble, the Wolf scratched her deeply across her bicep and chest before Red managed to throw her off. Swiftly, the Wolf snipped her leg, causing Red to cry out in pain, then jumped back out of reach.

They circled each other, each with a limp. Red steeled herself for another blow. Colliding again, they wrestled to avoid arrow and teeth, coming apart equally bruised and bloody. When Red pulled back, she waited for the Wolf to thrust forward before launching to the side. In her momentum, the Wolf slammed into a tree with a yelp.

Red drew her bow, arrow aimed at the spot between the Wolf's eyes as the beast crouched in a snarl. Pressure against her eardrums seemed to pop and she was suddenly aware of the crystal silence, the breath huffed over her lips, the arrow's feathers against her cheek. Here was the monster she'd been fighting for years. This growling beast she never wanted, who was forced upon her like a curse. She'd been running for so long, from her past, from Fang, from this Wolf. With one shot, she could end it all.

She yelled from deep in her throat in utter agony and dropped her bow. The Wolf didn't move from her stance, teeth bared, eying the weapon. Tears stung Red's eyes, rolled down her cheeks.

"I don't want to hurt you!" she exclaimed, her voice breaking.

Something in that proclamation released a wave of burdens within her. She was washed in exhaustion and relief, and the tears kept falling. She dropped to her knees, the bow and arrow beside her, and looked at the beast who'd been with her all this time. It wasn't the Wolf's fault – she wasn't the monster. The Wolf was just as much a part of Red as she herself was.

Soon, the Wolf stopped growling, muscles relaxed though her ears remained flat in suspicion. Red kept her hands in her lap. Cautiously, the Wolf approached as if she too did not want to end like this. She pressed her nose into Red's palm and her ears flicked up. Red gently placed a hand between the Wolf's eyes, then leaned in to press her forehead against the Wolf's brow.

"I'm sorry it's taken so long," Red whispered.

Pulling away, the Wolf whimpered short and sweet before she curled into Red's lap and lay there. Red bent over and buried her face in the thick scruff of fur. She didn't know what would happen now, but for the first time Red felt closer to the Wolf than she ever had before, and she wasn't ready to let this go.

*****

Gerda wanted to vomit as Häxan dug her wiry hands into a gash in the severed arm she collected, producing a bloody radial bone with a sickening crack from muscle and flesh. In awed submission, the witch presented her trophy. Gerda had no control when the Snow Queen took the wet bone in her grasp and turned to the mirror embedded in the wall behind her throne. She tried not to think about where the arm came from, whose bone she held in her hands, like maybe this was all a dream she could wake from and none of this was real.

But even she knew how ridiculous such thoughts were. No matter the circumstances, she had become the Snow Queen; and with every ingredient brought to her, that fact grew stronger in permanence. The Snow Queen let Gerda stew in silence, the cool gust of her consciousness curling around her mind like a snake.

Taking the marbleized breath Lupa had obtained from her pocket, the Snow Queen pressed it against the mirror's surface, the marble becoming a jellied substance upon contact. As the mirror accepted the offering, she breathed in this new power. Strength shot down her muscles. The crystalized armor blanketing her skin minimized to even smaller scales like diamonds. Exhilaration pounded in her chest as the Snow Queen now raised the bone and blew a rush of arctic air down its surface until the collagen flaked away and the calcium turned to dust, the particles sent flying into the mirror like snow.

She quaked from the energy pulsing through her veins. Her breath clouded for one, two, three gasps before there was nothing, her lungs filtering air colder than what surrounded her.

"I must rest," the Snow Queen spoke, her voice laced with Gerda's. Panting, she removed the polar bear fur around her shoulders and draped it over the throne. Häxan bowed deeply as the Snow Queen made her leave.

While the Snow Queen's presence flickered, soaking in her newfound power, Gerda felt her own consciousness solidify, her wakefulness aroused, the eye of the hurricane.

*****

It wasn't long before Red noticed the way the Wolf's breathing rattled and quickened. Her own breath grew short in her chest like the oxygen was slowly leaking from the world around them. She blinked, unsure what was happening. The Wolf whimpered. Red rubbed behind her ears. Maybe they were both dying now, together, just as they'd lived for a time. Her vision darkened, her breath wheezed.

The Wolf slowly stumbled to her paws as Red lay down on her side in the pine needles. She wouldn't blame the Wolf if she ended things now, killed her, lived. But instead the Wolf settled beside her, sniffed her face, and rested her head on Red's hand. Red struggled to keep her eyes open. Coldness seeped into her toes and fingers. The Wolf's eyes drooped, her breathing faint against Red's arm.

Everything was still and then it all went dark – and she was free.

Chapter Twenty-Seven
The Mirror Breaker

Frost snuck them into the castle through hallways carved from glaciers, floors padded in sealskin and bear furs. He held the real pickaxe wrapped tightly in his grasp. When the traveling party had separated, each held an identical weapon in hand to make finding it harder to track. But as Frost could lead them to the mirror, he possessed the authentic one.

Despite his fresh handicap throwing him off balance, Jack insisted on coming as planned, and ultimately Kai didn't want to leave him alone in this condition. So Jack stumbled forward between Frost and Kai's hold, scraping up the rugs as he went. At least Frost's treatment held fast.

They soon entered a chamber encircled by stalactite icicles, a blue glow pulsing from the ice core. The ceiling arched above like a dome before shooting straight up in piercing spires that penetrated the open sky. Through an ocean of stars, the aurora borealis rippled in ribbons of light.

Kai's gaze swept across this centermost chamber while Frost held up a hand to stop them. He heard it, the shuffle of feet over ice. Hidden in the shadow of a floor-reaching icicle, Frost and Jack remained frozen in place, but Kai gave them one look of caution before he tightened the grip on his broadsword and lurked further into the room.

Häxan met his eyes immediately, alone, the mirror hanging on the wall behind a throne lined in furs. Jack's severed arm lay mutilated on the ground, missing the radial bone in his forearm. Häxan peeled her lips back over yellow teeth.

"You're too late," she crooned. "She's not here."

Stomach twisting, Kai knew she meant Gerda. He'd just missed her.

Then Häxan trembled, her electric blue eyes iced over as some piece of the Snow Queen took over her body. "But I am."

"*Nej*," Kai corrected bitterly. Whatever this was, however the Snow Queen was able to use Häxan as her messenger, this wasn't the real Snow Queen. Her soul was in Gerda now.

Nothing was stopping him from killing this witch, though.

Kai launched to attack.

While a snowy tornado blasted into Kai, Jack followed close behind Frost as they wove around the tusk-like icicles encircling the chamber. Gritting his teeth, he restrained himself from going in after his friend, especially when he caught sight of what remained of his right arm. Bile rose in his mouth. He could still feel it, a throbbing in his right hand, his forearm against his thigh. He kept reminding himself it wasn't attached but lying on the floor in a mess of blood.

Ever since Jack could actually focus on his face, he realized how wretched Frost looked after healing his amputation. Frost appeared more human. Which lately wasn't looking good on him. Dark bags under bloodshot eyes, his skin was losing the albino effect and began growing fleshy and sickly. His hair was darkening at the roots and yellowing at the tips. He looked like he hadn't eaten anything in centuries.

Frost didn't lend a hand – *ha, funny* – when he darted up the stairs that led to both throne and mirror. Jack took them slowly, trying to remain quiet and not lose his balance. Behind them, Kai was launched into the wall. Icicles chimed together like glass at the impact. He tried not to think about it.

Jack was panting when he reached the mirror where Frost stood, about to question why Frost was dillydallying with destroying the blasted thing. But he did a doubletake as his blood ran cold. There was someone *inside* the mirror, a woman with crisp jade eyes and auburn hair. Recognition hit him in the chest.

"That's Anne Christiansen," Jack gawked. "That's Anne bloody Christiansen."

"No," Frost said weakly, arms limp at his sides, staring. "That's Babette."

Jack frowned. "Who's Babette?"

"*TRAITOR!*" The cry split from both the woman in the mirror, her face contorted in ferocious accusation, and the witch in a snow storm behind them.

Frost and Jack whipped around to face Häxan. Kai was sprawled on the floor screaming bloody murder. The witch had crystalline eyes boring into Frost who stood frozen, caught between two accusers. On impulse, Jack snatched the pickaxe from Frost's hand, whirled around, and smashed it into the mirror. A bloodcurdling scream erupted as glass shattered, sprayed, and melted away.

Stumbling back from the impact, Jack lost his footing and fell down the stairs. Scarlet spots speckled his vision. He groaned in pain.

When his sight cleared, he found the witch standing over him, a long icicle spear formulating in her hand.

"*Blasted bloody—*"

Kai jumped up behind her and took a swing at her arm with his broadsword, the wound digging deep. When Häxan whipped around to retaliate, he shoved his blade into her breast. She gasped. Crystal eyes flickered as blood bubbled up into her mouth. She grinned with crimson stained teeth.

"Everything has gone according to plan," the witch said to Kai between gargling breaths, her voice still not her own, "except for you. You were the only unexpected thing. I chose someone else before you came and postponed—" She coughed, sank to her knees. "I had to reevaluate... send you back to Wonderland to finish..."

Häxan was fading quickly. Kai shook her, demanded, "Finish what?"

The ice melted from her electric blue eyes as she tilted her head back to face the aurora borealis, blood over her chin. "You were never in control."

Häxan died like that, suspended and in awe. Kai tore his blade away while Frost watched from beside the throne having retrieved the pickaxe.

"We should go," Frost said gravely.

Kai shook his head. "This isn't finished yet."

"We have to go back, recuperate, strategize."

"Gerda is here. The Snow Queen is *here*."

"And we should leave before she finds us standing over the corpse of her most loyal ally."

"I'm not afraid of her like you are."

"Look at this!" Frost snapped, throwing out his arms from the slain witch to the destroyed mirror. "Look around you! We did what we came here to do."

"No, we haven't," Kai argued.

"And him?" Frost pointed at Jack. "He needs to get to the infirmary now."

"I feel fine," Jack lied, though he hadn't moved from where he lay sprawled on the ground.

Stepping down from the throne's side, his free hand curled into a fist, Frost pressed, "We've defeated her immortality. We can kill her. That's enough."

Kai worked his jaw and dropped his eyes. "Something doesn't sit right."

Suddenly, Jack burst out in hysterical laughter, the sound echoing through the chamber.

Frost frowned down at him. "What's the matter with you?"

"Kai!" Jack proclaimed, hugging his stomach. "I get it, I get it. Alice was right. Blasted bloody *borogoves*, she was right!"

"What are you going on about?" Kai asked as he stooped over to help him up.

Jack waved his left arm. "One handed mirror breaker!"

Tears began running down his face in ridiculous hilarity. Kai put an arm securely around him and heaved him to his feet.

"*Ja*," Kai said lowly. "I have a feeling we need to have a talk with her again."

It was one thing for Alice to suggest using the ghosts to free the giants, or to reveal her discovery of the Snow Queen's plans. But this was more than just insight. This was prophesy.

Chapter Twenty-Eight
Lost and Found

Kai stood before Lovisa's tree, wishing he could feel the throb of her heartbeat on his neck as he did before, just so he knew she was alive. The tree was a pyre of smoldering timber. A dead stump. Frost had assured him that Lovisa had survived the phoenix, but she had yet to return.

When the trio had stumbled back into the alcoves, Kai led Jack straight for the infirmary so the medics would tend to his amputated arm. On the way, Jack told him in mock positivity, "It's a bloody good thing I'm left handed."

He was in shock.

Kai had intended to stay with his friend, as he was certain panic would soon hit when the shock wore off – but like a ghost in the night, Red appeared before them wide-eyed and alive. They froze, utter disbelief emitting from all sides. Then she punched Jack's good shoulder and reprimanded sharply, "What the devil did you do?!"

Jack pulled a shaky smile, his lip trembling, before he broke down. Red caught him and held him tight as he sobbed into her shoulder. Squeezing her arm affectionately, Kai left them alone, thinking about how Alice stood guard over Red's body to prevent burial. Somehow, Alice knew the whole time. Kai swallowed bitter horror at the thought of what could have happened if they'd proceeded with the funeral.

From the battlefield, the troops were spilling in. There were minimal casualties, though all of the trapped wolves had escaped; and save for reports of their retreat into the woods, no one had heard from the Pack. But the giants had been rescued and the ghosts were freed before Kai had the chance to thank them. There was some peace this night, even if only for those already dead.

No sign yet had come of Esmeralda or most who had gone on the quest for the pickaxe. One Lost Boy had made it back, the one with a shock of orange hair, and of course Frost had returned. Soon the rest should be filing in.

Kai gave a long breath, hands deep in his pockets. The mirror was gone. Häxan was dead. The Snow Queen was just short of being defeated. Yet those words kept ringing in his mind, the last messages from the Snow Queen before Häxan faded:

Everything has gone according to plan...

You were never in control.

She'd said it even after the mirror was broken.

Kai knew he should talk to Alice, see if she had anything more to tell him, but every time he saw her sent a jab down his spine. He'd failed at protecting her and understanding her was worse than untangling a new dialect in a foreign tongue. The Hatter could help, but not Kai. He'd only disappoint her again.

Closing his eyes, he tried to recall all the things Alice told him before and after she lost her mind.

Why us?

Mind, Heart, Breath, Bone, Blood.

And Häxan said that *he* was the unexpected, the one who caused the Snow Queen to reevaluate her plans and send them back to Wonderland to finish fulfilling something out. But what? Why was it important to send them to Wonderland first and not directly to the Snow Queen?

257

Back in Giant Country, Alice had been obsessed with timelines. They spent hours in Liesel's attic trying to work everything out, how long each of them spent in their respective realms, how often. Kai's journey was the shortest of them, and Alice's second visit to Wonderland overlapped the end of his time in the Snow Queen's realm. Perhaps the Snow Queen got preoccupied with Kai and with piecing the mirror back together that she couldn't control much of what happened to Alice in Wonderland. To finish the job, they had to go back to Wonderland. What was so significant about that adventure in relation to Alice?

Realization snuck to the forefront of his mind. The Mad Hatter's heart. Alice returned the heart to Remus, linked their pulses and pains, changing her chemistry. That's what set their course into motion, one mission turned to something bigger than they'd ever dreamed of.

The thread continued between each of them: Wendy's flight, Red's Wolf, Jack's golden blood. They came from the same world and journeyed to another where something permanently supernatural changed within them.

Except where did Kai fit in? He wasn't imbued with magic. If he was the unexpected piece, how was he linked? The Snow Queen had prepared everything up to the day she kidnapped Gerda and Kai followed after her. Already, the Snow Queen had taken Alice's mind, Red's breath, Jack's bone. All that was left was the heart and blood.

But they broke the mirror; it was destroyed. She couldn't finish her spell without it. Except…

Kai touched the scar on his jaw, recalled how he got it when he'd first shattered the mirror and changed everything.

Someone stepped out from the surrounding woods. One glance proved it was Lovisa, a fairy on her shoulder. She couldn't tear her eyes away from the dead tree between them.

"I wanted to see," she explained, her voice somehow steady even if strained, "before returning to the others."

Kai's stomach tightened at the sight of her. Ash charred patches of her skin and singed her hair. Boils crept up her inflamed neck. Severe burns marred her hands and feet, and under her cloak her shift was in tattered ruin.

Tinker Bell jingled gently, but Kai couldn't understand. He couldn't bring himself to move as if afraid a single breath would scatter Lovisa to the winds. Brown eyes shone bright with tears. She blinked, trails down her cheeks, and looked at him. She didn't ask if they won or how bad the casualties were. She didn't mention that her immortality was stripped or that the tree she'd bound her life to had died in her stead. Just this one look at him, standing in forlorn silence, before together they left the tree to return to camp.

Passing through the grove of enchanted trees, Kai asked, "Where is Wendy?"

"She ran with the others to distract Häxan," Lovisa informed, though he already knew that. "Has no one else returned?"

"Few," he confessed.

At that, Tinker Bell spoke a quick line of rings before she uncovered her wings and flew off. Kai assumed she wanted to see the Lost Boys who returned.

Beside him, Lovisa said softly, "I have a confession to make."

Kai waited for her to continue, ignored the urge to wrap his arm protectively around her. He didn't want to agitate her burns with a misplaced touch.

"When I met with the Snow Queen, she informed me of something I did not disclose with anyone else for fear it would change things for my people. Or for you." She paused, lingering on her unspoken words. "The Snow Queen told me that our heroes are the very people she has always protected us from; that they are the reason my people hide in this land."

With a frown, Kai asked, "What does that mean?"

Lovisa raised her head, looking beyond the trees and alcoves to the brilliant display above. Rose, violet, and teal shone across her dark face and she was radiant. "I have never been beyond the mountains, Kai. The Snow Queen used to protect us from the those who live south, those who would wish my people harm, those like you and your friends."

Kai knew she wasn't accusing him of wishing her people harm, but he was still struggling to grasp what she meant by this. "What are you saying?"

"All this time we thought you came from another world." Lovisa breathed in the cool air. "It turns out we are from the same world, just different pieces of it."

"But does that mean Wonderland, Neverland, the others… is it the same?"

She shrugged. "Who can say? Perhaps no one has yet found the right connection."

Incredulous, Kai followed her gaze to where the mountains stretched pale against the night and beyond. How long would it take before he reached Anders? Were the realms all just some intricate puzzle?

"It doesn't change anything," Kai said.

Lovisa tilted her head, examined his face. "Yes it does. My people would question their trust in you. The nomads would lose the heroic myth they see in you. And you, already you wonder how far you could run home."

Kai swallowed, hating to admit the truth to her words. But in the end, it didn't matter how far he ran. He wasn't sure Anders would feel like home anymore, much less if he left everything behind.

"The world is a big place. Much bigger than I once knew," Kai said lowly, turning to face Lovisa, realizing how close he stood beside her. Steadily, she looked between his eyes. His stomach twisted, breath hitched in his throat.

"And how does it change for you?" he asked.

"I have yet to decide," she confessed, her warmth brushing his chin. "But the danger beyond our borders does not seem so great to me now. I no longer feel a need to stay behind such walls."

Heart pounding in his chest, he remembered the moment they'd shared and left behind long ago, or not so long ago it seemed. But this time she stepped away and he felt strangely thankful for it. Kai was wary of what sometimes flared up in him when they were alone. He told himself he could control it, and somehow, he made it true.

Upon their return to camp, Lovisa was met with cheers of relief from the forest people, a call like wind whistled through reeds. Even the nomads took up their chant of *Här kommer solen!* in victorious greeting. Her cousin Latham soon rushed her to the infirmary to have her burns tended to. As the news of her sacrifice spread, the forest people began filtering away to see Lovisa's tree for themselves, intending to memorialize it while the remnants still stood.

Kai noticed that more had returned from the quest, the Lost Boys grouped around Pan as he bounced anxiously on his heels. One Lost Boy and Wendy had yet to appear.

Like a grave shadow, Esmeralda slipped into the camp, claw marks raked across her collarbone, scratches down her arms. Dirt covered her face, her elbows, her knees. Clopin gave a shout and ran for her, clasping her in an embrace upon impact.

"Are you alright? Are you hurt? Were you bit?" he asked frantically. Each question was answered with a headshake. He wrapped an arm around her shoulder as they walked, kissed her on the head. "Good, good."

It wasn't long before Clopin started yelling at people to get bandages and aid for his sister. At his raging, Red emerged expectantly from a lavvu. Esmeralda dropped her arms, mouth agape. Red met her half way and hugged her tightly.

"Did you kill her?" Red asked over her shoulder.

"Yes," Esmeralda gasped, pulling away, grasping her friend's shoulders as if to assure herself this was real. "You're alive. *C'est impossible.*"

"Did you kill her twice?" Red pressed urgently.

Esmeralda frowned. "*Non.*"

"Cut off her head?"

"Slash," she explained, "across her stomach and throat."

Biting her lip, Red sighed and locked eyes with Kai. The look she gave him was strange, but before he could ask what she meant by it, a skinny boy with mousy hair flew into the glen with a false pickaxe strapped to his back.

"Is she here?" Nibs asked promptly, running around in circles.

"Who?" asked Liesel who stood nearby trying to calm her fiancé.

"Wendy."

A sick feeling coiled in Kai's stomach.

"Weren't you supposed to be with her, mouse-brain?" Slightly asked, knocking the boy upside the head.

"She was right behind me," Nibs insisted. "And then she wasn't."

"You mean you lost her?" Pan questioned, hovering inches above the ground as if ready to take off at a moment's notice.

Nibs grimaced but nodded.

"Maybe she just fell behind," Curly suggested though his brow was laced in worry.

One of the Twins piped up, "Yeah, maybe she'll come in any second."

"Any second," the other added.

They waited eagerly, arms folded over their chests. Wind ruffled their mess of blond hair. When Wendy didn't show, the Twins shook their heads and admitted, "Never mind, she's lost."

Like missiles from the sky, the Crows landed in a shower of black feathers before they shifted to their squat human forms. They immediately scrambled for Kai.

Hands on his knees, Mr. Crow puffed, "We've been flying all night."

"We lost track of the girl," Mrs. Crow said in deep concern.

Before anyone could stop him, Pan launched himself into the sky, Tinker Bell streaming after him.

As the Lost Boys made to stumble in pursuit, Mrs. Crow waved a hand and implored, "Don't go alone!"

Hastily, they paired up upon takeoff, Slightly dragging Nibs by the wrist. Mrs. Crow gave Kai's hand one quick squeeze before she shifted form once again, cawed at her husband, and took flight. Mr. Crow grumbled to himself before grumpily following.

Anxious, Kai turned to Red. "Can you find her?"

She opened her mouth to respond, but then her face dropped and for a moment she seemed to flounder. Kai didn't understand until Red opened empty hands. "Kai, the Wolf is gone."

His heart sank to his stomach, and he lowered his eyes to hide his panic. If there was ever a time they needed the Wolf, this was it. But he wouldn't let Red mistake his disappointment.

"Is Kezia here?" he asked.

She shook her head. "She stayed behind with most of the children in the Enchanted Forest."

His mind working rapidly, he said. "But not all of them. Gather whoever you can: Isbjørn, the gypsies, anyone. We have to find her."

Red nodded and Kai left. He quickly convinced Gretel to help him find Wendy before together, with Hansel and Inga in tow, they ducked into the woods to find Wendy. Deep in his gut, Kai knew this wasn't over.

Chapter Twenty-Nine
The Pirate

Wendy screamed as something sharp latched into her heel and slammed her to the ground with a force that knocked the wind out of her. Her foot erupted in pain, bleeding profusely from a deep puncture in her heel. The sky flowed in lime and emerald hues. Breathing fast, she pulled up on her elbows to find the culprit standing across from her in the night wiping the blood off his iron hook with a handkerchief.

"Hello, Miss Darling," Captain Hook said, ease oiling his voice. "I'll take that shadow back now."

Her heart pounding rapid-fire in her chest, Wendy clutched the cool steel of the lantern and swung it into a rock. Glass shattered on impact. The Shadow vanished into the trees.

When Wendy cast a venomous glare at Hook, he merely shrugged at her actions. "We'll do this without Pan then."

Scrambling back, Wendy hastened to her feet and stumbled when she put pressure on her injured foot, but she managed to gain speed as she ran. She tried to clear her mind and fumble to a hover in order to escape by flying away. But the trees began to cave inwards around her, branches blocking the sky.

"This isn't Neverland, Miss Darling," Hook shouted after her. "The land isn't on your side here."

She was limping now, her foot on fire and slick with blood. She was losing momentum. Tears streamed trails over her dirty face. But she knew she couldn't run far enough, not like this, and if the trees were turning against her then she couldn't fly away. The only weapons she had was long knife in her belt and a decoy pickaxe in her hand. That wasn't much against a pirate who possessed at least two revolvers, a cutlass, and an iron hook on his person at all times.

Still, if she could delay as long as possible, maybe someone would notice she was gone and come looking for her. She had to try.

With a start, the snow caved underfoot and brought her deep to her knee. She landed chest first into the snowbank, used her palms to push herself back up, then tried again to run only to have her damaged foot sink into the snow. Wrenching her feet free, she heard Hook catching up to her from behind. The trees were thin and close together, so Wendy grasped their trunks to pull herself through the deep snow. Rocks loomed to provide easy shelter, but with her bloody tracks, there was nowhere she could hide that Hook could not find her.

She plunged through the frosted brittle underbrush where the ground sloped into a clearing covered in fresh snow. The aurora borealis cast strange lights across the surface.

"Look at me, Miss Darling," Hook cried out behind her as she fell into the clearing.

Wendy looked around, panting, her lungs heaving hot clouds in the night. There was nowhere to hide, nothing to block the sky. But she couldn't find the strength to fly.

Steeling herself, Wendy drew her knife, spun around and threw the blade directly for Hook's middle. He swiped the dagger away midair with his iron claw.

"LOOK AT ME!"

She froze, a brown curl in her face. She saw him. Blistered eyes ringed in purpled circles, deep frown lines splitting his face, oily hair shot through with grey over slumped shoulders, rum-stained teeth, the tremor in his veiny hand. Hook was an old man, haggard.

"Look at what Peter Pan made of me," he spat, arms wide in presentation. "I am the manifestation of your worst nightmares, Miss Darling. The worst any child could face."

Wendy leaned into her good foot, holding tight to the decoy pickaxe. "Peter didn't make you into anything. You did this yourself."

"I am Peter Pan!" Hook exclaimed with such venom that Wendy nearly shrank back. She knew there had been Pans before Peter, but that wasn't what Hook was talking about. He heaved in surging anger. "I am him! I am who he will become. Bitter reality. He took everything away from me! When I get my vengeance, watch him become the very same man."

"You have a daughter," Wendy shot in retaliation, "who loves you, who would do anything for you."

The shifting northern lights hit his sea blue eyes like tidal waves. "Aye. I had a wife, too. Five boys. Do you know what happened to them?"

Wendy swallowed. "He was your friend."

"Is that what you call it? I'd wager that makes it worse, then. Never knew many friends who'd lay siege on your own home in the dead of night, who'd spark an explosion on a sleeping house, who'd turn everyone you used to call *friend* against you. Like it's all a game."

"You've got it wrong," she argued.

Hook laughed without any trace of humor, shaking his head in pity. "You think you know him, Miss Darling? You don't think he would turn on you, too, if suddenly you chose anything but him and his delusions? If you decided to grow up? Everything's a game to him, and when things get too dangerous, too serious, watch him flee like a *child*. Don't be a fool, Miss Darling. At least I'm not cowardly enough to avoid calling him what he is."

With as much strength as she could muster, Wendy took a swing at him with the pickaxe. The blow nicked his arm. When she grasped the handle in both hands to swing again, Hook lurched back, drew his cutlass, and in three fell swipes managed to throw her weapon from her hold. Wendy limped away, ready to run again, but Hook shoved her backwards to fall flat on the snow. He tossed his cutlass to the ground, and the sight of him standing tall against the fiery night sky shot a tense pang of saltwater down her spine. Wendy screamed as Hook grabbed her injured foot and dragged her to him. Frantically, she tried to wrestle him away, kicking and flailing her arms. His iron claw loomed dangerously close to her throat.

"Are you scared, Miss Darling?" Hook leered, his breath sour against her face. "Of me? Of what I could do to you?"

Panic shook every nerve in her body as the point of his hook pressed against her chest over her pounding heart. She heard Alice's voice in her head, a whisper: *You're the heart.* And something washed over her, an understanding like the highest wind rushing against her face. She was going to die. This was the end. She thought of her family waiting for her to return home, her Lost Boys crowding around her in Hangman's Tree, her friends sharing stories in the Facility's underground tunnels, and Peter. Peter who may never forgive himself for all the mistakes he made or the people who got hurt along the way, who would move heaven and earth for those he cared about, the boy she would always believe in.

And somewhere in the reaches of her mind, Wendy thought of Jane and Hook. This man was so broken and filled with hatred that he didn't understand how much his daughter loved him despite his vengeful obsession – and it was killing her. Sorrow rattled for him and all he could have been. Perhaps long ago he wasn't so different from Peter. But she had faith that Peter would never become Hook.

"Do you feel the hate, Wendy Bird, boiling out of you?"

This moment was important. She'd stand before God soon. Wendy wanted the end of her story to mean something. Her eyes blurred and there was light everywhere.

"I cannot hate you," she said, her eyes spilling over the sides of her face. "I cannot hate you."

Something rustled in the trees beyond, stealing Hook's attention so Wendy could only see sky. An open magnificent sky calling her home. With a growl, Hook scraped her cheek with the curve of his claw and slid a glass vial over the iron, catching the clear liquid before tucking the vial into his jacket.

"Thank you kindly, Miss Darling," Hook said with lips curled back, raising his claw to drive into her chest.

A shrill cry descended from overhead in fervent chaos. Whacking Hook in the head and pulling at his iron claw, the black birds pecked, scraped, and batted their wings. As soon as the pirate scrambled off, Wendy rolled out from under him. She hustled to stand, forced to favor her injured foot. By the time she gained her balance, the Crows were still a feathery flurry of beaks and claws until Hook bolted into the forest, and the Crows didn't bother to follow.

Her heart settled though she swayed on her feet. The night seemed suddenly colder around her, brilliant chartreuse streaking the dark sky. The Crows turned back toward her, one resting on the floor while the other came to perch on Wendy's shoulder, prune her hair, then went to bother her husband.

A cool rush passed under her feet and Peter Pan's Shadow stretched out beneath her, stark against the snow. It waved a black hand. Wendy raised her hand in turn, choked on a sob. The Shadow shortened as if it leaned forward in concern. But when her shouted name reached her ears and the Crows cawed in response, the Shadow somersaulted across the snow and disappeared.

Peter flew from the trees and slammed her into a hug, lifting Wendy off her feet. She held tightly to him and cried into his shoulder. The Crows cawed somewhere in the distance, and Tinker Bell rested delicately on Wendy's elbow while she still held her arms around Peter. She felt him as he rose slowly away from this place where blood sprayed the snow and her death hung close. Letting him carry her away, Wendy refused to let go.

Chapter Thirty
The Key

Inga's disappointment when Gretel led them full circle back to camp was more than she could bear, her black eyes gleaming with tears, her pouting lip trembling. Kai reached out to her as she slumped away, but she shook off his touch.

"*Lämna mig ifred*," she snapped.

Fists clenched and head bowed, she ducked into a small lavvu across the glen. Kai suspected her reaction had less to do with the lack of adventure and more to do with losing a distraction from Bae's death.

"She wasn't lying," Hansel offered, his lucky piggy perched on his mussed blond head.

A knot formed in his throat. He wished he could offer Inga some comfort, but Hansel was right. She wanted to be left alone.

After thanking Gretel and Hansel for their help and bidding that they get some rest, Kai joined his friends in Jack's lavvu where Wendy was getting caught up on all that has happened since she'd left the previous morning. He thought she took the news surprisingly well, about Red's death, the battle, the broken mirror. The hardest to swallow was Jack's amputation. She rested a hand lightly on Jack's right shoulder where most of his arm was missing, the rest bandaged. She remained silent for a long time as she soaked it in.

With a sigh, she said, "Just don't get a hook, alright?"

Jack cracked a smile. "Deal."

But Kai felt most uneasy about it, a churning disturbance in the pit of his stomach. Red and Wendy soon departed to bring Alice in with them, leaving Kai to sit with Jack in silence. Jack shifted uncomfortably on the cot where the gypsy healer, Drina, ordered him bedridden.

"You can just come right out and say it," Jack said with a nervous laugh. "Never should've shaken hands with the devil. It was stupid. I was stupid."

Kai rubbed his hands together and lowered his eyes. He still had blood on his sleeves from trying to stem the bleeding.

"Say something, Kai."

Jaw clenched, he sighed through his nose.

"I know you're upset. Just say it."

Pale blue eyes shone like glass when he raised them again. "Why didn't you wait for me?"

The question stung Jack speechless. Distress waned his face as he lay barely able to breath.

"Only a moment," Kai went on, his voice strained to the point of breaking. "You knew I was coming. Why did you feel *that* alone?"

When he couldn't answer, Jack squeezed his eyes shut, tears leaking through and wetting his lashes. Kai sniffed, blinking back his own tears. Then he stood to press his lips against his best friend's brow while Jack struggled to hold in the sobs, and they left this moment there between them.

When the girls returned, Red took her place beside Jack, holding his left hand tight. Alice stood silently in the back of the lavvu, her thumb knuckle against her teeth. She almost looked normal like she'd regained some control since being with Remus. While Wendy explained what had happened to her while she'd been missing, about Jane and the Shadow,

272

Hook and the Crows, Alice kept tapping her knuckle lightly against her chin. Kai clenched his fists just thinking about how close Hook had come to taking Wendy's heart.

"At least he didn't get anything from you," Red said, her voice low like she wanted to slaughter the pirate herself.

But Wendy rubbed her arm sheepishly. "I think he did. I don't think he needed my actual heart."

"What then?"

Wendy looked at Kai, at Alice. The words rose to the surface.

"*When little girls cry,*" Wendy started.

"We all die," Kai finished.

Alice started humming softly to herself, eyes distant.

With a huff, Jack muttered, "I wish mine was metaphorical."

"So that means the Snow Queen's only got one left," Red voiced. "Mind, heart, breath, bone—"

"Me," Kai spoke. Shadows fell over every hollow of his face, the light leaking in from the small hole in the lavvu where the northern lights still flicked.

"But I don't get it," Jack said with an edge of bitterness. "What makes us so special?"

"We are different," Alice spoke, hushed, her finger twitching as she struggled for control, "and the same. From the same place, accepted the same escape, embraced who she made us. Youth, madness, m-magic…" She rubbed her nose with the heel of her hand.

Raising an eyebrow, Jack looked around at the others. "Did anyone else get that?"

Kai rested his elbows on his knees. "The Snow Queen needed five ingredients, five of us—"

Alice cut him off in a sudden stream, "Five, yes, five she needed – now six. Five to six. Needed the body before the blood, not the blood, now the blood. Six now, not five. Only wanted five..." She rocked back and forth, knuckles to her teeth, and muttered, "History always tries to repeat itself."

Kai let this sift in his mind before sharing his recent discoveries, "First was Wendy. The plan was only beginning, a gamble, so the Snow Queen got a Shadow to hide in your room. A relationship developed, and you let Pan take you to Neverland. You kept going back. Somewhere along the way, you learned to fly.

"Then came Alice, another longer process so she'd make Wonderland home, so she'd follow a rabbit in a waistcoat again when the time was right.

"Then a bounty hunter was sent on the hunt for a new target, while at some point a magic bean was planted at an orphanage near Wales. Red was targeted and chased into the Enchanted Forest, Jack led his friends up a beanstalk that reached Giant Country. After a few years, Red was bitten and transformed to the Wolf, and Jack had gold shooting through his very bones.

"Not long after Red, Wendy, and soon Jack were captured by the Facility, Gerda was kidnapped by the Snow Queen. I followed. Alice journeyed again to Wonderland by the Snow Queen's bidding – then I broke the mirror. The Snow Queen faltered, lost track of Alice who was launched back to England before plans could culminate. And when we were all together in the Facility, Anne Christiansen – the Snow Queen in Babette's body – broke us out and sent us back to Wonderland. Why? So Alice could put the Hatter's heart back, link her heart with his. Everything since has brought us closer and closer to the Snow Queen."

"My flight, Red's Wolf, Jack's gold, Alice's heart," Wendy muttered to herself. "We're all some kind of magical concoction?"

"Except for you, Kai," Red observed with a frown. "Why you?"

Kai shrugged haplessly. "She never wanted me. I was unexpected. She was after Gerda the whole time, then I showed up and messed up the timeline. Now," he spread out open hands, "I'm not sure why she wants me."

"Doesn't matter, anyway," Jack said, shaking his head. "We smashed the mirror. Ole Hook just didn't get the memo in time. She can't use her ingredients now; the spell is finished."

Kai noticed how Alice stared at him, her cornflower blue eyes glittering in the dim light. He didn't know how long, but she knew he was lying. She knew what would happen and why. And somehow, she still had the good sense not to voice it – which confirmed all of his suspicions.

"There's still a war," Kai said at last, turning back to the others. "We should rest. Dawn will bring the beginning to the end of all this."

"History always tries to repeat itself," Alice said again in a whisper that could've been a scream.

Chapter Thirty-One
The Calm

Alone, Jack prompted Red to curl up in the cot next to him, his good arm – his only arm – growing numb under her shoulders. He didn't mind the sensation. She was here, they were alive, and they were together. He tried not to think about the strange tingling in his right forearm which he no longer had, how when he thought about holding Red's hand splayed on his chest, nothing happened.

"I think your hair is lighter," Jack said, his cheek against her head.

She tilted her head to look up at him. "What do you mean? And it's dark, so how would you know?"

Jack shrugged. "I just know. I think your eyes are brighter, too."

"You're ridiculous."

"Completely. Absolutely. But I am right. There's more amber or something. And your hair is more brown than black now. I'm serious!"

"I'll pretend I believe you."

"I'm just saying."

She kept picking at a wrinkle in his shirt, a flick of the fingernail. He wore fresh clothes now, but he could still picture the blood soaking his ribs, the dull absence.

"Are we going to talk about it?" Red asked with an unusual steadiness given the circumstances.

Jack swallowed the tightness in his throat. Thinking back on that moment was like focusing on a single car in a speeding train: he couldn't make sense of anything but the flash of color and the wind hitting his face as it swept by. "I thought you were dead."

"I know," she said softly. "But I can't be someone you stake your life on. You can't become suicidal if I'm gone – I won't have that kind of expectation. I'm not built to be your savior."

Jack's finger moved in little circles on her shoulder. "I know. And I can't, I won't... It's not like that."

She raised an eyebrow, glanced pointedly at his amputation. He rolled his eyes to the back of his head.

"Would you stop looking at my arm?"

"Or lack thereof."

"Point taken. But look, it wasn't you. I didn't, I wouldn't ever let anyone go through what I did with Bleddyn wondering if I could've stopped him. I was racked with so much grief, not just for you, but for my parents and Jill. I couldn't lose anyone else, so when that witch promised me not to hurt the others... And I know it's stupid, thinking back on it, I was reckless and impulsive, and if I had just waited a few more minutes, then... I don't know what would've changed, but maybe I'd still have two arms."

Red sighed, her breath against his collarbone. "I understand. When I found Lupa, she threatened the four of you, knew exactly where you were."

"That's right, you're the one who willingly swallowed poison."

"I knew I could have survived. You didn't."

"Fair enough," Jack admitted.

"Just," she stretched the thought, like she wasn't sure what to ask of him, "don't do it again."

277

"Which part? Making deals with witches or getting a limb amputated? Or doing stupid impulsive stuff?"

"I don't think anything could keep you from doing stupid impulsive stuff," Red said, chewing on a smile. "At least you're left handed."

"That's what I said!" Jack laughed, but it didn't stick like it should've. He rubbed a piece of her hair between his fingers. "But I want you to know this, too. I am staking my life on you, Rubes. It's staked, nail and hammer. There's no getting around it."

"No unrealistic expectations?" she mumbled into his chest.

"Just the usual ones," he teased, but she met his eyes and only the truth remained. "I just want you. It's always been you."

Gently, Red kissed him, pressed her forehead to his. Blood shot down his arm in tiny pinpricks. They stayed like that, close and steady. He could feel her pulse on his skin.

In a whisper, he confessed, "I'm going out there."

He knew he didn't need to explain. The impending battle had been hanging over their heads for years, even when they hadn't realized. He refused to let this new handicap get the better of him. He needed to go. He couldn't wait behind.

Red accepted this calmly. "Me too."

It was the same, Red without the Wolf, Jack without his arm. But their losses brought them here. Nothing could stop them.

The Lost Boys listened in rapt attention as Wendy explained what all had happened to her, from discovering she might fly on her own, to Jane offering her the Shadow, to Hook chasing after her. In the end, much of them lay in various states of sleep. Nibs drooled on the floor while the Twins leaned into each other, near to falling over. Curly lay flat on his back, his bear mask over his snoring face, his foot precariously close to the fire. When his shoe began to smoke, Tootles used a stick to push his foot aside. Slightly tried to balance a line of rocks along Nibs's sleeping form.

Wendy remained quiet for a long time, noticing that Peter was still missing his Shadow. She thought it best not to bring it up until they could talk in private. He dug his fist into his palm like he was processing all the information she'd given him. From his neck hung the silver thimble, and she watched as it swung, black and orange in the firelight.

"I think," Wendy started slowly, "after the battle tomorrow, we should form a peace agreement with the pirates again."

Slightly snorted a laugh, paused in his rock placements. "After everything they've done?"

"We've done much to each other. Someone had to take the first step."

"But does it have to be us?"

"It doesn't *have* to be us," Wendy answered, looking at Peter as she said so. "But it can be."

Slightly nudged Tootled with his elbow. "I hate when she uses English as if it means different things."

The Twins were awake now, though Curly and Nibs remained fast asleep. Their eyes narrowed as they tried to catch up with what Wendy was proposing.

"We could build a relationship with the pirates," she continued.

One of the Twins wrinkled his nose. "Ew."

Wendy gave him a look. "An alliance. We could even construct something as before, where Lost Boys would have the opportunity to grow up if they wanted, and we wouldn't stalk each other in the jungle any longer."

"But what about our adventures?" the other Twin questioned.

"Yeah," Slightly agreed. "Where's the fun in treasure hunting if we're not rubbing the pirates' noses in it?"

"The adventures won't stop," Wendy explained. "The Island provides enough dangers. Treasure hunts could still be competitive, maybe even a joint expedition as we've done with the Panther Tribe. We don't have to be at war to have fun."

Looking up from his hands, Peter met her eyes. "Hook will never agree to this."

Wendy sighed, admitted, "No. But he isn't our only option. Not all pirates are like Hook or look up to him."

As if he could read her mind, Peter added, "Jane won't rebel against her father."

"Her father might not last much longer."

"Neither could Jane," he said, casting a sheepish look around their small campfire. "Neither could any of us."

"And if we all survive? What happens then?"

"I don't know!"

The severity of his tone startled Curly awake for a moment before he collapsed into snores once again. Wendy didn't budge.

"I know the hatred between you and Hook has become so deeply ingrained it's suffocating. But that doesn't mean it's too late to do something about it."

"I can't forget what he's done," Peter choked. "I can't forget what I've done."

"I'm not asking you to forget," Wendy said, letting the rest hang unspoken in the air.

From the flickering pale night behind them, a grim voice said, "You will need a volunteer."

Peter turned and Wendy raised her head as Tiger Lily approached, the light gleaming amber across her features. She remained standing just beside where Curly lay.

Cocking his head, Peter asked, "For what?"

"This plan, if you can call it that," Tiger Lily responded with a huff. She swept a narrowed glance over them. "You will need a volunteer, an ambassador, someone sent to the pirates as a sign of good will. He would live with them, grow up with them, inspire the honest relationship you propose."

"I wouldn't have thought you'd be so keen as to draw up good relations with the pirates, Chief," Peter said, a hand on his knee.

Tiger Lily's expression remained rigid. "Tomorrow is the time for vengeance and war. But it means nothing if nothing changes." She paused a moment. "You will need a captain to rally behind, if not Jane then someone else. And the Hook must die."

Clenching his jaw, Peter looked to Wendy.

"You know I speak truth," Tiger Lily said gravely. "As long as the Hook is alive, there will be no peace in Neverland."

In the pit of her heart, Wendy knew she was right. So long as Hook was in the picture, he carried a threatening influence that would drive after everyone she loved, even if he eventually tore himself apart doing it. But how many people would go down with him? Did death have to be the answer?

Wendy supposed they could keep him imprisoned, but incarceration didn't always stop influence. If somehow Hook lost respect from his fellow pirates – but that would leave Jane, and Wendy knew she would die before she turned on her father. If he died tomorrow, Wendy knew Jane would case a Hook-sized shadow over her heart and never forgive herself for failing him. Beyond this, Wendy couldn't guess the breadth of Jane's reaction.

One thing was certain, though. Tiger Lily was out for revenge, or *justice* in her own terms, for her own father and all the other tribesmen who died under the iron claw. If any peace between Neverland's inhabitants was to be obtained as far as the Panther Tribe was concerned, Hook would have to die one way or another: battlefield, execution, assassination. The pirates would never agree to peaceful terms if Hook died of execution or assassination. If Hook was going to die, he had to perish on the battlefield.

"We could banish him," Wendy suggested in a low murmur.

Tiger Lily stared at her aghast. "And how would you banish him so he could never find his way back again? The sea has its own way of bringing people to Neverland."

"Perhaps. But it's worth a try. Banishment to the Mainland should he not die on the battlefield tomorrow."

"Jane would go after him," Slightly said, fidgeting with his hands. He seemed uncomfortable talking about Jane like this, and Wendy was reminded that Jane had been a Lost Girl to them for a time. She'd betrayed all of them.

Wendy sighed. "Then we would have to throw peace agreements at another captain."

"And who would be your ambassador?" Tiger Lily asked.

The Twins had already pretended to be asleep the moment Tiger Lily arrived, and Tootles played silently with a stick in the firepit. Slightly wouldn't meet anyone's eyes. Before anyone could speak, Peter said, "We will discuss it after the battle is over. We don't even know what will happen tomorrow."

Wendy nodded and Tiger Lily gave a tight grunt before returning to where her tribesmen slept. The Lost Boys quickly drifted off one by one until it was just she and Peter around a dead fire. She sidled closer, slipped her hand in his, placed them on her lap, and leaned her head against his shoulder. They remained like that, still and close, while the violet lights in the inky sky faded to jade and indigo brushstrokes.

"I love you," Peter whispered.

They'd said it a thousand times, each a renewed promise. They had no rings or formal arrangement. But they'd been together so long, through all their loyalty, friendship, and devotion, that they were as vital to each other as every breath they had yet to breathe.

Wendy nuzzled closer, watched the aurora borealis finally fade into darkness. "I love you, too."

Chapter Thirty-Two
The Storm

Kai spent the whole night pounding hammer to metal across a makeshift anvil, the glow of a furnace battering his face, his hands stained black and nails smoky. He talked as he worked with Liesel, Frost, and Lovisa, first about his creation's design, then about the details of the day's battle plans. But his most constant companion was Alice who was as sleepless as a moon sharing the sky with sun and stars alike.

As the armies assembled to take leave of the alcoves, Kai took his late-night work to find Jack and the others. They all stood together, a final moment before they were to part ways.

Jack turned from Alice, a smile on his face from some joke they'd exchanged, and his brow knit upon seeing Kai approach. "What's this?"

He held up the length of leather and steel. "For you, *bror*."

Jack grasped it in one fist, a wry expression on his face. "Thanks, I've always wanted one of these."

"He's giving you a hand," Alice sang with a grin.

"Very funny," Jack chided, making a face. "But really, what is it?"

Shaking his head in amusement, Kai helped him attach the prosthetic, securing the leather fittings to strap around Jack's shoulder and chest, tugging the sleeve over his padded bicep. Jack stared at the gift, wide-eyed.

"Did you make this?" he asked.

Kai shrugged. "Liesel helped design it. Granted, it was all I could do in such a short time. But it'll keep you balanced and provide a good swing."

Jack tested the metallic arm, proving it secure and mobile enough. He looked at his friend, glossy eyed. "I don't know what to say."

"*Thank you* usually does the trick," Wendy quipped. Jack pushed her away playfully.

"Thank you," Jack said, clasping his arm around Kai in a firm embrace. Kai clapped his shoulder.

An air of solemn foreboding weighed over them suddenly, the five standing together, unfathomable hope, fear, and love passing unspoken between them. Wendy's brown eyes shown bright with tears. Red clutched firmly to Jack's hand. A knot tightened in Kai's throat, but before anyone could say anything, Alice threw her arms open to grasp Kai on one side and Wendy on the other, pulling the five of them into a group hug where her arms could touch them all. She said nothing, but her embrace was strong, and her chin quavered as tears beaded her eyelashes.

Closing his eyes, Kai held his friends close. "I love you all," he muttered.

He tried to convince himself that this would not be the end of them here together. But he held his friends closer all the same.

"*Gubben*," barked the familiar tart voice behind him.

Kai gave final farewell to his friends before they parted ways and he turned to where Inga stood. Wisps of feathery black hair blew over her round face. She squinted up at him with her lip pouted, like she was ready to tell him off. Resting on his knee to meet her in the eye, Kai waited for her to continue.

"You are leaving again?" she asked, though she already knew the answer.

"*Ja*," Kai responded.

She gave a low grunt, shifted her weight from foot to foot, then produced something from her pocket and pushed it into his hands. "Here."

Kai examined the item, a knife, the very one Inga used to threaten him with when he was in her captivity. Its reindeer antler handle was adorned with traditional scrimshaw patterns, its sheath a soft russet leather. He looked back up at Inga whose gaze rested on the knife. Holding it up, he returned the short blade to her.

"*Tusen tack*," he said gently. "But you may need this more than I do. I'm counting on you, remember?"

Inga took back the knife in her gloved hands, staring down at it. "Will you come back?" she asked in a way to hide the strained edges of her voice.

Kai sighed, offering a small smile, and rubbed her shoulder. "I will do my best to return, *Lilla Rånareflickan*. I promise."

She nodded a smiled wryly. "Don't drag your feet this time."

He ruffled her hair which prompted a laugh. She made a face at him, but then pulled something else from her pocket. This time she held an ovular disk in her palm carved from a reindeer antler into the impression of an angel.

"For protection," she explained. "From one of the times Bae shed his antlers. I have another."

A warmth filled his chest. This time, Kai did accept the gift, stowing it safely in the pouch around his neck where he recently kept Gerda's engagement ring. He squeezed Inga's hand affectionately.

"I miss him, too," Kai said.

Her lip quavered, her black eyes welled. Suddenly, she threw her arms tightly around Kai's neck. He barely had time to hug her back before she pulled away and trotted back into camp, her face blotched as she struggled not to cry.

The sky toiled into a grey dawn and an early snow when Kai joined the ranks that filed out before the frozen lake. In this moment he wished for the comfort of Bae's soothing voice humming in his mind. He breathed the frigid air and allowed the memory of his friend to roll over him before he released it to be grieved another time.

Side by side, layer upon layer, their allies readied for battle. Wonderland cards stood at the front lines peppered with forest people. Behind them stood the belowlanders and giants, then the battalion of the Enchanted Forest. Lastly stood the Panther Tribe, the Lost Boys who'd serve to take the wounded from the battlefield, and a mix of nomads and forest people to defend the rear should they be attacked from behind again. Alice waited back in the infirmary with Aurore and the gypsies as well as much of the nomadic robbers.

Kai stood at the edge of the frozen lake with the leaders who waited for his command before they would return to their troops. From this distance, it was difficult to tell whether the haze at the Snow Queen's castle was just mist or a line of silent soldiers. Mounds lay scattered throughout the icy field from where fallen giants had frozen over during the night.

"Do you see anything?" asked Tweedle-Dee as he narrowed his eyes at the grim stillness before them.

"They're out there," Harry said with a dangerous smile, bouncing on the balls of his feet. "I can fell it."

"Don't be so dramatic," Cat grumbled sharply.

Red stepped forward, the soft wind catching strands of hair from her braid. Her eyes twitched. "They're coming."

"Have your wolfie senses come back to you, dearie?" Clopin chided. Despite the fact that his people were taking charge of protecting the infirmary, Clopin had chosen to join the fight along with Jim, both men taking up ranks with the belowlanders.

In response, Red pointed toward the ice castle where its crystalline wall seemed to part like rolling tides, dispensing indistinguishable shadows from its maw. Kai felt his stomach harden.

"So there," pronounced the Mad Hatter as if oblivious to the creeping sense of doom that had just fallen over them, "what's the call?"

"The call?" Wendy asked.

The Hatter shrugged. "We can't bloody well go screaming *For Wonderland! Neverland!* or whatever other blasted thing that comes to mind. It'd be chaos. We need unison." He turned to Kai, darkness sliced over one eye while the other sparked blue. The look reminded him of Alice. "We *all* need something to fight for. What'll it be?"

The weight of breath filled his lungs as Kai let the question sink in. After everything they'd been through, all the years of running and chasing, bracing against the darkness which threatened to consume them, what was it all for? What brought them all here from the farthest reaches of the realms to stand together and fight as one? The answer seemed overwhelming to him. But then Gerda's voice filled his mind, when they sat on the mountainside to watch the sunset.

Do you remember it, Kai? she'd said as the sky dusted her face in rose and gold.

And he knew with every longing heartbeat in his chest what the answer was.

"For home," Kai voiced at last. "Wherever home may be."

Ingénu nodded in agreement. "For home."

"For home," Peter Pan cheered with a resounding crow before he plunged over the armies to return to the Lost Boys.

"For home," Clopin shook his head with a scowl. "How very sentimental."

The statement passed from one mouth to the next, growing resolute with each repetition. As the leaders fell back to their troops, Wendy squeezed Kai's hand before disappearing after Peter. Jack and Red, instead of going back with the belowlanders, stayed to flank Kai on either side at the front lines with the Mad Hatter and the White Queen, readying the Wonderland battalion. Kai could see the enemy now as the mist faded, the silent figures of frozen complexion, the bestial creatures anxious in their restraint, the armored feet clanking against ice. And leading them all stood the dark silhouette of a lone woman – he couldn't yet tell who it was.

He gripped his naked sword in both hands, muttering a final prayer, *"Fräls oss ifrån ondo."*

The signal was passed. The White Queen gave sharp command to her troops, hefting an impressive double-bladed spear into the air. Together, the first ranks marched onto the battlefield just as hell broke loose before them.

Chapter Thirty-Three
The Bleeding Hearts

The figure who stood between the armies gave such a bloodcurdling scream that her head arched back in a gruesome crescent. Upon her cry, a lithe creature twisted up around her body and shot a jagged bolt of electricity into the air, the indigo light revealing the woman as the Queen of Hearts. Behind her rose a thin flock of jubjub birds taking flight, careening forward past the surging soldiers beneath them. They hit the Wonderland army with talons first, seeing the archers and spears too late in their decent.

"Archers!" the lizard Bill shouted, hefting his crossbow skyward. Red drew and aimed before the word hardly left his mouth, bringing down a carnivorous bird with an arrow through its open beak.

Celeste called with the might of a warrior queen, "Spades!"

A wave of spears shot into the air, diamond tips gleaming like stars. The jubjub birds screamed, some flapping back in retreat, but for most it was too late. Celeste tore down a bird with her double-bladed spear, tossing the body aside to skid across the ice where other soldiers dispatched the injured creature before it could snap up.

The few jubjub stragglers that managed to pull back in time flew to the enemy ranks in swift retreat. Other shadows closed the distance between the steadily marching armies. Celeste called again for spades, and those with spears shuffled to the front lines with shafts at the ready. The bandersnatch shot at them without hesitation, many skewering themselves on the extended diamond spades. But some beasts twisted through the barrier of warriors and tried to take them out from behind.

Kai and Jack helped the Brothers Tweedle bring down the bandersnatch that breached the front lines. Jack ripped through a snarling batch with his metal arm and short sword. Red quickly had his back before a set of sharp jaws could clamp around his leg, stopping the bandersnatch with an arrow in its flank. Jack flashed a smile at her, and she felt one tug at her mouth before together they became a whirlwind, him passing stray arrows to her, she keeping the beasts off the soldiers' backs.

Then the armies slammed into each other, losing formation and falling into chaos.

Boojum was released upon collision, the Dormouse and Dinah on his back giving shrill whoops as the snark hopped, glided, and landed on unsuspecting bandersnatch, knocking over cards like dominos with a sweep of his tail. For the most part, his objective was to go after the remaining jubjub birds that returned to battle.

Tweedle-Dum sidestepped his opponent, sweeping his blade in a fine arc before forcing his opponent to the ground. Beside him, his brother Tweedle-Dee danced around him, calling, "Time to bounce, brother."

On cue, Dum ducked with his arms spread out in a platform while Dee somersaulted into a stand on his shoulders. From the brief vantage point, Dee did something of a pirouette, flinging tiny poisoned blades in every direction before he leaped off again. Dum had done the same at a lesser arc below by flinging out his wrists and elbows. All around them cards collapsed, either dead or paralyzed.

The Brothers Tweedle worked from the leftmost flank to drive the enemy into itself, eventually allowing the Wonderland armies to surround them. But the fight was dense with hardly any way to look up or behind. In the haze of bodies, the Wonderland army seemed to gain ground on the leftmost flank which would mean a swift advantage.

Then came the stampede. A swipe of something massive took out three soldiers beside Dum. He blinked with hardly enough time to register what was happening until Dee cried, "Watch out!" and shoved him aside as a giant foot jammed into the spot where he'd stood. They were now in the midst of a different chaos, one that roared out from behind them in a sudden ambush that stole away their advantage. The remaining enemy giants had charged out from the forest, bolting for the battle. The Brothers Tweedle found themselves in the midst of it, the massive bodies like unstoppable boulders, each step threatening to crush them.

"RUN!" Dum shouted in desperate command to their soldiers as he and those around him wove between the giants' deadly footfalls.

They had no choice but to run headlong into the thick of battle, the soldiers weaving among the enemy to better hide from an overarching sweep of a giant's spiked club. Dee had to jerk Dum away from another such blow.

"Watch yourself," he said with a laugh.

Dum grinned, ready with another jab when Dee was suddenly launched backward through the air beyond enemy lines by a giant's sweeping weapon. Dum's heart dropped and he plunged in after his brother. Dee lay sprawled at an awkward angle, breath wheezing in short spurts, no doubt from broken ribs. Dum reached him, held out a hand to help him up, but Dee's arms seemed frozen stiff before his chest. When Dum made to get him up, they were immediately surrounded by cards while one tried to get a hold of Dee's sword.

Dum leapt into action, dispatching the card who tried to get Dee's sword with a slice at her arm then into her skull. He threw back the pursuing cards enough to yank his brother to his feet, earning a kick in the knee that caused his legs to buckle and him to cry out. He swung out another handful of poisonous blades every which way, clearing a path to drag his brother through with a painful limp. As Dee's injuries prevented him from helping, Dum secured his brother's grasp around the hilt of his sword, hoisted Dee over his shoulders, and legged it as fast as he could.

A stray spike shot past his ribs and he felt the sting of blood pulse from the wound. He stumbled along, risking the open chaos of running giants instead of the crowded world of swords and bodies. The ice and snow kicked up a kind of dust around them from the giants' footsteps. Dum's vision tunneled, blackened. They burst from the battlefield and reached the line of second ranks before his knees slacked. Dum collapsed, dropped his brother, and all went dark.

The Hatter was in full manic swing, a deadly whirlwind who dared to fight without care for his own self-preservation, making him all the more dangerous. He took risks without second thought. There were no boundaries. He overwhelmed his aggressors so much that he had to give chase to any who lay within sight.

The tick of a sparking tongue pricked his ears, and he yanked an enemy card's shield – arm and all – up before him just in time to deflect the surge of lightning shooting his way, the electrical stream bouncing off to launch straight into a crowd of enemy cards. The lightning sputtered off with hardly any damage to anything except the dislocated arm attached to the shield Remus held.

Tossing aside the hapless soldier, Remus trained his focus on the young jabberwock squawking at the surrounding chaos, its tail wrapped around the leg of his devilish big sister, the bloody Red Queen. Remus's eyes shone, a calm washed over him. Something drew him forward like a magnetic force. He hadn't faced her like this since the battle to rescue Alice, when Helena had torn his heart from his chest. He wondered how she felt about his little prophesy coming true.

Heads are rolling, highness. Nothing can save you now...

But the roar of giants ambushing their leftmost flank drew his attention. Adrenaline surged through his veins. The excitement was similar to facing a full-grown jabberwock. A challenge. He ran toward it with a mad smile, knowing he would never see his sister again. Of all the thoughts and emotions toiling around in his head, remorse was not one of them.

From behind, the second ranks joined the battlefield to take on the ambushing forces with the expertise of giant killers.

Celeste lost sight of the Brothers Tweedle long before the maneuver to lapse the enemy around the western flank, her brother also disappearing among the chaos. She noticed the giants' ambush but was comforted by the swift interjection of the second rank. Raising her voice in sturdy command, she ordered her forces to move east in order to give the belowlanders and giants room to overtake the ambushing adversary. Her double-bladed spear made for a steady signal to her troops and a lethal weapon to her enemies.

The surging violence tunneled around Celeste, the ozone tightening in her ears for a moment before she cried out warning to her soldiers and a blast of blue electricity flashed toward her like a ricochet bullet. She unleashed a spell to deflect the blow, white light parting the waters of her army in a momentary transparent shield until the lightning fizzled out. As the light faded, her vision focused on the figure sparking with scarlet and ebony. The Red Queen's eyes were black pools in her skull, bloodshot and raging. The baby jabberwock rested coiled around her shoulders.

"You!" the Red Queen spat venomously, stalking forward.

Celeste blinked, startled, because for the first time she did not recognize her own sister before her. She snapped out of this realization quickly as Helena unleashed ropes of ebony lightning careening towards her. Celeste met it with a braid of silver light, the collision exploding in a shower of sparks. The surging bursts of magic drove the surrounding battle away to give the two queens a wide berth. Celeste noticed how Helena was closing the distance between them, using the magic explosions as a distraction.

She broke the drive behind her spell enough to meet Helena's drawn battle axe with her double spaded spear. They stood at a struggling impasse, Celeste's shaft pushed against Helena's handle, the axe head precariously close to her neck. Face contorted with unfathomable rage, Helena bellowed deep within her throat. Celeste felt her arms shake as the axe drew closer, felt the blade press against her throat. Energy charged white hot through her limbs as she fought, Helena too distracted with the way her blade pierced her sister's skin to notice until Celeste burst away in a shock of light. Blood ran in crimson threads down her throat. Helena charged once again.

Their weapons sang of diamond and steel. The jabberwock slithered in around their feet, hissing at the noise. Celeste danced elegantly around the creature and her sister's continuous swing for her neck. Helena was the crazed executioner, and Celeste was already the ghost.

In one harsh maneuver, Helena's axe came down hard across the spear shaft, splitting the weapon in two. Each sister held one half of the spade, and Celeste knew deep in her core how this ended if she did nothing to stop it. Having won the upper hand, Helena dove for the kill with both weapons raised while Celeste spun into Helena instead of away, causing the blow to be too wide for such close quarters, and immediately Celeste drew upon the depths of her power to thrust her hand into Helena's chest. Both gasped, a moment of astonished suffocation before Celeste ripped out her sister's heart and jumped away with it pounding in her fist.

"*Stop!*" Celeste cried in utter desperation.

Helena stumbled, dazed. She didn't even look at the heart like a hostage in Celeste's hand, the spade at the ready. A glaze seemed to cast over her dark eyes.

But after everything, the bitterness, the vengeance, the betrayal, the blood; after Nix's execution and Helena's secreted stillbirth across Underland borders, after the overthrow and murder of their father the King of Diamonds, after the revolutionary rebellion and the hunt like a bloodhound for Celeste, after the heart ripping and imprisonment of their own brother Remus, after Alice was stripped of her sanity – and now this, the culmination of the destruction they'd caused. All of this poison between them and Celeste couldn't finish it.

"Stop this," she said, reaching for a shadow of the sister she grew up with. "Please—"

But the rage returned, hollow and destructive. With a scream, Helena charged like a bull without restraint, swinging the axe out to barely swipe the skin of Celeste's neck before hefting it again for an overhead swing, the spade held before her like a lance. Celeste recoiled, bracing herself to block the inevitable blow. Just as suddenly, everything froze before her, Helena a hand's breadth away from her face, eyes widened and face pale as a sheet. Celeste held her breath, feeling the blood drip down her throat, unsure if she'd yet been fatally wounded for the numb adrenaline coursing through her body. Helena made a choking gasp and there was blood in her mouth.

Celeste spared a glance down to where Helena had pierced her own heart with the broken spade, the convulsing thing bleeding in her hand. Panic seized her chest. She caught Helena by the arm as she leaned forward, but Helena shoved her away, stumbled back, fell on her knees. Scarlet lines dribbled down her chin like jam when she stuffed her mouth with raspberry tarts as a child, like paint dripping from ivory rose petals, like ribbons in her deep brown hair.

Then the axe fell from the sky where it had vanished a moment before. Celeste gasped, holding her stomach.

Overhead, the Cheshire Cat flickered with a stretched smile and sang, "Off with her head."

Chapter Thirty-Four
The Closing Dark

Jack knew the moment the giants entered the battlefield, felt the vibrations through the ice underfoot. He exchanged a look with Red – they'd been busy taking out the bandersnatch that were after the spearmen and archers. Blood sprayed across her face, making her look fierce in the pale morning light. Something passed between them as he realized that very few of the White Queen's cards would know how to take on a giant, and he couldn't remember for the life of him when the belowlanders and giants were supposed to engage, nor how long it would take them to reach the attack. Red nodded to him as if he'd spoken his concerns aloud.

"Go," she urged.

"Don't die again," Jack said as he plunged through the western flank toward the ambushing giants.

He arrived at utter chaos, ally and enemy cards alike running around like jackrabbits, leading some giants into a scrambled chase while others tried to plow into the thick pool of battle. The giants seemed to have forgotten whatever alliance they stood for, as they went after anyone under seven feet tall regardless of their red or white colors.

Fighting against the giants with any ounce of success was the strangest sight Jack had ever laid eyes on: the Mad Hatter somehow straddled a jubjub bird and was riding it around like a deranged ostrich wrangler, pulling the bird into giants to trip them over each other, or else he attacked the giants' heads if the jubjub took flight. Occasionally, the snark Boojum would join the mix, snarling at his towering aggressors as if he was angry that something was bigger than he was. But the Dormouse urged him into the battle again to knock out more bandersnatch and jubjub birds.

Jack took the scene in for a moment before he broke free, stepping easily into the movements he'd adapted as the Giant Slayer. He ran. And as he ran, he shouted instructions to the scrambling cards, telling them to bolt and go for the ankles and knees since the giant's armor prohibited much agility. He fell into his old habits quickly, stepped nimbly aside from a massive foot without even needing to look.

As the giantess bent her leg in poise for attack, Jack sped behind her and sprang He planted a foot against the meat of her calf, leaped up to catch the belt around her chainmail, made to scramble up her back – then realized in the instant that he fell backwards that he no longer had a right arm.

He landed in a clumsy roll, shoulders and ribs and knees. Pain split down his right elbow as the prosthetic shifted off at an uncomfortable angle. When he finally skidded to a halt on the ice, Jack groaned, forcing himself to sit up. He managed to slide the prosthetic back onto his amputation, though now it wasn't as comfortable as when Kai put it on.

Tremors from the ice up his heels caused the hair on the back of his neck to stand on end. Goosebumps rose all up his arms, or what was left of them. Fear tickled in his chest, and instead of caring enough to suppress it, he actually rolled his eyes with a huff.

"Hey Big Ugly," Jack greeted before raising his gaze. As soon as he locked eyes with Nozrok, all the rage and hurt from that night at the Well rushed to the surface. Jill was bleeding in his arms again. This was the giant who pulled the trigger.

"Little Jackie," the Giant King, Nozrok, leered in a low rumble, "all alone."

Jack tried to get to his feet but stumbled and fell hard on his knees. Nozrok laughed, shaking his head pitifully. Heat flushed up Jack's face.

"He's not alone."

At the voice, Jack turned to find Harry standing tall behind him, scraggly and grinning. He looked crazier than the Mad Hatter – who streaked by in the background on that jubjub to ride the shoulders a giantess – like some bedraggled Viking warrior. Liesel was there, too, those orbed explosives strapped to her belt. As Jack processed the arrival of the second ranks, the giant called Balthaz stepped into his shadow, a pillar of dangerous and steadfast fury backing him up.

"How long did you think that one up?" Jack asked his best friend.

"It just came to me, friend," Harry shrugged. "Got to have the dramatic effect."

Then Balthaz surged forward and slammed into Nozrok, barreling him backwards like a bull. Harry gave a whoop, hoisted Jack to his feet, and together they charged.

Tweedle-Dum woke on a cot in the makeshift infirmary, his knee stiff and sore to high heaven, a bandage wrapped tightly around his middle. Alice sat perched on the edge of his bed with her head cocked like a bird, face still as stone. Dum tried to sit up, but a pang split in his side and he lay back down – recalled the spike.

"What's happening, Alice?" he managed with a grin. "Have we won yet?"

She blinked.

Dum shrugged. "Pity." He looked around but it made his head dizzy, like he'd eaten bad mushrooms. "Where's Dee?"

She looked up at the ceiling. Her eyes shone rivers across the surface.

His smile waned, eyebrows creased. "Where is he, Alice?"

Calmly, she raised a hand, wrist up, fingers splayed downward. "There's a hole in the sky," she said softly, eyes still skyward, fingers coming together. "It's closing now."

"What are you saying?"

"It will open again. But not for him. He's already passed through."

Dum's stomach turned in knots. He licked his lips, shook his head. "But I saved him. I saved him; that can't be right."

Now she was looking at him, and her face became so mournful that he knew it was true. He passed a hand over his face, a wretched sob issuing forth. Alice held his hand. But he could only repeat himself, over and over, each time broaching the line between anger and despair, "But I saved him. But I saved him…"

He didn't notice when Alice left. No one did.

Kai knew something was wrong. A chill itched down his spine, over his limbs. Amidst the metal clashing around him, he heard screams, distinct and secluded in different areas throughout the battlefield. His ears pricked at each one. A warning.

In a burst of ice, an arm shot out from beneath the lake's frozen surface directly in front of him, the rest of the tainted water man following. The hole in the ice sealed over as soon as he emerged. Those around skidded back in shock, one of Wonderland's bestial solders screaming at the sight. The tainted man made a sword from the water dripping off his body, the weapon freezing solid in his hand. Kai wasted no time to attack and dispatch the tainted, a limp form at his feet that the lake took back into itself.

As if on cue, arms burst from the ice all around and throughout the battlefield. Stomach tight, Kai knew the numbers would keep coming, and already they'd deployed the second ranks to meet the ambushing giants. The third ranks were supposed to hold off until all of the Snow Queen's pieces were played; and the pirates still had yet to make an appearance.

Kai and the soldiers around him were trying to take the eastern flank in order to curve in around the enemy cards, but the tainted emerged in teems from the ice all along the east, regaining the advantage. Behind, Kai became aware of the chaos erupting on the lake's edge. The trees were coming to life. The Snow Queen had more forest people on her side than they'd anticipated, and they attacked the third and fourth ranks from the rear. The giants and belowlanders were still busy fending off Nozrok's fleet, and it remained unclear who held the upper hand.

Nearby, Kai found the White Queen like a beacon through the madness, her broken spear a spade in each hand. He approached her quickly. "We're surrounded."

Celeste looked around to take note of this herself, though she didn't seem any more worried than before. Her face seemed paler, a line of blood drying around her throat, giving her a ghostly appearance. She nodded curtly.

"Good," she said. "We can attack from every direction."

Kai frowned but shook his head. "We couldn't get one word in to form order in this chaos."

"But we can try—" But Celeste froze midsentence.

For a moment Kai thought the tainted had broken from the ice beside him, but then he heard it: the haunted drone of a wolf's howl. He turned toward the east where the army of tainted people clambered from the lake's frozen surface, and behind them charging from the forest toward the unsuspecting enemy came the Pack with Fang at their lead. The scene was soon a confusion of teeth and claws and water, but with the Pack entering the game, they'd gained the eastern front.

Chapter Thirty-Five
Vengeance and Justice

Being the Giant Slayer, Jack was the perfect distraction for the enemy giants, and losing an arm really revealed his true calling as an agitating human being. He'd accepted it since he couldn't do all the fighting maneuvers he used to. So as he weaved around the giantess Yldaa's feet, shouting insults and throwing ice chunks at her knees, she hardly noticed when Brann set her hair on fire.

"Hey hot-head!" Jack yelled, whistling as he twirled his finger around his own head.

She narrowed her stony eyes, sniffed the smoke, and as the realization hit her, she started screaming around in a running frenzy, holding her smoldering head. When Brann jogged up to Jack watching the result of his arson, Jack thumped him on the arm.

"What were you thinking?" he gawked.

Brann frowned. "What do you mean?"

Jack waved his arm at the giantess zooming around the battlefield. "Look what you did! There's nothing stopping her from squashing everyone like a bug!"

Brann grimaced, scratching the back of his bald head. They watched guiltily as the giantess forced belowlanders, cards, and giants alike to leap out of the way of her flaming typhoon. Jack flinched as a few soldiers from both sides got trampled.

Thankfully, Spider came to the rescue, hooking a silver rope into the ice before darting around Yldaa's feet and tangling the rope around her ankles. The maneuver shortened her damage area until eventually the giantess let out a frantic scream and crashed to the ground.

Jack cupped his hand around his mouth and called, "Careful! Don't crack the ice!"

Sheepish, Brann skittered over to join Spider with her giant writhing fly.

Jack shook his head, turned on his heel, and found himself once again in the shadow of the Giant King. Balthaz had disappeared somewhere in the haze. Nozrok looked like he'd just emerged from wrestling a bear – or a giant. Jack felt his stomach rise to his chest. Bolstering his courage, he raised his short sword. Nozrok was the last name on his list.

"Alright, tough guy," Jack yelled. "Let's finish this."

Nozrok swept toward him while Jack dodged between his legs, swiping at the giant's shins with his weapon. The blade glanced off steel plating.

Cheater, he thought bitterly.

Jack wasn't long behind him before Nozrok spun around and smashed his war hammer down like he was ready to split the earth in two. The hunk of iron and bronze barely missed. Scrambling, Jack hastened out of the way as Nozrok swung again and again. The third swing hit as Jack tried to dart out of the way, searing pain splitting up his right arm as something snapped around his chest. Panic hit before he registered that it was only his prosthetic that lay sprawled on the ground, the straps snapped clear off his torso, and most of the pain was all in his head.

"That's not fair," Jack muttered in complaint. At least he consoled himself that if he'd still had the arm he would've lost it anyway.

307

Nozrok froze momentarily when Jack's prosthetic fell off, his mismatched eyes glittering like dew. But then Jack realized the Giant King was seething with anger.

"You upset, big guy?" Jack taunted, indicating his stub of a right arm. "Someone beat you to it."

He flinched back as Nozrok raged again, silver rings and bones rattling in the giant's hair. Then Harry screamed into existence, launched into Nozrok's arm like a cannonball from Balthaz' catapult hurl, throwing the giant's blow off course. Swinging off Nozrok's forearm, Harry kicked his wrist until the war hammer dropped to the floor.

With a roar, Nozrok grabbed Harry and slammed him to the ground, his gargantuan fist keeping him pinned. Vision tinged scarlet, Jack burst forward with a cry, ready to ram headlong into his archnemesis. Nozrok looked up, caught his eye, smiled, and Harry stabbed him in the throat. Golden blood spilled all over Harry's face as Nozrok gawked, clutched his throat, gargled. Jack stumbled in to grasp Harry's arm and pull him away. Harry choked on the foul substance. Grey, Nozrok fell over on his side. Jack turned away to take care of his friend before the light even left the giant's eyes.

Harry wiped his face off in disgust, vomited on the ice. "*Blasted bloody* – that was disgusting."

"Fitting, though," Jack confessed.

"I am never killing a giant again."

"Here's to hoping."

Jack lent him a hand and helped him to his feet. They looked back to finally face the Giant King's corpse. Those mismatched eyes stared straight at them, blank as glass.

"I thought it'd feel different," Jack admitted to the body of his worst enemy.

Harry sniffed the frigid air and spat a glob of blood onto the floor. "You and me both, friend."

In all her years, Wendy had never really seen a warzone, and she never could've imagined it looking like this. Hazy sunlight in the dusted snow gave everything a dreamy sheen like fog. Chaotic terror battered mute against her ears. The tainted burst through the ice slick as eels. To the east snarled the Pack in wild attack, to the west rammed the giants in rapid collision. Between them battled cards baring white and red colors, the jubjub birds escaped or killed, the few remaining bandersnatch weaving throughout the armies like rats. A spark of lightning sporadically hit the sky to prove that the young jabberwock still lived. Behind at the lake's edge fought the Grimrose battalion against the tainted forest people, the trees rustling to life, roots snapping up from the ground.

Wendy helped the Lost Boys gather the injured from the battlefield, the eight of them flying in and out like vultures. It was easy enough to find the wounded but getting them out proved a challenge when the thick of battle bore in on all sides. What's more, the tainted who emerged from the frozen lake were difficult to fend off because if they returned to the frigid waters their wounds healed quickly and they rebounded in full attack at whoever stood near.

The cards left the Lost Boys alone for the most part, unwilling to come after a bunch of kids. In return, Wendy urged to Lost Boys to pull any injured soldier from the battlefield regardless of their allegiances. Better a prisoner of war than dead. The problem would come when the pirates showed up. They had no qualms with killing children.

Wendy landed in next to Tootles who'd found one of the White Queen's fallen soldiers, the reptile still clutching a crossbow in his scaly hands. She recognized him instantly as the lizard Bill who'd helped Alice and her rescue the Mad Hatter back in Wonderland. Tail smashed, the old lizard bled from his stomach and had an ugly burn on his neck that bulged with boils. Tootles tried to stuff a scrap of linen into the hole in Bill's chainmail where he was bleeding.

"I've still got some fight in me, sonny," Bill said, determined despite the strain in his voice. "Patch me up quick and I can take out a few more."

Tootles was shaking his head, his skunk mask hanging around his neck. Recognizing the urgency, Wendy readied to help carry Bill away when the crack of a gunshot split the air and silenced the lizard immediately. Wendy jumped with a start. Tootles's eyes bugged. Mouth slack, Bill's head lolled backward.

"Tootles?" Wendy said weakly as the Lost Boy's face turned ashen.

Tootles dropped his gaze from the lizard's life-snuffed body and stripped off his own jacket to expose the blood flowering over his ribs where the bullet had passed straight through and killed Bill. Wendy caught him before he could crumple, pressing his jacket to the exit wound on his ribs and her hand against the entry wound on his back. Tootles stiffened in shock against her shoulder. Behind him, she saw the pirate pulling back the hammer and aiming his pistol once again. Wendy dashed around Tootles with her back to the gun, still holding him close, and squeezed her eyes shut to prepare for the shot.

The gun fired into the sky as Peter appeared and shoved the pirate's arm up off aim. Gasping, Wendy looked back over her shoulder as Tink buzzed in to shower pixie dust over the gun, jamming its mechanics and causing it to float overhead. Before the pirate could make a leap for it, the Cheshire Cat appeared with a wide grin, took the floating pistol in his paws, and faded away once again. Wendy felt fleeting concern for what the Cheshire Cat planned to do with the gun.

As Peter fended off the pirate with his short sword, Wendy held Tootles tighter and lifted him to his feet. He was in such shock he could hardly move. She practically carried him forward through the thickening chaos. Her heart sped as pirates appeared all around them now, gunpowder and smoke polluting the air. The gunfire cracking her eardrums made her flinch, backstep, try a different route. Tootles clutched her arm and began to shake. Wendy urgently pulled him on, limping for the wound still throbbing in her heel.

Captain Hook stepped out before them, his ragged curls and scarlet coattails gusting in the snowy wind, his cutlass drawn at his side. Sliding to a halt, Wendy backed away as those sea blue eyes took in the vulnerable sight of them. Tootles's knees gave out and it was all Wendy could do to keep him from falling. Gravity was too heavy to spare them this time.

"Hello again, Miss Darling," Hook leered in mock greeting. "Where's the boy?"

"Right here, you old codfish," Peter snapped as he leaped out of the crowd to face the Captain. He quickly raised his sword with both arms as Hook swept down on him with his cutlass, the blades crossed between their sharp glares. Peter clicked his tongue against his teeth in disappointment. "Bad form, Captain."

Tootles was on the ground now and Wendy forced herself to tear her attention away from Peter and Hook, restrained her every instinct to leap up to help. But she realized Tootles was bleeding faster than anticipated, and unless she tended to him now, he could bleed out in her arms. She got on her knees and tore off his shirt to expose the bullet wound. Fumbling with her satchel, she pulled out a wad of bandages and cloths, absently pressing them against the open wound while she scoured for other tools.

She chanced a glance up as Peter and Hook were launched into a series of duel tactics, parries, and near misses. Frantic, she turned back to the task at hand. So much blood. Tears slipped down Tootles's cheeks. Snowflakes melted on his lashes. His breathing quickened, panicked, like a desperate plea in her ears.

I don't want to die, he seemed to say, though not a word left him. Wendy tried to calm him, but she was cut short when a cold blade pressed against her throat.

Slowly, Wendy looked up to find Jane standing over her, her messy black hair ruffling in her face, holding a cutlass to her throat. Jane's stance was steady, her jaw tight, breathing with exhilaration at the battle. Dark eyes gleamed.

"Jane, please!" Wendy begged, her face hot as tears welled in desperation. "He's dying!"

Jane looked from Wendy to Tootles bleeding out on the floor. Her cool stature faltered, and she looked back at the dueling enemies, the boy and the pirate, like her worst

312

nightmare. Then she lowered her sword but remained where she stood.

"Do what you must," Jane said.

Wendy nodded, glanced at Peter and Hook once again, then turned all focus on Tootles. She worked calm but quick. She wasn't going to lose him, not now, not when she could save him. Pouring the water from her canteen over the wound, she quickly checked for any bullet or bone fragments that may be stuck inside, but the morning light was too hazed by the fog to really tell. She made two thick cloth paddings to cover both holes, pressed them tightly against the wounds, then managed to sit Tootles up against her knee so she could securely wrap his abdomen in bandages.

A flustered outcry grabbed her attention. Both she and Jane whipped around anxiously to witness Peter stumble back with a grimace. Hook feel to his knees, a hand over a bleeding stomach where he'd been stabbed. Peter held both his bloodied short sword and Hook's cutlass, both pointed at the pirate's throat. The cutlass shaved a few hairs off Hook's chin.

With Jane distracted, Wendy quickly looked around and shoved Tootles toward a waiting Curly. "*Go!*" she whispered harshly.

Curly's eyes were wide as saucers, but he nodded, took Tootles in his arms, and flew away.

Hook growled at Peter. "Finish it, boy."

"No!" Jane exclaimed as she bolted forward only to skid to a halt just behind her father, afraid of the fierce look in Peter's eye and the sword at Hook's throat.

Knees sore and heel throbbing, Wendy rose to her feet. She hovered over to Peter's side, facing both Hook and Jane. She rested her hand lightly on Peter's arm. She could feel the horror trembling under his skin, the inner battle raging within him. She saw the shine of his fierce eyes, the tears there. Did he struggle to see the murderous pirate instead of the boy who'd grown up with the Lost Boys?

"Finish it!" Hook roared, thrown into a rasping fit of coughs that made his wound bleed more. "You blasted coward."

A war cry echoed somewhere behind them. The tribesmen. They were coming for the pirates, for Hook. Tiger Lily would soon be upon them with her vicious panther, ready to enact her vengeance.

Peter gave a yell in utter frustration and dropped his swords away from Hook's throat. Wendy felt the blood pump in her ears.

"Captain James Hook," Peter said forcefully, "I hereby banish you from Neverland forever."

"Why you little—" Hook sneered, starting up but quickly falling back to his knees and palm, choking on his own blood.

Wendy watched Jane take in what was happening as her father lay sprawled in seething indignation at Peter's feet. Her eyes widened, breaths heavy. Confliction seemed to press against her on all sides.

"Go," Peter ordered the pirate.

But Wendy held out a hand to Jane for the last time. "Come with us."

Hook lay gasping, head craned around towards his daughter. Jane looked between Hook, Peter, and Wendy. For a moment, she reached to take it, this final chance to turn. But she grimaced, shook her head. "No."

Resigned, Wendy dropped her hand.

Hook huffed, struggled again to rise, his bloodshot eyes glaring daggers at Peter. "This isn't the end," he growled.

Peter didn't move. Jane lunged forward on her knees and threw her arms around her father even as he resisted. Like she was holding him down.

"This isn't the last you'll hear of me!" Hook cried.

Swallowing the pain, Peter said solemnly, "Yes it is."

Jane tore something from under her shirt as Hook struggled against her, throwing the crystal on the floor. Hook's scream thrashed out, ringing in her ears, as he and Jane both vanished into thin air. A handcrafted leopard mask sat on the ice in their place. Snow spotted its yellow surface.

Wendy hugged Peter's arm, her eyes spilling over as they stared at the spot where their greatest enemy had disappeared. They could hear the Panther Tribe coming in around them now, Tiger Lily with them. With a sigh, Peter clasped Wendy's hand in his and shocked her with a kiss on the mouth, hand in her hair, right there in the middle of a war. She kissed him back, pulled away only just to look in his eyes. She knew he was hurting, but this relief was overbearing. They'd done the right thing.

The war wasn't done. But theirs was. For them, they'd already won.

Chapter Thirty-Six

The Tinderbox

The instant Red reached subconsciously for the Wolf, a ripping pain erupted through her head that caused her to scream and nearly collapse. Gasping, tears pricked her eyes. It was like she'd stabbed a raw open wound she'd forgotten about, a throbbing place where the Wolf used to be, gutted from her. She tried to shake it off, but the reaction had jostled her, and it was difficult to fall back into the swing of battle again.

"Rubina!" Jim appeared beside her, fending off the flood of tainted water people while she recovered. "Are you alright?"

"I'm fine," she said through grit teeth, pressing two fingers into her temples.

"Oh sure, sure," Clopin was there, too, mocking a cheery tone that set stark against his bloody face and raging eyes. "You're fine, she's fine, we're all fine."

"It doesn't look it," Jim observed. His eyes swept over her in a way that made her face burn.

"Didn't you hear her?" Clopin pulled a wry smile as he butted his elbow into a tainted woman's throat. "She's fine!"

"I never asked you to come," Red said, an edge to her voice at Clopin's complaints. "You volunteered."

"What are you talking about? I'm fine!"

Jim huffed and shook his head. Despite Clopin's grumbling, he had a pleasurable gleam in his eye as he cut through the frozen bodies around him, his rapier like a steel piano wire. Having run out of bullets, Jim used his pistol as a club alongside his sabre. When the pirates appeared running past them, he did a doubletake.

"Pirates?" Jim gawked.

"Don't get too excited," Red stated, gathering her strength enough to draw her bow again. "These ones are kid-killers. Not quite the gung-ho treasure hunters in your grandfather's stories."

"Still," Jim couldn't help the slight grin, "all my life I've chased after his adventures, and it's not even on the open water that I finally run into pirates."

"What are you talking about?" Clopin cried in a fluster. "You *joined* the pirates. You know what they say…" He gutted two tainted people before he continued, "Gypsies are the pirates of Paris! Or the Forest; the saying works both ways."

Red raised her eyebrows at Jim who rolled his eyes and chided, "Never heard that one before."

"Well now you have. *En garde!*" Clopin thrust his rapier at one of the Queen of Hearts' cards. "Just like Notre Dame."

Red only laughed, glad to know at least one man would remain unchanged throughout all this. Firing an arrow into the open mouth of a tainted woman, she turned and came face to face with Fang. Her breath hitched in her chest. She hadn't seen him since the Enchanted Forest when he was pushed through a swirling vortex by his aunt. He looked leaner now, scruffier, dark circles ringing his eyes like silver sinking into his skull. Despite everything, her stomach tightened with fear. She knew he wasn't the monster she once thought he was. But that didn't wash away the years of running from him, the trauma of his teeth in her flesh under a full moon.

317

"They told me you were dead," Fang said, voice strained. And the look in his eyes almost wiped all the darkness of their history away.

Red felt her own throat grow taunt. "Only a part of me."

He choked out a breath, his expression softened with relief and sorrow. "And Lupa?" he asked.

"Killed once," Red admitted. "But I don't know which came back."

Lips in a thin line, Fang sighed. Having won the eastern front, the Pack surged around them, snarling into the warzone. Behind him was a strange scene of calm, and Red frowned at it. Wisps of snow dusted down from the sky. Bodies littered the sheet of ice, some cards strewn throughout, but no tainted. Mostly what she saw were wolves slowly picking themselves up, glancing absently at the war before them, and turning away to walk into the woods. So many ghosts.

One body didn't stand, an Arctic wolf, his scraggly white fur matted in blood. Red wondered if he suffered two deaths or if neither man nor wolf chose to live without the other.

Through the haze cast by the grey noon sun, she saw a lone figure standing at the lake's edge among the trees, woken wolves trotting past. Gooseflesh crawled up her shoulders. Her grasp tightened on her bow. Touching Fang's arm, Red indicated the woman behind with a jerk of her chin. His jaw set, shadows over his eyes, he stalked forward. Red cast a fleeting glance at Jim who gave her a supportive nod, a sign that he had her back if things went wrong. With a breath, she followed after Fang, and together they walked across the empty ice to the forest where Lupa stood waiting.

Lupa easily stepped backwards until the three of them were off the lake, surrounded by a dying forest. A raw scar sliced from her throat to collarbone and her clothes were damaged from another healed wound at her stomach.

"So you did have the strength after all, Little Red," Lupa observed with an impressed air. "You overcame the Wolf."

Red's blood pounded, adrenaline spiking through her limbs. She wanted to contradict her, say she was wrong, that the Wolf died so Red would live. But it wasn't worth the effort. She struggled enough not to reach for the Wolf again and show how weak she felt. Lupa's golden eyes glittered.

"Do not speak to her," Fang growled, glaring at Lupa.

"You defend her now? Did I not tell you it was Little Red here who killed your wife?"

Something like confusion and dread twisted into Red's gut, confusion at this new information, dread that it was true. She glanced at the tattoo ringed around the finger on Fang's left hand. Had she done this horrible thing without knowing? Was another soul impressed upon her guilty conscience?

But Fang did not turn to her nor impress upon her this accusation. Instead, he answered, "You did say as much."

Lupa chuckled at his stoic posture, facing him comfortably, confident. "I thought the Pack never turned on its own kind."

Fang remained grim. "I thought so, too."

Before Lupa could respond, a raven flew up from the bare branches overhead, landing on Fang's shoulder and clicking in his ear. Red recognized the creature from when he'd picked at the hair of his former mistress Carabosse. At the strange language in his ear, Fang nodded. Lupa's smile barely waned before a murder of ravens suddenly streamed from above and descended upon her in a black cloud of feathers. Fang refused to turn away, fists clenched to his sides. A memory flashed through her head of when Red hanged the devil Bluebeard's burnt corpse from the skeleton of his own home. She'd felt nothing. This was the same, for her, for Fang.

He whistled sharply and the ravens retreated, swirling overhead in a haunting vortex. Lupa was crouched, bleeding, laughing in mania as if she'd proven a point. Still cackling, she stood with her flesh marred and hanging. From behind, someone jumped out and stabbed her in the neck. Lupa gasped, clawing at the hands which held the blade in place. But she crumbled, revealing the girl with amber-shot eyes, Quinn, standing behind her, face wet with tears, breathing heavily with every sob.

Lupa lay stiff on the ground, gold eyes like glass in the pale light. They felt nothing.

Chapter Thirty-Seven
The Boy Who Promised Too Much

Kai berated himself for coming alone. It was selfish. It wasn't part of the plan. But as soon as he found the opportunity, he slipped away from the battle and crept into the castle. He only bothered to be quiet self-consciously. He knew, or at least suspected, that the Snow Queen was expecting him.

He entered the throne room where his journey had accumulated over a year ago. This chamber was where he'd first confronted the Snow Queen, when he mistakenly thought he'd broken the mirror of her power. And this chamber was where they truly destroyed the mirror, where he'd killed Häxan last night. He imagined Frost standing here, too, swearing his life and loyalty to the Snow Queen, to the Ice Maiden, to his beloved Babette. Kai wondered at that. Was Frost as much the center of it all as the Snow Queen? His drowning caused Babette's possession, his love enabled the Snow Queen's power, his loyalty tricked Kai into coming here before, and his betrayal brought them the tools to destroy the Snow Queen forever. Now Kai was here, walking into the Snow Queen's throne room, broadsword in hand, ready to rescue his own beloved.

He wasn't prepared to see Gerda sitting on the fur lined throne, her skin glistening with thin ice crystals, a crown on her head. She was stunning and horrifying all at once, equally his foe and the woman he loved. His heart swelled even as his stomach convulsed. Seeing that crown on Gerda's head, to see her like this, made everything blaringly real. The sensation hit Kai so hard that it felt like his heart was being torn from his chest.

Gerda smiled at him. "You've come at last."

Kai blinked, shaking himself. This wasn't Gerda. This was the Snow Queen. Gerda was in there somewhere, but this wasn't her.

"You knew?" Kai asked through the knot in his throat.

The Snow Queen shrugged. "It is all part of the plan."

"Your armies are growing thin," he said, his voice edged with a growl. "You are losing."

"Am I?" Her eyes shone, Gerda's eyes, brown on the left and blue on the right. "Tell me, Kai, why did you send an army to my doorstep the other night? Draw out my wolves, my giants?"

An eel seemed to slick through his stomach, writhing. "A distraction."

"An attempt. But yes."

"So all these allies, all these villains, gathered here for the slaughter—"

"All for you, *min älskling*."

Kai flinched at the endearing term, the one he and Gerda called each other, with Gerda's voice and face but not *her*. This wasn't her. The words bothered him so much that he fought to grasp her meaning.

"You mean for this," Kai countered, rubbing his thumb over the scar along his jaw.

The Snow Queen cocked her head but did not deny it.

"It's the missing piece, isn't it?" Kai continued gruffly. "Blood mirror."

She grinned slowly, delighting in his discovery.

"And you expect me to give it to you? That's the key to your spell, isn't it? Free will."

"Clever boy," the Snow Queen said proudly. "I must admit, I am glad it was you. The one unexpected thing. I really should've known; there's a pattern to these things. But I am glad."

Kai shifted, fists clenched. He tried not to think of Frost. "So what happens now? I won't give it to you. And the very reason that brought me to this realm in the first place... I can't have her because you won't give her up. And I..."

"And you can't kill me without killing her," the Snow Queen guessed, leaning forward.

Kai did not respond but his silence was enough.

Standing from her throne, the Snow Queen began to descend from her pedestal, approaching him one step at a time. "You can still be with her, you know."

He hated the softness of her tone, the way they brushed over his defenses and made him feel weak. Kai fidgeted with the grasp on his broadsword. "How?"

"A trade," she responded. "A compromise. That way we both get what really matters in the end."

His heart raced as she came to his level. This close he could hardly see the icy layer covering her skin, except where the sunlight caught the surface like glass. She was Gerda. His Gerda. He swallowed painfully, resisting the urge to pull her to him. She looked him up and down, causing blood to rush to his face.

"You can be with her," the Snow Queen said gently, close enough to hurt. "Not ruling, but still by her side. I will transform her into the most powerful being in the realms, and no one will ever be able to harm her – and she will always be yours."

Kai wrestled with his words. "How can that be?"

"We will be one," she relished, and her expression dazzled in pure excitement and gentleness that he wondered if this truly was his Gerda. She reached briefly for his hands, but she brought them back to her side in hesitation. "With my power and her heart, she will be new and yet the same. You can be hers again. That is all you have ever wanted, to be together. I swear to you."

Setting his jaw, Kai dropped his eyes to the ground so she wouldn't see the tears forming there. His head felt like a blizzard, a cacophony of emotions he could barely hold back. Gently, she reached up and touched his face, bringing him to look at her – at Gerda – whose face was soft without the mask of ice and her eyes showed concern. He huffed out a shaky breath, chest tight, tears dropping.

"This is so hard," Kai whispered, trembling as he struggled to restrain himself.

Gerda brushed her thumb over his cheek to wipe away the tear lines. "It's alright," she said, so soft that he knew it was her, his Gerda.

She stood on tiptoe to kiss him on each cheek, then paused to look at him again, her own eyes shining now. She gave him a small smile like she was holding back how painful this was for her, too. And when she pressed her lips to his, he kissed her fervently back, dropping his broadsword to the ground, holding her face in both hands. She pulled back, a breath away, then retreated until she was out of his reach. She looked at him with such longing he felt it in his chest.

He didn't take his eyes off her as he unsheathed the knife at his belt. Carefully, he brought the steel blade to his jaw where he could feel the scar, squeezed his eyes against the pain, and drew the blade through his skin. He dropped the bloody knife, let it clatter on the floor. Bracing himself with a few breaths, he dug his fingers into the open wound until he pinched the glass lodged there, explosions of burning ice down his chin. He gasped in relief once he removed it, a thin line of broken mirror just large enough to see the shine, and he felt suddenly warmer like a chronic chill had lifted from his bones. He held the fragment between his bloodied fingers.

Glancing up at Gerda, he offered it to her. "Here."

He dropped the fragment in her open palm. Blood Mirror.

Dazed, he watched as she took a vial from her skirt pockets and poured the contents over the sliver in her hand. Tears and blood congealed and melted into the glass, glowing bright. In a rush, the icy scales shot over Gerda's skin and the Snow Queen gasped in exhilaration. Her head arched back in grotesque tension as power surged through her, the ice turning stark white and crystalline all around her feet. Kai's breath came out in clouded puffs.

Quickly her muscles slacked, her scream died, and the Snow Queen's power seemed to vanish as Gerda's knees gave way. Kai caught her just in time, grasping her arms as she did his. Gerda gulped at the air, her eyes widened in terror.

"Let me go, let me go!" she pleaded, shaky and desperate.

A fist seemed to lodge in his throat as Kai shook his head.

"Please, Kai. Please – she'll be back. She'll be back! Please," she begged.

Her face was wet with tears, her breath frigid against his skin. She clung to him, her full weight on him or else she'd fall. She struggled to look into his face.

"Set me free," she whispered.

Kai's chin trembled, and he ducked away from her pleading eyes so she couldn't see the wrestling turmoil etched across his brow, the weakness he felt all through his bones. "I can't," he choked, forcing himself to look at her.

Agony forced the breath from her and she leaned heavily against him, shivering uncontrollably. "It's alright, *min älskling*," her weakened voice fluttered into his ear. "I forgive you."

His vision was a blur of tears as he held her upright. It broke everything in him to see her under such anguish. But he couldn't bear to do what she asked. They didn't have long until the Snow Queen returned, and Gerda disappeared. So he held her, pressing his forehead to hers.

"I love you," he said, his voice breaking. "That day in our *smultronställe*, before everything, I wanted to give you this."

He tugged the chain around his neck with his thumb, revealing the ring he'd made for her and carried with him since he'd lost her. Gerda managed a smile, a laugh that sounded like a sob. Kai kept his gaze locked on hers.

"I wanted to ask you to marry me, *min sanna kärlek*."

"I would've said yes," Gerda breathed, joy under the strain in her voice. "A thousand times, yes."

Kai kissed her hard on the mouth, and he felt the ice freeze under his hands on her forearms, the chill between their lips. When he pulled away, she had paled just shy of transparency. Then she lurched into him in sudden convulsion, eyes and mouth wide as her breath jolted from her throat. The supernatural light raged in her eyes like a burning blue fire. Ice split around them, a chorus of sharp cracks underfoot. Her grasp on Kai's arms tightened and froze, a searing ice burn that would rip up his flesh. The light began to fade away until only Gerda remained from the storm, limp and falling against him. Kai stumbled, lowering her to the floor.

"I'm sorry, I'm sorry," Kai sobbed, holding her close, brushing the hair out of her face. She bled profusely from a deep wound in her back, the growing puddle soaking his knees. He blinked away the blur of tears. "I'm so sorry."

Gerda's eyes remained steadily on his face. "*Tusen tack, min älskling. Jag älskar dig.*" The words seemed to take her last breath with them as they brushed past his cheek.

Kai broke, clutching her tightly as if he could keep her there safe against him. He kissed her forehead, her cheeks, her nose. His tears glistened against her skin in frozen beads. But she was gone.

With a shaking breath, he looked up where Alice stood, the pickaxe bloody in her hand. She was crying, too. He remembered when he found her on the floor with wounded hands, asking him if he could feel the pain she couldn't. More than anything, he felt this. And he knew this time she felt it too.

Alice let the pickaxe slip from of her hand to clatter on the floor. The ground around them groaned, spiderwebs of fractures. He knew they needed to leave.

Gently, Kai closed Gerda's eyes and laid her on a long white fur with the whisper, "*Sov så gott, min älskling.*"

Sleep well.

Her honey gold hair fanned around her head like the sun. She was so peaceful she could have really been asleep. But she was too still, her breath gone, her heart silent, and the blood pooled around her soaking her bed. Kai's hands were warm, wet with Gerda's blood.

Alice took Kai's hand and pulled him gently away as the roof began to fall in on them and the sun shone in golden sheets across Gerda's body.

Chapter Thirty-Eight
Here Comes the Sun

On the battlefield, it stopped snowing. Pale sun streamed down from overhead, causing the mist to be blinding in its haze. Simultaneously the tainted dropped through the ice, but this time the lake did not freeze over their bodies, leaving behind sloshing holes. Jack heard the groan beneath his feet, as if a whale would emerge from below. He scowled at his toes. He wasn't sure if it was just him who noticed the way the floor seemed to darken. An inky blackness. And so many desperate faces screaming at him under the ice.

Jack looked up just as the first crack sliced past him, jagged and fierce, spraying water into the air, leaking over the surface. His stomach sank.

"Fall back!" he shouted with all the strength he could muster. The lake was melting. He broke into run.

All around him soldiers took up his cry, racing for the forest and solid ground. Some carried bodies with them, the giants especially. But one giant stepped through the weakening ice, sending out a spray of bitter cold water before he managed to pull free. A card in full armor slipped into the hole the giant's foot left behind.

Jack knew he should run straight for shore, but an overwhelming urgency took hold that he couldn't shake. He had to find Red. Bolting into the stampeding armies, he began to cry out her name, *"Rubes!"*

Everyone else already knew to retreat, so he took up his new cry in vigor, wary of the webbed cracks spreading over the lake. But even as he was running and looking, he wondered if maybe she'd already made it to the forest.

The ice split behind him, shifting up like a towering glacier, rolling soldiers over and into the frigid water below. Jack paused when he heard the scream for his name. Whipping around as the standing ice loomed overhead, he caught sight of a kid – Nibs – getting sucked into the water, clinging to the frozen edge and thrashing his legs. Jack rushed over, sliding to his knees and reaching for the kid. Water rained down as the ice prepared to flip.

"Take my hand," Jack exclaimed, grasping Nibs around one forearm.

Nibs held on with both hands. Jack tried to wedge his heels into the frozen floor to prevent himself from slipping in after the kid. But with only one arm, the struggle to heave out the waterlogged kid was near impossible for his strength alone.

"Come on, kid!" Jack urged through clenched teeth. "You've got to pull. Think sunshine, mud slides, chocolate cake…"

"What are you saying?!" Nibs screeched.

"Happy thoughts, happy thoughts!"

Nibs pulled, face scrunched with the effort. When Jack managed to drag him halfway up, Jack released Nibs's arm and fisted the back of his shirt to tug the rest of him up before the iceberg topped off and began to sink, water surging up around them. Jack dragged Nibs across the ice until they were well out of the way of getting sucked in.

Panting and keeled over, Jack waved towards the forest. "Go on, go. Happy thoughts, happy thoughts."

Nibs huffed a toothy smile, wiping his wet nose on his sleeve before he managed to run and hover away. Jack panted a moment more, forcing himself to straighten his stiff back. He looked around. Most of the armies had already fled the scene, the remaining being some stragglers of the Queen of Hearts' cards who hesitated at the thought of running into enemy hands. But something about the prospect of drowning or freezing to death made surrender more appealing.

Ice was cracking and splintering all around now. He scanned the area again.

"Rubes!" he shouted.

Someone slammed into him. It took Jack a second before he realized it was her, Red, smelling like blood and sweat but still hugging him like they were the last two people on earth.

"I found you," she gasped, pulling away with an exhausted laugh.

He squeezed her hand. "We have to get out of here."

"Wait!" She pointed behind him. The mist had cleared. The ice castle was crumbling, splashing into the lake, causing more frigid waters to lap over the melting ice. Running at breakneck speed from the place were three figures.

"Who is that?" Jack narrowed his eyes. He felt the ground groan beneath him.

"Kai and Frost, I think," Red said, breathless. "Is that Gerda?"

Jack shook his head, something twisting in his abdomen. "It's Alice."

The ice jolted under their feet, and Jack nearly lost his footing had Red not caught his arm. With one last glance over his shoulder toward their friends, Jack ran for the forest with

Red at his side, water shooting up in freezing geysers around them.

When they reached the edge where the armies stood waiting in wonder, Jack and Red whipped around to watch the three figures halfway across the hazardous terrain. Most of the ice had split, some towering onto their sides before splashing into the lake. The edge already turned to mush where they stood, lapping the shore for the chaos in its depths. Jack's heart pounded in his ears and Red squeezed his hand so tightly he began to feel burning pinpricks down his numb fingers.

To let loose the rising tension in his chest, Jack began to scream at them, beckoning them to hurry up, to run faster, to keep coming. Beside him, Red did the same, desperate and helpless. Then someone shot out of the woods behind them, skimming over the lake surface and pumping her legs like she was running on water. Wendy rocketed to meet her friends.

And then Alice stumbled, Kai started yelling incoherently at Wendy and waving his arms, and the ice crashed between them and those who waited anxiously on the shore. Jack and Red ceased yelling, holding their breaths. Red stifled a weak sob. The mist from the crash blocked everything from view. Water lapped around their ankles. Jack hardly noticed when Lovisa stood beside him, unsure how long she'd been there. But they couldn't see anything.

Kai didn't need Frost to tell him that the ice was giving in around them. As soon as the ice pillar landed directly before them, he bent his knees to brace against the shaking impact, the frozen ground splitting under his feet. He helped Alice up in a rush, thanking God that the iceberg hadn't crushed Wendy as she lurched toward them in a tumble.

"What are you doing here?" he exclaimed sharply as Wendy reached them soaked in frigid spray.

"Helping you! What does it look like I'm doing?" she snapped right back.

Alice stepped through the ice again, lurching forward. Kai caught her and Wendy did, too. Resigning himself, Kai pushed a stunned Alice towards Wendy. "Take her; go!"

Wendy nodded curtly, taking Alice by the armpits and managing to fly the two of them just barely over the fragile ice and water to the shore. Kai stepped aside as the ice separated under his feet, one piece floating away. He locked eyes with Frost, the man who'd led Alice to the castle, who gave her the real pickaxe so she could do what neither of them could – even he looked intimidated by all this. But Frost narrowed his eyes.

"What're you looking at?" he barked. "Run!"

The splashing hole lay gaping before them, and the ice was separating to widen expanse. Kai ran, Frost just behind, the ice cracking under every footfall. Before hitting the water, he jumped, arms wheeling, but the ledge was too far. He splashed into the black lake. His muscles stiffened instantly with the cold. Thrashing, Kai kicked his way to the surface and hit his head against the white sheet capping his escape. The impact caused him to let loose a stream of air, his vision spotting as his head pounded in pain. Somehow, he'd slipped underneath the very lip he'd meant to land on. Lungs burning, he pounded his fist against the ice ceiling that trapped him, but despite the web that appeared across the ice, the water made his punches sluggish. He was aware of the bodies approaching him from the depths, earning a flashback to mermaids who'd threatened him before. He wasn't sure if these water people were still tainted now that the Snow Queen was dead, but he wasn't willing to take any chances.

Fist against ice in ferocious repetition. Heartbeats in his eardrums. His chest lurched for breath. And when he remembered Gerda, a stillness overtook him, a kind of sorrow and yet a kind of peace. Her laugh as she raced him barefoot into the valley of their *smultronställe*. The way the sun hit her hair, like honey or gold, white at the edges in a glow. Gerda tucking a snowdrop petalled flower behind his ear, biting her lip even as she smiled, her mouth on his cheek whispering, *I love you.*

I love you.

Här kommer solen, min älskling.

A fist crashed into the ice above him, grasping his limp arm until Kai seized the lifeline in turn, and dragging him up and out of the blackness onto the wet ice. Kai rolled, vomiting water, straining to breathe.

"Don't die for her," Frost hissed down at him, the sun hitting his head like a halo. "Don't let her win."

All Kai could do was nod while coughing, take Frost's hand again to pull him up, and stumble into a run over the remaining distance into the forest where his friends awaited him.

Chapter Thirty-Nine

The Earth and Sky Open

Returning to the infirmary in the forest, they discovered the remnants of an invasion. Frostbitten roots bore up from the ground to strangle lavvus and goahtis, vines dripping in melted rime tangled the nomads' sleds, branches choked around purple corpses. The forest people, gypsies, and nomadic robbers as well as other individuals who'd remained to defend the injured stood as sweaty and bloody as those returning from the battlefield.

Tjuv greeted the returned soldiers in grim silence, her gnarled hands on Inga's shoulders. The survivors flanked her, nomads and forest people alike, in a moment of rest before the work would begin again.

Esmeralda and Aurore stood side by side with Gretel and Hansel, watching the incoming crowd expectantly until Clopin and Ingénu arrived carrying Jim barely conscious between them. Tears streaming, Aurore covered her husband's face with kisses while Esmeralda helped her brother get Jim to urgent care. Gretel sniffed back a sob, took Hansel's hand, and followed after the Woodsman.

Lovisa approached and spoke in hushed tones to her cousin Latham, urging him to lead the able-bodied forest people in gathering the dead and wounded. He nodded gravely, pulled her into a gentle embrace for her burns, and bade their people to disperse for the battlegrounds.

Kai took this all in as he slipped in among the returning ranks. Someone had thrown a wool coat over Kai's shoulders and he held it fast around him as he approached Tjuv and Inga, shivering and wet.

"I kept my promise, *Lilla Rånareflickan*," he said despite the quake in his voice.

Inga's lip pouted, dirt smudging her face, but she nodded and leaned in closer to her grandmother.

Turning his eyes to Tjuv, Kai whispered, "It's finished."

Tjuv cast a glance from the bleeding gash on his jaw to the puddle forming around his feet. "*Nej*," she said gruffly. "*Inte än.*"

Not yet.

The evening was for the wounded.

As some of the tainted had raided the infirmary during the battle, everything seemed to be in a perpetual state of frenzy as soldiers poured into the already hectic ward. Anyone not being treated or put on bedrest was expected to help with the medics.

Kai was demanded bedrest until his jaw was stitched up and the fear of pneumonia passed. Tjuv personally wrapped him in warm blankets, dried his head and feet with fervor, and threw him fresh clothes to put on in haste. He did as she requested only so she could move on to aid someone else who needed it more than he.

Wendy visited his small shelter, the half-dome made of woven branches and floored in mats, when she nursed her foot. The stab wound in her heel had reopened and needed new bandages. She informed him that Jack and Red were both well enough to be kept busy, and though Alice wasn't really well enough, she worked all the same.

Wendy didn't ask about what happened, didn't ask about his opened scar or the swollen rouge and alabaster ice burns shaped like hands on his forearms. All she did was wrap her arms tightly around him, a hand on the back of his head while he cried quietly into her shoulder. His eyes leaked when he squeezed them shut, but everything felt numb.

Pulling away, she squeezed his hand and asked, "What happens now?"

It was the same question he'd asked the Snow Queen when he stood before her and tried to convince himself they were at an impasse. As if no more choices lay before them. But he was a fool; there were always choices.

Kai breathed out a heavy sigh. "Now, we tend to our wounded and pray that most of us last the night."

Wendy nodded, offering a small smile before she took her leave. One of her Lost Boys had also fallen through the ice and threatened catching pneumonia as he did. Kai prayed that at least this boy survived.

The night was for rest.

Rest was all anyone could do. The wounded had been tended to, so those who remained sick and injured waited in awed tension to see if this would be their last night. Soldiers and makeshift nurses slept while they could or else sat in whatever calm they could gather within themselves. The camp was silent, holding a collective breath. Blackness blanketed the night, starless, void of the moon and aurora borealis. The only sound came from the surrounding forest, trees dripping from the melting ice.

At dawn, people began to wake, tentatively searching the beds to see who still breathed. The forest people constructed wooden caskets of braided branches, bidding the earth to part into deep trenches so the dead would receive a proper burial. The formerly tainted water people have brought many bodies lost in the melted lake to shore. Everyone soon emerged to discover who remained. Graves were organized by realm.

Heading the Wonderland burial, the White Queen foresaw that cards on both sides be buried equally. A line of scabs stretched across her throat, deep enough to scar, shallow enough not to need stitches. Already Celeste was called the Queen of Spades by her soldiers.

The Queen of Hearts was buried with her cards' graves lined behind, while Tweedle-Dee was positioned beside her as head of the White Queen's fallen cards. The honor equated the mercy bestowed for Helena. Dum held Celeste's hand as the bodies were lowered into the ground, distraught tears streaming down his face. Celeste held her head high, back rigid, like a heron looking over the grey washed before her. She was a picture of strength they both needed.

The Mad Hatter didn't stay long at the funeral, bidding his close friend and estranged sister farewell with a tip of his hat before he slipped away to search for the missing young jabberwock. The March Hare and the Dormouse went with him.

Very few pirates required burial, and those who survived were allowed to attend the funeral though disarmed and watched closely. Thankfully, none of the Lost Boys were slain, though Nibs and Tootles came close to it. The tribesmen who'd perished were sprinkled in oil, wrapped in cloths, and buried with an eagle feather on their chests. Among them was Tiger Lily's panther who'd been crushed under the fallen ice.

Peter approached the rotund pirate called Mister Smee who held a handkerchief to his scarlet nose and puffy eyes. Hands behind his back, Peter sheepishly told him about his captain's fate. Whether he believed it or not, Smee adjusted his foggy spectacles and nodded with a cracked thanks. Peter stepped away to express condolences to Tiger Lily, but she refused to look at him. She wanted to see Hook's body buried with the others. At least her silence suggested she would hold little hostility against him for his actions.

Aside from the Wonderland armies, the Enchanted Forest battalion lost the greatest number of soldiers, ranging between Grimrose to Chliobain to Lille-Havfrue. Their battle was primarily against the supernatural, fighting the snow bees and tainted who attacked from behind. Though the forest people helped as best they could, the casualties were great. King Thrushbeard had not survived the night after a tree branch had skewered him through the chest. With him lay his wife, Queen Euna, who died defending the infirmary from the tainted raiders, strangled by a holly branch. Tearfully, the massive Isbjørn lowered her body into the beautiful coffin.

"I'm so sorry, my dear girl," he whispered hoarsely, pressing his lips to his daughter's brow. He returned to the newly orphaned Princess Aurore, wrapped an arm around her, pulled her close to his side.

Jim had miraculously healed from a panicked case of internal bleeding. His face was ashen, his body weakened, but he watched the funeral with the gypsies as if thankful not to be one of those buried this morning. Hansel and Gretel held a hand on either side of him.

The Pack only had one body to bury. Much of their kind had only been half killed, leaving scores of wolves to wander wild in the forest. The Arctic wolf, Lev, was the only man not to come out of the battle. Quinn cried on her knees over his grave. Once, she raised her amber-shot eyes to see an old Himalayan wolf watching from the underbrush. She couldn't be sure it was Thaddeus, but it gave her some comfort to think so.

Lupa's body was burned without ceremony, Fang and Red being the only ones to watch as the flames consumed her. Nothing remained for even the ravens to feed on.

The belowlanders and giants burned their dead on the mountainside, a blazing fire as the ashes floated into the sky where they hoped their loved ones would find their way home. Balthaz stood solemn before Nozrok's raging pyre. They never found the stolen harp, but already Liesel talked about creating something similar for the goose, a music box or a sort of mechanical harp. The prospects weren't clear yet, but the chances were worth it if peace could at last be attained.

Later from the mountains came Mr. and Mrs. Crow with information about the lost witches. Their bodies were retrieved, long dead, ripped apart from an enemy the Crows could only assume was the snow bees under Häxan's command. The nomads took their remains and buried them under carefully piled stones near Bae's scree grave, the Lappish Witch to the east, the Finnish Witch to the west. In a ring around these three graves, the nomads buried their dead in similar fashion. Finally, in a larger ring, the tainted and forest people were buried without coffins, their bodies covered in soil, and trees were prompted to grow from their graves. Inga knelt in the very center where Bae rested and told him how the sun was rising.

Kai soon found himself again at the lake's edge, staring out at where the castle spires once pierced the sky. They never found Gerda's body. He had nothing to bury or say goodbye to. Not that he needed to see her to wish her farewell. But something about picturing her at the bottom of this lake, alone and far from home, wrenched a hollow pit in his chest.

The sun cast a golden wedge across his eyes. He held the ring like hammered moonrock in his hand, the weight heavy in his palm. In the stories, the ones inspired by him and this place, they said that Gerda was the hero, that she saved him and melted the ice in his heart, that her tears of love cured him of the Snow Queen's poison, that they made it home in the end. But this wasn't a fairy tale, he thought bitterly as his fingers closed around the engagement ring. Gerda was dead and his tears saved nothing.

Fisting his hand, Kai threw the ring as far as he could, watched it sail through the sun, hit the water with a silver shower, and sink to the bottom of the lake where Gerda waited. This was the closest thing to a burial he could have.

With a sigh, he closed his eyes and let the morning take his sorrow. He imagined a gentle hum filling his mind with something like peace.

"I know you are there," he said softly.

Behind him, he heard Lovisa's smooth voice, "I'm sorry."

341

He knew what she meant, heard it in her lingered silence. She was sorry for his loss, for Gerda's death, for losing what mattered most to him in the end. She was sorry that she could do nothing to take the pain away. Kai breathed in the cold air. Because he was sorry for it, too.

She remained a length away but stepped into the light with him. "So, what happens now?" Lovisa asked, just as Wendy had asked him last night, and he had asked the Snow Queen before. He supposed that at the end of the day, they all felt a little lost, looking for someone to show them the way. Kai looked over the water, his future as uncertain as it had ever been.

"I'm going home," he said at last. It felt right to breath the words into existence, to finally begin his journey home. He didn't know what waited for him there anymore. But through this adventure, he knew he was always going home.

Kai turned to her at last, the same question silent between them. She stood up next to him. The sun on her skin revealed the scarring burns, evidence of her human mortality. She was as much changed and the same as he was.

"I think it's time to see what lies beyond those mountains," she said gently, like a secret on the breeze.

Unsurprised by her answer, he asked, "And your people?"

"Latham is to lead them now. They will remain here with the new council to protect them."

Kai remembered her vision, the council of representatives for each people of the realm. "What will happen now that the witches are dead and the Snow Queen is gone? Who will seat a third chair?"

Lovisa sighed, her dark russet eyes blazing in the sunlight. "I believe that Frost has proven himself a viable candidate."

Kai didn't know if Frost would take the position if offered, but after everything, this somehow seemed right – or perhaps as right as it could be. His skin itched at the thought of how close he'd come to becoming the new Frost, to have a sliver of that mirror imbedded in his heart and eye until he'd changed into something cold and bitter. In this, the fairy tales got it wrong. It wasn't Kai's heart that melted in the end, nor was it Gerda who melted it. Alice was right. The key was Frost's heart, and he just needed one person to believe in him so he could melt it himself.

After a moment's thought, watching the woman standing beside him, Kai offered, "You could come with me."

Lovisa looked at him at last, revealing nothing. "To Anders?"

He shrugged though his shoulders were heavy. "Then wherever life takes us."

Searching his face, she gave the slightest of smiles. "I'd like that."

They watched the water, the sun glistening over its surface, a road to the sky. Somehow, Kai knew that Gerda had found her peace.

Chapter Forty
Farewell, My Friends

The White Rabbit was well equipped for a return journey. He planted one of the magic beans which towered overhead by the next afternoon, the stalk touching the clouds. With his instruction, a hollowed tree was enchanted by Aurore and Isbjørn, the split trunk fashioned into an archway to make easy passage. Five mirrors stood at varying heights against a large bolder, promising a journey back to England. The White Rabbit was still working with his cousin on the rabbit hole.

While the rest of the realms prepared to depart, the five friends came together again in the afternoon sun. It felt like years had passed since they first met in the underground facility. Like they'd known each other all their lives. Kai supposed they'd been connected since long before the Facility, their fates intertwined – but he liked to think that even though the Snow Queen was the force that brought them together, it was still their choice to become friends. She had not a thing to do with the love he had for them.

You were never in control, her words whispered in his mind, frigid and harsh.

Yes, I was, Kai thought to himself as relief passed over him. No one could control love. They could only choose it.

Alice slipped her hand in his, a familiar light in her eyes. The White Rabbit hypothesized that her healing mind and strengthening grip on reality had something to do with the connection she shared with Remus. Whatever sanity he held would be shared between them. But Kai thought the reason was beyond her link with the Hatter. Alice was strong, much stronger than anyone gave her credit for. Despite losing her sanity, she still fought through the chaos of her mind to tell them what was important. He thought back to what she did yesterday, putting an end to their mission, killing the Snow Queen. She did what he couldn't bear to do. Maybe her insanity saved them all in the end.

Then there were moments like this, when Alice held his hand and her face became honest and vulnerable, when she looked at him with smiling cornflower blue eyes. And it brought him back to the Enchanted Forest when she told him about her Unbirthday, when the sun caught her lemon hair in its glow, when she was afraid of losing her mind like her father did. He knew she was still the same Alice.

Kai squeezed her hand lightly, felt the slight twitch of her thumb. He needed her strength.

"This feels so strange," Red muttered, passing a hand over her face. Her bottle green eyes were tight with fatigue. "I don't even know... what comes next."

Wendy stared at a spot on the snow-spotted ground between their feet. "I suppose that's up to you, to each of us."

Kai remembered when Bae told him as much. What came next was for them to decide.

"Once we settle things in Neverland, I'm going back to London for a time," Wendy continued. "My parents deserve as much."

"Then you and Pan will live forever in Never Neverland," Jack quipped with a half-grin.

But Wendy thought about that for a moment before she shook her head. "No, we won't live forever. We visit the Mainland too much, and life is uncertain. But I think, at least, that Peter and I will grow up together, however long that takes. And when the time comes for a new Pan, we'll be there to help."

Jack gave a nod, but there was a truth to her words that weighed down on them all suddenly. Life was uncertain. After this moment, they may never see each other again. Perhaps there was a way, a bridge they could cross between their homes, reunions in an unknown future. But life would inevitably move on and transport them in different directions. They couldn't predict if or when they could see each other again. And Wendy, she would outlive them all.

Speaking slowly, Red took Jack's hand, "We'll go to England to see the orphanage. And I'd like to visit my grandmother."

"And after that?" Jack asked softly.

"We'll see," she answered. But they would do it together.

Kai felt an ache in his chest, small but present, a wish for the love he lost. He was glad for his friends, glad for the life they would share together. Something he would never have with Gerda.

"I'm going home to Anders," Kai said with the same assurance as he'd told Lovisa. "My family is waiting. And Gerda's. They deserve to know."

Silence returned, as if Gerda's name bore a reminder of all they had lost. A list that would only grow with time.

"I've made my peace with my family; I owe them nothing," Alice spoke casually, the only one of them certain not to step through the looking glass ever again. She would go home, they all knew it, but the home of her childhood would remain in her past. Her forever home was just down the rabbit hole. Then she raised her head, her voice calm, "People think we're fairy tales."

Jack huffed, "Some fairy tale."

"Fairy tales get happy endings," Red put bitterly. "If people knew the truth…" But she couldn't finish.

With the same tranquil assurance, Alice continued, "Perhaps the world isn't ready for the truth. Perhaps what they want, what they need, is a different ending. Tragic or moving or happy. They need stories that bring hope no matter the circumstances."

"You sound like a Christmas caroler," Jack muttered under his breath, earning a thump on the shoulder from Red. In response, Alice started humming a Christmas tune that Kai recognized with a smile.

Wendy's eyes shone as she took in her friend's words. "And that's what we need to do. We can't forget what we've gone through or who we've left behind. But we need to keep going forward, keep choosing hope and joy. It might take a while, and we probably won't recognize it when it comes, but I do believe – I have to believe – that someday we'll get our happy endings."

Jack's eyes were lowered now, but he managed a determined nod. "Just keep moving forward."

Red held his hand more securely.

Kai felt Alice squeeze his own hand. She swallowed, a vein in her neck popping. When she relaxed again, her humming ceased, and she glanced up at the moon which lingered in the afternoon sky.

"For now, let us be known as we are," she said, looking between the five of them. "The girl who didn't want to grow up, the boy who climbed so high he could touch the heavens, the girl who overcame the wolf, the boy who healed a frozen heart, and the girl who dreamed of a land of wonders."

Kai's eyes began to sting. At least for now Gerda would be known as the hero. She would be remembered as the girl who survived the darkness surrounding her. In his heart, she would be his, kissing the roses from her windowsill, coming home once her journey was done. He breathed in that memorial.

Then he found himself turning to Wendy. "But when the world is ready, you will tell them?"

She blinked at the gravity of his request, but he saw in her eyes that she understood. "Every word," she promised.

And that was enough. Now, he could move forward. Choking back the tightness in his throat, Kai brought them together in a firm and tearful embrace. He knew that somehow, someday he would see his friends again. They would always have each other.

This time, there was no pocket watch.

Their journey was done.

They would go home.

At the end of all things, there was no song;
so the legends lived on, until all that remained
were the stories she must tell.

There was a little café just outside of Kensington Gardens where Wendy liked to sit after her visits with the Darling family when it rained outside. Much of the family name had died out or taken on new surnames by now. But Wendy liked to keep in touch with her descended nieces and nephews when she could. Few remained in London. She could hardly keep track of them all.

Peter skipped up and placed a steaming ceramic cup on the table before her with a flourish. "Your tea, madam."

She laughed. "Why, thank you, kind sir."

He pulled his dimpled smile as he slid into the chair across from her. After about a hundred years since they'd returned to Neverland from the Realm of the Snow Queen, he'd hardly changed. The age made him roguish. He still wasn't used to the occasional stubble that grew on his chin when they visited the Mainland. He scratched at it now unconsciously and Wendy had a flash of déjà vu, remembering the tick Kai developed in scratching the scar on his jaw. Peter was probably now about the same physical age Kai had been when they'd battled the Snow Queen.

Peter cocked his head, leaning back in his chair. "You're thinking about them, aren't you?"

She nodded, hands wrapped around her mug, nostalgia churning in her stomach.

He lifted his own cup while he tapped the notebook that lay open between them. "Is that what this is for?" he asked over his drink.

Again, she nodded. "I just don't know where to start." She caught sight of the mobile number scrawled across Peter's paper cup and laughed. "And what's that for?"

He frowned and turned the cup to see what she indicated, then shrugged with an amused smile. "Guess she doesn't know about you."

"Or that you don't have a telephone," Wendy teased.

Peter rolled his eyes then leaned forward with elbows on the table. His eyes flicked down to her blank pages. "The beginning usually works, you know."

"I know that!" Wendy scoffed. "But which beginning? When I met you? Red's childhood as a thief; Jack's in the orphanage? Or do I go all the way back to Frost and Babette? I don't know."

"You're overthinking this."

"I know I am." She stared down at her mug, warmth in her palms. "I just miss them. I don't want to disappoint them."

His hand slipped over hers, squeezed, offered her a smile. She returned it. They knew each other so well by now, yet he could still spark a glow in her chest.

"Besides, I know how it should start," Peter said brightly as he downed another sip.

"How?"

He was standing now, slipping on his jacket. "Gosh, Wendy, you ought to know. It starts with all five of you."

She blinked as something settled in her mind like a missing piece. "Alice," she whispered, remembering that night in the Facility when she'd first met one of her best friends.

Peter grinned, knowing she'd figure the rest out now. "I'll leave you to it. There were some kids under the bridge and an orphanage I wanted to check out before we go home." He took up his drink, leaned over, and kissed her. "Love you."

"Love you, too," she said before he winked and was gone.

Wendy watched him disappear down the street and through the rain. A faint light trailed after him to keep him company. No shadow.

She returned to her notebook, her throat tight and a radiance growing inside. It began with Alice, then Wendy, Red, Jack, and Kai. All of them together to the end. So ordinary and unexpected.

Taking up her pen, Wendy scribbled down the words rising from her heart:

It was a dreary day in an unknown town in England...

THE END

Acknowledgements

The end of this journey is here, and I'm doing my best not to cry. This has been an ongoing project for over six years, and it's lasted through some of the craziest and most life-changing times of my life. I never could have done this without the help of some truly incredible people along the way.

Firstly, thank you so much to my family. You all have loved and supported me unconditionally, both in life and in my writing ventures. Thank you for picking me up, for pushing me forward, and being there for me through all the ups and downs. You've taught me how to love and be loved, and I hope that radiates throughout this book. Mom and Dad, I thank God for giving me to you. Girls, I don't know who I'd be without you – sorry for being sappy, but you do keep my life interesting, so thanks for the laughs and thanks for keeping me humble. I'm excited to see the astounding women you're becoming. You'll rattle the world.

More than anything, this book is about friendship, so thank you to all the friends who've joined their life with mine. You've helped me grow, you've left your mark. I'm forever changed because of you.

Special thanks to the Creative Writing faculty at Berry College – Dr. Donnelly, Dr. Meek, and Dr. Peters – for investing in me and developing my writing skills. You've nurtured a passion within me that will only grow.

To Lewis Carrol, J.M. Barrie, Hans Christian Andersen, the Brothers Grimm, Charles Perrault, Henry Cole, Joseph

Jacobs, and all the oral storytellers who've passed down the fairy tale legends – thank you for your stories. Thank you for creating the inspirations for Alice, Wendy, Red, Jack, and Kai. I'm forever grateful. Your tales touched me deeply, and I hope I paid homage to your originals as much as I developed my own stories.

This book is the ultimate culmination of legends and fairy tales throughout the series. But specifically, thank you to Hans Christian Andersen for the enchanting stories *The Snow Queen* and *The Ice Maiden*, as well as any other tale that leaked in. And of course, my thanks to the mysterious origins of Jack Frost, an unexpected character who played a vital role to the story.

Thanks to True Touch Lifestyle, Stefano Cavoretto, and dekolaine at Shutterstock for the beautiful images that have made up this cover, as well as Derek Murphy whose tips on DIY book covers have aided me well throughout the years. Thank you to my proofreaders whose advice polished the narrative – your vigilance is beyond appreciated.

Readers, thank you for taking this journey with me. Thank you for investing in these characters and for encouraging me throughout this process. It excites me that you've chosen this series to hold close all this time. I hope you enjoyed this last adventure!

Above all, thank you to my God who planted these stories in my heart – may You receive all the glory. I hope to shine Your light and life in all I am and all I do. Thank You for being my ultimate reason.

OTHER BOOKS BY EMORY R. FRIE

Heart of a Lion

THE REALMS SERIES:
Wonderland
Neverland
Enchanted Forest
Giant Country
Realm of the Snow Queen

Emory R. Frie is the award-winning author of debut novel, *Heart of a Lion*, and the Realms Series. She has a Bachelor's Degree in Creative Writing and Business at Berry College where she has also produced written works for the stage. When she isn't writing, Emory enjoys going on adventures with her friends and family. She is captivated with wanderlust and dreams of learning to fly. Raised in Oregon, she now lives in Georgia with her family and rambunctious Scottie pup.

Please visit emoryrfrie.weebly.com for more information.

www.ingramcontent.com/pod-product-compliance
Lightning Source LLC
Chambersburg PA
CBHW030551180626
46816CB00005B/1504